BOUNDARY

A Novel

Kevin Woodward

ISBN-13: 978-0692317969
ISBN-10:0692317961

For My Father
Edwin Lewis Woodward
1915 – 2005

ONE

Goiaina, Brazil, September, 1987

Dr. Deiter Gorn stared out the window, fear coursing through him like the staccato waves of heat distorting the symmetrical white lines in the emergency room parking lot. The cars, the palm trees and the pampas grass—all becoming insubstantial, going the way of his world.

"The man has radiation sickness," he said in a breathless whisper, more to himself than to the man standing behind him with the chart.

He stood outside room 211 with Cameron Craig, an abrasive ENT physician from some small southern U.S. burg. Their white lab coats were too short in the sleeves and sweat-stained beneath the arms in dark, yellow, half moons. Conspicuous in their height and fair complexions, they spoke in low urgent tones, though few of the short, dark native Brazilian hospital staff spoke English. The men had been in-country just 72 hours, part of a small "Doctors Without Borders" contingent brought in to evaluate a malaria outbreak in the poor villages outside of Goiania. In the face of the day's events, mosquitoes had quickly lost their allure. By nightfall, they would be forgotten altogether.

The American, balding with an unkempt salt and pepper beard, mottled skin and glasses shook his head, disbelieving.

"What about leprosy, pemphigus, hell, even syphilis?"

The other physician, a German, looked at his shoes and ran long fingers through a luxurious mat of jet black hair. He too shook his head.

"No, the wife and four year old daughter came in with him – extreme nausea, lesions, sloughing of the epidermis," the German said, his English halting, with a thick accent. "He said it was a blue paint or powder. That is as much as they could get out of the man before he passed out."

"Shit," said the American. "Living in this jungle – could have been some virus picked up from under-cooked bush meat – monkey balls or something."

"*Nein*!" said the black-haired German, impatience causing a brief lapse into his native tongue. "These people came into contact with a radioactive isotope. I have no doubt. And we have to find it before more people begin picking their skin from the street like brown banana peels."

Inside the room, as he lay dying, Victor Gallegos could not hear the doctors. He sensed the strands that held his soul to its earthly existence begin to fray. Pain greeted him like a blinding sun rising slowly above the horizon, through red eyelids, piercing his brain. The skin was falling away from his body in thin sheets, like an onion peeling in boiling water. He could not decide whether it would be better to hang on or tumble back into the depthless abyss from which he had only just awakened. From within that cloistered dark, he felt a straining, pulling…yearning even. He needed something. The need was amorphous and hollow, like the longing left by a lover in a dream. A part of him was missing. Something, no some*one* was missing. Soon the answer assembled itself from the jagged shards of his shattered memory and burst through the pain.

"Suzanna!"

TWO

Boundary Waters Canoe Area Wilderness, Minnesota
May, 2002
Wednesday, 8:20 AM

He found them on the Red Rock Lake side of the Red Rock/Saganaga portage—four men, two aluminum canoes, fishing rods and packs. An unremarkable sight in the middle of the wilderness boundary between Canada and the United States. Ranger Mark Toftey loved solitary travel, but occasional contact with other voyagers made the silences in between sweeter and more affirming. The utter absence of human beings turned the low murmur of distant voices into a siren song, a promise of comfort and camaraderie in what was at times an inhospitable place. Toftey's step had grown lighter as he approached the canoe landing, the trail leading him further and further away from the Seagull River, now a rushing torrent of snowmelt running between the two lakes. He was anticipating some friendly conversation and a welcome break from his own tired, meandering thoughts, when he rounded a bend in the rocky trail and saw the men seated on the ground.

"Mornin," he said.

All four men had comparatively dark complexions. They looked up but showed no immediate signs of comprehension. He smiled and looked them over – a brief assessment. Dark skin was, as the internal Forest Service bulletins put it, "not a well-represented demographic" here in the park. Toftey pictured the meeting in Washington where that pearl was penned – some environmental committee chair pontificating on increasing racial diversity in the Boundary Waters Canoe Area Wilderness park and that a commission should be formed to investigate before one more penny of Federal money would be spent, etc., etc. Toftey simply assumed that black kids from Compton didn't watch much "Outdoor Channel" – kind of hard to contemplate camping and fishing in miles of unbroken forest, lakes and rivers when your daily routine involves dodging gunfire and drug dealers on your way to school.

For Toftey it had been a long week. He liked solitude but seven days paddling and portaging a seventeen-foot canoe through miles of remote wilderness gave him about all he could handle. It was early in the season. Ice had only left the largest lakes a few days before he launched his slender craft from the landing at Trail's End, a small settlement at the terminus of the sixty-mile Gunflint Trail. The Trail, as it was known to the locals, was a two-lane paved artery snaking through the heart of canoe country from the small town of Grand Marais, huddled around its natural rocky harbor like a seaside Maine fishing village. At the end of the Trail, from the boat landing on the Seagull River, it was just a six-mile paddle to the middle of enormous Saganaga Lake, part of the pristine blue ribbon that was Minnesota's border with Canada.

Toftey had been lugging a bulky green canvas pack across the short rocky portage from the southernmost arm of "Big Sag" to Red Rock Lake. He left the canoe at the rock-strewn portage landing, preferring to "double-portage" rather than take everything in one backbreaking trip. Though only thirty-five he was beginning to feel twinges in his muscles from strenuous physical exercise and he was learning to make adjustments. It would be another three days before he would get to the Poplar Lake entry point where he would meet up with Border Patrol agent Garrett Hansen. It seemed like months since he'd made plans with his friend for the regular supply run to Grand Marais.

The portage to Red Rock was the length of two football fields; not long by BW standards, but under seventy-five pounds of food, clothes, first aid, ropes, fishing tackle, cooking supplies, compass, maps and other miscellany, "long" and "short" were relative terms. Toftey wore leather and GoreTex hiking boots that laced up just below his calf for extra ankle support. The mud and sharp protruding rocks made for a treacherous pathway. Given his distance from medical assistance or, sometimes, even another human being, Toftey was careful about every step he took. He knew that coming down wrong with that much extra weight on his back could snap a bone like a dead pine bough.

The warm temperatures of the past several days had encouraged the first hatch of bloodthirsty parasites and Toftey soon found himself slapping his neck and ears. The first mosquitoes, large, dark, and slow-moving, made their appearance along with hordes of black flies, swirling around and biting anything with a blood supply. Something about their bites, the anticoagulant he supposed, made him swell up spectacularly.

Thinking maybe the men sitting on the ground didn't hear his initial greeting, he continued, swatting at one of the little insects that had begun feeding on his left wrist.

"Damn things are horrible this time of year," he said, "But without 'em, we wouldn't have any blueberries come August. Guess it's worth it."

Still no response.

One man was older with salt and pepper hair. He wore the wrinkled and weather-checked skin of a man who spent much time outside in harsh conditions. His face bore a tremendous scar, which traversed much of the right side of his face in a beige line, puckering the corner of his mouth and raising it slightly in a look of bemusement incongruous with the rest of his harsh countenance. It's the face of a soldier, Toftey thought. Across from him sat a young slender man with a mustache. His eyes were downcast and he seemed preoccupied with a spot on his boot, rubbing and picking at it with his fingers. Next to him was a man of about thirty, with a medium build who, other than his ethnic features, was not remarkable in any other way. He stared at the ground, sitting cross-legged, listening, hands folded in his lap. Out of the corner of his eye, Toftey could see the man glance up and look at him, but when Toftey turned back the man had again directed his gaze to the ground. Finally, there was a man larger than the others, sitting slightly apart, elbows on his knees, head resting on clasped hands. His eyes were a brilliant green in the sun. As Toftey approached they offered no greeting but considered him cautiously, eyes peering intently from beneath their brows. With their hands they idly brushed away the persistent cloud of black flies surrounding their heads.

"How's fishing been?" Toftey asked, wondering if they even spoke English. He shed the big green pack and stretched his sore shoulders with a groan. He unzipped and removed his brown fleece jacket revealing his green uniform shirt and silver badge beneath.

As if jerked from a trance by this question, or, as Toftey would later suspect, by the badge glinting in the dappled sunlight, the larger man suddenly stood up and smiled broadly. He advanced on Toftey with an outstretched hand and brilliant disarming smile. Somewhat startled, the ranger extended his hand and it was enveloped and compressed almost uncomfortably by thick fingers and a warm grip; he had the sense of a bear trap whose straining jaws were stayed only by the thinnest of sinews. The man was strongly built and stood eye to eye with Toftey at six feet tall. His voice was friendly and, Toftey heard only the slightest hint of an accent.

"We haven't seen a fish during the whole trip. Not very lucky, I guess." The man released Toftey's hand and continued to smile, expectantly, as if waiting for a birthday gift or word of his Publisher's Clearinghouse winnings.

"Well, luck has a lot less to do with it than most folks would like to believe. Experience fishing in these waters counts for a lot."

Toftey stole a glance at the man's companions, still seated on the ground, but watching the interchange intently, distracted only slightly by the biting flies which they continued to brush away. Their stoic interest contrasted greatly with their newly animated spokesman.

"We have lost a lot of fishing tackle," the man said, sounding almost ashamed.

"I don't doubt it," Toftey said. "There's snags everywhere—boulders and dead-head logs from the logging camps. There's junk down there from a hundred years ago or more."

The officer glanced at the fishing rods propped up against a small cedar tree. He noticed that none of the rods had line strung through the rod guides. He followed the rod down to its base and saw that each open-faced fishing reel still wore the rubber band around its spool. When the reels were filled with line at the store, the line is secured with a rubber band to prevent the monofilament from peeling off the spool. The reels were plump full of line — they had never been used. He returned his gaze to the man before him.

"I take it this is your first trip?"

Toftey had a law enforcement background. He went to school for it, and served as a back-up officer for the Saint Louis County Sheriff's Department for two years. He was good and had been offered a permanent position many times. But his fiancée begged him to quit.

"I didn't sign up for this, Mark," she had said, those big brown eyes welling up with tears. "I don't want to be a cop's wife. I don't want to sit alone at night wondering if you're hurt or worse."

"You knew what I wanted to do when we met," he countered. "I never kept it a secret."

"I thought you'd see what a foolish thing it was," she admitted. "I thought that if you loved me enough you'd stop."

"And I thought you'd see how important it was to me," he had told her then. "I thought that if you loved me enough, you'd stand by me."

The sheriff repeatedly congratulated him on his sharp investigative skills. "You got a nose for lies, kid," he had said. But Mark left the work to appease the girl and applied for a Wilderness Ranger position with the U.S. Forest Service; he was lucky to have graduated with a forestry degree in college. In the six years he had been with the agency his fiancée left him anyway and his pauper's salary remained stagnant while friends in the sheriff's office saw promotions and pay that at least kept up with the cost of living.

Years had passed, but he hadn't lost any of his intuition. It was speaking to him now. With his last question he glanced back at the men on the ground and noticed that although the black flies had begun lighting on their necks, ears and faces, certainly piercing the skin with painful bites, they were no longer swatting them away.

"Yes," said the man in front of Toftey. "This is the first time for us. A friend suggested we try a camping trip in the Boundary Waters. He did not tell us we'd be eaten alive by swarms of insects. We will have a word with him when we get back, I assure you!"

"Where you guys from?" he asked.

"I cry your pardon?" the big guy said.

It sounded so over-the-top formal, out here with the bugs and the dirt and the woods, Toftey fought back a laugh. Maybe he's a prince or a sheik. "I asked you where you guys are from."

"Chicago," he said, almost too fast, like he was hitting the bell to answer a Jeopardy question or anxious to recite a well-rehearsed line.

"I meant originally. I detect a bit of an accent."

"Spain."

"Damn, I'm usually pretty good at guessing that. I would have said somewhere in the Middle East."

The man chuckled and smiled broadly once again, looking down at his companions whose answering smiles were less animated and enthusiastic.

Toftey had the feeling they didn't know why they were smiling, only that it was expected. It was as though with a look, the standing man had given them an order. And as their wooden smiles faded he saw their glances linger on each other, just for a second, and something passed between them. He couldn't be sure, but he thought he saw the slightest hint of a grim nod. It made his stomach flutter and he felt adrenaline rush warmly into his veins.

His fear made him angry. Why am I suspicious, he wondered? Because they look or sound foreign? Then again Mark, he argued with himself, you are the law 'round these parts, preservin' the public safety, keeping wayward bears and squirrels in line. It would be pretty chicken-shit to leave bad guys out here just to be politically correct. Plus, that "nose for lies" was still intact, and he smelled a whopper. He set his game face cleared his throat and continued.

"Gentlemen, I'm Officer Mark Toftey with the United Stated Forest Service. I'm a wilderness ranger, which means I get to help folks if they have questions or problems out here. It also means I check permits and ensure everybody complies with the law."

Toftey looked at the smiling man, who was no longer smiling. His expression was unreadable.

"I need to see your BWCAW permit," he said. "I take it you're the leader of the group?"

In the distance the rushing of the Seagull River rose and fell in its tumbling cascade from the sprawling "Big Sag." Chickadees flitted around in the nearby balsam firs, adding their nervous twittering punctuation to the white noise of the undulating river. A red squirrel began to chatter sharply from a jack pine just off the portage trail, berating the intruders with incessant scolding. Black flies circled over Toftey's head and swirled in front of his eyes as he looked at the man before him.

The gracious smile returned and the man said, "certainly" before turning and walking over to a small camouflage pack sitting on the ground.

Toftey quickly counted eight packs. There was a large green Duluth-style pack for each man in the group along with four large "fanny" packs designed to belt around the waist and carry smaller personal items. It was a lot of gear for four men, he thought, though "greenhorns" often brought much more food than they needed, as though starvation was the greatest danger for the wilderness traveler. It did strike him as odd how the packs were set so neatly next to each other. In fact, nothing was out of place. All of their gear was carefully arranged. That was usually the first sign of inexperience in a Boundary Waters tripper—the chaos of the gear. At the end of a long paddle or portage, usually the packs and paddles and life jackets and fishing rods are dropped as quickly as possible and left strewn about with no regard for other travelers. It is a sign of fatigue and disillusionment in the face of a daunting and unexpected physical challenge. Few first time voyagers had an accurate understanding of what was involved in a wilderness canoe trip. People pushed to their physical limits and beyond don't care about how neatly the gear is stowed. They just want to get someplace where they can lie down away from the bugs and dry out their socks and shoes.

As the smiling man bent down to one of the fanny packs, Toftey felt a growing apprehension. He had no reason to stop the man. There was nothing but a feeling and his imagination that made his heart race. If the guy pulled a weapon from the pack, Toftey didn't have a chance. Though he didn't carry a gun, it would have afforded him no protection in this scenario anyway. Even if he could have somehow unsnapped a stiff leather holster, pulled out a pistol, flipped off the safety and accurately fired a round, he sincerely doubted his ability to shoot a man. But instead of a gun, the man produced a piece of paper. It was a BWCAW entry permit which he handed to Toftey, and the officer felt a temporary wave of relief.

"Thank you." Toftey read the names on the permit. The leader and alternate leader were listed as "Richard Stallings" and "John Kurtz."

Toftey looked up. "So, you're Richard? Who's John?"

"Uh…John could not join us so we brought Adam instead," he pointed to the unremarkable man seated on the ground who nodded very subtly.

"I am sorry if that is not allowed. We did not think it would be a problem since I am the leader."

Leader of what, Toftey wondered? As the man was talking to him, he noticed how he had maneuvered himself between Toftey and the other members of the party. He had also moved somewhat closer, effectively limiting visibility and making Toftey uncomfortable. Toftey took a small step backwards still looking at the permit, but also trying to steal a glance behind the man looming in front of him. There was activity back there. Someone else was moving. He heard a pack unzip slowly, each pair of zipper teeth quietly snapping apart. The man in front of him took another step closer.

"Is there something wrong with the permit?" he asked.

Toftey couldn't see around him. "Could you step back, sir?"

The man kept coming and Toftey stepped back again.

"Sir, I need you to go sit down with your party while I review the permit."

Snap, snap, snap. The zipper opening for a candy bar? A compass?

"Is there something wrong," the man repeated. It was no longer question. The smile was gone, as was the friendly pretense.

Snap, snap, snap. A rustling of material. Somewhere behind this hulking figure the metallic ring of a weapon's action slowly being engaged shook Toftey from his paralysis.

He heard the soft click of a round being chambered as he ran.

THREE

Beth Adams sat alone in a field of five-foot-high dull gray cubicles, her desk hidden beneath a scattering of tattered document fragments, some with burned edges, some stained with what appeared to be blood. She wore a white lab coat, bright purple surgical gloves and a white paper breathing mask over her mouth and nose with a pair of clear plastic goggles over her glasses. Her shoulder-length blonde hair was pulled away from her face and tied in a tight ponytail. Her blue-gray eyes were intense as she concentrated on the mess before her. Fresh air was as scarce in the old building as decaffeinated coffee. She wondered if people would even need caffeine if they just pumped some oxygen into the old place once in a while. Wisps of hair that were once bangs now stuck to her damp forehead as she wiped her brow with the sleeve of her lab coat.

Though she automatically followed the standard precautions for evidence-handling, the documents were not particularly dangerous. They had already gone through initial screening and decontamination at Langley where each individual item was checked for chemical and biological agents, bagged and labeled with its area of origin, the date it was uncovered and the ranking officer in charge of the unit credited with the discovery. But protocol must be followed. Although she would have preferred a laboratory for such an investigation, lab time in the

Pentagon was tough to come by these days, even for long-time agents. The crash of Flight 77 had destroyed several forensic labs available to her clearance level. Beth, in only her third year with the CIA, had "an apple's chance in a pigpen" as her father used to say, of setting foot in an empty forensics laboratory.

The thought of her father made her look at the picture of him sitting on the top of her computer screen and her hand went instinctively to hold the small gold heart-shaped locket she wore around her neck. He bought it for her seventeenth birthday, but she hadn't worn it for years. It was only after she came home from his funeral on that cold November day that she dug it out of her jewelry box and slipped it over her head. Her mother had watched her and fastened the delicate clasp from behind.

"I remember when he gave this to you," she had said. "He was so worried that you would run off to college and forget about him. It kept him up at night."

"I remember opening it," Beth told her, "expecting to find a picture of both of you or Sadie with a tennis ball in her mouth. But it was this tiny sunrise picture, rising up over a lake, shafts of light coming through a few clouds. I didn't understand."

Her mother put her arms around her then and that was when she began to cry. "He told me, "It's your future. It's the hope and promise of a day you haven't lived yet. It's a chance to be anything you want to be and fix what didn't go right yesterday." He said `That's what I want you to keep in your heart, honey. Your future.'"

He had been a sheriff's deputy in northwestern Wisconsin and died in a car accident two years, seven months and three days ago. He had been driving the cruiser back to the office when a deer ran out from the ditch. He swerved to miss it but lost control of the car and hit a tree at about sixty-five miles per hour. Because he was in the cruiser at the end of his shift they said he was killed in the line of duty. Only now had she reached the point where she could smile about it, imagining her father's likely bemused reaction. One of his favorite jokes was to make up fake headlines, like "Deputy Dies in the Line of Duty, Ambushed by Venison." He was her basketball coach in high school and soccer coach before that. Mom was around, of course, but her father was the first man in her life, and also her best buddy.

In her heart she lived with the guilt of finding good in the events of September 11, 2001. She was swept up in the flurry of activity after the attacks. She worked fourteen-hour days, and then took the train home to work from her Silver Spring apartment until she passed out in a chair or on the couch. Her manic pace at work allowed her to hide from her own reality. And when she stumbled into the black chasm of her loss she could join in the country's grieving, her own tears for her father lost in the weeping of a nation.

Beth drifted out of the fog of her memories and the chaos of mangled papers materialized in front of her. This was a new box, delivered that morning from Langley. The box was marked "TB-127, Lt. B. Metzger, 020903, DBN-37426." "TB" meant the shipment came from the Tora Bora region of Afghanistan, where the extensive al-Qaeda cave network lay, and "127" was its consecutive number. "Lieutenant B. Metzger" was in charge of the unit that found the intelligence, "020903" was the date it was catalogued and "DBN-37426" was the document batch number, telling her that 37,425 boxes of document fragments had been fought over, killed and died for, captured, recorded and shipped to information officers like her somewhere else in the Pentagon before this one ended up on her desk. Beth felt the burden of that responsibility every day, that those who fought and sacrificed to gather this evidence could be confident that it was delivered into the hands of people committed to using every tool at their disposal to extract value from the contents. She believed the stories buried in these piles of paper could save lives.

Most of the papers were religious writings. She read Arabic fairly well, though she would never speak it because she knew it came out oafish and virtually unintelligible to a native speaker. Many copies of the Qur'an were in those caves judging from the volume of pages she began to set aside in a pile at the upper left corner of her desk. As she placed pieces on the pile, phrases caught her eye and she would stop to read them as best she could:

"Surely those who disbelieve from among the followers of the Book and the polytheists shall be in the fire of hell, abiding therein; they are the worst of men…those who believe and do good, surely they are the best of men. Their reward with their Lord is gardens of perpetuity beneath which rivers flow, abiding therein forever; Allah is well pleased with them and they are well pleased with him; that is for him who fears his Lord."

She imagined the caves of Tora Bora full of men believing with unwavering faith that they were "the best of men" and all their actions were justified against "the worst of men."

In addition to fragments of the Qur'an there were crudely printed propaganda pieces sporting pictures of Osama Bin-Laden and various influential Muslim clerics, the messages below the pictures, by inference, endorsed by them. These writings were all essentially the same, demonizing the United States and its allies as killers of their Arab brothers and defilers of God and the Muslim faith. "The infidels will meet their deaths, praise Allah, if you are strong in your faith and pure of heart. The way is just and the foreigners that destroy us and occupy our land…." The rest was torn off, but there were many copies and Beth could recreate it if she found it was relevant later on. She began another pile on her desk for propaganda.

"Find any Playboys in there yet Adams? Maybe the Hamas Hustler?"

The voice startled her. She had been so engrossed in the materials in front of her that she hadn't heard the man walk up behind her. Richard Gilmore had been a field agent for twenty years and enjoyed "charming" the young women when he was in the office. Richard seemed to emanate the same stale, "grandma's basement" odor that permeated the Pentagon air exchange and all the dark lower levels of the place. Beth thought he was a crude pig and did not share her coworkers' tolerance. The other women in the section treated him like a cute old uncle, laughing off his smarmy comments as if they were visiting a nursing home and one of the male residents got a little "frisky." Beth knew Gilmore was a smart man. He would not have reached this level in the organization without having attained a certain degree of respect and a winning investigative track record. He took his innuendo as far as possible, just before it became actionable. Are you a pig accidentally, she wanted to ask, or do you have to work at it?

He laughed at his own joke and continued, "What about Bhurka Babes or Muslim Mamas?"

"No, Richard, sorry to disappoint."

She slid a few pieces of paper around as though looking for something. She tried to appear too busy to talk, absolutely engrossed in the work at hand. Though she was in a long white lab coat, she suddenly became aware of bending across her desk and him looking at her from behind. She sat down with a torn photograph in her hand and began studying it intently. The glare from the goggles over her glasses made it difficult to see so she removed them and placed them on the desk. In their reflection she could see Gilmore still standing behind her, looking over her shoulder at the items strewn across her desk.

"Not disappointed, really. I don't need to confiscate porn; that's what the Internet's for." He moved closer to the back of her chair and loomed over her. "What have you got there, really?" he asked her.

His clearance was two levels higher than hers so she didn't feel any hesitation in telling him what she knew.

"Stuff from Afghanistan, the caves."

"Why aren't you in a lab?" he asked. "You don't have enough room to change your mind in this cube."

"They're all booked," Beth sighed, "and have been for weeks."

As she turned to look at him, she pushed the stack of Qur'an fragments off the desk and they scattered across the floor and under her cube and desk.

"Shit!" she cried and bent down to retrieve them.

She felt like an idiot—a vulnerable idiot, on her knees in front of Gilmore picking up her scattered papers like a clumsy schoolgirl. She didn't expect that he would help her, and he didn't, but she was still taken aback by his rudeness as he stepped over the fallen documents and picked up her phone. He dialed an internal extension. Beth heard a female voice answer.

"Hey darlin.' I know, I know. I'm a horrible person, but you pity me and that warms my heart. Do me a favor? I need 708 for a couple of days."

Beth looked up at Gilmore's reference to one of the largest forensics labs in the building. Every technician in the Pentagon coveted it. It was on the tour during orientation. She remembered the revered silence as all the scientists in her group admired the facilities, the lights, the tables, and the equipment—all so clean and inviting. Back at Johns Hopkins, her dreams of working in a government laboratory were a crystalline vision of what she saw behind the gunmetal gray door marked 708. Gilmore looked down and winked at her. She looked down and admonished herself for the excitement in her eyes, a look he probably misinterpreted as encouragement, gratitude.

"I'm sure he has," Gilmore continued into the phone. "You know he's had it for over two months now and that he's in Jakarta until August. Come on, darlin,' help out an old man?"

Whatever goodwill he may have purchased by helping Beth evaporated with the condescending tone he just used on the phone—a tone that implied, to Beth, a debt payable only with sexual currency. She shook her head, gathered the last shreds of the Qur'an and her dignity and stood up. Gilmore finished the call.

"Thanks honey, I love ya!" He made smooching noises into the phone, as though he were coaxing a dog to its food, and then hung up.

Beth was disgusted. She stood frowning defiantly before him, the hastily collected armful of papers held awkwardly over her chest.

"There you go," he said. "You've got ten days in one of the finest forensic labs in the world, starting today. Better get your…" he looked down at the jumble of documents before her and raised his eyebrows, "…stuff organized."

Then, it just slipped out, like a fleck of spit during conversation.

"Do you talk to all the women around here like that?" she said, looking for a moment as though she wasn't sure who spoke. She tried to cover. "I…I mean, don't you see how talking like that to a wom…a female colleague might be offensive?"

His growing, smug smile confused and angered her. What an ass! He may be a senior agent, but really!

"I don't think this is fun…."

Before she could finish, Gilmore held up a hand. He reached over one more time and hit the redial button on Beth's phone. On-hook, the speaker phone feature activated automatically. A young woman answered pleasantly,

"Lab Desk, can I help you?"

Gilmore spoke, looking directly at Beth as he spoke. "Honey, I think I forgot to say I love you."

"No you didn't, silly," the young woman said through the speaker. "I love you too, Daddy."

Beth looked blankly at him a moment, then dropped heavily into her chair, dislodging the papers in her arms and sending them fluttering back to the floor in a chaotic heap. She stared up at the ceiling and listened to Richard Gilmore's cheery whistling and footsteps fade as he walked briskly down the corridor.

FOUR

The man's hands were bound behind his back. Over his head a black cloth hood with no ventilation was tied snugly around his neck. The utter blackness within the hood, the stifling heat it trapped, the constriction he felt around his neck and the difficulty in drawing breath through the tight weave of the fabric contributed to his sense of panic. He had been stripped and searched in front of clothed soldiers, men and, to his horror, women. One of the women had painfully grabbed his ears, pulled his head to her crotch and ground her pelvis against his face while the other soldiers laughed and smoked cigarettes.

Several days before—he had lost count exactly—in the middle of the night, he'd been taken from his home and thrown in this cell with a concrete floor and no toilet. He called out many times to be taken to a facility to relieve himself but a cattle prod was used to silence him and he was forced to defecate in a corner. Beyond the darkness of the hood there were echoes of footsteps, clanking cell doors, soldiers speaking and yelling in English, laughing, faint prayers to Allah, desperate whispers and screams.

He lost track of time in the constant darkness, but soon he learned to tell night from day. At night the concrete floor grew damp and cold and the constant drone of flies, attracted by the growing pile of excrement, ceased. Rats prowled from cell to cell searching for scraps of food while the scratching of carrion beetles wrestling over the shit in the corner replaced the buzzing flies. Since the man's capture in his Baghdad home, no one had spoken to him.

He prayed in silence. He first asked Allah for forgiveness; he was disoriented and did not know in which direction lay the Holy City. It was clear that everything the clerics preached in the madrasah was true. These were an evil, God-destroying people. All the sacrifices he had endured and those yet to come were worthwhile if he could play some small part in their demise. Martyrdom was freedom. Sitting naked in the darkness, it was the only freedom he could imagine. He bent his head, touching his forehead and nose to the floor, feeling the damp concrete pull the warmth from his skin even through the material of the hood. Quietly he spoke the final supplication of the day's al-Salah, the al-Fatihah:

"In the name of Allah, Most Gracious, Most Merciful. Praise be to Allah the Lord of the Worlds; Most Gracious, Most Merciful; Master of the Day of Judgment. Thee do we worship, and Thine aid we seek. Show us the straight way, the way of those on whom Thou hast bestowed Thy Grace, Those whose portion is not wrath, and who go not astray."

FIVE

Pentagon, Arlington, Virginia
May, 2002
Tuesday, 7:00 PM

The low rush of air running through an advanced carbon and ion filter system was the only sound in the brightly lit laboratory. It was a scientist's playground of autoclaves, centrifuges, microscopes, freezers, refrigerators, and computer stations with which, she assumed, one could create graphical representations of data streams for trending models and postulations of infinite breadth and scope. There were no windows. The known physical universe had no place here. The empirical was only a necessary foundation for the fanciful musings of esoteric thought indulged within these walls, like coarse and featureless concrete blocks supporting the architect's artistic vision. Splitting the atom was just such a vision. Room 708 was a rare thing in this vast temple built to the gods of war. It was a place of imagination and fantasy, if not made real, then at least entertained within a generous budget.

After her initial bout of open-mouthed awe, looking at the stations and equipment sitting idle throughout the facility, which she guessed to be about the same size as the house in which she grew up back in Wisconsin, Beth found an empty inspection table, complete with a magnifying glass/lamp on an adjustable arm and a backlit table surface. With her foot, she pushed aside a padded metal stool, turned on the lights and laid her chaotic burden of papers onto the table. There were goggles, aspirators, clean suits, latex and non-latex gloves stored in cabinets around the room, but Beth decided against using them. The room itself felt safe to her and she enjoyed the clarity of looking through glasses not clouded and distorted by the warped plastic of the goggles.

She spread the pictures across the table and resumed the sorting she had begun at her desk the night before when Gilmore had embarrassed her. She knew that was not a fair assessment. She was being hard on him out of her own insecurity. She looked around again, still amazed by her surroundings, and then looked down to focus on the task at hand. Beth found binder clips in a desk drawer well stocked with office supplies. She grouped and bound the pile of Qur'an fragments, propaganda leaflets, both Taliban-generated and those from the U.S., and other miscellaneous documents: supply lists, personal letters, weapons manuals, American magazines—*Field and Stream* appeared to be a favorite. When she was finished, one piece of paper sat in the middle of the lighted tabletop.

It looked like a conventional 8-½"x11" piece of white copy paper, charred around the edges. A corner approximately four inches square remained, with only the center of it recognizable, though yellowed by smoke. Looking through the desk drawer once more, she found a pair of spade-tip forceps that she used to pick up the charred fragment. It was a satellite photograph of what appeared to be small bodies of water, though "small" was meaningless conjecture until she could determine the scale of the image. In a glass-fronted cabinet on the wall she has seen several sets of "magni-focusers" hanging on pegs next to the safety goggles. She plucked one of the devices from its perch, adjusted the headband and placed it over her head. She was pleased to discover that the lenses fit perfectly over her glasses.

Returning her gaze to the burned paper before her, she could see ink spray at the boundaries of the image, a hallmark of an ink-jet printer, so commonplace in homes and businesses. Looking past the ink, the picture revealed a densely forested area, interspersed with open patches of low vegetation. The trees were conifers and it appeared as though there was snow on the ground. It was either mid-morning or mid-afternoon judging from the shadows projected by the trees across lakes—if that's what they were—partially covered with ice. Whether it was spring or fall was not clear at first glance; the angle of the sun could determine that. She'd need some comparison photos of similar terrain. And that presented the most compelling question: Where was this? She didn't know much about Afghanistan, but she knew there were mountains and there was snow. Perhaps there was a "pothole" region where snowmelt created vernal ponds, small depressions holding water for at least two months during the spring. She'd obviously have to do some digging on the geography of Afghanistan.

She turned the paper over. There was nothing on the back. Laying the tattered scrap face down on the illuminated table, Beth followed the burnt edge around its perimeter. On the right side, emerging from its ragged, flaking border she saw, under the magni-focuser, small hand-written characters. It was Arabic and appeared to be the tail end of a sentence or phrase. Given what she saw in the picture, the small ponds and low vegetation amidst the spruce, it made sense, sort of. It appeared to be the word *Marais*, which was French for "swamp." Why would an Arab write a French word, she wondered?

What bugged her even more was why a satellite picture of a swamp would be in the Tora Bora caves. Perhaps it was a fresh water supply contaminated with a biological agent. Or a breeding ground for typhoid, encephalitis, or malaria. Or worse yet, something engineered.

That her first thoughts were of destruction and evil disappointed her. It was not what her dad taught her.

"You can't meet people and start out not trusting them," he said, "thinking the worst. If you've already condemned a person, you always question their motivations. Everything they do from that moment on has a double meaning."

Beth knew her pessimism was a symptom of a world stunned by violence on a dramatic scale, where mercy and justice were sacrificed and human life became the only universal currency. Transactions made in blood earned interest in fear. Fear paid dividends to those with nothing to lose or nothing more to gain, both poles bereft of dreams and desire, left only with greed and envy. She worked in a climate that rewarded paranoia. In her job, being paranoid and wrong was easily defended. Lackadaisical and wrong would not be tolerated. Nobody wanted to be in the hot seat as the congressional committee began asking, "With so much at stake, why didn't you check further, dig deeper, and listen harder?"

But was there any other reason why a picture of a swamp would be in an al-Qaeda facility, if one could call a cave such a thing? The CIA had captured other aerial surveillance photos, but most were taken from airplanes or were very old satellite images. There was no telling how old this image was, at least not without further study. By finding out where this was taken and comparing these snow cover patterns and shadow angles with recorded images, a date, within days, could be determined. The date of the photograph could be instrumental in determining whose satellite provided the image. That could be significant, unless, as was often the case, the trail led back to the hulking five-sided building squatting next to the Potomac in which she now sat.

SIX

A year before the battle for the Afghanistan Tora Bora caves, Asad al-Muhammad sat outside at a Moroccan café sipping strong coffee with lots of cream, tapping his fingers lightly on the wrought-iron table. Across the ancient cobblestone square a line of palm trees reminded him of green fountains, the way the fronds spouted from the center and arched outward then toward the ground. They sparkled in the bright spring sunlight, swaying against the gun-barrel blue of the Mediterranean beyond. He was over two hundred miles from Casablanca where thirty-three people had been killed in four bomb blasts only a day before. There was no rhythm to his finger tapping, like a child pretending to send a telegraph, typing nonsensical Morse code. He wore a loose-fitting tunic-style shirt that hung low over cream-colored khakis. Powerful forearms lay on the table, the only hint of his military-tuned physique. His dark eyes watched people moving through the square, looking for…he wasn't sure exactly, but he would know it when he saw it. He was meeting a man who was in Casablanca yesterday—he had news, details. Asad was hungry for information. It was his most ambitious project to date and important people were watching. Not only had he orchestrated one of the most complex simultaneous operations since New York, but also had done it in Morocco. The Moroccan king and his father before him walked the line of allegiance between Muslim Arabs and the U.S. To Asad and his associates, there could be no compromise. A side must be chosen. He would force a choice.

This man, whom he knew only as Ibrahim, would bring first-hand news of the operation and a blessing from the Sheik. It was the Sheik who would choose the man who would lead the ultimate assault on evil. Asad's victory in Morocco was crucial if he was to enter Hell itself and slay the monster in its den. Only a just and righteous man could do this—a man of faith. He hoped that Casablanca had proven to the Sheik and his clerics that Asad was this man. It was only logical. After all, it had been his plan in the first place.

He had been going to school in New York, studying medicine and English at Cornell University. After undergraduate study in Ithaca, he planned to finish his medical studies at Weill Cornell Medical College in Doha, Qatar. At home, he was always fascinated by the American wilderness. As a boy he eagerly awaited his father's return from diplomatic travels. Along with candy bars and other sweets, his father would bring western magazines, which he would devour as eagerly as the candy. Field and Stream and Outdoor Life were his favorites. He found it hard to believe a place with as many trees and as much water as he saw pictured and read about in those articles. In his first year at Cornell, he signed up for a trip with the university's "Wilderness Reflections" program. The student-run organization offered wilderness adventures as preparation for the rigors of college life and opportunities for personal growth and team building.

His trip included hiking and canoeing through the Adirondacks of upstate New York. The canoe trips coursed through wild, largely inaccessible country, through chains of lakes like Fulton, Long and Saranac.

That trip, through the deep woods, warm water, sunshine and cool evenings of August, changed him.

There had always been a general apprehension in him, a distrust of things unknown. New people, new places, new experiences all produced anxiety which manifested itself in a constricted chest, sweating palms and, when he was younger, running away and hiding. He lived a sheltered life as a child. He came from a privileged Saudi family, on the fringe of the Royals, feeding on their table scraps. His diplomat father was in charge of polishing the Saudi royal family's image overseas and stroking their egos at home. His mother was a paranoid, doting woman who demurred to her husband's every desire and command. Asad was tutored along with the royal princes by excellent American teachers hired by the government. He spent most of his days speaking English, only allowed Arabic with his friends on the streets, though he soon began to see them as peasants, adopting the aloof air of his more privileged associates.

After college in America, he began to "hang with" the princes, hovering on the fringe, looking in on their lives of sex and drugs and all the thrills money could buy. Soon he found escape from his ubiquitous and permeating fear in cocaine. High, he could talk to and even make love to women. High, he could fight outside a busy Cairo bar and feel invincible. High, he could dance, sky dive, hang glide, sail, race boats and cars. High, he was loved and respected and envied. And feared. But when each episode finished in the action-hero movie that had become his life, the void in his soul was bigger than before and he struggled desperately to fill it. More cocaine, younger girls, or even boys, bigger boats, faster cars, more chances.

Ibiza was a favorite playground of the Saudi royal family and a well-known Mediterranean party destination. The small Spanish Island, famous for its beaches, nightlife and wealthy international clientele, knew how to please its super-rich Arab visitors. Here they owned beachfront properties, clubs, sports cars, HumVees, yachts, airplanes and helicopters. The merchants of Ibiza Town, along with the drug dealers, prostitutes, police and petty bureaucrats, all celebrated the bottomless well of Middle East cash. The occasional overdose, rape or murder was just the cost of doing business. Tourism fed the little island's economy, but bribes bought the champagne.

One night outside a busy club in Ibiza City, Asad met a young woman standing in the queue. He had been working his way through the loud throng of twenty-somethings waiting to get in to drink, snort coke and dance. Asad was heading to the door to get to Assiz, the club's bouncer, to let him in. By now he carried much the same clout as the Royals, many club owners unwilling to take the chance of offending the royal family by asking whether "this Asad" was deserving of the privileges apparently bestowed upon him.

Asad saw her and wanted her immediately. He had snorted several lines of coke in the Ferrari only moments before and like electric current it hummed through his body, bringing every sight, sound and smell into almost painful focus, revealing in crystalline relief its underlying beauty. Her dark eyes sparkled under the neon lights. Her midriff shirt and tight jeans made her look very American, so he spoke to her in English.

"How do you breathe in those pants?" he asked, leaning in close and smelling perfume mixed with her sweat.

She turned and met his eyes. There was defiance and a reckless confidence there. She shook her head and shoulder-length black hair flowed behind her, shaking side to side like a horse's tail.

In Arabic she said, "You'll lose your soul speaking the infidel's tongue. That's what my father says." Her smile and black eyes quickened his pulse. "Anyway," she said, "my ass doesn't need to breathe."

His lust churned with anger at her impetuousness. He expected some sign of respect, downcast eyes, a nervously whispered "Your Highness" or something that acknowledged his position in the social strata. There was nothing. After several years of looking and acting like one, Asad had begun to see himself as a Royal. Hypersensitivity to perceived insult and injustice were results of this evolution. The social freedom to right these wrongs and legal indifference to the manner in which they were resolved made Asad, the pretend prince, a dangerous man indeed.

But he wanted her so he held his voice even and flashed a brilliant disarming smile of his own. He gave her a bold exaggerated appraisal, looking her up and down, his gaze lingering on her buttocks.

"It looks like a living, breathing thing to me," he said in Arabic, and placed his hand on her back pocket. She did not remove it.

"Do you like waiting in line like a peasant?" he asked the girl, flashing his beautiful teeth and striking green eyes. In his silk shirt, tailored pants and Italian shoes, the gold necklace, Rolex and rings against his olive skin, he was a strikingly handsome man.

"If I am a peasant, why do you lower yourself to speak to me?" she said.

"It is enough to know that I did," he said, still smiling. "There is nothing in there," he told her, pointing to the door of the club, "that I cannot give you. Come with me; take a ride in my Ferrari. We can come back if you wish. I can get you in here anytime."

He promised they would return after midnight for an exclusive, invitation-only party. Despite her bravado, Asad knew the young woman, like most he met, assumed him to be a prince. He had the clothes, the jewelry, the cars, the drugs, the connections. To have a royal ask her into his car, to show interest in a common girl such as she, was an opportunity not to be missed. She was Cinderella to his Prince. Pretend Prince Asad. As he expected, she accepted his offer.

He drove her to a small villa in Jesus, northwest of Ibiza Town, calling ahead first to ensure it wasn't already in use. Asad had access to twenty-seven apartments, bungalows, luxury hotel suites, and villas, all maintained by the royal family and stocked with food, alcohol and drugs. Security staff controlled access to each location and defended judiciously the property of the Crown. Before the wrought-iron gate at the villa's entrance, a large Arab in a dark suit with a machine gun slung over his shoulder looked into the Ferrari. Recognizing Asad, he stepped aside and opened the gate. They drove up a circular driveway and parked in front of a two-story white stucco structure that sat on a hill, looking over the sparkling lights of the city. On the second floor they drank champagne and did lines of cocaine on the balcony railing as they looked out on the flickering lights of Jesus.

Asad stood behind her and slid his hands over her breasts, pulling her close.

"I want you," he whispered in her ear.

She set down her champagne glass, placed her hands over his and removed them from her chest.

"I would like to know more about you than the length of your dick before this night is over," she said quietly, still holding his hands.

To him, her tone was still maddeningly defiant. The sting of her earlier insult at the club had not abated. This rejection was gasoline to his smoldering temper. Still behind her, he slowly, affectionately caressed her long dark hair, then slowly wrapped it around both of his hands.

"Mmmm…that's nice," she said as she closed her eyes to the softly illuminated skyline and enjoyed the feeling of his hands playing in her hair. "What is it like," she asked him, "to live as royalty? To get anything you want?"

"It is a privilege and tradition to be honored. It is destiny," he said coldly. "Tell me, what is it like to be the thing taken?"

He kept his hands in her hair, separating the strands, and then bringing them back together again. Her hair was fine and smooth. It still smelled of soap, as she had not entered the smoky funk of the club. He hated that smell on a woman, the smell of old cigarettes and booze. It was rebellious and disrespectful.

"Will you be king one day? Girls want to grow up and be the princess," she observed, leaning back against him. "Men always want to be the king."

He could never be king, of course. He could never even be a prince. He would forever stand at the fringes, alone, his blood inferior like the peasant girl before him. No better than a mongrel dog at heart. His façade was fragile and this whore had just stabbed at it with her stupid childish words.

With two fistfuls of her beautiful hair he gritted his teeth and felt an incredible rage squeeze his hands tightly together. He heard her gasp as he dragged her backwards to the bed, her heels clicking across the ornately tiled floor. She began to scream as he stepped backwards up on the bed and lifted her as though she were a heavy suitcase to be opened and unpacked. She reached up to hold onto his wrists and relieve some of the pain in her scalp, her long nails digging into his flesh. He leaned down and savagely sunk his teeth into her hand, tasting the blood flow into his mouth. Her screams grew louder, but he was not concerned about the open window or the guard below. The man had surely heard similar things before. The woman's little finger was between his teeth and Asad bit hard, moving his jaw back and forth until it came loose in his mouth. He spit the finger onto the bed, bitten off at the second knuckle.

The cocaine and the alcohol and the struggle and her screams converged in his brain exciting him to greater and greater violence. He sat on her chest and beat her face with his fists, cutting them on her teeth, mixing her blood with his own. When she stopped struggling, he stripped off her clothes and raped her. Looking down at her bloody, disfigured face, she had ceased to be a human being to him. He rolled her onto her stomach so he would not have to look at her grotesque face. She was moaning now, a low animal sound that added to the impression that this was some injured animal. He raped her again, his appetite and capacity for brutality insatiable. He wanted to feel her die beneath him, an animal sacrificed to his whim and pleasure. Within the ornate buckle of his leather belt lay a small Shebriya dagger, its gold and silver handle etched with a crown and tangled vines. He removed it from its hidden sheath. Grabbing her hair once again he jerked her head back and drew the knife quickly across her throat. The shock sent her sinuous body into violent spasms, its wild, panicked thrashing fueling his desire. Blood flowed in waves from the gaping wound and soaked into the bed covers. An underwater gurgling sound issued from her open throat. Soon all sound and movement stopped, his lust temporarily satisfied.

The episode was easily concealed, at first. Witnesses not of sufficient social status were threatened, while the more influential ones were bought. Asad was mildly chastised by elder Saudi Royals for his indiscretion, though his actions won the respect and admiration of the young princes. But this relative indifference to rape and murder would be short-lived.

The girl, it turned out, was the daughter of a well-respected merchant back in Riyadh who had connections in the government. These were connections for which the father had paid handsomely. He saw the investment as insurance for an event such as this. His purpose in pursuing the matter had more to do with saving face and getting his money's worth, than seeking justice for his slain daughter. The fact that it was a daughter and that he had three more tempered his anger slightly. Instead of insisting on the assailant's head, which was well within his right once he discovered Asad was not royalty, the merchant agreed to financial compensation and the promise that his daughter's killer would be sent into the military. Asad's father lost his job as a diplomat and became a driver for one of the princes. Asad lost his medical scholarship and was sent to the Saudi military where he soon found himself helping the United States liberate Kuwait. It was there he would turn the agony of losing everything into a hatred of those who still had it. A hatred that would ultimately lead him to implement a plan to avenge himself in the name of Allah.

SEVEN

The U.S. Border Patrol Cessna 185 banked sharply to the south, as Officer Garrett Hansen made a slow circle twelve hundred feet above Gunflint Lake. The lightweight plane rattled and moved with fickle low-altitude breezes. He never got tired of seeing this country from the air. If you like wild country, he thought, you couldn't do any better than Minnesota's Arrowhead, the triangle of land bordered by Canada and the big lake. From his high perch he could see the rugged coast of Lake Superior, the largest body of fresh water in the world, bright gold in the morning sunlight. In the distance was the scalloped line of the Sawtooth Mountains rising almost two thousand feet above the rocky shoreline, covered with unbroken miles of pine, birch and maple forest provided a postcard setting for visitors and residents. Grand Marais was a welcoming ambassador to this wilderness, sitting on the only highway linking Canada and the United States between Duluth, Minnesota and the border. Interstate 35 ended in Duluth and state highway 61 carried traffic the remaining one hundred and fifty miles to the border, just north of the Chippewa Indian village of Grand Portage and a half hour south of Thunder Bay, Ontario. The narrow two-lane, serpentine road primarily followed the shore of Superior, crossing wild tumbling streams and threading its way through lighted tunnels blasted through tons of solid granite. Road improvements continued to inch northward, but the route was still dangerous, offering many perils like fog, wind, deer, moose, wolves and all forms of precipitation, sometimes all within a five-mile stretch of asphalt. Head-on collisions were common.

Hansen was a local. His father used to set gill nets in Superior's forty-degree waters for herring, whitefish and the occasional lake trout. Hansen helped him while he was growing up, but the U.S. Navy's promise of money and adventure drew him away from Grand Marais. He ended up in the Military Police, sometimes on ships, sometimes at military installations. He spent most of his time in Newport News, Virginia, busting drunks and breaking up fights. After eight years and a decent savings account, he traveled around the states, mostly out west. Somewhere along the way he picked up three tattoos, an earring, the clap, and a pilot's license for single-engine planes. When a job came up for border patrol agent he used his military connections and just a hint of blackmail—even Lieutenant Colonels drive drunk with young ladies in their laps on occasion—to secure a post in the Grand Marais office. In all that traveling, somehow he had lost himself. Returning to his birthplace felt like a natural thing to him, like a salmon swimming back to its river of origin to spawn. Either that, he speculated, or he just couldn't think of anyplace else to go.

Below him, the tentative green of new leaves washed the landscape like the first pass of a watercolor brush. The deep clear waters of Gunflint Lake sparkled in the bright spring sunlight. It was a sunny morning and he could see the plane's shadow floating across the shimmering surface. This was a routine daily patrol, but Hansen found nothing routine in flying above this country he loved so much, sharing the sky with bald eagles or watching moose cows and their calves swimming below him. He'd seen wolves tracking deer, watched bull moose locking antlers in battle, spotted wildfires and searched for campers lost in the woods. But one thing he'd never seen, in fact the very justification for him being in the air, was someone sneaking across the border.

In fact, he thought, it was laughable to think he would ever see anything worthy of follow-up. Regularly flying over a million acres of roadless wilderness he knew that if someone didn't want to be found, it would be damn hard to spot them from the air. On the ground, it was the wilderness rangers' job to check permits and handle the day-to-day management of the park, though there were only a few of them in the enormous park at any given time. Unless they reported something suspicious, he doubted his ability to distinguish an illegal alien in a canoe from anybody else. As a new agent, he brought it up to his supervisor, who told him, "Boy, the BWCAW border is protected by a billion of the most vicious border guards in the United States!" Hansen laughed it off at the time, but learning that the security of the United States depended largely on the voracity of biting flies and mosquitoes left him a little unsettled.

Hansen guided the plane toward the southeast, crossing four-mile long Loon Lake, the narrow twisting Iron Lake and Portage Lake. Further to the east he saw the long narrow blue finger of Birch Lake and the nineteen hundred-foot hills marking the Laurentian Divide. The divide splits the North American continent in two, directing the flow of water through the land. Rain falling on the north side of the divide runs to Hudson Bay and, ultimately, the Arctic Ocean over one thousand miles away. On the south side, water is bound for Lake Superior or the Mississippi and finally the Gulf of Mexico. He'd always found that fascinating, that he could stand in a place on the earth where things changed depending on which way you faced. He likened it to standing atop Everest, which he had never done, or the Equator, which he had. It was proof of the nature of things, that the world could be a place of permanence and reliability, that reality was not a subjective thing. If he were a drop of rain falling on this spot on the earth, depending on which way he tumbled, he would always know where he would end up. There were few things in the world, he thought, so assured as that.

Hansen brought the Cessna down on the huge expanse of Poplar Lake, the pontoons bouncing lightly across the choppy water, then sinking in and dragging the small airplane to a halt. Poplar was a motor lake, at the edge of the BW. There were many lake homes and cabins on the shore, along with a couple of small resorts, which offered the relative luxuries of indoor plumbing and electricity along with outfitting services for trips into the primitive Wilderness. It served as a transition between civilization and the wild, the contrasts between the two made more striking by their proximity.

He taxied to the fifty-foot seaplane dock in front of Cosgrove's Poplar Lodge and watched as Billy Cosgrove walked down its length grinning and waving. Billy grabbed a pontoon strut with a thick-callused hand and tied the plane to a cleat. The slowly drifting plane reached the end of the thick short length of rope and stopped with a jerk, sending a vibration down the wooden platform. Hansen opened the door of the airplane and jumped down onto the dock, extending his hand which was grasped and shaken enthusiastically.

"Up there burnin' my tax money again, I see!" Billy said. "It's noon somewhere. Come have a beer with me."

"You do this every time, Billy," Hansen said. "I'm on duty, you know that. Stop testing me damn it!"

"Well, at least have some eggs and bacon. Libby's got the fire hot and the coffee's blacker than a moose's ass at midnight!"

"You know it's tempting when you put it like that." Hansen straightened the Border Patrol cap on his head and removed the polarized aviator-style sunglasses he wore. "Tell Libby, a few scrambled eggs and Tabasco sounds perfect. Then you can tell me where the damn big walleyes are out here this year!"

"I tell you every year, but you fish like my grandmother fucks. Anyway, you shouldn't be fishing when there's All-Kinda in the bushes." Billy leaned close to Hansen and whispered, as if in confidence, "I hear the terror alert is orange now. Can you tell me what the hell that means? Does that mean somebody called in a threat or is Dubya bored with his Legos?"

"It's pronounced al Qaeda and I could arrest you for disparaging my commander in chief, you know. Anyway, I don't know any more than you do. It changes more often than gas prices. Let's eat and forget about politics for a few minutes, huh?" Hansen suggested.

"Amen to that, brother," Cosgrove said. "Amen to that! Boring shit anyway. By the way, haven't seen your partner in crime in a while. Shouldn't Toftey be paddlin' in here by now, looking like Jesus Christ hisself, the long-haired, bearded wonder?"

"He's coming down from Sag," Hansen shrugged. "Should be here in a couple of days. I'll drive down and meet him here. Then it's into town for a shower and supplies."

"And pussy." Billy added. "Hey, don't give me that look! I was young once."

Hansen looked around, an exaggerated look of shock and incredulity on his tan, weather-beaten face, looking older than his forty years, and said, "I thought this was a *family* resort?"

Billy scoffed, then made a sound of modest surprise, as if the action reminded him of a neglected chore or a curious phenomenon. He took a deep rattling breath and sent the results of a productive cough far into the crystal-clear waters of Poplar Lake.

"Let the fuckin' tree huggers get that through their micro filters."

They headed up the long dock toward the main lodge. Hansen could see movement inside. As he got closer the smoky, greasy scent of bacon and the promise of strong coffee greeted his nostrils.

"Billy," Hansen said, his mouth watering with the smell, "whatever you do, don't lose that woman. There's not another that would have you."

EIGHT

Federal Bureau of Investigation Headquarters, Quantico, Virginia
May, 2002
Wednesday, 10:00 AM

The punch came from an impossible angle. At least that's how he would remember it after he woke up. And when Brian Setty came to, lying on a cot, slowly focusing on the fluorescent lights over his head, he was angry and wanted a second chance. The throbbing at the base of his skull, however, quickly tempered his zeal.

"Ah," said a rough voice to his left. "Sleeping beauty awakens."

"Am I on the train?" Setty managed groggily.

"What train?" said the man to his left.

"The train that hit me."

The disembodied voice laughed. "He came right up the middle, baby. Bout lifted you off your feet!"

A large bearded face came into view, blocking the light as dark brown eyes looked down on him. "Good thing you had your mouth closed, for once. Otherwise you'd be gettin' your jaw wired shut right about now." The bearded man laid a warm cloth across Setty's forehead and continued. "I told you at every goddamn break you need to back off when he comes inside on you!"

"I thought you were messin' with me, Kirby. I heard something like `Back off when he comes on you!' or some such shit." Setty grinned. "I thought it best not to turn my back on him. That's what I get for having a gay boxing coach. Mixed signals."

There were two boxing rings in the FBI gym complex in Quantico, one with fourteen-foot inside ropes and one eighteen-footer. Setty was decked in the big ring by a field agent, Eddie Rutherford, who had won the academy tournament for the past three years. It wasn't shocking that he lost. He'd had his ass kicked by Rutherford on several occasions. What frustrated Brian most was that he made the same mistake every time. Eddie led with a long left jab, probing and poking, keeping Brian off balance and unable to set himself for an effective punch of his own. Usually Setty could only withstand this for two rounds before he would become exasperated and wade in, lulled into complacency by the repetitive and relatively gentle punches. Before pursuing this ill-fated strategy—Kirby called it 'the walking testicle', vulnerable, full of testosterone and no brain—he would feel that he could simply overpower Eddie with strong body-to-head combinations. Then, sometime during the "wading in" process, Rutherford would land two devastating right hooks to Brian's ribs and, as he doubled over from the blows, Eddie would land an uppercut that seemed to start near the floor somewhere and gather velocity like a rocket launching, until it connected with Setty's chin. Kirby liked to call that part "the time machine," as Setty would invariably wake up elsewhere later in the day.

"Here's a mixed signal for you," Kirby said. "I sucked your dick while you were out. Now you're gay too."

Setty was regaining a sense of humor along with his consciousness. "Aha, I wondered how that worked," he said. "Kind of like vampires and werewolves I guess."

"Yeah, you get eternal life but the full moon brings cravings for red pumps and Rodgers and Hammerstein."

Kirby Lutz lifted weights and rode a '57 Harley Electra Glide, his only true love. It was emblazoned in a blue tattoo across the back of his bulging neck, the words streaming though the center of a plump red heart. He was the perfect fit for undercover work and the Bureau shipped him around frequently, from drug busts of motorcycle gangs to white supremacist weapons violations, even once to infiltrate a prison crack ring in Folsom. He was afraid of nothing and loved putting on a good show. He took great pleasure in judiciously executing his duties as a federal agent, particularly against criminals in whom he recognized even the slightest hint of the arrogance and cruelty of the school kids who had ridiculed him, back when it became clear he was different.

His best friend since the first day at the academy was Brian Setty. Setty's self-confidence bordered on swagger, but held none of the intolerance or cruelty that Kirby recognized almost telepathically in others. He respected the kid's investigative sense. Though ten years his junior, Brian Setty deciphered patterns in the most obscure and/or scant evidence before Kirby or any other agent could swallow their first sip of coffee.

"Next time," Setty said, sitting up slowly and rolling off the massage table in the locker room, "I'll kick his ass."

"Take a shower, then let's go get some lunch, killer," said Kirby.

"I can't," Setty told him, grabbing a towel from his locker and slinging it over his shoulder. "I've got a DHS border briefing at one o'clock. I might be going to Minnesota." He stopped, and then turned back to Kirby looking puzzled. "Know where that is?"

Kirby shrugged his huge shoulders and made a "no idea" face at Brian. "I think it's over there around Nevada."

Setty looked at the big man, exasperated. "It has to be on the border somewhere, genius."

"Oh no! Are the Mounties planning an offensive?" Kirby adopted his flaming hairdresser persona and said with a flourish, "Girlfriend, the only things offensive on those boys are their hideous red suits and baggy knickers! Tailor, tailor! Emergency!"

Setty shook his head, turned on the shower and yelled over the rushing water, "I'm so glad you won't be passing on your genes."

Kirby watched the cloud of steam billowing from the shower room and grunted. He looked down at Setty's dress clothes lying on the massage table. He picked them up, deposited each individual item in a separate locker and left the tropical funk of the FBI locker room behind.

NINE

Morocco, December, 2000

Across a cobblestone square, as pigeons nervously strutted, fluttered and lighted amid the constantly moving mass of people, Asad picked the man out of the crowd, like a lion separating the vulnerable beast from the herd. His body language was hesitant and slow, appearing uncertain of his movements and direction. The man was surveying the crowd from behind sunglasses—the slight downward cast and furtive glances betraying his apprehension and caution. He wore the garb of a religious man—not a holy man, but a man of devout faith. On his head was a simple white taqiyah and a gandora flowing behind him in the warm saltwater breeze. In the long white shirt, buttoned all the way up to his neck, he was slightly conspicuous in the crowd of people wearing a mixture of western clothes and traditional Moroccan dress, mainly modest colored jelabas. It was not unusual enough to comment on, but to Asad he stood out in stark contrast to those around him.

He briefly thought how easy it would be to kill him. That evaluation was second nature to him now, like praying. It was no longer a conscious effort. Every meeting, every situation began with an almost instantaneous measurement of distances to cover, possible methods of attack, routes of escape, natural and manmade features, lighting, noise, obstacles, hostages. He would position himself as best he could to take full advantage of natural barriers to bomb blast shrapnel, like brick walls, delivery trucks, even crowds of people. If he was to die, he did not want it to be through chance or fate. It would be

Allah's will, just as it was Allah's will that he should be careful.

Finally the man saw Asad sitting at the café and crossed the square toward him. Asad stood as he approached. They embraced and kissed each other's cheeks, taking seats across from one another. Ibrahim ordered tea and did not speak until it arrived. Then he spoke in a soft voice, barely raising his mouth from the tea cup. "The Sheik is pleased, Asad. You have done a great thing, praise Allah."

"Thank you," Asad said, picking up his own cup. "It pleased me as well."

Ibrahim set his cup down on its saucer and removed his sunglasses.

"It was well executed and it showed great vision, planning, leadership and faith, praise Allah."

The soft-spoken man paused to sip his tea once again.

"The Sheik requests your service for the trip next spring, a journey through the wilderness. He wants your leadership, your dedication, your loyalty and your strength. This is your time, Asad, your moment to make history here and in eternity. You stand bravely before evil. Do you accept this great honor?"

In the midst of this solemn occasion, Asad al-Muhammad felt a smile threaten the corners of his mouth. Here in this Moroccan café, with the smell of the sea and fish assaulting his nostrils, the shade from the table's umbrella barely keeping the afternoon heat at bay, Asad took the assignment with all the zealous conviction of a man whose life had been taken then given to him once more. It would be his chance to strike at the heart of those who dishonored him. It was America who empowered the Saudis. To hurt the dog that was America was to hurt all its parasites—fleas, like the House of Saud. To Asad, who had lost so much, it was a chance to grab them by their bejeweled throats and squeeze the arrogance from them. With effort he reminded himself that this man before him and their leader saw the mission as an attack on infidels, non-believers, enemies of Islam. Asad saw himself as a good Muslim who believed in the martyr's path to paradise. That Allah's wrath and his own would converge was truly glorious. All this and Heaven too, he thought.

"I do," said Asad. "With all of my Earthly being I give myself to the just and righteous path. All my brain and muscle and blood, praise Allah! I am his will."

At this, the soft-spoken Ibrahim finished his tea and rose from the table. The man looked down at Asad through mirrored sunglasses. Asad could see his own paired reflection staring back at him—two Asads: the religious crusader and the avenger of his own wounded pride.

"You must rest now," said Ibrahim. "You look tired. Go home and we will find you when the time is right."

He dropped a few coins on the table then walked back across the square, the gandora flowing behind him, pigeons fluttering in his wake.

The exhaustion hit Asad all at once. Ibrahim was right; all he wanted now was sleep. He paid the café and headed to his flat in the city.

TEN

Abu Ghraib Prison, Iraq
May, 2002
Saturday, 6:30 AM

"Get up, sand nigger!" A terrifying clatter woke him from a fitful sleep. He sat up and panicked in the blackness until he remembered the hood over his head. The door to his cell clanged open and footsteps approached. Hands grabbed him roughly under each arm and hoisted him to his feet. He was dragged backwards out of his cell then led down a long hallway. He heard a door open to his left. He was dragged again then thrown down into a hard metal chair. The plastic tie that bound his hands was cut, as was the one around his neck, which kept the black hood in place. The hood was not removed. A single set of footsteps exited the room and clicked smartly down the hallway. He could still sense a presence in the room; he could hear the breathing of another person.

"Take off the hood," ordered the male voice to his right. It was hard not to follow the instructions but it was imperative he feign ignorance. He assumed this was typical treatment for all new prisoners—a few cursory attempts to extract knowledge after weakening his condition then he would be remanded to a less secure area and held. For how long he did not know.

He expected torture. He expected beatings, electrocution, burns, strangulation, drowning. He had been through much of it in Saddam's prison, under the cruelty of the Secret Police. Suddenly the hood was removed from his head and the light in the room blinded him. His eyes adjusted slowly. In front of him was a table on which sat two plastic bottles of what appeared to be liquor. There was a paper cup sitting next the square bottles of caramel-colored liquid. Also on the table was a plastic funnel attached to a three-foot length of garden hose. Next to the funnel was a portable stereo system. Looking up, he saw that the walls were covered with pornographic images, mostly of homosexual sex acts between men and sado-masochistic scenes. There was a large television set in the corner playing a pornographic video of an all-male orgy. The sound was turned down. He turned toward the soldier next to him, but before his face could come all the way around he was zapped by a painful jolt from a cattle prod.

"You have two choices," the man told him. "You can drink the Jack Daniels or I can help you booze bong it. Trust me, you don't want my help, partner"

He made no sign that he had understood anything the soldier was saying. The soldier rapped the cattle prod sharply on the table, and then slowly swept the cup and plastic bottle closer.

"Drink, you motherfucker!"

Ibrahim did not move.

The soldier held the cattle prod against the man's shoulder for several seconds. Ibrahim screamed then slumped in the chair, muscles twitching involuntarily. He heard the soldier's voice once again.

"Look at me, al-Takar."

Weakened by the pain in his back he turned at the sound of his name. As soon as he did so, he felt something inside desert him. He assumed it was hope. His head grew oppressively heavy and sunk to his chest. They had his name and he had just confirmed it.

"Yeah, I know who you are and I know you speak English. Now, have a fucking drink."

"I do not drink alcohol," he managed weakly.

"You do today."

As if on cue three soldiers entered. Two men handcuffed Ibrahim's hands behind him while another with forearms like tree trunks put him in a vise-like headlock and tilted him back until he was staring at the fluorescent lights on the ceiling. "Don't choke him, Barnes—he's gotta Linda Lovelace this fuckin' hose. Epps, help him open wide."

Epps resembled a grain silo in fatigues, huge and vaguely cylindrical.

"You got it, Sarge," the soldier said, and then pinched the Iraqi's nose closed painfully while clamping an enormous hand over the man's mouth.

The sergeant opened a bottle of whiskey.

"Vince, get over here and fill up the bong."

Vince, a skinny kid with almost translucent white skin and a fuzz of red hair on his scalp, dumped liquor into the funnel until it was full, holding the end of the hose above it so the liquid would not run out.

The sergeant said, "When he takes a breath shove that fucker down his throat like he was some sloppy crack ho."

When Ibrahim began to struggle, Epps asked, "Ready?"

Vince nodded. Epps removed his hand. As Ibrahim opened his mouth to take a breath Vince shoved the hose into his mouth and pushed until it passed brutally into his gullet. The sergeant raised the funnel and the golden liquid disappeared in a second. He pulled the hose from the gagging man's throat and they all stepped back.

"Dude, he's gonna puke," said Vince, giggling.

"Nah," said the sergeant, "at least not until the room zooms kick in."

The sergeant was a young man, like the rest of them, with steely close-set blue eyes and the flat top crew cut typical of old-school Special Forces. He bent down close to Ibrahim, so close their noses touched.

He whispered menacingly, "Sit back, relax and enjoy the best that American culture has to offer. We're gonna put your soul in Hell, you terrorist piece of shit."

He then turned on the boom box and cranked the volume up high. The relentless thrashing guitars and drums of Metallica's "Blitzkrieg" thundered from the speakers. Before he left the room, the sergeant walked over to the TV and turned up the volume equally high, filling the room with a cacophony of moans, shrieks and profanity accompanied by the pounding heavy metal.

"Enjoy!" he shouted as they all left the room.

ELEVEN

Goiaina, Brazil
September, 1987

The surrounding jungle was still in the thick sodden air of midday. Insects buzzed and bird calls echoed from deep within the dark shade of the tree canopy, but only the waves of heat, undulating mirage-like across the gravel parking lot, brought motion to the still life.

A small cloud of dust rose sluggishly above the trees in the distance and hung there, marking the path of a car on the road below. Soon, a little red Fiat rattled into the open of the parking lot and pulled to a shuddering stop before the chaos of metal and glass that once was "La Clínica de Familia Goiania."

Victor Gallegos peered through the dusty windshield at the remains of the abandoned and partially demolished clinic. Much of the building lay in a shimmering heap at the edge of the gravel lot, surrounded by the Amazon jungle's tattered hem. Already its threads had begun to unravel and creep back into the clearing, eager to reclaim the land lost to developers years ago. The clinic was the enterprise of three cancer specialists: a German and two Americans. They overestimated the willingness and income of Goiania's 760,000 people. Those who discovered their cancer were often too poor to do much about it. To the rest who died from the disease it was accepted as the will of God and they made their peace. The German and American doctors talked to their lawyers, signed a few papers and soon found themselves on a chartered plane to Rio, wondering how life could be so unfair and if the

Cipriani on Copacabana Beach would be serving the veal marsala that night.

They wrote-off the property, they wrote-off the building and they wrote-off its contents – the couches, the beds, the desks the equipment. The imaging machines and the radiation therapy instruments stayed there too. And, of course, they wrote off the residents of Goiania.

Victor open the car door, which squealed in protest, and got out. Two junk dealer friends who were salvaging the site told him he could take anything he wanted. They had already picked it clean of copper and aluminum. There was little left, but Victor was good at making a little go a long way. He stepped through the door-less entry, scattering small green and brown lizards with each footfall. Kicking through the debris, he noticed many ceiling tiles still intact and pieces of drywall large enough to sell. Some wall outlets and switches remained. He could make enough for groceries, maybe a new pair of shoes for Maria. Victor didn't want the other kids to make fun of her tattered sandals. There had been no shoes for him growing up…no school either. Things would be better for his daughter.

All the shingles had been removed and water had leaked into the structure from above. Victor splashed through the puddles and investigated the remaining rooms. Most were empty examining rooms, the tables and chairs removed along with light fixtures. In the last room he was surprised to find a complicated machine on the floor. Some of it had been torn away, but a large metal arm remained along with a cylindrical silver canister. When he bent down to pick up the canister he discovered why it was still there. It was incredibly heavy and still attached to the metal arm. Victor walked back to the Fiat, unhooked the rubber strap holding down the trunk lid, and removed a large heavy pry bar. He returned to the machine and after several minutes of effort, separated the cylinder from the frame of the device. He assumed there was an engine within, or perhaps a sensor of some kind with fine optical equipment. Whatever the contents, it was heavy, and Victor knew, that often meant it was valuable.

As he hefted the silver can and waddled with it back to his car, he noticed a blue powder on his hands. It appeared luminescent in the sunlight and glowed a deep azure when he passed through shadows of the hallway. It was mesmerizing. Beautiful. He could see he had ruptured the metal canister with the crow bar and the powder was coming from inside. He had never seen anything like it. It will make Maria smile, he thought. Victor would do anything to see his little *ardilla* smile.

He sat the cylinder in the trunk and went back into the building, gathering sheets of drywall and ceiling tiles. He collected all the little car could carry. He tied these to the roof of the Fiat and headed home to his family.

TWELVE

Boundary Waters Canoe Area Wilderness
Minnesota, May, 2002
Wednesday 9:00 AM

Branches slapped Toftey's face and arms as he ran through the trees. He ran wildly in a zigzag pattern, hoping to dodge the inevitable bullet, fighting the weakness in his knees at the thought of being shot in the back. Even more frightening than his panicked thoughts were the thudding, crashing footsteps behind him. He heard no human voices, just animal grunts, snapping branches, footfalls and his own thundering heart. He dared not look behind him for fear of tripping on the multitude of obstacles before him. He plunged on into head-high hazel brush, with no thought of direction, just an unconscious instinct to run away from the men with the guns. A waist-high blowdown or a fallen limb would be the death of him so he tried to look ahead with his arms raised, fending off the branches that whipped him. He knew he was in plain sight as the budding leaves were not adequate to conceal him. He also knew he was picking the best path for them as well. The steps behind were getting closer. Why didn't they shoot?

A thought fought its way through the torrent of adrenaline coursing through his body. To the north of the portage a ridge rose up to Saganaga Lake and dropped straight down to the water below. The lake then emptied into the Seagull River, swollen and surging with spring run-off. He didn't know how deep the water was there, but reaching it was the only plan he had. He figured it was about a hundred yards away. He could see the open expanse of the lake through the bare trees. The roar of the river was growing louder and filled his head, softening the sounds of his pursuers. Ahead of him was a huge fallen spruce tree, its tangle of limbs creating a wall of sharp broken branches and hanging moss. On one end its root ball rose twelve feet out of the ground, roots, rocks and other trees all torn from the ground. The top of the tree disappeared into a confusion of other fallen trees and undergrowth. There was no going around it. He hoped his momentum would carry him through, though he didn't have time to check if the branches would easily snap or hold him back. Without breaking stride, like a hurdler Toftey cleared the trunk of the spruce, snapping several branches with a sharp crack.

On his way over the tree he felt his right leg catch on something, rip his pants and tear at his thigh. On the other side the uneven ground made him stumble, but he was able to regain his footing and keep running. As he regained his stride, he heard a tremendous crack behind him and assumed that the shot had missed otherwise, like a deer running with its heart mangled by a hunter's bullet, he was simply dead on his feet, running on adrenaline alone. For the first time he chanced a quick look back and saw a man struggling, draped over the trunk of the tree as though trying to crawl over it. But just before he turned back, he saw the group's leader leap onto the struggling man's back and launch himself toward Toftey in one fluid powerful motion.

Toftey ran for the open lake. The roar of the water was all he could hear now. As he neared the cliff a brief rush of renewed panic threatened to choke him. Then he broke through the woods and jumped into empty air.

To Toftey, who was still expecting a bullet in the back, it took a long time to hit the water. He had no idea if he would land on a boulder in six inches of water and crumple like an accordion. His eyes were closed, teeth clenched and body taut when he splashed and sank beneath the surface. He knew it would be cold, but he was not prepared for the shock. It was all he could do not to gasp for breath. As his body slowed its descent he fought through the pain of the cold and began stroking with legs and arms toward the cliff face. His eyes were open now and the clear water let shafts of shimmering sunlight into the depths, illuminating the world beneath. Below him was impenetrable darkness; he had no idea how deep the water was. In front of him now was the dark stone of the cliff. Upon reaching it, he surfaced. Looking up he could see that it overhung the water slightly and that against its base he could remain hidden from above.

The river roared twenty feet to his right; its current pulling at his body while uncontrollable shivering overtook him. Suddenly behind him a tremendous splash made him think one of the men had followed him in. Turning he saw only waves rippling from the impact. He drew breath and ducked under the water to look for someone rising from a dive, but saw nothing. Then another tremendous splash and Toftey watched a large rock sink into the darkness and out of sight. They were throwing rocks at him. Then he realized; they *can't* shoot me! They didn't want the attention a gunshot could bring. Even with the park as lightly traveled as it was this time of the year, sound carried for miles across the water.

This realization gave him the confidence to move. He crept along the base of the cliff as quickly as his stiffening limbs would carry him. The current was stronger now and it pulled him to the cataract. The rock wall was slippery and cold. His grasping fingers began to fail him. In an instant, with a heart-sinking gasp he was sucked beneath the surface and pulled into the tumbling vortex.

THIRTEEN

Pentagon, Arlington, Virginia
May, 2002
Tuesday, 9:40 PM

It was getting late, but Beth's brain was busy formulating hypotheses around the picture fragment she'd found. From one of the computers in 708 she had put several investigative processes into motion. First, after making several photograph-quality copies of the image, applying various degrees of enlargement, she scanned the image and emailed the resulting "jpeg" file to Darryl Allis, an imaging expert with the CIA's National Photographic Interpretation Center.

She'd worked with Darryl on many projects and didn't know anybody better at wringing a story out of a seemingly inconsequential photograph. She had seen him solve the murder of a Colorado woman whose boyfriend reported her missing in the spring after a hiking trip in Estes Park. The man claimed that they had taken a trail that wound through the foothills. He told park rangers she had grown tired and sat down to rest. He left her to take some pictures of butterflies in a meadow. When he returned, she was gone. The pictures he took that day were entered into evidence, though all of them were close-ups of flowers and butterflies—nothing containing a landmark or any other point of reference to tell investigators where the pictures were taken. Beth remembered Darryl explaining it all to her in his nasal, manic delivery, running his fingers over his forehead and through his long dark hair repeatedly to keep it out of his eyes. She thought he looked like one of the Ramones.

"I was looking at the pictures. They were awesome, you know, really great color and composition, interesting instead of American Gothic, National Geographic, you know, everything smack-dabbed in the middle of the frame? Not to mention the butterflies—really cool, white wings with black dots and red or orange centers. Then I looked at this guy—not an artistic tooth in his fat head. Wouldn't know a butterfly from a butthole. No elfin' way dude took these, no way!"

Beth just nodded and watched Darryl spin through his story, frantic and breathless, bouncing around like a dust devil on a dirt road.

"So, I got a wild hair and I checked them against bug and flower field guides. And guess what? No, no, guess?" He looked at her expectantly. It was clear he wouldn't go on without her response.

"Uh, they were from somewhere else?" she guessed.

Darryl cleared his face of hair, eyes wide and said, "Dude! No wonder you're a CIA mega-sleuth! They were from the genus Parnissius; they're pretty common in parts of Colorado, just not in the part of Colorado where this dude said they'd been hiking. See, you only find Parnissans above seven thousand feet. Dude said they were hiking a trail that never gets higher than five thousand feet. There's also a flower you only find on Mount Evans, about three hundred miles from Estes Park."

"That's incredible, Darryl! Now who's the mega-sleuth?"

"But wait, wait, there's more! Like I said, whoever shot these was really good. Everything was dead clear, like looking through outer space. The close-ups of the flowers were so clear that I could see stuff reflected in the dewdrops. I could see butterfly wings, flower petals, even grass and the hillside. So I enlarged a few and sure as my grandma's mustache, in one of the drops I saw her."

"Your grandma?"

He ignored her remark and lowered his voice to achieve full dramatic effect.

"The photographer."

"You said, *her*?"

"Yeah, dude didn't take those pics. His old lady did."

Darryl raised the dark curtain of hair once more revealing eyes like saucers and whispered, "She's speakin' to us from the other side, like a restless ghost, demanding justice. Freaky ain't it?"

Not only did the man lie about where they were, but his entire justification for leaving his girlfriend alone in the woods was proven a lie by Darryl's work. Faced with these facts "dude" confessed.

Now, Beth removed her glasses and rubbed her eyes, which felt like someone had thrown sand into them.

"God, what a long-ass day," she said. Looking at the large round institutional clock mounted over the doorway of the lab, she was overwhelmed by a sudden memory of her father, sitting in her fourth-grade classroom, talking to the kids about a sheriff's daily work. She remembered beaming with pride watching this man, so handsome in his brown uniform and trooper-style hat, so at ease with the children, commanding their rapt attention and respect. She could hear his words, smooth and soft with a barely contained enthusiasm, see his big hands gesticulating in concert with his voice, like a conductor urging them on, infusing them with his own passion. As a nine-year-old girl, Beth felt giddy satisfaction watching her classmates, especially mean Mary Jane Keller who teased her about her glasses and many other things, sit in awe before her dad. She was invincible when he was in the room.

The clock's long black minute hand clicked loudly as it met the hour hand on the twelve. The memory dissolved and left her staring blankly at the wall, as if she had arrived too late to the station and watched forlorn as the last train pulled away. A ghost train, she thought. Time to go home, you loopy workaholic.

Before she left, Beth did a quick Internet search for "Marais" the word she had found written on the back of the tattered aerial photo. She found a dead South African folk singer, a trendy neighborhood in Paris, a small Michigan town on the South Shore of Lake Superior and a small Minnesota town on the North Shore of Lake Superior. There were other references, but it was the last two that most intrigued Beth. The Michigan town was near Sault Ste. Marie, a popular border crossing between Canada and the U.S. The Minnesota Grand Marais was close to another busy border crossing, Grand Portage, only thirty miles from Thunder Bay, Ontario. The proximity of both towns to busy Canadian borders made her uneasy, though she had worked on enough investigations to know that usually things are not what they seem.

As she put the documents away, she felt the visceral pang of disappointment that returned every time she prepared to go home to her small Bethesda, Maryland apartment. She told herself it was only because she loved her job so much and that she was tired of the thirty-minute train ride. Every morning she'd grab the red line Metro south from Bethesda to the Metro Center station at eleventh and G, then transfer to the blue line train down to Pentagon station, joining the jostling throng streaming to the sea of cubicles within the huge stone edifice. It was hard not to make the "ants into the anthill" comparison. She knew there was more to her malaise, but Beth Adams wasn't in the mood for self-discovery. It inevitably lead to sadness and she was tired of feeling sad. No, she thought, no honesty tonight. She opened the desk drawer she'd been using and locked the files inside, dropping the key in her briefcase. She swiped her access card past the reader at the door and entered her PIN. The metallic click signaled the magnetic lock had disengaged and she pushed the heavy door, which swung open, silently. The hallway was empty. It was a long walk to the station and the last train would pull away in ten minutes. She'd have to hurry. Her quick footsteps clattered and bounced around the walls like marbles tossed down a stairwell.

FOURTEEN

Asad stood atop the sharp cliff face looking over the edge to the water, looking for a sign of the man who had just made a fool of him. He knew how cold the water was and had no intention of following the ranger's desperate leap. None of them were experienced canoeists and they had already dumped each of the canoes twice at rocky portage landings. Fortunately their volatile cargo was well sealed in waterproof bags and cushioned within the bulky canvas Duluth-style packs.

Asad took a deep breath in an attempt to steady his voice and turned to the three others who now joined him above the calm water. The roar of the nearby river required him to shout. He must, he thought, appear calm and in complete control. They must obey him or all would be lost. He looked into the eyes of each man, appraising their states of mind. His dark eyes settled coldly on the man they knew as Saad. None of the members of the team knew the other members. Not even Asad had any knowledge of these men. The Sheik had told them that if their mission was successful they would meet in the afterlife to celebrate their martyrdom as the real men they were, the men Allah meant them to be. The bodies they inhabited here on earth were merely vessels to hold their souls—hands and legs and brains to serve Allah, inconsequential flesh and bone. They were not to place any value on their physical beings except as tools to accomplish the greater good. Their deaths would be a glorious beginning.

"If any of you are that foolish again I will kill you," said Asad, still looking at Saad, watching the old man's scar turn to crimson. "There can be no shooting here."

He paced in front of them now, as he had done when berating his unit in Iraq after perceived challenges to his authority.

"Do nothing without my orders. I am in charge of this mission! Do any of you doubt this?" All eyes were downcast and they shook their heads in unison. "Anwar, Saad, take those large rocks and throw them into the water," he ordered. "I want him distracted while I go down to the river in case he tries to escape there. Kadir, go to the head of the trail where he left his canoe and carry it to ours, then wait there. If you see him, kill him."

Then he ran down the slope toward the rushing stream.

Kadir had been a student in Tangiers when world events and sympathy for the suffering of his Arab brothers and sisters in Iraq brought him closer to his religious roots. One day, at a mosque near the university, a cleric from Tehran spoke passionately about the duty of all Muslims to come to the aid of those dying for their beliefs, dying at the hands of non-believers. It was as simple as that — Muslims were being persecuted in their own countries by invaders carrying the destruction of Islam wrapped in the guise of liberation from oppression. The cleric asked the audience of mostly students if they felt oppressed. He reminded them of their freedom to learn, to travel, to grow, their freedom to use their learning to form their own opinions, and, most importantly, their obligation as world citizens, moral human beings and followers of Islam to fight, in prayer and deed, for their faith, regardless of the personal cost. "For a righteous man," he said, "has nothing to fear in this world but the loss of his faith."

Kadir was a thin young man, sensitive about his round boyish face. He wore a thick mustache to appear older, though it only succeeded in drawing further attention to the contradiction. He was not happy to be off on his own, away from the group. This place frightened him, especially at night when sounds unlike anything he had ever heard assaulted his ears. He had been given books to read about the forests of northeastern Minnesota, which apparently they called "the Arrowhead Region" due to the shape of the state as it squeezed to a point between Lake Superior's northern shore and the Canadian border. He had seen pictures of squirrels, beavers, eagles, deer, moose and, most worrisome to him, bears and wolves. But none of those books described the various sounds made by each animal. At night he lay wrapped tightly in his sleeping bag, eyes open and searching the darkness for movement, imagining each twitter, chirp and twig snap was a prelude to the attack of some dangerous beast. As a result he was already exhausted when the rigorous daily routine began again.

He did not share his fears with the strangers in the group. He expected it would be seen as the weakness of a boy in over his head. But, occasionally, he would glimpse a hint of similar apprehension on another man's face. Their eyes would meet for a second then, just as quickly, they would look away. That is except for Asad. There was nothing to learn from his face. It was as unforgiving and cruel as the cold rock-strewn country in which they now found themselves. Kadir would not meet his gaze for fear he would see into his soul and find the doubt hiding there.

In his daily prayers he asked Allah for the strength to continue—the strength, when the moment arrived, to carry out his mission and die a martyr, to live eternity bathed in the pleasures he had not known as a mortal man on earth.

FIFTEEN

Garrett Hansen raised the three-pound splitting maul over his head and brought it down on the thick spruce log sitting on the stump in front of him. The log split cleanly with a loud snap and each half fell to opposite sides, the maul embedding itself in the wide cedar stump beneath with a heavy thud. The pile of stove-sized logs beside him were the remains of trees cut earlier in the day. He had spent the chilly morning cutting white spruce and balsams that had blown down during heavy winds the previous fall. He hadn't had time to clean up around his little log home last November, with deer hunting season upon him and splitting maple for his stove a priority. Plus, of course, there was his work with the United States Border Patrol.

Away from the politics of the office, everybody at the Grand Portage station knew the workload was light. Sure, there were reports to file and the occasional border run by some kid freaking out over the bag of weed under the seat of his pickup truck, but by and large, the challenges were few. There had been enough excitement in the military to last him the rest of his life. Collecting a regular government paycheck for flying and driving around this country was ok with him.

The heavy maul came down in the center of another upright log and two more pieces fell neatly cleaved in two. He wanted to get his work done before he drove back to Poplar Lake to pick up his friend Mark Toftey. He was looking forward to hearing news from the wilderness over a beer and a burger in Grand Marais.

He found in Toftey a man who, like himself, embraced the wilderness while shunning what he called the redneck ethic. In explanation, Toftey once told him, "The redneck ethic says the common good is a myth perpetrated by those who would steal my freedom. They see government rules and policies as fascism or socialism but they wouldn't be able to tell you what either of those words mean." He continued, "They're the folks who yell for less government while supporting policies and leaders that actually tighten the hold the government has on the only true personal freedoms, like expression, thought, association, spirituality. The redneck," Toftey said, "sells his soul for football on Sundays and the right to drive his gas-sucking pickup to get cigarettes. Losing the right to think for yourself isn't scary to someone who's never had an original thought."

"Well, I've stolen a little freedom in my day," Hansen admitted, "and I don't regret a single arrest, soldier or civilian. When I was an MP, I just started hating people," he had said. "I hated the drunks that swung at me, that spit on me, kicked me. I saw them puke, piss and shit on themselves then ask me for a cigarette. I saw men on base beat their wives into unrecognizable purple flesh, stab and shoot them. I've seen women do the same. I've seen them do it to their own babies. I broke a dozen thumbs, three noses, chipped lots of teeth, dislocated four shoulders and handed out probably a dozen concussions by slamming hammerheads against car hoods and sidewalks. Nobody brought a lawsuit, I got no reprimands, no backlash of any kind. With every arrest I was more convinced of the worthlessness of humankind."

"So," Toftey asked, "why sit here talking to another worthless human?"

"Maybe I value honest friendship, uncluttered by agendas, expectations, passions."

"Maybe you should get a dog."

"You don't hump my leg," Hansen said, raising his empty bottle, "and you bring beer."

He found northeastern Minnesota held much of the honesty he was looking for. He found that people here lived close to the edge—the edge of convenience, the edge of comfort, and if they chose, the edge of survival. They built their lives tenuously on the rocky shoulders of Earth's ancient crust, taking sustenance from its scant bounty and from those who would come in slack-jawed wonder to see its scars—the lakes and rivers carved into its skin and the wilderness that grew around them. By the thousands they paddled its crystalline blue lifeblood, slept on shores strewn with pine needles and moss, staring up at a sparkling chaos of stars, vast beyond imagining, dreaming for the first time of infinity.

Hansen had little patience for the local hypocrites who derided the tourists responsible for their daily bread. Without the naïve fascination and child-like awe of the "citiots" or "berry pickers" or "leaf peepers" there would be no economy in Grand Marais. He thought the locals could use some good old-fashioned wonder to reconnect with the beauty around them. If they had to rely on jaded misanthropes like themselves to visit and spend money looking at trees, water and rocks, they'd be hard pressed to last one winter.

Sure, he had taken to living in town on occasion—since both he and Toftey had friends there. Hansen's on-again-off-again girlfriend, Malorie, was a bartender at the

Harbor View Inn. He liked her full lips and what he called the "porno star" tattoo of a flying heart on the small of her back, just above her ass. When they weren't fighting they were approaching a fight or recovering from the last, which meant drinks, laughs, sex, then the brief familiar path back to fighting, culminating in a simultaneous "Fuck you!" and slamming door.

Hansen brought the maul down on the last piece of wood, striking it dead center and sending the halves flying. The pitch in the conifer made it unsuitable for his wood stove. As it burned it deposited a volatile mixture of resin and carbon on the chimney and became a fire hazard. This was fuel for the outdoor fire pit, a ring of large rocks where many an evening of drunken philosophizing had been spent. He liked a campfire and cooked on it every chance he got, whether it was wrapping vegetables in foil and burying under coals or grilling venison steaks over the open flames. Sitting in front of the fire, watching northern lights dance overhead or satellites sail across the sky, the bats squeaking and wheeling after moths drawn spinning toward the flames, shooting stars plummeting to their fiery demise…and the silence, the soothing quiet like a blanket surrounding him, it healed him. He could feel it every day he spent in this place, as if his body and mind were reassembling themselves after being torn into ragged strips and dropped in a haphazard jumble at his feet.

It felt as though he had lost too much time with hateful people and that made him angry. The irony was not lost on him. He feared that, like the stove containing the resinous flame, the residue of all that hatred clung to him somewhere and would ignite one day in a terrible conflagration. He confided his theory to Toftey that same evening drinking beers around the fire pit.

"Maybe that's why you drink so much," his friend offered.

"Because I'm angry?" Hansen asked, clutching the bottle, his bleary eyes reflecting the flickering orange flames.

"Not exactly," Toftey said. "I think maybe you're just tryin' to put the fire out."

SIXTEEN

I-95, Virginia, May, 2002
Wednesday, 12:30 PM

The hum of the Audi TT laid an extra satisfying base track for REM's "Welcome to the Occupation." Brian Setty liked to feel his music. And he liked to feel speed. It was a two-hour trip from the FBI training facility in Quantico, Virginia to the Pentagon for most drivers on I-95. But Setty prided himself on making the most out of every opportunity and he saw rush-hour traffic as an opportunity to work on his highway slalom. He was a catalyst for road rage, a vector. He never developed it himself, but carried the illness and spread it as he wove in and out of traffic, cutting off those behind him and tailgating everyone else.

Setty felt the responsibility of his position as an agent for the federal government's primary law enforcement agency. He woke with it, slept with it—every moment was an exercise or a study and every assignment a practical exam. He based his physical regimen loosely on the daily training routine of his hero, Alexis Arguello, lightweight boxing champion from Nicaragua. He had read an article in Boxing Monthly, an issue from the early eighties, when Arguello was at the top of his game, which described in detail what the man ate and the grueling daily course he set for his body, ten-mile runs, thirty minutes on the speed bag, thirty minutes on the heavy bag, three hundred sit-ups and an hour of heavy sparring with ten-ounce gloves. The realities of a 50- to 60-hour workweek prevented that kind of extreme dedication, but Setty devoted some time every day to at least one or two items on Arguello's list.

In front of him an SUV and a minivan hung together perfectly parallel as they drove just slightly below the posted speed limit. Brian swung from the right into the left lane and pulled intimately close to the minivan, matching their pulses in speed, looking for the chance to quickly jump into the right lane and pass. The SUV on the right began to gain some ground against the van, so he swerved back into that lane expectantly. But the SUV slowed once again, effectively boxing him in. He eased the TT onto the shoulder and looked ahead. The path was clear, though the next opening was one mini-van and two semis away. He did a quick calculation. The TT could get up to one hundred from fifty-five in about six seconds. There was an overpass further ahead where he would run out of room and at one hundred miles-per-hour, it would be spectacular. He shifted back into fourth gear and punched it. The car responded with a throaty roar that drowned out Michael Stipe's vocals and pulled him back into the leather seat. He shot past the minivan and the first semi, the weeds on the roadside a green blur. The concrete column of the overpass was speeding toward him. He glanced down to the speedometer and saw it shivering at one hundred and twelve. As his back bumper cleared the front of the second semi he swerved in front of it, the angry drone of its air horns fading as the Audi surged forward toward the next clot of vehicles.

He didn't like the Pentagon, though he seemed hell-bent on getting there in record time. The first few times he entered the building he hadn't noticed the dreariness of the pale institutional walls and scuffed tile floors. And then there was the smell, reminiscent of an old closet or an attic. No, on his early visits, when he was new to the Bureau, the place affected him the way it was designed to. It left him in awe. Homeland Security briefings on various subjects happened there every week. Unless he had an assignment in the field, he would attend them. This one was different.

His region chief, Ed Williams, had called him two days earlier to ensure his attendance. Williams was direct, as usual, "Nine a.m. DHS briefing. Tuesday. See you there."

"This one goes out to the one I love. This one goes out to the one I left behind..."

Michael Stipe sang his ironic love ballad as Setty smiled at the liberating sight of a mile of clear left lane. If this is something big, Brian thought, I want in on it. The Bureau had been working closely with the Border Patrol for the past three years, enjoying the influx of money from the President's war on terror. Setty had followed up on reports of Arabs passing themselves off as Mexicans as they crossed the Rio Grande. He'd spent five months of the past year flying down there to eat dust and sit on the filthy southern U.S. border, looking for leads on terrorists. Very little attention had been paid to the northern border. He wondered why. It was a hell of a lot longer! And the Canadians allowed more freedom of movement into and out of the country for certain nationalities that America found "of interest," like Syrians and Pakistanis, for instance. He was looking forward to asking a few questions today.

"I am, I am, I am Superman, and I can do anything...."
Setty sang along with Mike Mills. As he sang and nudged the TT to ninety miles per hour in the half-mile stretch before the next pack of cars, his mind wandered back down to Mexico. He'd been trying to block the thoughts

since his return. He'd had a scare in the desert north of Mexico City.

A scare—that's what Williams called it, as if being held at gunpoint by smugglers in the middle of nowhere was some innocuous prank.

The memory left a sick feeling in the pit of his stomach. He imagined his fear as a snail, occasionally protruding obscenely from its shell, then passing slowly, leaving a slimy glistening trail to mark its way. He tried to reject fear—simply refuse to believe in it. It angered him when it oozed out of its fragile curly shell uninvited. He was a professional, after all.

Kirby told him once "Fear is the only antidote for testosterone."

Setty had answered, "Fear is for old queers in high heels."

After Mexico, he felt like asking Kirby to help him pick out a pair—size eleven bright yellow pumps, like two bananas on stilts.

The TT hummed at one hundred and ten and the pack of slower cars seemed to speed toward him. He looked for an opening on the right, but there was a bridge approaching and several exits after that. He would have to settle for the relatively languid pace of sixty miles per hour for the next ten miles and an obstructed view of the road ahead. It made him claustrophobic, but gave him plenty of time to work on his denial. Because, he told himself, it was only denial that kept the snail in its shell.

SEVENTEEN

After three days and nights of drunken stupor,
pornography and heavy metal, Ibrahim al-Takar was no
longer sure who he was. On the morning of the fourth day
he awoke, as he always did, back on the stone floor of his
cell. The odor of puke, urine and feces was over-powering
and he usually awoke vomiting. He found himself wishing
for the days of the black hood. To his ailing brain it seemed
like a comfort, before the sickness and the filth and the
headaches. His days were an unending series of depraved
visions and suffering, his nights, when he finally was
allowed to sleep, an empty dreamless blackness. He had
few lucid moments not occupied by the effects of alcohol
and the vile images that bombarded his waking hours.

This morning, however, he would receive a reprieve.
After he was given medication for his debilitating
hangover, he was taken to a washroom where he was
allowed to wash his face and put on clean clothes. His
filthy ones were saved in a sealed plastic bag. He would
have to put them back on before returning to "Vegas," the
name bestowed on the pornography room by some of the
Special Forces grunts in charge of interrogations.

After his toilet, Ibrahim was led handcuffed to a sparse
room with no furniture or windows. There lingered a
pleasant odor reminiscent of sandalwood and lilac. The
walls were painted in earthen tones and there were two
multicolored blankets on the shining tile floor. Between

them was a tray on which sat a silver teapot. Several teabags, creamer cups and sugar packets sat on a small plate next to the pot along with two white ceramic cups. A spoon lay nearby. In one corner a small green arrow had been neatly painted indicating the direction for prayer. The young female soldier who had escorted him removed the handcuffs and told him to sit and wait. "There's tea bags and hot water there," she said, then turned and left, closing the door behind her.

Ibrahim sat motionless on one of the blankets. He looked at the silver teapot. After several minutes of staring at it, Ibrahim reached out slowly and took the teapot in a shaky hand and poured water into the cup, trying not to spill any for fear it would invite punishment. He carefully unwrapped a teabag and dropped it in the steaming water. Into the water he poured cream and sugar, stirring it with the spoon. When he brought the mixture toward his lips he could smell the tea and feel the steam rise to his face. He sipped from the cup and the hot liquid ran across his tongue, scalding the tip, leaving a trail of warmth and sweetness through his mouth and into his stomach, spreading throughout his body like a warm bath. Setting the cup down he turned toward Mecca, bent his head to pray and began to weep.

An hour later he was taken from the room, stripped of the clean clothes and brought back to his cell, along with the bag of filthy rags. At first he refused to put them on but he was shocked with the cattle prod until he complied. Then he was taken back to Vegas where, after the first day, he began drinking the liquor from the cup until he was drunk and watched the video of the day. It was not always pornography. Sometimes it was episodes of "Baywatch," sometimes, "Different Strokes," sometimes a Christian televangelist. As the day wore on he began to believe that the time in the clean room had been a dream. He was pleased that his dreams had returned and that this had been a pleasant one. Dreams had always been important to Ibrahim. His father was a pious man who taught his sons that God spoke directly to them through dreams and they were not to be taken lightly. He thought of the clean room many times that day. It became an escape from the relentless sensations assaulting him in Vegas. And then, as he lay on the concrete of his cell, as far from the growing pile of his own filth as he could get, before alcohol-induced slumber overtook him once more, he prayed that the dream would return and that God would speak to him once more.

His prayers were answered the next morning when, once again, a female soldier led him to the washroom, administered medication for his alcohol sickness, gave him fresh robes and brought him to the clean room. The pleasant scent greeted him as before, but this time a man was seated on the blanket facing him. The man wore simple robes like his own and a red-checkered headdress. Without looking up, he motioned for Ibrahim to sit. Then he turned in the direction of the green arrow and prayed. Ibrahim followed suit and also bowed his head in silent prayer.

When they had finished the man poured them cups of tea, preparing each with sugar and cream, just as Ibrahim had done the day before. He handed a cup to Ibrahim, who took it, nodding his head in thanks. For the first time he really looked at the man. He could see an aquiline nose and full lips, but the man did not look up from his tea. Though sitting, it was clear he was a tall, angular man. Ibrahim al-Takar was struck by a sense of familiarity, but did not want to make the man feel uncomfortable. He did not want to do anything to endanger the longevity of this vision. It was a lucid dream and his hold on it felt tenuous.

They sat in silence, sipping tea. Ibrahim stole surreptitious glances at the figure before him, but never fully saw the tall man's face. For the first time in many days he felt his mind open to thoughts beyond the walls within which he had been imprisoned. He thought of his family and his brothers in the Jihad. He felt a pang of excitement at the devastating blow that would soon be dealt to his arrogant captors. The mission had consumed him for over a year and he longed to speak of it with one sympathetic to the struggle. He had worked so hard and now it was in motion. He prayed daily to Allah that he would be free to celebrate the martyrdom of his brothers in the United States. Though he was prepared, he prayed that his martyrdom would not come first.

When the door opened and he was led away he fought back tears. He would do anything to stay in this wonderful dream. As he was led out he hoarsely whispered goodbye to the man on the floor. He waved his hand as though giving a blessing but did not look up as Ibrahim was led away once again.

EIGHTEEN

Victor drove through his busy neighborhood very slowly, past simple tiny homes like his own. There were children everywhere. The dirty street was their playground and balls and sticks and bicycles littered the cracked and crumbling asphalt as the kids ran back and forth across his path. He pulled the car into the dusty yard, past a small chicken coop surrounded by drooping wire. Victor came to a rattling stop in front of a 2-room house of adobe with a simple roof of green corrugated tin and got out of the car. The sour smell of chicken shit assaulted his nostrils, but as always, he quickly grew used to it.

"Papá, papá!" A young girl in an adult t-shirt which dragged along the ground ran out to meet Victor. Her black hair was long and bounced behind her like a horse tail. The girl's dark brown eyes seemed almost too large for her face. A bright smile greeted him as she leapt into his arms.

"You really are a little squirrel, aren't you?" he said, kissing her on the cheek. "What have you been doing all day, Maria?"

The little girl squirmed to get down and he set her feet on the ground.

"I helped Claudio dig for bones for his dog," she said, "and we found buried treasure and made a treasure map because we needed to be pirates and steal the treasure we found…"

"My," he said, looking onto her excited eyes, "I would like to see that treasure map."

"You can't," his daughter said, suddenly grave. "It's only for pirates."

"How do you know I'm not a pirate?" he asked.

"Because you don't have a patch or a wooden leg and you don't know where the treasure is," she asserted.

He smiled down at her with eyes the same color as her own. "Ah, but I have my own secret treasure," he said mysteriously.

Maria's eyes widened. "What is it," she asked him.

"I'll show you what I found as long as you show me what you found." He turned and walked back to the heavily-laden Fiat.

She looked distraught. "But Papá! We were just playing pretend. We didn't really have any treasure. Mostly rocks and bottle tops."

"Well," he said, back at the Fiat, "I guess you can't see what I've got."

"Papá! Please!"

He laughed heartily. "Venido aquí, mi pequeña ardilla."

"I'm not a little squirrel, I'm a pirate!"

"Well, you certainly are the cutest pirate I have ever seen," he said, rumpling her hair as he walked past. "Look in here."

From the Fiat's rusted trunk he pulled out the silver canister. Victor looked up at the slamming of the screen door to see his wife hurry down the stairs. The evening sun turned her dark skin to honey. He watched her breasts jump beneath the thin loose cotton dress. It amazed him how much she still thrilled him, even after almost 10 years of marriage. When he met his amigos for beers every

Saturday he could only sit in silence while they complained about their wives and girlfriends, all the while thinking how lucky he was to have a woman like Suzanna.

"Mama, Papá found buried treasure!"

Suzanna encircled Victor's waist with a strong arm and kissed him, her tongue brushing his lips sending electricity through his body. "Oh has he now?" Her eyes were lighter than his or his daughter's, looking copper in the setting sun. He secretly wished his daughter had her mother's eyes.

Victor picked up the pry bar and forced it beneath the cap of the canister. It appeared to be spot welded, but it was no match for the heavy iron bar and Victor's strong shoulders. The lid popped off and all eyes, both dark brown and copper, stared at the contents of the silver container.

"It's beautiful," Suzanna said, mesmerized. She reached down without hesitation and dipped her hand into the powder. It had the consistency of baby powder. It felt warm to Suzanna as it drifted through her fingers. "What is it?"

"I don't know," answered Victor. "It must be a chemical for developing the x-rays. It glows in the dark."

"Can I have some, Papá?" Squeaked Maria. "Can I have some to play with please?"

Victor looked at his wife who had brushed the substance off her hands and onto her dress. "Sure," she said, never taking her eyes off her husband, a crooked smile flashing brilliant across her face like lightning, burrowing into a dimple on her cheek, igniting his desire. "Take it and show Claudio. I'm sure you and your friends can find a game to play for an hour or so. I'll call you when it's time for dinner."

"Thanks, mama!" said the little girl, staring at the material glowing inside the container. "Hey, can I have something to put it in?"

Their daughter went on her way with a glass jar full of "magic powder" and several more containers for her friends. Back in the house, Victor and his wife closed the door and pulled the shades. An oil lamp burned dimly on an orange crate bedside table and illuminated their bed in a small flickering circle of golden light. Outside the small circle darkness hid the functional clutter of their tiny home – the dishes, the sink, the clothes, the vegetables and tortillas sitting on the dining table. All of the mundane and minutia of their daily existence faded into shadow until there was only the two of them in the lamplight. On the other side of the bed sat the silver canister. From the open top a faint blue light emanated, like some phosphorescent creature beneath a deep tropical ocean.

"You are beautiful, you know," Victor told her softly.

"And you talk too much, *mi marido*," she said, putting a finger to his lips.

Though the sun had set, the house was still warm. The pulled shades kept out the cooling night air. Victor sat up and admired his wife's body. He ran his hands over her glistening skin, sweat reflecting the lamplight. He kneeled over her and kneaded her shoulders. Her dark hair clung to her face and forehead as her eyes closed giving into his roaming hands. Reaching over to the silver container he scooped out a generous portion of glowing azure powder and sprinkled it onto her breasts and stomach.

"What are you doing?" she asked, giggling.

"Shhh," he said, smiling. "Now who is talking too much?"

He massaged it over her, the blue powder mixing with the sweat from her body, covering her breasts, illuminating his hands. He painted her thighs and hips with the powder on his hands then reached over and shut off the light. She glowed beneath him like a velvet painting in black light. She looked down at her body and rubbed her hands over her breasts as he had done, feeling the nipples stiffen. She reached up and took his face in her hands, brought him down to her lips and kissed him deeply.

"*Te quiero*," she said.

He did not know it then, but he would never hear those words from her again.

NINETEEN

Cold water filled Mark Toftey's nose, ears and mouth as he bobbed and tumbled down the river toward open water, bouncing off rocks and logs caught in the raging current. He could not control his descent and knew it was just a matter of time until the current threw him headfirst into a boulder. All thoughts of his pursuers left him, as survival became his physical being's only directive. There was little room in Toftey's panicked brain for hypothesis or strategizing. "What ifs" were a luxury his numb and battered body could not afford. He had to get out of the river.

The cedars along the shore were passing at an alarming rate, little more than a green blur moving up and down like the countryside from the back of a galloping horse. The opposing whorls and driving currents spun his body around regardless of any attempts to right himself. Each time his head surfaced he had two imperatives: first, take a breath, second, turn his head to look downstream and try and pick out something to grab or avoid as he flew by. The longer he stayed in the water however, the less likely it was that he would be able to hold on to anything. He felt his extremities shutting down to preserve warmth in his vital organs and the absence of pain when he careened off of rocks scared him even more. He could have broken bones and not even know it until he thawed—that is, if he ever got the opportunity.

As he spun his head around he caught a glimpse of a chance at escape coming quickly. A large spruce had fallen across the stream and lay just above the froth of a cataract where the river was constricted between two boulders, like water through a pinched hose. He fought his body around to meet the log head-on, raised his arms in front of his face and braced for the impact. Just before he reached the log the current raised him up and he met the tree at his midsection, below his ribs. The collision drove the air and water from his lungs and he folded around the log like a wet towel. He clung there exhausted, struggling for breath, feebly working his way higher on the log, attempting to straddle it. The river held onto his legs as if giant hands grasped his ankles beneath the water. As he recovered his breath he slowly pulled one leg out of the torrent, then the other. Hey lay there like a shipwreck survivor washed upon the shore, his body refusing to move, ignorant of his precarious position.

He lost track of time since jumping into the water, but he could feel the warm sun on his back. By observing the height of the sun in the sky he guessed it to be late morning. Looking toward the shore in front of him, he saw that all the snow was gone; that would be the northern shore, catching most of the sun's lengthening arch in the southern sky. The southern shore behind him still held the occasional white mound, hidden in the shadows of the cedars lining the stream. He had to head southeast, toward popular Seagull Lake. He figured that was his best chance at finding help. But first he had to get out of the middle of the river, out of sight. Then there were wet clothes and the looming threat of hypothermia to deal with. If he didn't dry out and warm up, he'd never make it to Seagull. Then of course, the portage trail lay between him and Seagull.

There was no way around it if he meant to get to the shoreline of the big lake. Hopefully they were not waiting for him. Hopefully, their timeline did not allow for chasing him down. Hopefully, his canoe and gear were exactly where he left them and the men had simply fled.

Toftey knew that was an awful lot of hoping.

TWENTY

Kadir reached the portage trail and walked carefully toward the ranger's canoe. It was possible that the man had somehow reached the landing. It would certainly be the most reasonable course of action. As he neared the last bend in the rocky, root-bound trail he heard sounds that convinced him the man had indeed made it back. Kadir had received extensive hand-to-hand combat training and was formidable with the knife they had each received, blessed by the Sheik himself. He grabbed the weapon's ornately carved handle and pulled it from the sheath in his belt. He slowly crept to a large boulder that sat several feet from the landing. He crouched there and listened to the man struggling with the packs, grunting with the effort and ripping the pack in frustration. Kadir assumed he was looking for a weapon of his own. His heart was hammering in his chest, so loud he expected the other man would surely hear him. There was no other sound but that of the stranger he was about to kill frantically ripping open his packs. He could not call for help. There was no time and it was expected he could do this thing on his own. Allah was with him. His faith was true. With a quick prayer and a yell he jumped from behind the rock and raised the knife over his head, its wicked curved blade glinting in the bright sun.

"Aaaaaye!"

His war cry turned to a yelp of surprise and fear at the sight before him. He didn't even notice the knife drop from his hand and clatter to the ground. Two pig-sized black animals were looking at him, their clawed paws buried in plastic bags that they had savagely removed from a shredded canvas pack. Their mouths were red with strawberry jam, their jaws and tongues working frantically to remove the remaining peanut butter sandwich from the roofs of their mouths. For a moment the bear cubs regarded him with wide eyes like children caught stealing candy. Then with bawling cries they ran to the nearest fir tree and ascended it quickly with powerful thrusts of their clawed feet. Kadir was frozen to the spot, looking up at the cubs that were now staring down at him from the relative safety of the tree. He recognized them now as black bears, but was surprised at their size. In the books he read their size could reach three hundred pounds—these two were barely sixty pounds. Then with a stab of fear in his bowels he understood his situation. This dawned on him just as he heard a soft, deep "huff" from the trail behind him. He had read something about rolling into a ball and covering the back of your neck with interlaced fingers if you were attacked. This lesson crossed his mind too quietly to be heard above the din of blood thundering in his ears. He ran.

The sow probably would have only bluff-charged the man, except that Kadir ran directly into the woods past the tree where her cubs were hiding. To her it was an aggressive move toward her offspring and in response she launched herself through the forest and caught the man by the back of his left thigh. She bit him several times there and tore at his back with her claws. He screamed hysterically, with a pitch and volume that seemed to surprise the bear as she jumped off him and looked back toward her cubs. But Kadir tried to get up and the movement brought the bear's attention back to the creature that still appeared to her as a threat. With a swat of her front paw, she knocked him down on his side and began biting his exposed ear, removing much of it in the process. Blood from the gaping wound flowed freely into his mouth and eyes. Whether from panic or shock, Kadir fainted. His suddenly limp body ended the sow's attack. The mother bear turned back to collect her cubs, which slid down the tree trunk like dispatched firemen and fled into the woods close behind their mother, who heard footsteps and frantic human voices approaching.

The whole attack took less than two minutes and when Anwar and Saad arrived at the portage landing, they found the shredded packs but no sign of Kadir or the bears. They had heard the terrible screams and, finding the packs smeared with what appeared to be a great deal of congealed blood, their hearts raced and their breathing grew fast and shallow. Like the young student from Tangiers they had read the books on the local animals. It was clear that something had attacked Kadir. It just wasn't clear what animal had done so. Had it dragged him away to feed on him? The men crept toward the canoe and packs apprehensively, looking around them for any sign of movement. Then they heard moaning in the woods nearby and followed the sound to where Kadir lay. The left side of his head was covered in blood that still flowed from an open wound where his ear used to be. His pants were torn at the thigh and soaked with blood. He was moaning quietly but was otherwise motionless.

Anwar looked at Saad and said, "Go get Asad. He'll know what must be done. Hurry."

Saad ran back to the river to get their leader, unhappy to be the bearer of bad news. He knew somehow it would be his fault that Kadir was lying in a pool of his own blood after an animal attack. During their trip Saad had grown to hate the man with his American education and his constant threats. Saad could see that behind the fearful demeanor was a petulant and frightened child. He had seen enough of the young Saudi princes to recognize a boy who was given privilege instead of earning it. Saad was a Saudi and had been a sergeant in Prince Faad's army for many years. He felt this unbalanced man was not worthy to lead the assignment they had been given, much less to give him orders. It was out of his sense of duty and respect for the Sheik that he bit his tongue and followed orders. He was a good soldier and would not break the chain of command. At least not until the moment of truth arrived. Nobody would ever know who pushed the button, he thought. This Asad will be dead before the deed is done. Allah will understand.

By the time Asad arrived Anwar had cleaned the wounds, applied antibiotic ointment and bound them with bandages all found in the ranger's pack. Looking more closely at the scene, realizing the red substance was jam not blood, he was able to recreate with some accuracy what had happened to their comrade.

"I suspect he interrupted a bear eating food out of the ranger's pack," Anwar told Asad, "and he was attacked."

"Can he travel?" asked Asad curtly.

"It depends on how bad the leg is injured. I am no doctor, but it looks like flesh wounds. I think as long as the bleeding stops and there is no infection, he will be ok."

"I am not worried about infections. I am worried about being found on this portage with an injured man and someone else's canoe and packs. I did not see the ranger so I can only assume he drowned. You two get his gear to the other side. Float the canoe and fill the front and back with rocks. Then put a couple of big rocks in the packs and set them in the canoe. We will tow it out into the lake and sink it all. Go, now!"

Anwar and Saad exchanged glances but did as they were told. Asad looked at the young man lying on the ground beneath him and rolled up the sleeves of his lightweight khaki shirt. Kadir was still unconscious, though he seemed to be sleeping peacefully, looking very young beneath the bandage on his head, like the sick children he had seen in the teaching hospital in Qatar. Asad took a moment to appreciate Anwar's fine job of bandaging Kadir's wounds. He knew that Anwar had some military training, obviously first aid as well. He gently laid his hand on the young man's forehead and ran it slowly over his hair to the back of his head, tilting it so that the neck was exposed. Asad al-Muhammad removed his small knife with the curved blade from its sheath and drew it across Kadir's exposed throat. Warm blood gushed from the deep slice and flowed over his hands. The body jerked in electric spasms, then calmed as the flow of blood slowed and finally stopped. He never woke up. Asad dragged him into a depression well off the trail and out of sight beneath thick balsam trees. He then returned to the portage, washed his hands thoroughly in the cold waters of Saganaga Lake and walked the length of the portage to meet the men waiting on the other side. He could see that his orders had been followed. The ranger's canoe was riding very low in the water, a pile of large rocks in both the bow and the stern and the rock filled packs sitting in the middle.

"You two get into a canoe and tow that one. I'll take our remaining canoe. Let's go."

Anwar and Saad watched as Asad filled Kadir's personal pack with rocks and threw it in the ranger's canoe.

Anwar asked, "Where is Kadir?"

Asad opened his own pack and removed a small camp axe, which he laid on the bottom of his own canoe. Then he hefted the packs into the boat.

"He died."

The other two men paused, exchanged a quick glance, and continued deliberately in their work.

The three men and three canoes headed out into the middle of Red Rock Lake. Asad pulled up next to the ranger's Kevlar, now loaded down with rocks, and swung his camp axe against the floor. Water squirted up from the narrow opening. Asad chopped six more holes in the bottom of the boat and they all watched it slowly sink out of sight.

"Let's go," said Asad. "We have many miles to travel."

The canoes slipped quietly through the calm surface of Red Rock Lake, leaving a "V" of ripples and tiny whirlpools behind each craft.

TWENTY-ONE

Boundary Waters Canoe Area Wilderness, Minnesota
May, 2002
Wednesday, 9:30 AM

With agonizing care he tested the stability of the log to which he clung. Then, slowly, he swung his left leg over, pivoted and swung over the right leg so that he was once again straddling the spruce, facing the opposite direction. The sun felt good on his face and he craved a flat shoreline rock upon which to lie face down and let the sun do its work on his clammy skin and soaking, tattered clothes. The nights were still chilly and he doubted his ability to last even one night in wet clothes and no fire. Of course, his matches and multi-tool, with its pliers, knife and saw blade, were in his fanny pack, tied on his canoe.

Sliding along the spruce sent flakes of its rough bark into the rushing river below. He could hear nothing over the sound of the river. He looked up and down the shore as he moved, imagining he would see his pursuers emerge from the trees at any moment. But eventually he reached the other side and stepped safely onto dry land. Walking slowly on unsteady legs Toftey kept the sun in his right eye, estimating that to be the southeast track that would take him to the western shore of Seagull. He knew there were several campsites there and one of them might be occupied. If not, there should at least be some traffic on the lake and he could hail a passing canoe. Worst case he could follow the western shore around to the north and reach Trail's End which he figured was about five or six miles from where he now stood. Tough bushwhacking, but doable in a day of motivated hiking. And motivated he was.

Toftey wanted to walk carefully, but until he was farther from the river, he would not be able to hear a threat, so he moved quickly, looking nervously in every direction, shivers wracking his body as he went. The roaring of the river subsided behind him and soon he arrived at the portage trail. He could see it through the woods before he stepped onto it and spent a few minutes looking up and down its length for danger. Satisfied and eager to find his gear, Toftey stepped out from the trees and onto the rocky portage. He walked quickly to the Red Rock Lake side of the portage and saw that everything was gone—the canoe, the gear, everything. As he neared the water's edge a glint of metal caught his eye, shining at the base of a huge boulder just off of the trail. Toftey bent over and picked up a small, evil-looking knife with a carved handle and a short curved blade. It was incredibly sharp.

At the landing there were pieces of green canvas that looked to be from his pack, a torn plastic sandwich bag and bear prints in the mud. Looking around, Toftey found human footprints as well leading away from the landing and into the woods. Hesitantly, Toftey followed the tracks and soon found blood. He tracked it until he came to an opening where grass and brush had been trampled down and spattered with blood. There was a trail through the grass, toward the edge of the forest. It was bloody and looked as though something large had been dragged there. A little further, in a shallow depression, Toftey found the remains of one of the men who were chasing him. It was the thin young man with the mustache. He had what appeared to be bite marks on his legs and hands, but it was the neat slice across his neck that Toftey found most interesting. They had killed one of their own. Now they were three. He felt some relief at the thought. Not because the odds were suddenly more in his favor, but because losing a quarter of their team was a significant event and he suspected it probably made them a little more intent on reaching their destination and leaving distractions like him alone. It was a selfish thought, he realized, because no matter where these guys ended up there was going to be trouble for anyone they met.

Toftey checked the dead man's pockets and to his relief found a small waterproof container of matches. In another pocket he found a pocketknife and slipped both items into his wet pants. He briefly considered exchanging pants with the young man, but they were about as wet as his own and were torn as well. Around his waist the dead man wore a belt that fastened with a large buckle. Upon removing the belt, Toftey saw a sheath built into the buckle. He inserted the knife he had found and it slipped in, a perfect fit. Finding nothing else of value on the man, Toftey left the body and continued across the portage and on to Seagull Lake.

TWENTY-TWO

Beth walked into the briefing room with a heavy leather briefcase slung over her shoulder, bulging with files, an ancient laptop computer and assorted cables, batteries, a mouse, a port replicator. Portable my ass, she thought. She winced slightly at the stale bitter smells of tobacco breath, coffee and perspiration infused with the ever-present hint of must, mold and mildew that lived in the walls. Beth wondered if it was just age or if the old building had caught something foul and cancerous from sixty years of black ops and nefarious whisperings.

Her day had begun with an hour spent rifling through her meager wardrobe searching for the right combination of clothing for the day's meeting. Her fatigue and frustration had grown with every ensemble that fell, discarded, and onto the chaos of her tousled bed. The litany of criteria disgusted her: not too masculine lest she seem like she was trying to be one of the boys, as if she couldn't compete as a woman solely on substance, yet not too feminine lest she appear as though, once again, she was trying to distract from some deficiency in knowledge or ability. Red is too aggressive, while pastels too unsubstantial and easily dismissed. Black seemed to her like a copout—the stealth color employed to hide imperfections and divert attention, the modern woman's hoop skirt, the feminist girdle. She finally settled on the navy blue suit she interviewed in three years ago, straight knee-length skirt, matching jacket over a simple white blouse. She agonized over the shoes. The suit called for heels, but heels carried with them the very real threat of destroying any credibility she may have built with her conservative clothing and provocative data. It had happened before, the sudden abrupt upending as the pinhead surfaces upon which she so precariously balanced, below her weak and traitorous ankles, found some microscopic imperfection in the floor. The horror of it made her shudder and reach for her plain navy flats. Better to look a bit frumpy and stay upright than chance a Three Stooges moment in front of senior members of the nation's security community.

The dark room was dominated by a large oblong conference table surrounded by dark gray office chairs with high backs. The shape prevented anyone from sitting at the head of the table, implying that each opinion deserved equal consideration and carried equal weight. Beyond one end of the table the wall held a large screen, which descended slowly with a quiet mechanical buzz over a bank of whiteboards that ran in a four-foot-high band around the room. At the opposite end of the room in one corner sat a small table with a large coffee pot, a dwindling stack of white Styrofoam cups, a round box of sugar and, in an odd juxtaposition, individual plastic creamer cups heaped into an elegant silver bowl filled with ice. Sitting next to the creamers was a large white plastic pitcher sporting a yellow sticky note with the hastily scrawled words "cold water."

A quick count revealed twenty-four chairs around the table. Notebooks, PDAs and cellular phones sat in front of all of them. Some people were seated already, engaged in conversations with each other or on their phones. Many were in uniform; most were men at least twenty to thirty years older than she was. She recognized a few of them simply from working in the Pentagon. A couple she had seen on TV. She felt her mouth going dry and headed to the water pitcher. She was relieved to see the familiar squat form of her boss, Kevin Stiles, standing there filling his coffee cup. He looked up with his droopy bloodhound eyes as she walked over. He flashed her a brief smile but it was quickly replaced by a look of concern as he spoke.

"You look nervous."

"A little," she admitted with a nod and a slight smile of her own.

In truth she wanted to run away and not come back, but she knew that was not an option unless she wanted to look for another job. She felt like she was selling her theory, which in a sense she was. She had already convinced Stiles, a skeptic if there ever was one. So she knew it was possible to sway a tough crowd. She also knew she had a bit of leverage. The alternative to not acting on the information she was about to share with this esteemed group was, obviously, to ignore it. But in the current political and social climate of fear of terrorist attack, that was about as likely as her sprinting out the door.

"You'll do fine," he said. "You've done important work and it's worth checking out. Let's get some support here for an agent on the ground so we can start filling in the blanks."

"Um, sir?" she said. "Where do I sit?"

"Sit?" Stiles looked at her quizzically. "I'd suggest a bar stool by the time they're done with you."

He winked at her and went to his seat near the front, leaving her standing alone by the coffee pot with her cup in her hand.

Most of the audience had taken their seats as Beth adjusted focus on the LCD projector, which displayed the title page of her PowerPoint presentation on the screen before her. It had taken her several agonizing hours to prepare the slides, triple checking and transcribing her notes, embedding photos and other images.

She figured she had probably strained the limits of her professional relationship with photography expert Darryl Allis about as far as it could possibly go without hearing "Dude, you, me, pizza. What do ya think?" She was certain he had a crush on her and though the thought made her feel guilty, she suspected it helped her get what she needed from him.

Once the slide, which read "SOI (Subjects of Interest) Movement Through the Northern Wilderness Border," was clear to her satisfaction, Beth shut off the lamp and the screen went blank. Looking at the clock, she saw there was less than five minutes before the scheduled start time. Conversations faded into hushed tones and eyes began to wander up to her expectantly. She looked around at the raised faces and a warm and not wholly pleasant flush of adrenaline shot through her veins. She looked down and slowly backed into the corner, wondering if she would be able to speak when the time came. She resisted the urge to dry her moist palms on her skirt, as she would have on her white coat back in the lab. If only I could do this from the lab, she thought. There she was in her element, with the gentle hum of finely tuned equipment, the bright lights, the cleanliness, the unwavering concentration on what one can see, touch, hear, smell, taste and feel with curious fingertips. And of course, there was no audience. She hadn't inherited her father's unwavering confidence in himself, though many times she had wished for it. She had grown accustomed to hiding the anxiety by working harder than anyone else. But that was a fragile defense, and challenges like this exposed its shaky foundation. For a moment she heard her father's voice reading the headline: "Agent Seized by the Moment: Briefing Brief."

A large black man in a perfectly tailored charcoal suit with a sharply pressed white shirt and turquoise tie stood up from his seat next to her boss and walked to the front and center of the room to Beth's left and faced the now silent attendees of the weekly Department of Homeland Security Threat Briefing. She recognized him as regional chief Ed Williams. Williams had a storied record with the CIA and commanded great respect inside and outside of "The Club," the name those inside the Beltway gave to senior members of the D.C. security community. When he walked into a room, his commanding presence was a result not simply of his bulk but of his reputation as an expert in protecting the nation from external threats. He'd earned that reputation as a covert agent in North Africa, exposing key terrorist infrastructure and leadership hierarchy in countries like Morocco, Syria and Libya. Many thought him to be the obvious choice for Secretary of Homeland Security, though the administration felt otherwise.

Just as Williams was about to speak the main door opened and a young man, dressed as impeccably as Chief Williams, slipped quietly into the room. Beth watched him acknowledge Williams with a slight wave of his hand and assumed he was another CIA agent. She looked at Williams who just stared at the man unhappily for a few moments before beginning. Her eyes lingered on the young dark-haired agent for several seconds as he silently drifted across the back of the room and took a position in the corner diagonal from her. As he settled in his perch he glanced at her and smiled warmly. She returned it without thinking, something automatic from somewhere behind her brain, a reflex, like a sneeze. She looked down, rattled, and felt her face flush.

Williams cleared his throat and began speaking, his voice deep and hoarse.

"Today, we are going to deviate from our usual protocol." He scanned the room as though looking for dissent. There was none.

"Those of you responsible for presenting weekly status reports," he continued, "will email them to me and I will disseminate to the group. This meeting will be dedicated to a briefing and discussion on a potential imminent threat via the northern border. We have some compelling evidence recently gathered from the caves in Afghanistan and some remarkable analysis by Agent Adams here," Williams indicated Beth, who was little more than a shadow in the corner, "I want to reach consensus on next steps." Williams turned to Beth and beckoned. "Agent Adams?"

Beth emerged from the shadows and replaced Williams in front of the screen facing the stoic, attentive group. Using the remote control she clutched in her hand, Agent Adams pushed the button to turn on the projector lamp. Unprepared for the bright flash that resulted she reflexively brought her hand up to shield her eyes and the hard plastic remote control hit her forehead with an audible crack.

"Ouch!" she exclaimed, more in surprise than pain, and dropped the remote, which skittered across the table and onto the floor.

There was complete silence in the darkness beyond the light. To her right Brigadier General Richard Westguard pushed his chair away from the table, picked up the wayward controller and handed it to Beth, who felt herself seizing up with embarrassment as she bent down to take it from him.

"Thank you," she managed quietly, fighting to hold back a flood of tears or profanity, she wasn't sure which.

The general held the remote a second and Beth met striking blue eyes of disarming kindness. In a hushed tone just for her Beth heard him say with the hint of a Texas drawl, "Think of us all in our underwear. In fact, Colonel Gillis over there is wearing fishnet stockings and a garter belt."

He released the control and sat up straight in his chair, stoic demeanor restored, the picture of military authority in his stiffly pressed dress uniform with its colorful cascade of ribbons and medals hanging on the chest.

Now it was laughter she fought to suppress. "Thank you, General," she said and allowed herself a lingering smile.

Sufficiently recovered, the blind spot in her vision fading, Beth dove into her presentation. She summarized her observations and research, following along with her slides. She projected a scan of the original torn image from Tora Bora and then on the next slide the copy Darryl had digitized and enhanced. Pressing the remote control a template of drawings appeared across the image. With the laser pointer she followed the lines on the screen and explained them, her voice gaining strength as she expanded on material she knew so well.

"After exhaustive analysis in our photography labs, through species identification of these conifers, this shoreline, the angle of these shadows, snow-cover and a comparison of readily available satellite images we were able to identify not only the exact location of this photograph but when it was taken within a three-day window."

The next slide showed a map of the United States. After several clicks of her keyboard the image had zoomed in to northeastern Minnesota on the north shore of Lake Superior. A few more clicks and Beth had zeroed in on a section of the map that showed more water than land. To the southeast lay a huge expanse of blue, which was Lake Superior. In the center of the screen the shoreline ran diagonally from top right to bottom left. Beth activated the pointer built into the remote control and moved it to the upper left corner of the screen, circling a confusion of streams and narrow lakes which ran primarily northeast to southwest.

"This is the Boundary Waters Canoe Area Wilderness, about a million acres of lakes, rivers, swamps, rocks and trees. North of the boundary is Ontario's Quetico Provincial Park, another million acres of road-less wilderness. This represents over three hundred miles of, for all intents and purposes, unprotected border between the United States and Canada. Over two hundred thousand visitors enter the U.S. park every year. Numbers are lower for the Canadian side."

The next slide showed a photograph with a map overlay so that the topographical contours matched the features on the image below.

"Below this map is the image we found in the caves in Afghanistan. It is a picture of the southern part of Lake Saganaga and several lakes to the south. Although a significant portion of the picture is missing, the fact that these lakes represent an established yet lightly used route from Canada into the United States is of concern. All of these lakes," Beth said, moving the pointer from Saganaga at the top of the screen down to Sawbill at the bottom, "are connected either by navigable water or portage trails across the land. To the south is a series of county roads which ultimately lead to the lightly patrolled Minnesota state highway 61, which in turn connects to U.S. Interstate 35, which originates in Duluth."

"Excuse me, miss."

Looking to her left about halfway down the table she identified the alleged fishnet stocking-wearer, Colonel Gillis. His tone was condescending and dismissive and though he addressed her, he looked around the room and spoke to those around him, not once glancing up to where Beth was standing.

"This is no great revelation," he said. "I mean, we all know we have vulnerabilities. For God's sake, we're looking at thousands of miles of border with on average one officer for every twenty or thirty miles. The northern boundary is a sieve. Hell, so's the Mexican border and we've got somebody standing every thousand feet. I don't need her," the man waved a hand in Beth's general direction, "to tell me terrorists might take a goddamn canoe trip into the U.S. Imagine any scenario—if we followed up on all of them…."

He let the comment linger unfinished and shook his head disgusted as though the subject was unworthy of more breath.

Another voice came from somewhere in the darkness toward the back of the room.

"I have to agree with Colonel Gillis. We've discussed this scenario before and I believe we came to the conclusion after more than a little study that it just isn't feasible for a credible terrorist threat to come via a wilderness route. There are cultural obstacles, physical obstacles…. There are easier ways to get into this country. Let's face it, political correctness aside for a moment, half the rednecks at our southern entry points couldn't tell an Arab from a Mexican."

There was some nervous laughter, and then other voices joined the chorus of skeptics. Beth felt her confidence beginning to drain. She was only halfway through her presentation and already she'd lost them.

"Excuse me. Excuse me, gentlemen, ladies." It was Williams. "We need to allow Agent Adams to finish her briefing before we argue its merits. None of us needs to be reminded of the dangers of closed minds in the face of evidence, no matter how obscure or unlikely. Agent, please continue." The big man looked around the table slowly, communicating clearly his displeasure with the group's behavior.

"We'll reserve comment, other than requests for clarification, until after you've finished."

"Thank you, sir," she said. "In addition to the image and reference to Grand Marais, Mideast operatives have been reporting increased chatter between SOIs in Pakistan, Iraq and Morocco. This is similar to the increased communications we heard before 9-11, Yemen, Kenya and the bombing in Casablanca. In these transcripts there are many references to wilderness within the usual religious quotations. For instance, `Through the wilderness our martyrs will prevail…from the wilds will come a great cleansing of evil and death to our enemies.'"

On the screen there were several excerpts from intercepted communications similar to those she read out loud. All were dated. The next slide showed a line graph that showed a steady increase across a period of six months.

"This slide," she said, "shows the increase of references to wilderness, trees, lakes, streams. More disturbing is the increase in talk of `God's fire of truth' or `the fire of God.' This has historically referred to a nuclear device. When you overlay these trends for the same period you find an interesting corollary."

Beth heard the faintest shifting and grunts of surprise as she displayed the slide. The lines ran almost perfectly parallel. She clicked the remote once again, showing another slide.

"Here's the chatter analysis six months before Yemen." She clicked again.

"Here's Kenya." Clicked once more.

"And 9-11."

Her last slide overlaid them all. They all matched with uncanny precision.

"Something is going to happen, and the evidence I've analyzed thus far points toward the wilderness of northern Minnesota."

Beth was satisfied by the silence that followed her last slide. She had got them back. Then a voice came from the back of the room. Though she couldn't see him, she knew from the direction that it was the young well-dressed man who came in late.

"Agent Adams, someone mentioned earlier that this scenario had already been studied. I'd just like to put it up to the group for discussion, has this specific scenario been run? What Agent Adams has just presented is a pretty compelling threat and I think the first thing we better do is get this thing modeled and get an agent or two on the ground up there."

The dark-haired agent came forward into the edge of the reflected light from the screen. He spoke directly to Beth.

"You are suggesting the introduction of a nuclear device onto American soil via a wilderness land and water route from Canada. Is that a fair summary?"

She answered, "Yes, that is accurate."

Colonel Gillis found his voice once again.

"How in the hell is someone going to drag a radiological weapon through lakes and rivers, over rocks and through the forest? Anything significant you're probably talking a hundred pounds of nuclear material and explosives. I assume we're talking about a dirty bomb here. Unless we're now suggesting that al-Qaeda has tactical nuclear weapons. Though maybe we should, since we're all sitting here contemplating fantasies."

Chief Williams' distinctive voice grated through the murmurings, side conversations and sycophantic witnessing for Gillis' remarks.

"Agent Setty is right. We need to model this thing while we're investigating in the field. Brian, I want you to pack your bags. You'll need to coordinate your efforts with the border patrol office up there in Minnesota. We're not ready for full disclosure at this point so play it close to the vest. Stop by my office after the meeting. Agent Adams, please stop by as well. You need to be part of this conversation. Billings? Billings, are you out there?"

"Yes sir." A small balding man in a white shirt and poorly tied yellow necktie hanging askew stood up from his chair. He looked eagerly at Chief Williams like an expectant dog waiting hungrily for a treat.

"Billings, please get this scenario into the computer. I want a report on my desk in the morning."

"Yes sir," the little man said and scurried away, a brief shaft of light entering the dark room the only evidence of his exit.

The feeble yellow ceiling lights were turned on and illuminated the room as best they could. People began filing out. Beth began disconnecting her laptop from the projector. She felt someone standing behind her and turned to see agent Brian Setty looking though a file he had removed from her bulging briefcase. He looked up at her and said, "Hope you don't mind. That's pretty scary stuff you laid on them today. I think you scared them."

Beth continued packing up her laptop.

"What about you?" she asked.

"This," he said, brandishing the folder, "doesn't scare me as much as people like Gillis. He's an ignorant prick. I hope he didn't get to you. This is good stuff. It's not often you find an information officer who puts the whole picture together. They're usually stuck in the tall grass."

He returned the folder to her leather satchel.

"Well, sounds like you're going to end up hip deep in it so I'm glad you appreciate my work. What do you know about Minnesota?" she asked.

"Nothing. I'm a beltway boy. I've had assignments from L.A. to Boston, but somehow I've avoided the upper Midwest. At least I'm not going in January. I hear it gets pretty cold up there."

Williams, who had been talking to General Westguard, walked over to Beth and Brian.

"Beth, I want you to devote your time to this one hundred percent. I spoke to Chief Stiles and he's going to reassign your other projects. As of right now, you're mine," he said motioning to Setty at his side, "so is our loaner here from the bureau."

Surprised, Beth glanced at the younger man, then back to Williams.

"Agent Setty is FBI?"

"Patriot Act, Adams," Williams said, smiling. "Setty has, shall we say, blundered into some counter terrorism actions on the southern border." Williams raised one large meaty paw and slapped Setty's back in a fatherly gesture. "Foiled some serious monkey business down there."

She looked at Setty again who shrugged with a "just lucky I guess" smirk on his face.

"I used a little-known provision of the P.A.," Williams continued, "to kidnap his ass from the Bureau. So come on, kids. Let's save the free world."

The two agents followed the hulking man out of the conference room deeper into the bowels of the Pentagon.

TWENTY-THREE

Abu Ghraib Prison, Iraq
May, 2002
Wednesday, 1:30 PM

For Ibrahim al-Takar, time had become as incomprehensible a concept as quantum physics. His life had become a trinity of disparate and disorienting experiences: the pit where he slept, head often covered in a stifling black hood, hands bound, amidst the foul products of his own mortal flesh. Then there was the orientation room the non-believers called "Vegas" where his senses were assaulted by at best banal, at worst obscene overdoses of Americana. And, finally, here in the quiet room where his humanity was restored for a few precious moments. The most affirming manifestation of humanity—speech—he could no longer avoid. He was compelled to speak to this man with whom he shared such sublime moments of peace. He wanted to ask a question, but he was afraid of the answer. On the fifth day, after prayer and much internal vacillation and trepidation, Ibrahim finally spoke.

"Please forgive..." he began, but his voice was hoarse and weak from lack of use and only an unintelligible croak emerged. He cleared his throat and tried again. "Please forgive me, but are you real or is this a dream?"

The man did not look up, but asked in Arabic, "Are you happy here?"

At the sound of his native tongue and the unexpected kindness in the man's voice, tears filled Ibrahim's eyes once again. He wiped them with the back of his hand.

"I feel at peace in this room with you."

Without looking up the man returned the teacup to his lips. "Then what does it matter?"

Ibrahim, emboldened by the man's response, continued.

"I fear I have failed."

The man stared into the teacup for a long moment before speaking again. "What is it you have failed?"

Ibrahim thought carefully before he answered. The question, from this man, in this oasis in Hell, seemed to carry significantly more weight than its obvious meaning. He tried to recreate past events, but the journey to this place blurred into a shimmering heat-haze obscuring reality and presenting mirage as rock solid fact. He picked his way carefully, but even so progress was impossible to measure. He had been doing work for the Jihad, for God's glory, for martyrdom and eternity in God's holy grace. That is what he knew for certain.

"Allah," he said in answer.

The man answered without hesitation. "You cannot fail Allah. You can only fail yourself." The man put down his teacup and straightened his robes over his knees. "Do you see the vanity in your words, the arrogance?" He picked up the teapot and poured more hot water into his cup. "How can you fail Allah?" he asked. "Do you believe his plans are thwarted by your personal success or failure?"

The Holy Warrior was confused. "I am doing his work," he said. "I am doing as the Prophet has commanded in his name. I am destroying the infidel in his lair and uniting all Muslims in his name. I have only tried to serve him. But what can I do in here?"

"You have suffered for Jihad, for Allah, be praised. He has not deserted you."

It was what Ibrahim wanted to hear, as though the words came from somewhere within his own tortured brain.

Suddenly the door opened and, as always, the female soldier walked in and stood next to Ibrahim, handcuffs dangling from her left hand, right hand resting on the handle of her sidearm, his Charon waiting to ferry him back to Hell. He wept like a woman all the way back to the cell, which made him feel even more wretched. He felt the hood and bindings were a just punishment and he dutifully lay on the concrete and resigned himself to whatever Allah revealed.

TWENTY-FOUR

Boundary Waters Canoe Area Wilderness, Minnesota
May, 2002
Wednesday, 7:00 PM

Asad paddled in the stern of the canoe and found the experience frustrating. He placed an extra pack in the bow which leveled the craft. Each pack weighed roughly eighty pounds and kept the front down out of every errant gust of wind, but steering was still difficult. As the boat's solo engine, he expended a tremendous amount of energy just to keep it moving forward. Adding to his frustration, Anwar and Saad had pulled far ahead and he could not yell for them to slow down. He worried that if they met another person on the next portage, the disaster that had only hours before threatened their entire mission would repeat itself. "Ignorant fools," he said aloud.

Despite his worries, the next several portages went without incident, except for the ever-present circling black flies biting any exposed skin surface. They rotated duty in the single canoe and Asad was pleased with their progress. By the end of the day, according to the GPS unit he carried, they had put more than ten miles between themselves and the dead forest ranger. They had successfully crossed several portages and two large lakes, Gabimichigami and Little Saganaga. During that time they had passed only two canoes and those were at a distance. They met no one on the portage trails. They were back on schedule, spending the night on an island campsite on Mora Lake. The group was now entering the seldom-visited interior of the BWCAW. The lakes along this path were small and far from the entry points off the Gunflint Trail or the southern border of the park. They expected no human contact here, which suited Asad well.

Each of them carried a GPS unit that contained their entire route. Asad had planned it meticulously, researching each lake, each portage with a book readily available for purchase on the Internet. The book provided detailed descriptions of each portage, including the conditions of the trail in various seasons, elevation changes, hiking difficulty, estimated time to complete, and, most importantly to their mission, the popularity of each route. On a laptop computer loaded with topographic mapping software, Asad marked key locations on the map, including portages, campsites and contingency routes in the event of natural or man-made obstacles. All of these locations were uploaded to the individual GPS units which were in turn distributed to the group. The Sheik and his clerics were not pleased to hear that the mission's plans would be stored in four small devices that could possibly be lost or captured. Asad assured them that it was the only way to ensure that the fate of one man could not endanger the entire mission. It would be disastrous if they were to become lost somewhere in those vast road-less forests.

Their campsite faced east and each man prayed as the glow of the setting sun faded behind the skyline, jagged with the black spires of endless conifers. Saad built a fire and boiled a pot of rice seasoned with salt and herbs while Anwar and Asad pitched their tent. Though no one mentioned it, they were all thankful for the additional room provided by Kadir's absence. They sat cross-legged on a ledge of ancient bedrock sloping gently into the lake and ate their simple meal in silence. Around them sounds of the approaching evening filled the still air. Loons yodeled their eerie calls while white-throated sparrows sang their pure descending notes signaling the end of another day. Frogs were beginning to peep and croak from vernal ponds deep in the darkening woods. And, as a subtle but insistent accompaniment, the growing hum of mosquitoes and midges moving from the forest out toward the water. Anwar was the first to speak.

"This place does have its beauty, praise Allah," he said. "The stars are so clear. They look as if Heaven itself is descending upon us."

"In a way, it is," Asad said, and chuckled at his own joke. "It will have finished its descent in three days. One could say we are bringing Heaven down."

Saad spoke in his low rasping voice, "I prefer to think that I am rising up to meet it. Allah does not lower himself to take me. I must aspire to his height, his beauty. It is blasphemy to expect God to lower himself at your convenience, at your beckoning."

Asad looked at Saad as though seeing him for the first time. He probed the older man's weathered countenance— years of death and suffering had hollowed him, though some humanity remained. That was his weakness.

"You think like a peasant," he said, as one might say, 'it's raining.' "Your world is a simple place of two dimensions," he continued, rising to pace around the fire. "As there is up, there is down, just as there is black and white, night and day. So it goes, if there is evil, there must be good, but somewhere just out of our reach. It gives you something to live for because if you examined your petty accomplishments here on earth you would jump in front of a truck at the inconsequence of it all. A pile of shit and your squirming prodigy—the legacy of the masses."

The firelight played upon Asad's handsome features, twisting them into grotesque caricatures as he strode around the pulsing flames, adding an ominous air to his oration.

"You believe in your God and your Heaven to the exclusion of all others, just as your enemy does. We all believe in the same God. None argue that there is only one God, not the Jew, not the Christian, not us. It is simply the rulebooks we dispute. But all of these intricacies, these shades of gray are lost upon the peasantry."

At this he stopped and looked down at Saad, whose own face was contorted in rage, the scar on his face as red as the campfire.

"Lost on you in your blinding misplaced rage," he said pointing a finger at the old soldier. "And thank God, says the wealthy Jew, the wealthy Christian, the wealthy Muslim. Praise Allah for the idiots we rule!"

Saad could contain himself no longer. He leapt up and roared in Asad's face who stood his ground.

"You are not worthy of this great honor! You are a whore, a whore of a thousand fathers!"

Saad turned and stormed off to the tent, muttering to himself as he walked.

Asad looked down at the remaining member of his team. Anwar calmly stirred the dying fire with a stick. Quietly he asked Asad, "What were you trying to accomplish? I see no value in turning us against each other."

"What you don't see could fill volumes," Asad snarled. "We are here in this endless, parasite-infested swamp for our God, are we not?"

Asad reached down and pulled a burning branch from the flames and heaved it into the dark water stretching out before them. They watched it fly through the air like a comet then hit the water with a splash and a soft hiss.

"What else do men discuss who are doomed to glory?"

Anwar rose and dropped his stirring stick into the coals.

"I am here because I believe in our mission," he said. "I am here for my family, for my Muslim brothers and sisters, and yes, for my God. I say that without confusion, without hesitation, without shame. I am here because death will not stop for us until we bring death to them. So spare me your schoolyard taunting. Make no mistake, I will see that this succeeds regardless of your doubts."

He turned and followed Saad into the tent, leaving Asad alone staring into what was left of the fire with nothing more to say.

TWENTY-FIVE

Hansen stepped up into the old Ford pickup and sat upon the torn vinyl bench seat. The rusting brown F-250 was a gift from his father. The old man took it hard the day he had to admit, from the hospital bed after his second stroke, that he could no longer drive the truck, much less haul in herring nets. His right side was paralyzed and he couldn't manage it only with his left hand, though he would try several times, struggling mightily in his eighteen-foot dinghy on the pitching, steely waters of Superior. And Hansen couldn't find it within himself to say the words he knew his father longed to hear. The subject came up in silent moments at the end of halting, barely intelligible conversations that both men found exhausting. Stroke or not, it was always that way with them. There was never debate. Neither held out any illusion that the other would see his side. Every disagreement scabbed over in this way, became a coarse and lifeless callus, devoid of feeling. Over the years it had become harder and harder to find subjects where the advancing borders of that desolation did not encroach. As a typical contrary teenager, Hansen had vowed to get out, away from the constant stink of fish, the frozen fingers and rope-burned hands. But the years and distance turned empty rebellion into pig-headed resolve that not even a deathbed could crumble. So with the old man thinking, "If only he would offer," and the young man, "If only he would ask," the end came too soon in a few shuddering, rasping breaths leaving Hansen suddenly convinced that a few more moments would have made all the difference.

Now he pulled the old truck out onto the Gunflint Trail and it rattled its way south toward Poplar Lake Lodge where Mark Toftey would be waiting for a ride into town. Hansen hadn't called Billy to check if the ranger had arrived. First, Toftey was nothing if not punctual. The weather had been perfect for traveling all week. There was no reason to believe he'd encountered any delays. Second, Hansen didn't have a phone. Cook County, Minnesota was a place where you couldn't take it for granted that a person had a phone or electricity. He had neighbors he could ask in a pinch, but most shared a pioneer spirit that took pride in overcoming minor difficulties with ingenuity and independence instead of soulless, pre-packaged solutions. And sometimes, he was just stubborn.

Hansen parked the truck in front of the main lodge, an impressive two-story cedar log structure built in the late 1940's by Billy's father. Billy's wife opened the screen door and leaned out, smiling at Hansen.

"He's down at the dock, hon. Some knucklehead ran one of the boats up on a rock."

Hansen rolled his eyes.

"I'm sure that's made his day. Thanks Libby."

He walked around the lodge and down the grassy slope to the docks and boathouse. The main dock was eight feet wide and stretched fifty feet into the crystal waters of Poplar Lake, ending in a "T" which supported two benches and a series of cleats for docking the occasional floatplane. The lake lay before him, sparkling blue, rippling in a late morning breeze, growing as the spring sunshine warmed the sweet-smelling air. On the far shore Hansen admired the varying shades of green that marked the annual awakening of the forest. Halfway down the dock, on the left side Hansen saw a man and a boy standing, looking down at Billy who was removing a twenty-five-horsepower motor from an aluminum fishing boat. The man wore khaki shorts, a tee shirt with a moose on it that said, "Families Love Poplar Lake," flip-flops and a khaki Tilley hat. The boy wore the same. Hansen could hear the cursing before he reached the dock.

"Shit, shit, shit!"

Billy was loosening the two clamps that held the motor securely to the boat's transom. His knuckles were bleeding from scraping them against the motor cover which was cracked and missing a large section of fiberglass. He stood abruptly with the one hundred and twenty-pound, long-shaft outboard in his hands.

"Look out!" he yelled.

The man and boy jumped out of the way as Billy threw the motor onto the dock. The Mercury thumped onto the wood decking with an impressive crunch. But instead of staying put as one might expect, given the weight of the unit, it bounced, perhaps gaining some spring from the wooden dock, stood briefly on its end, then tumbled over and flipped into the water with an impressive plop and splash. What remained of the shattered engine cover lay on the decking, rocking back and forth, after popping free upon impact. Billy watched it all, red-faced, veins bulging, from the boat. He stepped from the seat up onto the dock, walked over to the broken cover and kicked it mightily into the water where it floated momentarily then sank slowly out of sight.

"Shit."

Hansen was afraid the man and boy would be next and hurried onto the dock.

"Had a little motor trouble I see," Hansen said unnecessarily. The man was clearly relieved to see another person on the dock.

"Yes, I did. You know, you can't see those gosh darn rocks out there. Treacherous, really! Someone ought to get them out of there. It's a real hazard. You'd think the Forest Service or somebody would blast them or dredge them out of there. I mean, someone could get killed!"

As if suddenly aware of his own growing agitation, the man put his arm around the boy and finished with, "My son was scared to death."

The boy looked up at him, puzzled, apparently not fully supporting his father's version of events.

"Come on, Benny, let's get out of Mr. Cosgrove's hair so he can fix the boat," the man said and walked quickly past Hansen with a nod, his son in tow.

Billy stood on the dock looking down at a growing rainbow slick of oil and gas spreading from the spot at which the motor entered the water. When Benny and his father were out of sight, Billy Cosgrove looked sideways at Hansen.

"Only thing that kept me from feeding that numb-nuts my busted prop was his kid was watching. I told him where that goddamn reef was ten times! I showed him on his map. He said, I'll mark it on my GPS, that way I can't miss it!"

"So how did he miss it?" asked Hansen, smiling.

"Batteries died. So my motor is fucked 'cause he couldn't spend three bucks on a Duracell! Ignorant piece of shit!"

"That's what insurance is for," Hansen offered.

The old man produced a wry chuckle. He looked up at Hansen and asked, "What are you doing here besides pissin' me off?"

"I thought I'd find our local wilderness ranger here by now looking for a ride to town. Any sign of him?"

"Nope, nothin.' Probably show up this afternoon. Stick around and help me fish this fuckin' $2000 anchor out of the drink. I'll buy you a beer. Don't tell me you're working." Billy eyed him up and down.

"You look like a fuckin' farmer. How you expect to get laid, hillbilly? Know how to operate a razor?"

Hansen rubbed a hand over the three-day growth of beard on his chin and watched as Billy took the anchor rope from the disabled fishing boat and expertly tied a beautiful slipknot at one end. Looking over the edge of the dock he could see the motor through the oil haze, lying on the rocky bottom. Cosgrove pulled a tackle box out of the boat, opened it and removed a heavy sinker on a chain. This he attached to a short wire leader and tied it to the bottom of the noose.

"Why not just jump in there and get it, ya lazy bastard?" Hansen asked.

Billy laid on his belly and lowered the noose over the edge of the dock, through the oil slick toward the motor below.

"That fucking water's forty-five degrees, genius. You go ahead."

A few moments later Billy and Hansen were on shore, pulling on the rope until the battered motor emerged from the cold water. Hansen could see that one blade of the propeller was missing and the other two were badly damaged with sizeable nicks torn out of the aluminum.

"Damn!" he said.

"Come on," Billy said. "I'll drop this off in the boat house, then we'll get us a beer or three. Might as well wait in comfort for the prodigal son, get a head start on your evening."

Hansen looked down at his watch. "It's only eleven o'clock, Billy!"

Billy picked up the motor and began walking toward the shed.

"So, you can pour it on some pancakes."

————————————

By five that evening, Hansen had a good buzz going, but not enough to relieve a slight pang of concern that had been growing for the last hour or so. As he sat at Billy and Libby Cosgrove's bar, drinking strong Jack and Cokes, his gaze drifted more and more often out the picture windows to the pine tree shadows creeping steadily out onto the placid surface of Poplar Lake. He'd been sitting here alone for the past few hours, alternately watching the Twins get brutally out-pitched by the Mariners on the TV and staring at the lake. Billy had disappeared to tend to "resort operations" as he called them, usually restarting stove pilot lights, filling boat gas tanks or snaking tampons out of cabin toilets.

"It's not always this glamorous," he would say.

Libby brought Hansen a burger and fries after he finished a bowl of bar pretzels.

"You need some sustenance, honey," she told him. "Something to soak up that rot gut you drink."

He let her baby him, not that he had a choice. In the Cosgroves he'd met two people who were incredibly forthright with their emotions. When they were mad, they yelled at you then promptly forgot about it and moved on.

When you made them happy, they hugged you or slapped you on the back and it was like a warm sun shining on you when you're cold. He felt like their kid sometimes. It was a good feeling.

"You worried about him?" Libby asked from behind the bar as she cleaned glasses.

It took Hansen a moment to return to the here and now. "Uh, no, not really. I mean, I'm sure there's a good reason he's not here."

"That's ok," she said and put a hand on his. "I won't tell the boys that you're a worried mother hen." She patted him, gave him a wink then resumed her chores.

She's right, he thought. I am acting like a mother hen. Jesus!

"You're right," he said. "He's a big boy, he can take care of himself. I'll check back tomorrow."

He drained his glass, got up and slapped a twenty-dollar bill on the bar. Just as Libby protested he raised his hand and said, "buy yourself something nice." Then he headed for the door.

"Thanks. I'll remember you in my will, honey," she said as the screen door shut behind him.

TWENTY-SIX

Goiaina, Brazil, September, 1987

In the afterglow of their lovemaking, Victor lay awake and let his mind drift in an out of sleep, vaguely aware of Suzanna fixing dinner for Maria, shushing her excited twittering voice, "Let your papá sleep." This was such a rare luxury, his daily thoughts so often consumed with the next day's, the next hour's demanding chores, the narrow space between each task, if it even existed, was reserved for mindless physical recovery. When he allowed himself these moments, what he found always surprised him. It was a part of him that spoke of greater things, of plans, and dreams and romance beyond what he thought of as his "peasant's existence."

It had been a good day, though Victor was too humble a man to gloat. He had been taught to be humble, as Jesus had been. And there was so much to do. There were the endless repairs of their modest home – the tin roof, the chicken coop, the fence, the little dusty yard. With Maria he cared for the chickens, carried water from the community well for Suzanna to boil, and there was the unrelenting vigilance required to keep the things they worked so hard to obtain. Victor was patient with those who stole, almost paternal. Where he lived nobody stole to get rich or even with the thought that their actions would hurt those from which they robbed. They stole to feed their family, to keep their home, to simply *have* something and in so doing affirm their place on God's good earth and the world of men.

He had done it himself, when Maria was only 2 months old and he could find no work. He had once taken several loaves of bread from outside a bakery in town. The rack of still-warm loaves had been dropped off by the delivery van before first light and the owner had not yet arrived. Victor had been walking to a construction site where he would jostle and yell with a crowd of men like him, tradesmen and laborers, desperate for a day's work. Then he saw the loaves. He hesitated, for just a moment, until he saw the faces of his wife and his baby daughter. He was sure that God had put their faces before him to help him decide. God understood and would forgive him this trifling sin, he was sure. Allowing his family to go hungry when God had just provided would have been the sin. He took the bread and fed his family and it felt right.

He dreamed. Shimmering blue curtains billowed from an open window. Through them he glimpsed his own face along with Suzanna and Maria. But they were not looking at him, not the Victor he saw by their side nor the voyeur Victor, watching them through the curtains. They looked over their shoulders, as though someone they knew was approaching from behind.

Suddenly he awoke, disoriented with a feeling of dread At once he realized Maria was calling his name from outside. He didn't know how long he had been sleeping, but it was dark. Suzanna was by his side, eyes closed, breathing deeply. Maria knew not to go outside alone in the middle of the night. Growing worried and angry he slipped on his boxers and sandals and stepped outside. The air was humid and warm, the acrid smell of chicken guano burning in his nostrils as he breathed. Distant traffic, dogs and his neighbor's voices greeted his ears as

Maria ran toward him, her bare, calloused feet slapping the ground in rapid succession.

"Papá, papá!"

"What is it, Maria? You know you shouldn't be out here," he scolded, but his anger melted as he looked into his daughters dark eyes. Excitement sparkled there like a thousand stars in the inky black of space.

"Come, you have to see them!" She grabbed his fingers in her own little hand and dragged him toward the chicken coop. They reached the fence and a young boy slightly older than Maria, tall and thin, opened the gate so they could enter.

"Hey, Claudio," said Victor, greeting the boy. "What's this all about?"

Victor felt bad for him. Claudio lived with his young mother who left him for hours, sometimes days, alone. Neighbors speculated that she spent her evenings on Avenida Araguia, selling her body on that busy downtown artery to foreigners looking for a more intimate connection with the indigenous populace than that afforded them by the many resort enclaves around the city. Suzanna checked on Claudio when the woman was gone and he often shared meals with them.

"It's an invasion," the young boy whispered, looking around conspiratorially. "Aliens."

"Aliens?" Victor asked, smiling a little, his playfulness engaged by the earnest children before him, consumed by their fantasy. He felt a pang of longing there as well, a wish that he could once more visit such a world, where the fantastical was commonplace and journeys of the mind were exhilarating expeditions to undiscovered lands. Such thoughts, when they dared surface, were quickly drowned amid the harsh, insistent clamoring of responsibility and obligation that ruled the world in which he lived – the world of adults.

"Yeah, Papá," Maria said, leading him into the dark humid funk of the coop. He could hear a great deal of excited clucking from inside.

"They're aliens that came down from space to suck our blood," said Maria, with dramatically overwrought disgust.

Victor walked into the coop, but it wasn't dark at all. In fact he could see surprisingly well. Because, of course, all the chickens were glowing.

TWENTY-SEVEN

The Georgetown Hotel, Georgetown, Virginia,
May, 2002
Wednesday, 7:40 PM

"The real danger of an RDD isn't the radiation at all." Brian Setty sat at a small table in the lounge of the bustling Georgetown hotel. He wore a white cable-knit sweater, jeans and tennis shoes and slumped in a red lounge chair.

He sipped his beer and continued, "It's the panic." The morning had energized him and he had spent the remainder of the day reviewing Beth's files from the briefing.

Across a small cocktail table sat Beth Adams, who was feeling stiff and self-conscious in the same suit she had so meticulously selected earlier in the day. She had not been prepared for Chief Williams' orders at the end of the briefing.

"Get the hell out of this place," Williams said. "There hasn't been an original constructive idea hatched in this cave since Truman's day. Kick back, get a beer and some dinner and talk this thing to death. I want the most probable scenario by tomorrow."

It was Setty who suggested the venue, primarily because he was staying at the hotel and could avoid driving around D.C. trying in vain to park. It had grown so much more difficult to get around in the capital since the towers came down - concrete barricades replacing parking meters, walls replacing invitations. It was a sign of the times.

They had removed the candle from their table as well as the plastic sign displaying the happy hour specials to make room for Beth's laptop and documents. The bar was busy with business travelers and government office workers, there for the cheap drinks and free snacks. It was noisy, but as good a place as any to anonymously discuss the scenarios under which a "radiological dispersion device" might be smuggled into the country and detonated, causing widespread panic in the general populace.

Beth looked at Setty, puzzled by his last remark. "I can understand there will be panic, sure, but I would think people dying of radiation burns and poisoning would be a pretty significant danger all on its own."

She took a sip of her beer. She wasn't used to drinking it, but anything to help her cloud the memory of her gaffs in the briefing was worth a try.

Before being stationed at the southern border, Setty had learned a lot about the potential threats he was sent to sniff out. Among them were radiological weapons, what the popular media liked to call `dirty bombs'—any sort of radioactive material wrapped in conventional explosive of sufficient quantity to disperse the material over as wide an area as possible.

"They call them `weapons of mass disruption,' he said, "because the point isn't to vaporize as many people as possible, like a regular nuke. The idea is to scare the shit out of as many people as possible with the side benefit of leaving an area dangerous and inaccessible for a couple hundred years or more, depending on the isotope."

Beth looked down and saw that her beer was gone. The empty glass surprised her. The bitter taste of the cold beer lifted her spirits while her conversation with Agent

Brian Setty was taking on a pleasant hue. It was clear that he was someone who was into his work as much as she was, but without as much of the macho, jarhead mentality displayed by so many field agents, most with military police backgrounds and something to prove to their daddies, whom they all called "Sir." She looked around until she caught their waitress' eye and circled her finger over the table to order another round for the both of them. She could feel the tension of the day slipping away.

Setty looked at her and raised an eyebrow and a smile. "You go girl," he said.

She suddenly felt embarrassed and hoped the dim light hid the blush rising in her cheeks. This was a professional discussion with a defined goal. The expectations of the agency and the security of the nation were on the line. It was not a time to get too comfortable in front of a fellow agent, an agent who obviously had the ear of her boss' boss. For the second time in a day, she wanted to bolt out the nearest door.

Brian Setty noticed the subtle change in her demeanor. He was an expert at reading body language. It was a survival skill and it had saved his ass in Mexico. Back then it had been the unusual tension in a voice he had come to know. It was the forced character of a shoulder shrug when it should have been the most natural thing in the world. It was the look in the truck's rearview mirror that told him he was being driven to his grave.

"Hey, I didn't mean to embarrass you," he told her.

"I know," she lied.

She didn't know anything at the moment. She certainly didn't know him well enough to guess his intentions. She assumed he was being sincere, but then again....

"It's okay to loosen up a bit." He made the same circular motion above the table with his finger.

"I like that you know your way around a bar."

"I'm not sure `knowing my way around a bar,' as you put it, is an admirable skill," she said.

"I like that you are insightful as hell with your data analysis and can order a round of beers like a sailor on shore leave. That is admirable in my book, Agent Adams. We have a lot to do and I'd rather do it with someone who can help me keep the glasses full."

Beth hoped that Brian Setty didn't equate that to making his coffee. Stop it, she thought, you're being a dolt! She allowed herself a brief smile as the waitress arrived with two beers.

She raised her glass in a toast and said, "Thank you."

Their glasses clinked and they drank. Beth wiped foam from under her nose with a napkin and tried to put her most recent awkward moment behind her.

"So," she began, "are you saying nobody gets radioactive?"

"No, I didn't mean that at all. People closest to the blast who aren't immediately killed by the explosion could be burned by radioactivity or show symptoms of radiation sickness within hours. The efficacy of the release depends on several factors: the amount of explosive used, the amount of radioactive material used, its consistency. A powder, for instance, like cesium, is great for dispersal over large areas in a brisk wind. So, the weather is a big factor, where the device is placed, for instance on public transportation, say maybe a subway tunnel or airport? While it would be good for effect, from al-Qaeda's perspective, for people to be on the news with horrific radiation burns, it's pretty unlikely. They'll pay the price twenty or thirty years from now in lymphomas and leukemia. Another thing to remember is the more potent the isotope, the more dangerous it is to the handler and the less likely it can be concealed and moved."

"You said where it is placed is one of the factors, right?" she asked.

"Yup."

"So, the best scenario would be some way to maximize panic without having to deal with large conspicuous amounts of radioactive material and large conspicuous amounts of explosive."

"Correct again."

He was casually looking at a copy of the tattered aerial photograph that had led them here.

Beth was staring at her beer and thinking feverishly, her excitement beginning to rise.

"Obviously prime targets for a spectacular conventional explosion are places where large numbers of people congregate—large buildings, stadiums, public transportation. But those places would contain the radioactivity, making a dirty bomb less effective."

Brian noted her growing enthusiasm. He liked the vitality that animated her face as she spoke—her eyes sparkled with it. "The typical RDD models identify large outdoor venues, like Times Square, as high-probability targets."

She took a couple of swallows of beer and felt the carbonation burn in her throat. It made her cough.

"What about a nuclear facility," she ventured. "A power plant?"

Setty shook his head.

"Nope. Even if you could somehow get conventional explosives in there, which you wouldn't be able to do since visitors get everything but strip-searched upon entry, you'd never get past the radiation-sensing equipment, unless of course you could somehow nonchalantly muscle in a lead box to hide it in. But you're still faced with the issue of limiting contamination to the interior of the facility."

"True, but it's a *nuclear* facility. What's going to happen when people hear that there's been a blast at a nuclear power plant and that radioactivity has been detected? It's a win/win for a terrorist: If the story is that it's radioactivity from the plant, then people assume it's been damaged by a bomb and they panic. If they find out it's radioactivity from a dirty bomb, then the magnitude of that fact alone spreads panic. I mean, it doesn't matter whether Mr. Terrorist was in the monitoring station outside the cooling towers or sitting in HR filling out a job application. Once that bomb goes off anywhere in a nuclear facility people are gonna freak."

"Well, you still have the problem of getting enough explosives and radioactive material past a pretty formidable array of security measures." Setty drained his beer glass and set it down.

"I think it would be a hell of a lot easier for the terrorists and scarier for Joe Six-Pack to have it go off at the local state fair or some outdoor sporting event, like the U.S. Open or the Indy Five Hundred."

Beth was getting buzzed. She caught the waitress' eye once again, glanced at Brian to make sure he was watching, and swirled her finger above the table again.

She looked back at him and continued, "But unless you yell `Praise Allah, I've got a dirty bomb and I'm not afraid to use it!' People might not know right away there's a nuclear threat. Don't you think the bad guys want us to know right away? If it went off at a nuclear power plant, everybody would assume radiation."

Setty laughed, then looked at her intently.

"Why are you so stuck on the nuclear power plant angle anyway?" he asked. "What do you have that we didn't see today?"

She looked slyly over the top of her beer glass, winked and said, "Oh, I've got a lot you haven't seen!"

As soon as she said it, she knew it was bad. She looked down at her beer but the glass was empty, so there was no hiding her red face behind the raised glass. Explaining herself now would make it worse—make it a thing worthy of further discussion. She frantically tried to think of something to say, but her brain was slow and fuzzy. She had to say something. She forced something out and it came out too loud.

"I have to pee."

She got up horrified and tried not to run to the restroom.

TWENTY-EIGHT

Boundary Waters Canoe Area Wilderness, Minnesota
May, 2002
Wednesday, 7:20 PM

It was taking longer than Toftey estimated to get through the woods. Thousands of blown-down trees from a devastating windstorm in 1999 crisscrossed the forest at waist height, making cross-country travel a rigorous, bruising, scraping ordeal. Darkness was descending. He was facing a night in the woods. Under normal conditions, sleeping under the stars would have been an enjoyable prospect. He had taken many trips into the BW without a tent and only his canoe as shelter from the rain. But several factors made tonight less attractive. First, he was still wet. Though his travel thus far gave his clothes a chance to air out some, everything was still clammy. He couldn't tell how much was from sweat and how much was Seagull River water. When the temperature dipped to freezing tonight, it wouldn't matter. Hypothermia would be almost inevitable. Second, he was afraid to build a fire, aware that the light and smell could guide the men back to him. Third, related to point number two, he could have his throat slit in the night. Soon it would be too dark to see, so he decided to take a chance on a small fire.

He found a suitable sheltered spot beside a natural stone wall jutting out of the forest duff. On a shelf of rock he laid dead balsam boughs, then a temple of progressively larger sticks. He surveyed his creation, looked around the congealing shadows once more, then pulled out the matches he'd salvaged from the dead Arab and lit a fire. Immediately his plight seemed somehow less dire. The warmth and light of the snapping flames raised his spirits and gave him hope. It was obviously the right thing to do.

Once he had established a steady blaze, he stripped and hung his clothing as near to the flames as he dared. He stood by the fire naked, waiting for his clothes to dry, turning to alternately warm his back and his front. The mosquitoes all but disappeared with the onset of darkness and the black flies, he knew, were active only in the daylight. Anyway, he knew the smoke from the fire would keep away any remaining bloodsucker. If his friends could see him now, he thought, standing bare-assed naked in the middle of the woods, burning his butt or his pecker, jerking his head around at the slightest rustle of leaves or snapped twig, expecting to see that big guy charging him like a hungry lion.

It hit him, how alone he was. For the first time in the Boundary Waters, even after all the years spent paddling and camping by himself, he finally felt utterly alone—as alone as the only man left on the planet. He couldn't just turn around and head back. He couldn't yell for help. Maybe you don't feel alone until you need somebody, he mused. Maybe most people need somebody more often than I do, so being in the BW alone would never suit them. Maybe, he wondered, I'm just full of shit and scared and want my mommy.

He circled the fire, throwing more wood on, looking past the rising sparks into the impenetrable darkness beyond. Strange how fragile he felt without that thin layer of cotton between him and the night. Loons called forlornly from the waters nearby. Only their song and the crackling fire intruded on the silence of the wilderness night shift. He wondered how the Arabs were spending the night in this place. It must be unsettling, to come from a culture and environment so vastly different from where they now found themselves. He assumed they came from arid or desert lands of the middle east, so all this water and wildlife must really be fucking with their heads about now. Good luck finding a dry grain of sand up here— nothing to remind you of home. He looked to the sky— maybe the stars? But no, they would be probably be unfamiliar as well, their position strange in the sky, if they even thought to look at them. He remembered staring at the stars for hours on his solo trips, laying on a rock still warm from the summer day's baking sun. From his back he watched distant glittering suns, hurtling satellites and falling stars animate the otherwise cold black dome above.

Those men today meant to kill me, he thought. He'd had folks mean him harm on a few occasions, but he always knew why. Usually because he'd been writing them a ticket or, on a few rare occasions, arresting them. But he had never seen murder in another man's eyes. And for what, he did not know. That was the most disturbing part, because as far as he could tell, these guys showed up already with a reason to kill. The *who*, it seemed, was incidental.

To hasten their drying, Toftey swung his pants around over his head and out over the fire. Fortunately the weave was loose and the material lightweight. Soon they were comfortable enough to slip on over his boxers and socks, which had dried quickly. Then the white "T" and over that his long-sleeved uniform shirt. It felt really good to be dry. He broke off some balsam boughs thinking, "no-trace, my ass, this is survival!" and made a surprisingly comfortable nest near the fire. He stoked it as much as he could, lay down and was asleep in seconds.

TWENTY-NINE

Abu Ghraib Prison, Iraq, May, 2002
Wednesday, 2:30 PM

"If he drinks much more Jack," said the sergeant, "he's gonna be askin' for NASCAR and bass fishin' on the TV! Ain't ya, Ibby? Gonna be stickin' a number three on yer camel's ass."

The other young soldiers laughed. Vince, giggling, walked over to where Ibrahim sat in silence and kicked his chair, sending their prisoner and the chair crashing to the floor.

"Knock that shit off, numb-nuts!" yelled the sergeant. "If that fucker cracks his skull then we all end up in deep shit!"

"What's one more dead camel jockey?"

The sergeant went over and helped the man back onto his chair.

"This here's one important camel jockey. Ibby was a bag man for al-Qaeda, weren't ya Ibby? A courier for messages, cash, supplies, drugs. He was in Morocco, they figure buyin' weapons. Get this, one of his own kids turned him in for a hundred bucks!"

"No shit? That's fuckin' cold!" Vince bent down and looked into Ibrahim's face. "Dude's a regular gangsta, ain't ya?"

Vince began strutting around the room, alternately stabbing the air with his outstretched fingers and grabbing his crotch. He rapped, "Ibby got camel he like to fuck, Ibby got bomb in the back a his truck, he don't got no girl with titties to feel, he down in the dungeon keepin' it real, uh huh."

The soldiers were beside themselves with wild laughter. Barnes wiped tears from his eyes and caught his breath. "Damn, that's some funny shit!"

With that the door flew open and all the men whirled toward the sound, their minds and bodies taut from training and combat, ready for anything.

They were confronted by a deep, booming voice, "What the hell are you grunts doing? Turn the damn TV on and get out of here."

Ibrahim was startled and looked up to see a tall man in a military uniform, impeccably clean and pressed. A vague familiarity nagged at his brain, but Ibrahim was drunk and could not pull it into focus. Epps lumbered over to the television and turned it on. Then he and the other soldiers filed out of the room, eyes downcast. The tall man followed. Ibrahim turned back to the television, his will long since vanquished, and watched as a woman performed sex acts with a large dog of varied ancestry. He drained the cup of brown liquid and prayed to Allah that he would soon pass into oblivion once again.

THIRTY

How long she stayed in the bathroom she wasn't sure. It seemed like a long time, but checking her watch when she entered had not been the first thing on her mind. In fact, nothing had been on her mind other than escape.

At one of the sinks she splashed cold water on her face and looked up into the mirror. Oh my God what a mess! she thought. Wet strands of hair had escaped her ponytail and hung across her eyes, which were bloodshot and puffy from the pointless silent weeping she had done sitting on the toilet in one of the stalls. "Damn it!" she shouted out loud. Then, embarrassed, she bent over and looked under the stalls for feet. She was alone. Get back in there—you know this shit! she told her reflection.

When she returned to the table there was a large glass of ice water setting in front of her chair and a steaming cup of coffee. Brian Setty was still in his chair. He was smiling kindly.

"So, no jokes about search parties or falling in?" she asked.

"Look, I know you're out of your element here."

"You mean, in the bar? Well, you're right," she agreed.

"Yeah, that too," he said. "But I was actually talking about D.C. You're a scientist, you know logic, you know proof—empirical data. That stuff's like oxygen to you and the air is pretty damn thin up here on the hill. Reality? That's for the public. They don't live on reality up here."

She picked up the coffee cup. "No kidding."

"But," he said, "you hit a home run in there today." He raised his almost empty beer glass to her. "You had 'em all quaking in their loafers."

"So," she said, "when are you going to Minnesota?"

"Tomorrow morning. I'm riding jump seat on a C-130 heading to Duluth at five a.m. Then I pick up a company car at the Resident Agency and head north for a couple of hours to Grand Marais. Wanna come?"

The question caught her completely off guard.

"Uh...I'm not a field agent."

"You're a CIA agent on an investigation with Homeland Security implications. You can go anywhere you damn well please."

She could see he was serious. Her brain was spinning. She wanted to go and see if she was right, but the thought of a field assignment scared the hell out of her. But Brian's enthusiasm was infectious and she was intrigued.

"My boss wouldn't let me go. I have too much to do at the Pentagon."

"Yeah, but my boss can beat up your boss."

She laughed out loud. It felt good. She sat her coffee cup down and looked at him.

"It's been a long time since someone's made me laugh, other than by being an ass."

She toasted him with the water glass. "Thank you...and thanks for the change in beverage. You must think I'm a real flake."

"I don't know you that well." He smiled at her. "I do think you spend too much time worrying about what other people think."

"You sound like my dad."

"Sounds like a smart man. Give him a call and ask him if he thinks you should come to Minnesota with me."

"I wish I could," she looked down and sipped the coffee.

Setty realized his gaffe immediately. "Sorry."

"He would have said 'no' anyway." Beth said, "I think I can be more help to you from here. I've got more research to do and I may find out a few things you can use up there. Make sure I have your cell phone number before you go."

"If I had a buck for every time I've heard the old `Give-me-your-number-so-I-can-help-you-find-terrorists-in-the-wilderness' line, I could quit this dead-end job."

Setty put his beer glass down and looked at her.

"If a terrorist cell is coming in through the wilderness, what do you think is their objective?"

"I don't know," she said. "I...I think they need to get whatever it is accomplished as quickly as possible upon entering the country. I don't see them emerging from the woods and embarking on a long cross-country trip, exposing themselves to capture as they drive to a population center on either coast. There are targets right in Minnesota. There're two nuclear power plants, an international airport, three major stadiums and the largest shopping mall in the world. Why go anywhere else?"

"Makes sense," Setty said matter-of-factly. "How far away is the closest power plant from the woods?"

"Monticello is less than four hours away from Grand Marais," she said, "and you don't have to take any interstate highway to get there. It's been identified as a significant target in past scenarios. That's where I'd be going."

"I'm still stuck on them getting into the plant. I was on a special ops detail to probe security measures at Three

Mile Island, of all places. Though every plant in the U.S. is privately built and operated, they must all adhere, without exception, to a very comprehensive and rigid set of security protocols. From background checks that could find dirt on Mother Theresa to physical measures like biometrics, entry scales, man traps…."

Beth looked up, saw the waitress and signaled for the check. She wasn't feeling good and wanted to end the evening with whatever shred of dignity she had remaining.

"Look," she said, "I don't know how, yet. But who really knew about September 11, how effective their techniques would be? A coordinated multiple high jacking and suicide mission was unheard of before it happened. Sure, there was speculation, but nobody thought it could actually be done. Terrorists exploding a bomb inside a nuclear facility? Just as far-fetched, so probably just as possible."

"All I'm saying is we were good, my unit," Brian continued. "Really good. We came up with some very ingenious countermeasures. But we got caught. And every other ops team with that mission has been caught."

The waitress arrived with the check. Setty produced a credit card and gave it to her.

"The least I can do after getting you drunk is to pay the bill."

"Thank you, agent Setty," she said. "Something is compelling me to say, 'be careful.'"

"Maybe you want to see me again?"

"Maybe. Or maybe I don't have much confidence in you."

He looked at her intently, frowning, nodding his head as though puzzling over her comment. Then he shook his head emphatically and said, "Nah!"

Beth smiled as she packed her laptop, gathered her files, and rose to leave. "Just remember, agent," she said, her smile fading, "the one thing these guys have on their side, something that no special ops team ever had—they know that success means they won't be coming back."

THIRTY-ONE

Goiaina, Brazil
September, 1987

Victor awoke to his daughter screaming. He could tell it was morning from the bright light coming in around the shades, which were still pulled. But this time it was not joyous excitement he heard in her voice. It was panic.

Outside she ran into him crying, burying her face against his thigh, clutching his leg with desperate strength. He looked behind her and saw the chicken coop gate open and the egg basket lying on the ground, empty.

"What is it honey? What's the matter? Did something scare you? Is there a skunk in there?"

Maria was sobbing and could not form words or gather enough breath to answer his questions. "I didn't mean to," she sobbed. "I didn't mean to!"

"Mean to what honey? What happened? Are you hurt?" He began looking her over, afraid she had injured herself on the sharp ends of the chicken wire. His heart pounded in concert with her own, fluttering against him like a hummingbird.

"It's the chickens, Papá," she sobbed, the sound muffled against his leg. "They're all dead!"

Suzanna heard her daughter's cries and joined them outside. "You go with your mother, Maria," Victor said. "I'll check on the chickens." He disengaged from the girl and walked into the chicken coop, looking around. It was true. All of their chickens were dead. He looked at them closely. Many had discoloration and sores on the exposed skin of their combs, feet and around their eyes. All were covered with blue powder to varying degrees. He felt fear pierce his body just as his wife called from the yard. Back outside of the coop, in the warming sun of early morning, he saw his wife kneeling with his daughter. Maria was throwing up and couldn't seem to stop. As he ran toward them he heard her retching and crying. Drawing near he saw blood in her vomit.

"Get her in the car," he told his wife, trying to keep his voice level. He could see the fear in her eyes.

"Was it the powder?" she asked, her voice shaking. "*Madre del dios*, was it the powder?"

"Just get her in the car," he said quickly. "We have to go to the doctor."

THIRTY-TWO

The White Mountains, Afghanistan
August, 2000

The surface of the Afghan desert was one hundred and twelve degrees Fahrenheit, but sixty feet underground, it was little more than half that. Life survived in the labyrinth of rock and wooden timbers, cooled and watered by the pure crystal runoff from countless snowmelt streams tumbling out of the mountains. These streams, fed by the deep melting snows that buried the mountains every winter, flowed noisily through gullies and canyons in the spring and summer. From their frigid genesis in the rugged mountains above Tora Bora, the little streams joined and formed ranks, carving ravines into solid stone. The pure waters gave life to the people below, quenching their thirst, feeding them and their livestock, washing their bodies and clothes to stay clean as required by Allah and the Qur'an. And the waters brought riches as they irrigated the beautiful fields bringing white, red and blue to hundreds of square miles of tillable acreage—rich bottomland soil. From the seed pods of the flowers, stretching like a rippling magic carpet across the valleys of the White Mountains, came a solution to pain and suffering that the world had used for thousands of years. Over a third of Afghanistan's economy came from the poppy. The opium and heroin enslaving millions of people around the world funded freedom for a country struggling to find its place in the world.

They sat on rugs in a circle inside a cave whose ceiling stretched high into darkness above them. The cold air of the mountain evening was creeping in and chilling their backs, while a fire warmed their faces and hands. Inside the windless cave the smoke stretched straight up like a gray serpent searching for the small vent hole high overhead. There was magic in the air as the Sheik spoke softly to them, his words like velvet in the pure stillness of the night. Peace and tranquility emanated from him and they felt safe and right with the world. From his lips came wisdom and truth. They began to glimpse, finally, their purpose in the world and the reason for the suffering that had befallen their families and friends, not only in their memories, but also for generations past. God had a purpose and it was within their grasp. Their faith would be answered with beauty and love and, most important of all—the thing that they strained for, reached for like the poppies stretching up for the mountain sunlight— understanding.

"It is the evil they have created that we will turn against them," he said. "It is the hatred they have created that we will turn against them. We have lost so many to the Godless path of revenge. But we must use them, as Allah would use the wind and the waters to do his bidding. Just as he would use the righteous and holy to teach his word, we must use them as tools to protect and serve our master, praise Allah."

"They speak of Jesus, Peace be with him, as if they know him. But to them he is a tool for their greed and bigotry. Our brothers whom we have lost treat Allah the same. We must remember these blind people are only the tools born of the same evil, and it is the righteous and holy who will use these evil tools against each other and triumph at the end of the glorious battle, praise Allah. You are the righteous and holy. You will use them and not be soiled if you do not join them in your heart."

A woman walked toward the circle of light with a wooden tray, her face covered, black robes rustling as she brought the men tea made from a mixture of jasmine and poppy seed extract. Muhammad would probably not approve, but it was a small indulgence they allowed themselves in these severe and Spartan surroundings. Conversation ceased. Steam from the hot liquid swirled from plain ceramic mugs. Thin white clouds rising in the increasingly cool evening air. The woman knelt beside the Sheik and held the tray, her eyes downcast. Each man rose silently and, careful not to look at her, took a cup of tea from the tray she held and sat back down. When the last cup had been removed she arose with the empty tray and returned to the depths of the cave. The Sheik sipped the hot tea and spoke once again.

"Our brothers and sisters who now know only hatred suffer from a deadly disease that cannot be cured. We can help them find peace for their tortured souls. We can help them find Allah once again, praise him, cleansing the evil from themselves and cleansing it from the world with the death of his enemies."

As though on some hidden cue, one of the seated clerics stood and disappeared inside the cave. He returned a moment later with a large silver box, handles on both ends. He obviously struggled with its weight. He put the box near the fire and opened the lid. Inside were several small glass jars, their lids made of metal with clamps that held the lids on tight. The cleric reached into the box, pulled out one of the jars and held it up to the flickering firelight. Inside the jar was a beautiful powder-blue substance that sparkled in the changing light. It shifted within the jar like sugar and sparkled as it flowed.

The Sheik reached for the jar and the cleric held it out with both hands, his brow furrowed with concern. He released it reluctantly once he was sure the large man's hand gripped it firmly. His hands lingered for a few seconds, fingers retaining the shape of the vessel, poised to catch it should it fall. The Sheik dismissed him with a reassuring nod and spoke to the group.

"This is the culmination of their evil. In my hand is the power of the universe, second only to the will of God, praise Allah." The Sheik held out his hand and opened his fingers until the jar sat balanced in his open palm. He looked around the ring of orange faces, shadow and light playing across them as they stared transfixed by the blue jar, a mixture of fear and reverence in their eyes. "It is with this they steal our homes, our oil, our hope, our freedom. But they cannot steal our God. In our righteous hands Allah will turn their own power against them."

The effects of the warm opium tea crept through each of them like a woman's fingers, gentle and soothing, opening their minds to the wisdom of these calmly spoken words. It was all so obvious, so reasonable. There was an answer to all the suffering they had endured, all the sadness. The power to end it was within their grasp. In this jar burned The Fire of God, they could feel the seductive power within its serene, magical beauty. It both frightened and compelled them. They would do anything this man commanded them to do. It was clear to them all—his was the voice of God.

THIRTY-THREE

Gunflint Trail, Cook County Minnesota
May, 2002
Thursday, 9:20 AM

"I have to baby-sit some FBI tourist from Washington."

Hansen sat once again at Cosgrove's bar nursing a beer and looking out at the brilliant blue chop on Poplar Lake, sparkling as its waves pulsed toward the sandy shore in front of the lodge. And still, a day later, there was no sign of Mark Toftey. Libby wiped the bar and the strong smell of bleach assaulted his nostrils.

"What's that all about? Drugs?" she asked.

"Nah, something about illegal immigrants coming in through the Boundary Waters."

Libby Cosgrove snorted, "You kiddin' me? This time of year, with the bugs, the cold nights, not to mention getting lost. It's like those poor people from Cuba that tie milk crates together and paddle them across the ocean to Florida. I saw on TV once where they had an old outboard motor on a '57 Chevy. I say let 'em come, if they'd go through all that bullshit to get here."

"You're starting to talk like the old man," Hansen said.

"Oh, Garrett, you know he doesn't recognize anything as conversation unless it begins or ends with a cuss word. I used to sing in the church choir before I met William. Now, he's got me goin' straight to hell."

"So where is the ornery old cuss?"

"He took a trip over to Mesaba Lake to check on a group that should have come out yesterday. A husband and wife—greenhorns. Probably lost their canoe in the wind. You know, he worries like an old woman even though he'll call 'em names until Christmas. Of course he's going to keep an eye out for Mark while he's out there."

"Well, I'll be taking the plane up tomorrow, FBI agent or not, if that dumbass isn't back here by tonight."

"Which one? Yours or mine?"

Hansen laughed. "Mine, I guess."

Libby sat down and poured herself a short beer.

"Been to see your mom lately? I'm not asking to guilt you, hon."

She patted Hansen's hand. "I was going to send along some of that pin cherry jelly she always loved so much."

Hansen sipped his beer and continued staring out at the lake.

"She'd like that, I know." He took a deep breath and turned back to look at her. "It's only about 45 minutes to Duluth in the plane, but Libby, coming back after seeing her is the longest goddamn trip you can imagine."

"That nursing home was the only thing you could have done. She'd be the first to tell you that. Spending the next ten or twenty years caring for your ailing mother is a waste of two lives. She'd have kicked you in the ass for even thinking it."

Hansen laughed weakly.

"It's just hard to let her go while she's still sitting there, looking at you."

Libby put her hand back on Hansen's and squeezed.

"You don't have any choice, honey. She left you years ago."

"Ok, you tryin' to make me cry now?" Hansen pulled away and stood up abruptly.

He reached into his pocket and pulled out a five dollar bill and slapped it on the counter.

"Go grab dinner and a show."

He kissed the air in her direction and walked out into the warm spring sunlight.

He stood a moment and looked up to the sun. Closing his eyes he felt its warmth flow through him, watching the blood-red glow of his eyelids. Things were slipping through his fingers, he realized. They always had. His father, his mother, lovers, jobs…he always seemed to be busy doing something else while life slipped by unnoticed. Hansen opened the door to the old pickup truck and as he did, he struck his shin on its sharp corner. The heat of the sun, the swirling thoughts, the worry, the guilt, the breathtaking pain in his leg reached their flash point in his pressure cooker brain. He grabbed the edge of the door and swung it closed with a burst of uncontrolled vicious anger. The door slammed with the sound of a gunshot and the driver's side window burst and fell to the ground and floorboards in a shower of green glass pellets.

Behind him he heard Libby exclaim "What the hell?" just before the screen door opened.

"You ok?" she said. "What happened?"

Hansen pulled himself together with a deep breath and turned to face her.

"Shit," he said. "Call me grace. I stumbled over my own big feet and fell against the goddamn door."

"Oh no!" Libby said. "Damn cheap crap. Here, let me get some cardboard and duct tape."

"No, Libby, don't bother. It's a beautiful day. Who needs a window on a day like this?"

She smiled at him. "Break out the other three and you've got yourself a redneck convertible."

She turned to go back in, then looked back at him one more time.

"Hon," she said, "you're a good man. Don't forget that."

She turned and headed back into the lodge, saying as she disappeared, "I'll get the shop-vac later. You go on."

Standing amid the shattered remains of the window, he felt like a little boy after a tantrum, pieces of his favorite toy scattered at his feet. Twice in ten minutes he'd felt like crying. He decided to get into the truck and drive fast, hoping to avoid the emotional hat-trick.

THIRTY-FOUR

Goiaina, Brazil, September, 1987

Before they reached the hospital Suzanna was nauseous and complained that she felt hot. Her skin did look red, as though sunburned. Their daughter, in contrast was deathly pale, her stomach contracting in spasms but there was no more liquid to bring up. She lay unconscious in her mother's arms.

"What have I done? What have I done?" he whispered over and over again as he sped toward the hospital, willing the little red car to go faster, leaning forward and squeezing the steering wheel tightly. His daughter's unnatural silence frightened him unlike anything he had ever known.

In the emergency room the triage nurse took the little girl from Suzanna who was herself becoming more ill as the moments passed. She vomited twice before they were able to find an empty bed for their daughter. Soon they wheeled in a second bed for Suzanna.

An older nurse entered the room with a friendly, reassuring smile for Victor. Without speaking she went immediately to Maria's bed and placed a stethoscope to the little girl's chest, now rising and falling with quick shallow breaths. He heard the nurse softly say "*Qué sucedió poco ángel?*"

Victor found his voice and stood. He held up a small glass jar full of blue powder. "I think it was this," he told her. As she stared at the striking contents of the jar, Victor saw his wife begin to shake on the bed next to them. Her head thrashed from side to side and she vomited onto herself and the pillow. The nursed yelled for help. "Hold her," she told Victor, "so she doesn't fall." Then the nurse left him there.

"Suzanna," he whispered to her as she thrashed, her beautiful black hair flipping from side to side, soiled by the contents of her stomach and sweat. He held her tightly and began to cry, "Suzanna! Suzanna!" Victor glanced over at his daughter, laying so quietly on the other bed, so small. Her color, like a chameleon, had changed to the pallid white of the sheet beneath her. Her beautiful darks eyes were closed and only her jet black hair defied the deathly transformation. He could not see her breathing.

More people rushed into the room. Doctors or nurses, he would not remember. He would only remember the black hair of his beautiful girls and the last time he heard his wife say "I love you."

THIRTY-FIVE

Billy Cosgrove paddled the old Grumman aluminum canoe up a shallow stream infested with lily pads and thin reeds that vibrated in the soft morning breeze. It was a rare indulgence, this solo trip into the park. This was probably the only chance he'd get until deer hunting season in November to get into the wilderness. Living here, "on the edge," folks seldom had the opportunity to appreciate the beauty around them for its own sake. For most year-round residents who made their living from the land, nature was something to be either battled or exploited. Usually, there was not one without the other. It's bullshit, Billy thought, the romantic notion of living where you loved to visit, thinking that magic would somehow sustain you—like living on love. He'd seen, too many times to count, people with unrealistic expectations of what it meant to call this place your home. Even if you made it through the mud and black flies in the spring, the oppressive humidity and mosquitoes in the summer, the frost and early snow in the fall, there was always winter stalking you, like the matador with the muleta, waiting to plunge the cold steel deep between your shoulder blades. But if you made it through the hardships there were days of utter perfection where the sky could not be any bluer, the trees any greener, the water any clearer, the breeze any sweeter. And if, for just a moment, you could raise your head up out of the rut you'd worn into your daily existence and rub the sleep from your eyes you would marvel at the wild brilliance before you. For an elusive, fleeting instant, you felt the presence of a higher consciousness. Cosgrove once tried to describe it to his wife. It was the closest he would ever get to poetry: "It's like you caught a whiff of God."

Today, Billy thought, was just such a day: perfect. There were no clouds as far as he could see and a light breeze kept him comfortable beneath an unusually warm spring sun. He had seen a few boats and canoes on Poplar, but since leaving that busy lake and crossing the almost mile-long portage to Skipper Lake he left all obvious signs of civilization behind him. In the canoe was a fishing pole, a tackle box and a bota bag. On his back he carried a small pack that contained a tarp, a sleeping bag, a fleece jacket and some beef jerky. He was only staying one night and would sleep on the tarp, under the canoe for shelter. "At least take a foam pad," Libby had told him, but he had refused. "For one night I'm not takin' all that shit," he said. Though his stated objective was to check on a husband and wife he had outfitted a few days earlier, he didn't expect to find them in any trouble. They were heading to Cherokee Lake which sported around twenty campsites along its ten miles of shoreline and he wasn't about to check every one of them. He planned to paddle and portage to his favorite lake trout water, Mesaba Lake, about 15 miles from Poplar. It would take him most of the day, but he figured he'd arrive just in time for "the witching hour," the hours just before and just after sunset when fish usually fed most aggressively.

Cosgrove, at 55, was still very strong in the canoe. His powerful arms drove the craft forward in rhythmic surges, leaving evenly spaced whirlpools spinning in the water behind him. Efficient "C" and "J" strokes kept the craft tracking in a straight line regardless of what side he paddled on. His technique had won him many canoe races in the surrounding area over the years, the most prestigious being the races held every year at the Gunflint Lodge near the end of the Trail. He'd tried paddling with Libby as his partner a few times, but she quickly tired of him barking orders at her. He remembered the last words he ever spoke with her in the same canoe.

"Keep the goddamn blade flat to the fucking water!"

At his suggestion, Libby pulled the wooden paddle dripping from the lake, turned the blade perpendicular to the water's surface, as instructed, then hit him sharply on the side of the head with it.

"Flat enough for ya?"

His left ear bled spectacularly into the canoe as they leisurely returned to shore, a barely hidden grin on her face. He still had the scar.

From Cherokee, Billy headed north through Gordon, west to Frost then into the Frost River, which carried him quickly to the northwest on its swollen current. There were a few hairy spots along the way where boulders split the water and threatened to dump him. It was the rocks he couldn't see that he most tried to avoid, marking their hulking presence just below the surface by the roiling and churning above. It was moments like these when he was glad for the indestructible old Grumman, which bounced off rocks like a pinball. As long as he kept her nose headed downstream he knew he'd make out ok.

Even so, he was relieved when the current finally dumped him into the calm waters of the small, shallow Afton Lake, then on to Fente where he would find the long portage to Hub Lake. At almost a mile, the portage was difficult more because of the change in elevation along the way than the distance. The trail lost one hundred and seventy feet about halfway as it sank toward a swampy stream, then climbed back to its original altitude. This was high country, about one thousand feet above Lake Superior, which already lay six hundred feet above sea level. Stepping out at the Fente Lake landing, Billy grabbed his loose gear, then reached across the center thwart of the canoe and in one fluid motion raised it above his head and rested it on his shoulders. Beneath the shadow of the canoe Billy walked carefully, but quickly, not wanting to waste valuable fishing time walking on the trail. He unloaded the canoe and rested on a log at the low point in the trail, near a stream that was flowing across the top of the portage. Normally the water would seep under the path, but snowmelt had infused the creek with new energy and it rushed on to Hudson Bay like all flowing water here on the north side of the Laurentian Divide.

Billy sat and breathed deeply the smells of the wakening forest, buried for so long under a deep blanket of snow. Afternoon shadows were beginning to lengthen across the portage. The woods echoed with the sounds of birdsong and flowing water. He was just one lake and one more portage from his goal. He was tired, but he knew that first cast into Mesaba's deep crystalline waters would rejuvenate him instantly. He took another deep breath, hefted the canoe once again, and pressed on up the hill before him.

Billy reached the end of the portage and looked out upon Hub Lake. The day was clear and on the far side he caught a glimpse of a canoe sitting at the portage to Mesaba. What the hell, he thought, I've had a pretty good run so far. Bound to run into someone eventually.

"Fuck it," he said, a bit disgusted.

Hopefully they weren't heading for his lake in search of trout. He dropped the canoe into the water and started paddling. He had to find out if they were carrying fishing poles and learn their intentions. As he drew closer to the landing, he saw a canoe and a pack lying there, but no fishing poles. So far, so good.

Billy jumped out of the canoe and dragged it up onto the rocks of the landing where the hollow metallic banging shattered the silence of the woods and echoed across the water. The rocks wore the colors of generations of canoes that had been similarly beached here—red, green and the silver of plain aluminum.

Billy looked down at the large Duluth pack sitting at the trailhead. It was customary to help someone in the bush who had a greater load than you. And, as an outfitter, it was just good business—word of mouth could make you or break you up here, he knew. Since Billy had only his light solo canoe and a little pack he decided to do someone a favor and hefted the pack onto his back. But when he did, the weight of it almost pulled him over backwards.

"Jesus H. Christ!"

Normally he wouldn't snoop into other folks' packs, but he thought he could maybe offer some packing suggestions when he caught up with them at the other end of the trail. He unbuckled the leather straps and folded back the green canvas to reveal a square silver box which filled the pack completely, almost as though it was made to fit in perfectly. Billy Cosgrove assumed it was some sort of homemade food pack, with hard sides and insulation to protect fragile items like eggs and maintain cold for perishable foods. They had to be carrying a couple gallons of milk or, he thought with a smile, maybe a dozen of Libby's bran muffins. The metal case had a latch with a clip that held it closed. Billy unclipped the latch and opened the silver lid.

He had no idea what he was looking at. The thick-walled box was half full of what appeared to be small oblong blue balloons. He reached in and picked one up and held it in his hand. It was actually a clear plastic balloon about the size of a fat Vienna sausage filled with a beautiful sparkling blue powder. He rolled it between his fingers and it was iridescent under the sun as the substance shifted in its tough rubber skin. He brought it up to his nose but could smell nothing but rubber. It smelled a little like a new tire. He was tempted to put one in his pocket to show Libby, but then he wondered if it might be drugs. Billy had never seen cocaine. He thought it was white, at least that's what he saw on TV. But, he figured, if they can make beer green on Saint Patty's Day, how hard could it be to make cocaine blue?

"Drug-smugglin' sons-a-bitches," he said under his breath.

Billy looked at the knot holding the thing closed. Dumb bastards couldn't even tie a decent half-hitch. He tugged a little at one of the cut ends of monofilament holding the balloon closed. With surprising ease it let loose and the blue powder spilled from its container and onto his hands.

"Shit!"

It suddenly hit him that if these guys came back now he'd be in deep dung. Hastily he tied the balloon back up with a simple square knot, dropped the blue sausage back into its box, closed the lid firmly and replaced the clip. He brushed the spilled blue powder from his hands then secured the leather straps on the pack. Billy stood, and looked around for any evidence of what he'd just done.

Seeing none, he left the pack and returned to get his gear and canoe. Glancing once more at his hands he saw some of the shimmering blue powder still adhering to his fingertips. He touched it to his tongue, like the cops did on TV. He tasted nothing. He spat several times and washed his hands off in the lake.

He was unsure what to do next. He was a quarter mile from his one opportunity to fish this year. It promised to be a perfect evening of casting and trolling on calm water for big hungry trout. He'd hauled ass all day to get here. Even if he left now, he'd have to paddle and portage most of the way in the dark, which was not an attractive proposition given the myriad ways he could break a leg, arm or his neck. They're in the same boat, he figured. They would have to camp tonight too, so it's not like they're going to get far. Hell, maybe it's not even drugs.

"Fuck 'em!"

Billy Cosgrove shouldered his canoe once more and headed towards Mesaba Lake for what he hoped would be a great evening of fishing.

THIRTY-SIX

The ponderous C-130 Hercules roared down runway 9-27, one of only three active runways at the Duluth International Airport, home to the 148th Fighter Wing. The 148th occupies about one hundred and fifty acres at the northeast corner of the small airport—a scattered collection of aging administrative and industrial buildings occupied by three hundred civilian and military personnel. The steady drone of the Herc's four big Allison turbo-props left Brian Setty's ears ringing an hour after he got off the plane.

Once he retrieved his service weapon and gear from the hold, he called the Duluth Resident Agency who would bring him a car for his drive to Grand Marais. He didn't relish spending two hours in the FBI's standard-issue, basic brown Ford Crown Victoria. He felt the cars were a hazard—too much power and weight, which made them about as responsive as a tugboat in a tidal wave. In tactical situations where fast, aggressive driving was necessary, he didn't want to spend time recovering from over-steering and fighting gravity and physics on every maneuver. In D.C. they gave him a choice of a car allowance or a company car. He took the allowance and bought the Audi TT.

Speaking to the secretary at the RA he learned that they didn't have a car for him and that he'd have to rent one. Though the inconvenience of it irritated him at first, he realized he could get something a little more enjoyable and stylish than the old Crown Vic. After checking in with airport security—he didn't want any misunderstandings if someone caught a glimpse of the holster under his jacket— he saw that both rental counters were serving long lines of people. He joined one line and asked a round elderly man with wingtips and a white belt riding the center of his belly like the equator on a globe what was going on.

"Vegas revue at the DECC starting tonight!" he relayed, obviously excited. "I hope you've got a reservation, otherwise you might be walking!"

"The deck?" Setty asked, puzzled and frowning.

The old man raised his eyebrows.

"Not from around here, huh? It's the Duluth Entertainment Convention Center, DECC. Wayne Newton and Engelbert Humperdinck are headlining. Gonna be shows all weekend!"

"Wonderful," he said, suddenly thankful he was heading further north.

He stood in line anyway. The man he was to meet in Grand Marais was Garrett Hansen, a border patrol agent who worked the northern border. He was a local who supposedly knew the area well, both from the air and the ground. Setty was not thrilled about the assignment. Not that the subject matter didn't interest him, because it did. He just didn't like roughing it, not anymore. He'd had enough of that in Special Forces. He hoped he could find a clean hotel and some good food up there. Since it was a tourist destination he was optimistic that someone up there might even have a decent bottle of wine.

The trip was an evaluation, plain and simple. His job was to assess the possibility that a terrorist cell could infiltrate the country via a wilderness route—how they might do it, where they would go, how long it would take them, how difficult it would be to find them once their mission began. They had no absolute proof that terrorists were operating up there. Just Beth Adams' research and analysis, though that had proven very compelling indeed.

"Do you have a reservation, sir?"

The clerk behind the counter was a frail-looking man of indeterminate age. His mannerisms suggested elderly, but his features were youthful. He moved slowly and spoke even more so.

"No I don't. I just need a car for a few days. Something sporty would be nice, maybe a convertible. I don't suppose you rent Audi?"

The man stared at him for several moments, blinking. Finally he said, "No."

"Well," Setty said, "what do you have available in a sports car?"

The man looked down at his computer screen and pressed a few keys.

"I only have two vehicles not reserved. Would you like a minivan or Ford Ranger?"

Now it was Setty's turn to stare, blinking.

"Ranger. That's a pickup truck, right? You're telling me I have to choose between a minivan and a pickup truck?"

"Uh, yes sir."

He glanced back at the screen.

"The pickup is red, the minivan is yellow," the clerk said, as though that detail would make the choice obvious.

All Setty could picture was a fire truck and a lemon. Pointing at the competitor's counter, Brian asked, "What about them?"

The man looked around Setty as though he had to confirm the subject of the inquiry himself, though it was the only other rental agency in the building.

"Yeah…no, they ran out of vehicles about two hours ago."

Setty signed the documents and walked out to the lot where he found the specified number painted on the asphalt behind the bed of his fire-engine-red pickup truck. The red was more startling than he had imagined it could be. It seemed to glow like a big briquette, throwing red light onto every surrounding surface. He opened the door, removed his suit jacket and laid it over the passenger seat, then threw his bag on the floor. The interior was red as well. He felt hot and opened a window. It was going to be a long way to Grand Marais.

The trip up the north shore of Lake Superior was, to Brian Setty's surprise, spectacular. It was a land of rugged beauty, with much exposed rock, endless pine forest and steely blue water. He hadn't been prepared for the topography. Brian thought it would be flat like the rest of the state, but it was clear that some cataclysmic geologic forces had been at work here. Rock beds driven up into the air at severe angles, ledge rock shorelines beaten by the cold waves of the big lake, torrential rivers pummeling their smooth ancient stone chutes as they had for thousands of years.

The truck was noisy, but not because of excess power under the hood. It was noisy because the tires sported an overly aggressive tread. It was noisy because the little six-cylinder engine strained mightily whenever he passed someone, which happened often. It was noisy because the driver's door didn't fit right and air whistled through a gap in the rubber seal. There was also an almost subsonic rumble coming from somewhere underneath the truck—

probably bearings, he figured. He tried to drown out some of the noise with the radio but found an overabundance of country music. He opened the passenger window and listened to the rush of air as he caught glimpses of the infinite expanse of water to his right.

Small towns appeared every twenty miles or so: Beaver Bay, Silver Bay, Schroeder, Lutsen. He got so used to driving through them he didn't even realize he was in Grand Marais until he reached the city's only stop light and had a moment to contemplate his surroundings. There was a Holiday gas station, a restaurant called "South of the Border," a grocery store and Como propane gas each at their respective corners. The U.S. Border Patrol office was a mile or so past the traffic light. Setty pulled the truck into the gravel parking lot, the tires crackling over the stones and raising a small cloud of dust. He walked into the small metal building and found it empty. He called out and checked the few offices but found no one. After leaving a note with his cell phone number he decided to drive up to the border and see if the guy was there. Maybe someone at least knew where the hell Officer Hansen was. Setty didn't want to be here any longer than he had to and wasting time tracking down his guide was not the way he wanted to start the assignment.

THIRTY-SEVEN

Boundary Waters Canoe Area Wilderness, Minnesota
May, 2002
Thursday, 6:20 AM

Toftey awoke early to the warbling of loons. He was cold, but not as cold as he thought he'd be. He had more difficult walking to do. As he rose from his pine-bough bed, his joints creaked and his stiff muscles protested painfully. Looking around, he saw no signs of other human beings. While he was convinced that his pursuers had left him for dead, it was clear they were comfortable with desperate measures and deadly force to accomplish their objective, whatever that was. He could tell his rest had been a fitful one, like he had spent much of the night with one eye open.

He guessed that Seagull Lake was just a couple of miles to the southeast. He just had to follow the sun and he'd be fine. Worst case, if he didn't see anybody on the lake within hailing distance, he would follow the shoreline to Trail's End. He had to call Hansen, not only because he knew his friend was probably worried by now, but because he could call in the cavalry and have local and government law enforcement in the woods in a matter of hours. Toftey couldn't imagine anyone he would rather have in his corner when it all went to hell. He recalled the last twenty-four hours as if remembering scenes from a movie. It did happen to me, he asserted somewhat hesitantly. With the realization came the compelling need to move, fast.

Toftey's intuition and training was painting a scenario in his brain that scared the living bejeezus out of him. Here were four men— well, three now—military-trained and battle-ready, probably from the Middle East, willing to kill without hesitation anyone who challenged them. Within those four huge canvas packs they carried something they were willing to kill for. It could be drugs, of course. You could get a lot of cocaine or heroin in a single Duluth pack, he imagined. It would certainly be worth the trip to pack in millions of dollars in drugs through the Boundary Waters. But that's where his intuition objected. That didn't feel like the right answer. He saw their eyes—there was more at stake here than money.

He walked quickly through dense forest, through bogs and cedar swamps, up over ridges and across countless small streams. Butterflies fluttered ahead of him while above, birds sang from the trees and sky. He looked up to see a pair of eagles screeching and diving at one another. Suddenly they locked talons in a dramatic courtship display, spiraling toward the ground and releasing their grasp only when contact with the ground seemed imminent. Tough way to get a date, he thought, allowing himself a smile. The natural rhythms soothed him and cleansed his soul. It was his church, a sanctuary of simplicity. But his brief reverie was short-lived and the nagging tension returned and tightened the knot in the pit of his stomach.

Toftey kept the sun in front of him and moved as quickly as he dared, climbing over deadfalls, slogging through swamps, negotiating steep ridges. His face and hands were slapped and cut with branches. Regardless of the obstacle, he did not deviate from the path. The going was slow and he marked the passage of time by the position of the sun slowly advancing through the sky. The walk might have been pleasant, if it weren't for the nagging suspicion that he was racing to prevent a terrorist attack somewhere on American soil.

He'd done a lot of reading on terrorism over the past few years, trying to understand how things had gotten so out of hand. Some said it was U.S. colonialism or world domination, others, the rise of radical fundamental Islamic states in the wake of European divestiture, or simply the escalating Arab hatred of the Jews and the U.S. by association. And as always there were convincing theories on the American manipulation of foreign governments to help satisfy its insatiable appetite for oil, just as there were equally convincing theories that foreign governments used terrorism to manipulate the United States in order to effect political change and strengthen entrenched "moderate" governments. But in all of these conflicting hypotheses, one element must be present: an infinite supply of motivated zealots willing to give their lives for their beliefs.

As long as you had some nut willing to strap on a belt full of explosives and walk onto a bus full of people who had committed no crime other than to be born under a certain political system, or to be sitting in close proximity to one who was, and blow them up, there was no end in sight. Reason being, there is no solution to such a conflict. It is like hating bees for stinging you when you throw a rock at their nest. You certainly can destroy it, but the bees will just build it again, because that's what bees do. Beavers build dams. You can kill them and blow up the dam, but another beaver will move in and dam the stream in the same spot, because that's what beavers do. People believe in things. That's what people do. But what do you do when your belief precludes, even destroys another's. And there's the rub. You simply can't stop people from believing in what they believe in. Tell them to, and they get angry. They prefer to stop you instead.

But all that philosophizing, he realized, was useless in his current predicament. There were killers in his woods and he had to get them out. Looking up, he began to see an opening in the trees far ahead, revealing what he hoped would be the broad expanse of Seagull Lake and the path home. The urge to run overpowered him, so he ran.

THIRTY-EIGHT

Boundary Waters Canoe Area Wilderness, Minnesota
May, 2002
Thursday, 8:00

The two canoes and three men neared the portage to Mesaba Lake. They were making good time and expected to be back on schedule by the time darkness fell over the woods and lakes. Asad al-Muhammad's hands were sore and blistered from the wooden canoe paddle. He rested the instrument of torture across the wooden gunwales of the canoe and looked at them in disgust. It was a disgrace that his hands had become so soft, "Like a woman's," he sneered under his breath.

It seemed to him an eternity since the Jihad camps in Afghanistan where he trained for almost a year after deserting the Saudi military. He deserted with several other soldiers who were heading to Afghanistan to train in terrorist techniques and bring the fight to the Americans. Asad held no religious loyalties but once at the camp he was exposed to the fiery passion of the Sheik and other Muslim clerics who inextricably wove the coarse fibers of religious fervor, obligation and vengeance into a tapestry of deadly single-minded purpose for the glory of Allah. Asad's daily regimen of intensive military training in guerilla warfare and modern weapons along with radical Islamic teachings in the madrasah helped him rationalize and channel his amorphous anger and hatred for those who rejected and deserted him. In the service of God he could exercise the violence within him while following the path to eternal glory.

The Sheik spoke of Asad's former homeland as "The Land of the Two Holy Places," Medina and Mecca. "We do not speak the name here," he said, meaning Saud. "No person can own a country or its people. Arabia is morally corrupt and in the evil service of the United States. They want to steal our faith in our god to steal our oil. They want to bury us in the depths of poverty and hopelessness, then throw down a little food and water to keep us grateful and weak," he said, his voice rising with his passion. "We will not be buried. We will not bow down while our faith is destroyed. We will turn the mirror upon them and make them gaze into their own ugliness. The suffering they have caused, let it be their suffering. What they have stolen, let them find it missing. Let them call their children and hear only silence. Let them look from their windows and see the wrath of Allah. Then they will know God's judgment."

Asad heard his own disillusionment and bitterness given voice by this man. Within days he felt comfort and confidence unlike anything he had experienced before. He observed the hierarchy within the camp, insinuating himself within the group of higher-ranking officers, Saudis like himself, quickly befriending them until they had forgotten he was just another new recruit. His royal bearing and physical presence gave him an air of control that others assumed was due to some official rank as yet not displayed. He hoped that none of the men recognized him. He was not so derelict in his empathy that he would deny the suffering he had caused others. For Asad, however, awareness did not equate regret. He harbored no doubt that his actions were just.

His ruthlessness and intelligence caught the eyes of al-Qaeda leaders quickly. He soon found himself called up to conduct limited operations in the Middle East, North Africa and even Europe as part of small terrorist cells conducting surveillance and quiet assassinations of individuals deemed enemies of the Jihad. His ability to travel easily in many cultures, with his handsome features and command of English, and his willingness to kill without hesitation, helped Asad's star rise quickly in the organization. His assignments became more ambitious and he played an increasingly important role in their development. The bombs in Casablanca had been his operation, his team. It had all led up to this operation. It would be his masterpiece. Just when they thought they were safe once again, a fear unlike anything the infidels had yet experienced would suffocate and paralyze them. The moment of his death would be glorious and he was ready for it. In fact he awaited it with intense excitement and anticipation. The world would see his greatness and tremble at the mention of his name. From paradise he would watch their suffering and see awe and respect in the eyes of the Sheik and his followers.

As soon as the men arrived on shore the onslaught of black flies resumed. Saad was most profoundly affected. Apparently reacting to the strong anticoagulant in the tiny fly's saliva, the seasoned holy warrior was afflicted with dozens of large red welts on his face and neck. Some were bleeding, as the man could not prevent himself from scratching them. Along with the scar, his new blemishes made his face even more formidable. They unloaded the canoes, swatting flies the whole time. Saad and Anwar were clearly miserable in their surroundings and their mettle was tested several times a day, not only by nature, but also by Asad's relentless drive and condescension. He lavished most of his attentions on Saad.

Hearing the older man curse the parasites yet again, Asad said, "You, with the glory of Allah on your lips, would demonize his creations?"

He shouldered one of the heavy green packs and then a canoe. His voice resonated from within the hollow craft over his head, giving it an unusual depth when he spoke again.

"This is a pilgrimage, a purification of our souls. We must prove that we are worthy of this honor."

"Honor?" Saad snorted, picking up a pack and the fishing rods. "What do you know of it?"

Anwar took a third pack, leaving the final pack and canoe for a second trip.

"This useless bickering must stop," he said firmly. "You're like old women at the market. There is no time for it."

They would camp on Malberg that night with the final leg of their wilderness journey ending tomorrow at the Kawishiwi Lake campground. In the parking lot they would find a white minivan with Minnesota license plates purchased by a local operative over two years ago. The van had been parked in the gravel lot for several days, lost amid the many vehicles left there by wilderness travelers. Kawishiwi was a popular wilderness entry point, due largely to the nearby campground that served as a convenient spot to layover the night before paddling into the park. Once they reached the van there would be no delays for sleep. The van would be loaded and they would drive five hours south to meet their destiny.

Asad ignored Anwar's comments, which struck him as unusually bold for the usually reticent man. Perhaps he would kill them both and complete the assignment himself. It was not as though they were necessary. He was leading them through the wilderness; they would be lost here without him. The incident with the ranger proved that. Had it not been for his damage control they surely would have seriously jeopardized the mission, more so than it was already.

After a brief period of adaptation to the alien climate, the moisture, the ever-present cool in the air, he had actually grown to appreciate the beauty around him. Whether it was the accelerating path to his demise or a resurgence of his naturalist tendencies, he was enjoying himself in the northern Minnesota woods. Birdlife abounded in the trees and sky, while tracks in the mud along the portages showed signs of larger animals such as deer, wolves, bear and moose. The first time he saw a moose hoof print he briefly forgot his status as a leader of their jihad and excitedly called the other men over to see it. If this was America, these woods and lakes and wildlife, like those in Field and Stream and Outdoor Life, the America of his dreams, then he could live contented in this place.

Asad left Saad and Anwar at the Mesaba side of the portage and returned for the remaining pack and canoe. The second trip allowed him an opportunity to look around without the burden of a pack or the canoe over his head. The smells were glorious, with plants blossoming in profusion, their perfume mixing, blending with the rich earthly scent of the awakening forest. It reminded him of his college days on the Atlantic coast. He could not remember that young man any longer, so free of the world's injustices, naïve and simple. He pitied his memory as he pitied Saad. How comforting it is, he thought, to live in such a small world before all its unspoken promises are broken.

As the trail dropped down toward Hub Lake, Asad was surprised to see a man with a canoe on his shoulders walking quickly toward him. Asad felt his heart begin to race as he quickly took stock of the situation. He had already considered the possibility that someone would be looking for the forest ranger and the remote but considerably more disturbing scenario that the man had somehow escaped and related the previous day's events to law enforcement. Asad made a quick assessment of the man: older, though he couldn't see his face he could see the gray hair on his thick sleeveless arms, in good shape—no labored breathing or unsteadiness of gait, powerful. He would be a formidable opponent in a hand-to-hand struggle because of his compact stature and musculature developed from physical labor as opposed to a bulging physique born of vanity and self-aggrandizement. Confidence emanated from him. Asad would have to decide quickly whether to kill him or not, before the man saw him and he lost the advantage. Asad moved his hand to the hilt of the knife in his belt. In that split second the man stopped and raised the canoe so he could look up the trail. He locked eyes with Asad who removed his hand from his belt and waved instead.

"Hi there!"

"Afternoon," said the man. He ducked back under the canoe and continued approaching Asad, who stepped off the trail to let him pass.

As he did so, the man said, "Thanks," and kept walking.

Asad considered running back to the other men but that would certainly draw unwanted attention. He just hoped the lecture he gave them after the ranger incident was still fresh in their minds. He moved quickly now to gather the last pack and the second canoe. Though the pack was heavier than all the others he stood with it easily and strapped it onto his back. He then bent over and raised the craft over his head, standing the bow on the ground and walking forward until he reached the fulcrum point where the narrow boat slowly rose up of its own volition, the padded yoke sitting gently upon Asad's shoulders. He sprinted up the trail and soon reached the Mesaba landing where Saad, Anwar and the stranger were gathered. The old man showed no interest in sticking around to converse. As Asad approached, the man dropped a fishing rod into the bottom of his boat and climbed in, paddling with strong deep strokes without looking back. The three holy warriors watched the gray-haired man's broad back grow smaller as he pulled quickly away from the shore and soon disappeared around a rocky point to the south.

"There are three campsites on this lake," Asad said to no one in particular. "He is of no consequence. If he is in our chosen site, we pick another one. Let's go."

THIRTY-NINE

Abu Ghraib Prison, Iraq
May, 2002
Thursday, 7:00 AM

Sitting on the blanket, holding his tea, Ibrahim al-Takar floated above the desert. Far below him a train of four camels with their burdens strapped to their distinctly misshapen backs struggled through shifting blue sand that blended into a cloudless sky, creating an indistinguishable horizon. The luminous sand flowed like water and swirled up around the camels, consuming them in a vortex until they exploded into bright azure flames.

He awoke startled and disoriented.

The man in robes and headdress sitting across from him said, "You've spilled your tea."

Ibrahim looked down and saw a stain on his own white linen robe. "I was dreaming."

"What did you see?" asked the man.

"I saw camels, burning in a sea of blue. I believe it is a message from God."

"And what does God's message tell you?"

Ibrahim knew what the dream meant and it filled him with joy. But some lingering poisonous doubt prevented him from sharing his joy. He longed to share it—his very being craved an honest, caring connection with the like-minded soul sitting less than a meter from him. As though sensing his longing, for the first time the man looked up and into Ibrahim's eyes. Though the prisoner had suspected it all along, it was then he knew it was true. The leader of the Jihad was here with him. Allah had answered his prayers. The Sheik was with him. Relief flooded through him.

"I am here to help you," the Sheik told him, "to guide you through the evil you have found here. In return, I ask that you help me to fight them and to serve the benevolence and grace of our God, praise him."

With these words, he felt his brain's stubborn resolve melt and with it any hint of suspicion he may have held toward this holy man.

"I give my earthly being to him and my soul," said Ibrahim. "We will celebrate his glory soon. I have heard from our martyrs."

At this the Sheik looked intently at Ibrahim.

"We have many martyrs who deserve our admiration," he said. "Fear grows in the hearts of our enemies every day. Of which battle do you speak?"

"Our brothers who carry the fire of God through the wilderness. They will succeed. I have seen it. They were consumed in the holy fire. They will bring god's fire to that evil temple. They will be martyred in the destruction of that place of false worship and greed. It will be glorious. The polytheists will suffer for generations and the monument will stand forever, reminding them of the power they squandered and lost. They will not be able to hide it as they have the shame of their fallen towers."

"But we have heard nothing from them. I need your help, Ibrahim. We must find them and help them complete their mission or all may be lost."

From somewhere deep in Ibrahim's tortured mind a voice was warning him. He felt a sense of dread and sadness overcome him, feelings that seldom intruded into this peaceful place.

"Ibrahim, I do believe that Allah speaks to you through your dreams. You are truly blessed. But your vision could be interpreted another way. Perhaps it is a call for help. You know what this means to the struggle. If the mission is in danger it is your duty to ensure it succeeds, your duty to the Jihad, to Allah. It is not your place to deny them their place and rewards in paradise."

Tears welled in Ibrahim's eyes and ran down his cheeks. He was so tired.

"If you could help them, but do not," the man continued, "you will face harsh judgment in this world and the next."

The man leaned in toward Ibrahim and whispered "If you do help them, your martyrdom will be assured and you will live on in the hearts and minds of your Muslim brothers and sisters for eternity."

The man reached out and took his trembling hands. For the next several hours, Ibrahim al-Takar could not stop talking.

FORTY

Less than 24-hours after her controversial Pentagon briefing, Beth had been summoned for another one. Riding the train from Silver Spring station, Beth fiddled with the heart-shaped locket around her neck and noticed that in the pre-dawn light of her apartment she had chosen two different color nylon stockings. After her shower she had dressed in her bedroom by the light from the bathroom across the hall. It was warm and she left the window open to catch a rare breeze. Not wanting to close the shade and lose the breeze, especially after a hot shower, she left the window open and the light off. Now she stared at the result: one sheer stocking, one tan. Had there been time to shave her legs it wouldn't have been a problem—she could have simply removed them. But she figured the five o'clock shadow on her ankles would not convey that professional aplomb she was going for. Well, she rationalized, if they base their level of respect on my stockings they probably weren't inclined to give me any respect anyway.

Chief Williams himself called at four-thirty a.m.

"What do you know about cesium-137?"

Though she usually had trouble waking up, the word "cesium" hit her like ice water on the face. For those in the intelligence community few substances caused greater alarm than the radioactive isotopes of that substance, particularly 137.

"Uh…I believe it's usually used in industrial monitoring devices and, ironically, in the treatment of cancer. Large, unsecured stores can be found internationally, in just about every developed country."

"Uh huh," Williams grunted into the phone. "Do you know what it can do?"

Beth knew. If an inanimate object could be evil, cesium-137 certainly qualified. "It's almost like it was engineered to destroy human beings," she told him. "It passes freely into the body, *invited* in wouldn't be an exaggeration, by replacing potassium. Once inside it wreaks chaos on the body's cells that divide most quickly—the skin, the hair, the gastrointestinal tract, and the bone marrow. Of course, blood cells come from the marrow, both red and white. As a result, the victim may experience hemorrhaging, since they have no platelets for clotting, and serious complications from what should be minor infections, since they can't make white blood cells."

"What about exposure in an incident?" Williams asked.

He was really beginning to scare her. Had something already happened, or was this a test?

"Sir, I don't know much about dispersal patterns, but I know it depends on the release, of course," she said. "For those on the perimeter of an incident who receive less radiation, say less than one hundred REM, they can look forward to cataracts and leukemia fifteen or twenty years down the road. Within the kill zone, over two hundred REM, you'll see vomiting, blood changes, hair loss, hemorrhaging, burns—death rate around 80%. You've heard of Goiania, sir?"

"Yeah, I remember it," said Williams.

Silently, she berated herself. Of course he knew about Goiania, you knucklehead! He was probably down there!

Everyone in the intelligence community, the 'I.C.', knew of Goiania, Brazil. In the fall of 1987 this small tropical tourist city was the site of a radiation disaster second only to Chernobyl in human and environmental impact. Beth had studied the incident in preparation for work on a system to track the deployment and disposal of domestic radiological substances used in industry, medicine and research.

According to various accounts, a radiotherapy device from a demolished clinic was salvaged and sold to a local junk dealer who pried open a shielded canister containing a large amount of luminous blue powder. He thought his family would appreciate the beautiful substance, which glowed and sparkled in the sun. Nearby family and friends received gifts of the powder as well. Within a week of the man laying his hands upon the canister of magic blue powder, almost two hundred and fifty people had been exposed to what would later be identified as cesium-137.

The government of Brazil had underestimated the problem and did not know how to deal with it. The nuclear agency technicians did not wear protective overalls, hoods, gloves or boots while decontaminating. Ambulances transporting victims from Rio de Janeiro's Santos Dumont airport to the city's naval hospital were not decontaminated for several days. Contamination spread. Finally, Brazil's nuclear agency called in the International Atomic Energy Commission, which helped quantify the disaster, facilitate treatment for the victims and coordinate the cleanup of the site. At one point, the AEC and local officials herded 34,000 people into Goiania's soccer stadium and checked them all with Geiger counters.

Government-dispatched medical teams found the most seriously irradiated victims had received doses up to 1000 rads, levels not seen since Chernobyl. Nineteen of the most critical cases had radiation-induced skin burns, and all were internally contaminated, which meant that they were being continually irradiated from the cesium that they had inhaled or accidentally eaten. The people themselves had become radioactive. The cesium seeped into the soil as quickly as it seeped into the residents, poisoning ground water, plants and animals. The junk man's neighborhood was razed, the houses dismantled and stored in giant concrete barrels designed for radioactive waste. The man's little daughter was buried, as were three others, in a lead coffin, her grave sealed in concrete. In fact, under the direction of the IAEC, contractors entombed several city blocks in cement, sealed tight for a century's festering slumber – another monument, like Chernobyl, to the devil in man's genius.

"Has something happened, sir," she had asked hesitantly, holding the phone away from her ear as if it might burn her.

"Just get down here as soon as you can," he said abruptly. "That little fire you started yesterday just had some gasoline poured on it."

———————————

When she arrived at the Pentagon, Security personnel met her at the south entrance after she was scanned and her ID was checked.

"Ma'am," said the young marine, "Mr. Williams asked me to escort you to the situation room. He said he'd get you the proper clearance later today."

"Thank you," she said and hurried to keep up with the marine's quick, long stride.

There was a tense urgency in his movements. He couldn't be over twenty, she estimated, trying not to let the "Ma'am" send her into a funk. Beth couldn't imagine herself at twenty years old working at the Pentagon. Even after college and several years of this place under her belt, she still felt like a kid walking in disguise among the adults. Moments like this she missed her dad most of all. He could always dispel her anxieties, at least for a little while, with a laugh or a hug. His timing was always impeccable.

They stepped into an elevator and the marine passed his security card in front of the reader and pushed a button that was not labeled. The elevator dropped them several levels below where they began and opened into a shining lobby. At the end of the hall, opposite the elevator, stood two more Marines. These men, unlike her escort, had side arms strapped to their hips. The young Marine stayed in the elevator and told her, "Through those doors, ma'am. They're expecting you." She stepped out and the elevator door closed behind her, leaving her standing in silence about fifty feet from two armed soldiers guarding dark mahogany doors with shining brass handles, doors she was supposed to enter. She had never felt more profoundly inadequate than she did at this moment. What am I doing here? she asked herself. In the long bright corridor she felt about three feet tall, like Alice through the looking glass. Suddenly, one of the marines at the end of the corridor spoke. His voice sounded hollow as it bounced off the walls. It wasn't only the sound that startled her. She had assumed that, like London's Buckingham Palace guards, these guys didn't speak. The marine mistook her hesitation for confusion over protocol.

"Ma'am, you can go right in. They're expecting you."

"Uh, oh, yes, of course."

She walked forward, hoping they wouldn't notice her mismatched stockings. Each soldier grabbed and turned the nearest brass handle with white-gloved hands and opened the doors.

"Thank you," she said and walked into the room.

The big doors closed behind her. She was immediately relieved that she was not the center of attention. The large room was bustling with activity. On the walls were screens, maps and clocks and along one wall were several workstations with glowing monitors and uniformed personnel sitting at each, wearing headsets and looking intently at their flickering blue screens. In the center of the room was a large dark table. Unlike the conference table where she had given her presentation the previous day, this table did have a head end and a chair was positioned there. There was a round emblem on the chair's headrest— the Presidential seal. She felt sweat coating her palms. Williams stood talking to a small group of uniformed men. He saw her and motioned for her to join him.

"Gentlemen, I think you remember Agent Adams from our briefing yesterday." One of the men was General Westguard, the man who had corralled her wayward remote control. They all nodded politely, though she could see immediately there was no room for levity in these conversations.

"Agent Adams, we've received some solid intelligence out of Abu Ghraib that supports the evidence and analysis you presented. According to our source, the terrorist cell is already here, possibly still in the woods or on their way to their destination. We're scrambling to put contingencies in place and getting agents on the ground in Minnesota."

"Do you know where they're heading?" she asked.

"Apparently," Williams said, pausing to take a breath as though he was about to dive into deep water, "their plan is to detonate four RDDs within the Mall of America."

Beth stood in shock for a few moments. The men in the little group must have recently gone through a similar experience as none of them spoke while the concept sank in.

"Are we closing the mall?" she asked.

"Well, that's what we're here to discuss."

Williams turned from them and walked to the front of the room. In his commanding voice, he said, "Everybody. Please take your seats."

Beth took a seat next to the doubting Colonel Gillis from the day before. Smiling slightly, she remembered General Westguard's comment about Gillis' provocative undergarments. She wondered if maybe Gillis had a matching stocking she could borrow. For the next hour, nothing else would be so amusing.

Williams began. "As you all know by now, we've received some very credible intelligence that points to the realization of the scenario so aptly presented to us yesterday by Agent Adams." Williams nodded in her direction. "Now, I'm going to turn it over to Special Forces Colonel Stuart Kimball, who took the red-eye from Iraq to be with us this morning. Colonel?"

A tall angular man with a distinctive aquiline nose and full lips stood before them wearing a stiffly pressed dress uniform sporting significant hardware on his breast. He had obviously been in Iraq for a long time as his skin was darkly tanned. His voice was deep and, like Williams,' commanded everyone's full attention.

"Yesterday we completed a targeted interrogation on a subject of interest, one Ibrahim al-Takar. He was identified several years ago as a key man in OBL's inner circle, in charge of establishing and facilitating communication with terrorist cells in the field."

Behind the colonel a picture of Ibrahim appeared. It showed a man with a full, round face, dark hair, light skin, pale eyes, and a bright smile, sitting on a couch in western-style clothing—a blue Oxford and khakis. The picture appeared to be part of a larger image. Beth thought it looked like a family portrait. There was the outline of long dark hair partially obscuring his right arm—perhaps a child.

"Yesterday during interrogation," continued Kimball, "Mr. al-Takar painted a very disturbing picture. In a nutshell, there is a terrorist cell in Minnesota actively engaged in a mission whose objective is to detonate several radiological dispersion devices within the biggest retail space in the United States—the Mall of America in Bloomington, Minnesota, a suburb of the Twin Cities of Minneapolis and St. Paul."

First a map of Minnesota was flashed briefly on the screen, and then several pictures of the mall, both inside and out, were displayed.

Kimball continued. "Also of concern is the mall's proximity to the international airport—less than a mile."

An aerial view of the area showed both facilities. Kimball used a blue laser pointer to circle both sites, though they were clearly the two largest items in the photo.

"The manner in which the cell plans to disperse the substance demonstrates that the suicide bombers have reached a new level of sophistication, creativity and dedication."

Behind him appeared a picture of what looked like an evidence table upon which were several bricks of a white substance Beth assumed was cocaine, along with several balloons filled with the white powder, presumably for hiding inside the smuggler's body. It was still the most effective method for avoiding detection at airports and border crossings.

"For years," said the colonel, "the DEA and border officials have struggled to capture smugglers who swallow balloons full of drugs and cross undetected into the United States. This method foils all traditional detection methods, leaving discovery to x-ray technology."

A picture of an x-ray clearly showing a pile of dark, oblong shapes in a human stomach appeared behind him.

"And mishaps with the containers happen quite frequently, causing serious illness and often death."

"Mr. al-Takar told us that OBL had been experimenting with new methods to bring radiological weapons into the United States. However, to get a sufficient amount through the border undetected, then into a highly populated area seemed to be an insurmountable challenge, especially after the increased security post nine-eleven. The physical characteristics of an effective RDD make it a bulky thing to carry around. You not only need a substantial amount of explosive if you're going to get it up into the air, you also need to consider the heavy shielding around the substance. You must have some shielding around the isotope so you don't get too sick to carry out your mission. So, if you have shielding, you have to blow through that to fully disperse the material, which means more explosive and a bulkier bomber belt around an already bulky shielded container of radioactive material. Again, not practical in locations with security and a vigilant public."

"Cesium powder, sealed in an impermeable yet flexible membrane made of silicone and latex, in fact the same material used for breast augmentation, experiences little radioactive bleed-through and would not noticeably affect the health of the host for several hours. Months ago, we found dog kennels in two of the Tora Bora cave sites. The dogs inside were dead and emitted dangerous levels of radiation. The animals' remains were quarantined and have been in secure storage until now. After receiving the information from Takar, we autopsied the animals and found this in their stomachs."

There was an audible shifting of chairs and rustling of stiffly pressed uniforms. Next to her, even the suspected lingerie-clad Colonel Gillis hissed, "Holy shit!"

On the screen was an autopsy photo of a dog's viscera. The stomach had been cut open. Inside were several clear plastic balloons filled with a blue substance, which caught the light of the flash like fresh snow in headlights. Even amid the gore, it was beautiful.

"According to al-Takar, four men have been dispatched on a suicide mission. They are carrying several pounds of cesium-137 in dozens of silicone balloons. They will ingest these balloons at the target, strap on a standard suicide belt, without the shrapnel to save on bulk and weight, and proceed to several central destinations chosen for maximum exposure and detonate. Each blast will immediately distribute material to a radius of up to three hundred feet. The superheated air from the explosion will carry the talc-like powder high in to the air. Airborne particles not hindered by contact with the bomber's bodily fluids will drift through the air distribution system, effectively permeating the structure. Without causing any structural damage, they will essentially destroy the building."

There was a moment of complete silence. Colonel Kimball returned to his seat and Williams returned to the head of the table. He looked around the room slowly, and then spoke. He sounded weary.

"We clearly have some decisions to make about how to approach this, but we have to do it within the next thirty-minutes. That's when the president of the United States will be sitting in this chair," Williams tapped the emblem on the back of the chair before him, "looking at you all for an answer."

Williams looked expectantly at the leaders of the United States intelligence community who sat looking at their hands, their feet, the ceiling or each other for what felt to Beth an uncomfortably long time. Suddenly, Chief Williams was pointing to her.

She heard him say, "Yes, Agent Adams?" Then, a little exasperated, "Go ahead."

Then she realized her hand was up. She couldn't remember doing it, but she looked up and there it was, hanging up there suspended as though from a balloon. Then she heard her father's voice in her head, "CIA Agent Floats Arm, Finds Balls." She dropped her arm and said, "Uh, sir, we have to find them." There were a few dismissive huffs, the loudest from Gillis, though it may have only seemed loudest because he was closest to her. Ignoring him, she stood and walked over to the map of Minnesota which was back on the screen.

"What I mean is, where these guys are will determine our approach, from the standpoint of both neutralization and damage control."

She held her hand out to Colonel Kimball and asked him for his laser pointer. As he handed it to her, her fingers closed on it in a death grip, fearing it would escape as the unruly device had done the day before. She used the pointer to project a small brilliant blue dot on the map and circled the extreme northeastern part of the state.

"If we catch them here, in the woods, we have a better chance at preventing an incident. They will not be wearing the explosive on the trail and the material will likely be safely contained and shielded."

She moved the pointer to a road labeled "61" running parallel to the shore of lake Superior.

"If they get on the road, our chances are less promising, but still reasonable north of Duluth. If they get to a city, or any populated area, our chances for avoiding an incident are still decent if we can neutralize them before they can prepare themselves. But if they know we're after them, they'll probably detonate at the first populated spot they can find."

Gillis scoffed. "After all this work and expense and expectation, you think they're just going to pick some no-name, one-traffic-light berg and blow their big chance on a place nobody's heard of? They're not going to just give up."

Beth mentally balked at his confrontational, dismissive tone, but she realized she knew what she was talking about and this cross-dressing officer—she couldn't get that out of her mind—did not. She glanced at General Westguard, who gave her a barely perceptible nod and frown of encouragement.

"No, Colonel, they won't give up. They will detonate their payload and no matter where they do it, they win. What would be more frightening to the American public? A radiological weapon detonated in a popular shopping mall in a major metropolitan area or a weapon detonated on Main Street of rural, God-fearing, small-town Middle America? They key is not the where, but the what. The goal is radiation on U.S. soil. They don't care whether it's paved over or there's corn growing in it."

She paused for a moment to catch her breath and look around the room. All eyes were on her. It was Chief Williams, leaning on the chair over the seal of the President of the United States, who broke the silence.

"So," he asked, "what do you propose?"

Without thinking, she said, "We have to kill them…uh, obviously. But we can't go in guns blazing or we could rupture the containers holding the cesium or inadvertently detonate explosives stored around it. We need a sniper or something to pick them off before they know what's happening. But you have to get all four of them almost simultaneously. If they have the material booby-trapped, I'm sure they have all been trained to detonate it at the first sign of capture."

Another military officer with a thick Texas drawl, breast bejeweled with ribbons and medals, said, "So what y'all got if your little sniper drill comes off without a hitch? Best case, ya got four dead A-rabs and no intel on other cells, future ops, whereabouts of key players…. Worst case, ya got a nuclear bomb goin' off somewhere."

"Excuse me, sir," Beth interrupted, "it's not a nuclear device. We're not talking about a nuclear explosion."

The officer looked at her and tilted his head. As though addressing a slow child, he said, "Listen, with all due respect young lady, yer average American ain't gonna make that distinction. They hear 'radiation,' they'll be runnin' for the hills."

He turned from her and faced the whole group. "We need to take these bastards prisoner. Interrogate 'em. We're expendin' a hell of a lot of energy on four scouts while the whole damn Apache nation could be waitin' over the next hill. We're throwin' a lot a eggs in one big ol' basket."

Colonel Gillis spoke up next.

"That's what I've been saying all along. We're rushing to conclusions here. We've got some," he glanced at Beth, "very preliminary, unverified evidence of a glorified boy scout trip and the ramblings of a prisoner, who, if I may be so bold here, was likely under, shall we say, extreme duress."

Gillis gave Colonel Kimball a wry smile that implied a level of knowledge much deeper than he was letting on. Kimball smiled back, his very white teeth almost startling against the dark tan of his face.

"Extreme duress can bring with it liberating clarity. Maybe you should try it, colonel? I would be happy to facilitate."

He watched the smile retreat quickly from Gillis' face. He spoke then to the rest of the group.

"We have evidence from Agent Adams of a plot," he said, holding out one tanned, long-fingered hand palm up, "we have a completely independent interrogation effort," he said, extending his other palm, "conducted across the world which corroborates that evidence exactly."

He brought both hands together and clasped them elegantly. "That is more than enough to warrant an aggressive and immediate response. Agent Adams is right. They must be terminated, but as delicately as possible."

Williams spoke next.

"Okay, I've heard enough. We have an experienced agent on the ground already with Special Forces training from Fort Bragg and JFK. I'm putting him in charge of base operations. Colonel Kimball will call operations from here. Agent Adams, I want you on a plane to the Twin Cities today. I want you to set up shop near the Mall of America. I want you to scope the place out and help direct our security team on likely target sites within the building when they arrive tomorrow. General Westguard, Colonel Kimball, Colonel Gillis, General Greer, let's make sure we're on the same page before the President gets here. Everyone else, move out!"

Except for the few men Williams mentioned, the room cleared quickly. Beth sat for a moment looking at the map of Minnesota still displayed on the screen and contemplating the monster she had unleashed. What if I'm wrong, she wondered. Worse yet, what if I'm right?

FORTY-ONE

After his conversation with the Sheik he was returned to his filthy cell. He was not bound this time nor were his old clothes returned. He took a moment to look around the room. In one corner feces was ankle-deep. Sawdust had been dumped around the pile to contain the urine. A squadron of flies circled it endlessly. There were numerous dark stains on the floor and walls. A pallid yellow light seeped in from the hallway beyond the iron bars. There was another cell directly across from his, though he could not see into it. It was too dark.

How long he sat on the cold concrete floor, staring at the light coming through the bars, he could not tell. He knew a night had passed when the flies were replaced by the marauding rats, which he watched with fascination as they investigated every inch of his cell. They paid particular attention to the dark stains, licking at them with little pink tongues—a sound he could hear in the silence.

Sometime after the rats had disappeared and the flies had returned in full force he heard several sets of approaching footsteps echoing in the hall. When they reached his cell he saw the tall officer who had visited him briefly in Vegas, accompanied by two soldiers: the thick-necked sergeant and cruel red-headed Vince. All three entered Ibrahim's cell. Vince gagged at the smell.

"Fucking animal," he said, coughing.

The tall uniformed man ordered Ibrahim to stand. He did so. The man held out his hand to the sergeant who unclasped the holster for his service revolver, removed the weapon from the tight leather which squeaked in protest and placed it in his superior's outstretched hand. The tall man clasped the grip and looked down, hefting the pistol's substantial weight.

Still looking down, he told Ibrahim, "I made you a promise yesterday. A martyr you will be."

As the man leveled the gun to the prisoner's temple, their eyes met and Ibrahim saw it was the man from the quiet room. It had been a tenuous fantasy to be sure, believing this man was the military and spiritual leader to whom he had devoted his earthly existence. But the thought had sustained him these past days. He found it surprisingly easy to drift back into the feeling of peace and well-being he felt each time he sat in the room and sipped sweet tea from a simple white cup and prayed to his gracious and benevolent God. He was grateful for the seconds of calm he felt just before the bullet shattered his skull and left yet another dark stain on the concrete floor.

FORTY-TWO

Goiaina, Brazil, September, 1987

Victor Gallegos felt the strands unravel, gossamer threads peeling away, carried off into the descending void. A gnawing pang of fear swept the pain aside as darkness fell. A question probed him "What if I was not good enough?" Would God take him or would he let go and fall into the abyss. He would not find them there, his wife or his daughter. They would be with God, but would he find himself cast out for sins not forgiven, separated from the only love in his life by the millennia? "No," he sighed. "Voy con el Dios." He opened his hands and stretched his fingers to Heaven.

FORTY-THREE

Gunflint Trail, Cook County Minnesota, May, 2002
Thursday, 10:50 AM

Setty drove the red pickup down a narrow, rutted trail
that wound through a mixture of dense conifers and
aspen. He closed the driver's side window after getting
slapped in the cheek by a passing branch. He heard the
squeaking of sticks against the paint and for the first time
gave thanks he wasn't driving his own car. As he bounced
along the rugged goat path he began to wonder if the
officer at the Pigeon River border station was having a
good laugh at his expense. This damn road probably leads
to some shoot-first-ask-questions-later hermit who thinks
anybody with a full complement of brushed teeth might be
suitable romantic companionship. His right hand
instinctively reached to the reassuring bulge of the Ruger
9mm under his jacket. It helped vanquish the visions of
"Deliverance" that flashed through his mind.

The trail turned uphill, then suddenly the woods
opened up into a park-like setting, revealing a small log
cabin sitting on a ridge overlooking distant scalloped hills.
As he pulled up to the cabin he noticed a small storage
building to his right with an overhanging roof under
which was a pile of neatly stacked birch firewood. In front
of the pile were scattered several recently split logs. The
splitting maul stuck out of the top of a large log sitting
near the pile and a pair of gloves lay nearby on the
ground. It looked as though the project had been hastily
abandoned. Further from the cabin, along the ridge, was a
small narrow building with half-log siding and a small

galvanized pipe sticking out the top. The outhouse, he assumed. "Jesus!" He parked the red truck directly behind an old Ford pickup with a broken driver's side window and rust overtaking the body of the vehicle in a pox of brown and orange spots. Once again, he wondered anxiously if this was the right place. "What are you doing with your money, Officer Hansen?" he said to himself before getting out and walking to the door.

The door looked homemade—other than hinges, there was no hardware, only a handle made of deer antler. A couple of moose antlers lay propped up on the small covered porch along with a chair made from some sort of light-colored wood with dark diamond-shaped knots. Next to the chair were a couple of beer bottles. Not a women around here for miles, he thought to himself. At least he hadn't recently brushed his teeth. He thought of his friend Kirby He's gonna love this!

"Hello? Officer Hansen?"

Setty pushed the door open a little more with his foot so he could see inside. It creaked and moved stubbornly. It was dark in there, though he could make out a table and chairs, a counter and a fridge.

"Can I help you?"

The voice was right at his ear and it made him jump and whirl around. A large blond-haired man stood before him with a couple days' growth of reddish beard and many lines on his forehead and at the corners of his pale gray eyes.

"Jesus! Where the hell did you come from?"

"Sorry," said Hansen, "sneaking around is an old habit."

He extended a hand.

"Garrett Hansen. Pleased to meet you. You're Brian Setty, from Washington?"

"Yep, nice to meet you. I like your cabin. It's…uh, rustic, rugged. Looks like a good place to get away from it all."

Setty wasn't sure what to say about the place actually. He couldn't find anything pleasant in the scene. It had taken him twenty minutes to drive down the trail to get here and that was after about thirty minutes from the nearest town, which had about as much culture as Fort Bragg. The woods were claustrophobic, biting flies were already attacking his exposed skin. His local resource, with the plaid shirt, stained blue jeans and scraggly beard looked like Jeremiah Johnson's stunt double. God, what a sentence it would be to live here, he thought.

"Yeah, it usually is," Hansen said, walking past the agent and into the cabin.

He grabbed a small camouflage backpack from a hook on the wall and began stuffing it with items on the kitchen table, matches, jerky, a GPS, a compass, maps. He began filling a bottle of water from a large plastic jug that sat at the edge of the sink.

"Look," he said, "I know you probably want to jump right in, but we're going to have to postpone getting together until tonight or tomorrow. I've got a little search and rescue operation right now."

Setty backed out of the doorway as Hansen bustled through. He wasn't ready to fill this guy in on the real reason for his visit, but he also wasn't interested in sitting on his ass for most of the day waiting for Grizzly Adams to emerge from the woods.

"I don't want to get in your way or anything…."

"Looks like you already have." Hansen nodded toward Setty's truck sitting directly behind his own.

"I figure I shouldn't be in the air more than a couple of hours. This guy's a friend of mine and I figure something happened to his canoe or he's hurt and I've gotta check on it. He should have been back a couple days ago."

Setty heard "canoe" and guessed, "He's in the Boundary Waters?"

"Yeah, he's a wilderness ranger. I'm gonna run over to Gunflint Lodge and get the plane. Like I said, it won't take long. I can meet you in town tonight," said Hansen looking back at Setty's truck once again, making his impatience clear.

"No trouble finding that in the dark," he commented.

"Like I said, I don't want to get in your way, but I came a long way to get a feel for the country up here and this sounds like a perfect introduction. You said you're flying over the area in a plane?" Hansen nodded, looking displeased.

"I'd like to go up with you. I'm not staying here all that long and I can't waste any time."

Hansen considered the FBI agent for a moment. Setty had the feeling of being sized up, as a boxing opponent or poker player might do. As if suddenly deciding something, a brief smile flashed across the officer's scruffy face and he said,

"Sure. Follow me."

With that he jumped in the old truck and it sputtered to life with a choking cloud of bluish smoke. Setty wasn't sure why they couldn't ride together, but he got into the Ranger and backed out of the way so Hansen could get past him. After turning their trucks around they bounced and rattled back down the trail single file.

Hansen was worried about his friend and the last thing he needed was some tourist with a badge tagging along asking about the flora and fauna. He wasn't interested in being a tour guide today. There was a muddy logging road about halfway down the driveway. It was a sharp right around a sharp corner and he thought he could lose the Fed if he did it right. He stepped on the gas and urged the old truck forward, taking the turns and ruts a little more aggressively. He needed a bit more room between him and the agent in order to disappear.

Driving behind Hansen, Brian Setty wondered if his little truck would hold together as it bounced and twisted over the moguls and rocks. So, when Hansen sped up, Setty hesitated. But as he rounded a sharp curve in the road he saw that his guide had disappeared.

"Shit!"

Immediately, Brian shut off the truck and brought it to a halt. He heard the rumble of Hansen's old Ford off to the right, but saw no road entrance. He backed up and there in the mud were a fresh pair of tracks seemingly heading off into the woods.

"Redneck!" Setty exclaimed as he turned a dial on the dashboard to "4WD" which caused a small amber light to appear below the fuel gauge. He found the absence of any related mechanical sound both unsatisfying and worrisome. Regardless, he drove the truck into the brush, hoping to find a road somewhere. Once he pushed through the initial undergrowth, he found a trail similar to the driveway to Hansen's cabin.

Apparently an old logging road, it wound its way through more aspen and conifer forest, climbing and descending high, steep ridges. He could clearly see Hansen's tracks in the road and from the summit of one ridge he saw the old Ford's tailgate disappear over the top of another. Brian pulled the seatbelt across his chest and clicked it into place. Then he stepped on the gas, sending two arcs of mud flying behind the red truck.

Hansen saw a flash in his rearview mirror and was shocked to see the FBI agent's bright red truck topping a rise and covering the distance between them.

"Shit!"

His old truck roared as he pressed the gas pedal down even further, launching his own rooster tail of brown slop. He held tightly to the steering wheel to keep from hitting his head on the roof of the truck as the old rig jumped over rocks and uneven ground. The road, like many in this network of old logging tracks, would come out on the Gunflint Trail. Though he had never done it, he assumed this was what bull riding felt like. At several points looking for Setty in the rearview, Hansen could only see the bed of the pickup as it rose up behind him and flew over another nasty bump.

Setty fought to keep the lightweight truck on the trail. It bounced around like a rubber ball over logs and rocks, threatening to career into the trees standing just off the trail. A set of muddy ruts ran the length of the road and Setty kept the little truck out of them since the soggy ground grabbed the tires and slowed him down. With that strategy he gained quickly on the rusty old truck until he was within ten feet, mud spattering his windshield, blurring his vision.

Hansen checked his rearview and saw the cab of the red Ranger directly behind him. "Shit!" Hansen looked back too late to react to the fallen tree lying across the road right in front of him. "Shit!" The old truck's front wheels hit the log at about thirty miles per hour, launching

Hansen into the roof with a loud thud. Then the back of the truck followed suit, flying up behind him. This time, with a horrific metallic clunk, the tailgate was dislodged. The heavy five by two foot rectangle of steel was thrown upward like a playing card and came down on its edge like a brick wall, directly into Brian Setty's path.

Brian hit it. Hard.

For a moment, all was white. He thought he'd hit the windshield and was passing out, but then he realized, as it deflated, the airbag had deployed. He didn't remember doing it, but his leg was locked and his foot had mashed the brake pedal into the firewall. He slowly relaxed his leg and let things sink in. His hands were shaking. Through the windshield he could see no evidence of the impact. There was nothing in front of him. The last thing he remembered was the back end of Hansen's truck suddenly appearing in his windshield, as if it had dropped from the sky. Then the crash. Now he saw Hansen's truck backing up slowly and noticed that the tailgate was gone. It stopped and the big man got out and trotted back to Setty. "You ok?" he asked.

Setty threw the door open and hopped out of the disabled truck. He stood slightly less than six feet tall and cut a slim figure. He boxed because no other physical training activity taught with such perfection how to generate incredible destructive power from balance, speed and leverage, while proving an elusive target using those same attributes. Not a particularly imposing man, he had to rely on using what he had to the best of his ability

The decision to hit Hansen was not premeditated. But as the large man stood before him, after attempting to lose him like an annoying little brother in these bare desolate woods, with biting bugs descending upon him and a mission of national security weighing heavily on his shoulders, Setty felt compelled to take the initiative and assert his place in their embryonic relationship. There was no time for any more games. Brian squared his body, pushed off of his right foot and threw a straight right hand, his best punch, hitting Hansen square under his left eye.

The border officer wavered a second, then dropped to one knee and stayed there for several moments, rubbing his face and regaining his balance. Standing over him, Setty clenched his fists and prepared for retaliation. He knew he'd have to maintain the advantage and keep the bigger man down. If the guy got a hold of him, Setty wasn't confident of the outcome. He watched Hansen carefully for tension in the muscles, subtle adjustments in footing and orientation—things a calculating but rage-bound man might hide before he attacks. But, looking down at the big Scandinavian, he only saw resignation.

Brian relaxed slightly and said, "Look, we don't have to be friends. I do, however, expect your cooperation. We both have the same boss and we should act like it. I came up here on an assignment for the United States government. I couldn't care less whether or not you think that's important. I'm telling you it is. It is because my boss said so and his boss said so and his boss is the President of the United States. Are we clear?"

Looking up at the FBI agent, standing in the woods with his dark suit and shiny black shoes in the mud, Hansen said, "Yeah, I'm sorry. I was being an ass. You'd think after so many years I'd learn to recognize it before I got punched for a change."

He held up a hand to Setty, who reached down and helped him up.

"Sorry," Hansen said. "Really."

"Apology accepted," said Setty, anxious to put it behind them.

"Now, can we get the hell out of here?"

"Yeah," Hansen said.

They reattached the old Ford's tailgate, and then Setty used a hunting knife from Hansen's truck to cut off the remains of the airbag hanging from the steering wheel. After driving another thirty minutes at a more reasonable pace they emerged from the woods not far from Gunflint Lake. The Cessna waited at the end of the resort's longest dock where he'd left it the previous evening.

———————————

Brian Setty looked out the plane's small window at an endless forest of evergreens and the greenish gray of budding deciduous trees. The expanse of trees was only broken by lakes and streams, brilliant blue reflecting a clear sky. The sun was high and it shone into the crystalline waters, illuminating a profusion of boulders and logs beneath the calm surface.

"So, which way's Canada?" he asked.

Hansen, who sat to his left wearing a headset, hands firmly on the wheel, nodded to his right. Setty just saw more woods.

"What makes you think you'd ever see your friend out here? It seems like a needle in a haystack!"

"If you want to be found," Hansen said, "it's not that hard. There's a lot of exposed rock on the shorelines of most lakes. Lots of places to be seen easily."

"And if you didn't want to be seen?"

Hansen looked over at the agent.

"You wouldn't be."

He returned to his instrument panel, then said, "He was coming from Big Sag and heading down to Poplar Lake. I'm just going to run down his route, starting at Poplar. If he's in trouble we'll see him somewhere along those lakes or portages."

Hansen banked the plane and headed southeast. He stayed low. To Setty, it felt like they were skimming the tops of the trees. The little plane jumped around a lot. He could feel every movement of the air around them and the little dips and bumps reminded him vividly of their precarious position, suspended above certain death by a little straining engine propelling this pop can with seats. Looking out the window watching the trees, rocks and water rush by it was clear there would be no "emergency landings" in this country.

"It's funny," he said, "eight years in Special Forces and I don't like to fly."

Hansen glanced over at Setty for a moment.

"So, what happened, why don't you like to fly?"

"Jumping out of planes for the Army, I always had a chute. It was like a security blanket—no matter how hairy it got, it gave me confidence. Flying without one now seems wrong—like I'm naked."

"Special Forces Army Rangers, eh?" Hansen nodded knowingly. "At least I don't feel so bad about getting decked. You probably could've killed me seven different ways with a toothpick."

"I don't use toothpicks," said Setty, trying to lighten the mood. "Bad for your gums."

Hansen ignored the joke.

"Yeah, I pulled MP duty at Bragg for a couple of years. It was scary...you guys, badasses all. Get a little liquor in you..." he trailed off and shook his head. "I'd always go in with a Taser. I'd seen other grunts taken down, their wrists snapped and knees popped, lying on the ground before they had a chance to say word one. I was glad to get reassigned."

Setty was feeling a little off balance and not just because he was a few hundred feet off the ground. Why is this guy busting my balls?

"I guarantee you," he said, "any Rangers you found in a bar drunk off their asses washed out of the program."

"Unfortunately they got the training and attitude before they washed out. Too bad you guys don't 'untrain' folks as effectively as you train them."

Setty frowned, cocked his head, and said, "You were an MP, right? You went through the same advanced training in hand-to-hand. You know that restraint is part of that training."

"Yeah, well, in my experience," Hansen said, "restraint is the first thing you forget."

They spent the next several minutes in silence, the drone of the engine and the occasional rattle of loose items in the plane the only sounds. Setty's mind wandered to Beth Adams. He wondered if she would actually call him before he called her. He planned to call her tonight and ask her about any progress she may have made in her research. He figured he could do it easily without seeming too eager, given their working relationship. He found her attractive and engaging. Her natural honesty and quick mind left him energized. He enjoyed the prospect of seeing her again.

Eventually they flew over a large lake where Hansen banked the plane over what appeared to be a resort. Setty saw a large building, presumably the lodge, and several small cabins in a line along the shore. From the lodge a long pier stretched into the water. Several fishing boats and canoes were tied to the dock or pulled up on the sandy shoreline.

"That's Cosgrove's resort on Poplar Lake," he told Setty. "That's where Mark should have ended up a couple of days ago." They circled once, and then followed the big lake to the west until they reached a narrow bay.

"Look down," said Hansen.

"You'll see the portage wind through the woods. The portages are pretty easy to spot now with the leaves just starting to come out. In another month, you won't see a damn thing."

They flew a course roughly northwest, following the faint line of portages to lakes and streams. At each opening in the canopy, Hansen would circle the plane and search the area. Then he'd move on. They saw no one on the portages or on the lakes beneath them.

Suddenly, Setty cried, "What in the hell is that?"

He was pointing down to a stream below them. Hansen brought the plane around until he could see what caught the agent's attention. Half-submerged in the wide, murky, reed-lined stream, stood a large dark bull moose with its palmate antlers still small and growing in velvet. The giant deer thrust its head into the water and then surfaced, bringing with it long green strands of submergent vegetation hanging and dripping from its large mouth. It seemed oblivious to the airplane circling above its head.

"My god," Setty said, "that's magnificent! I've never seen anything like that. Are there a lot of those things around?"

"Yeah," said Hansen. "They're more common than deer this deep in the wilderness. Snow's too deep and it's too cold this far away from Superior for whitetails. The lake moderates the temps a few degrees and all the exposed ground along highway 61 thaws grass before any place else, so the deer hang out there. It's like a damn obstacle course during the winter along that road, at least until green-up. Nobody who lives up here gets through a winter without hitting at least one deer."

Hansen circled once more, then headed to the next portage, Setty straining to catch a final glimpse of the incredible animal.

"I've never seen so much land without a single human being," Setty remarked, his face still glued to the window, looking for the next moose.

"How can you possibly be expected to police so many miles of wilderness?"

Hansen laughed.

"You can't! We were supposed to see an additional two hundred and forty-five agents by 2004 on the northern border after 9-11. We haven't seen half that. Even if we did, there's something like half a million people crossing the border with Canada every day. It's a sieve. If I really wanted to bring drugs into the U.S., hell, I'd fill a few Duluth packs over in Canada, take my canoe and paddle it over. I could bring in fifty kilos of coke every day without coming within two hundred miles of a drug-sniffing dog."

"You think it happens?" Setty asked.

"I know it happens. I know people who do it almost every goddamn day through the summer. Maybe not one hundred pounds, but we've busted folks with everything from a joint to a kilo of coke. We don't get many, but with only a couple of law enforcement agents covering a million acres, you can bet we miss the vast majority."

The words sent a shudder through the agent seated in the small single-engine float plane. As he looked down across miles and miles of roadless forest the enormity of the problem hit him. Bags and bags of illegal substances smuggled without fear of discovery. Beth was right. He felt it. If they weren't out here, they would be soon. Just a matter of time.

"You always like to fly this low?" Setty asked, his anxiety still percolating.

"Yep, because I like it and because I can. Except for authorized uses, air traffic below four thousand feet was banned by Truman in 1949. A lot of local resort owners and developers had a cow cause it effectively ended fly-in fishing trips into the "Roadless Area" as they used to call it. Even before that, the Federal government bought up private properties to get ready for wilderness protection, which passed in 1964. After that, in '78, they passed the BWCA Wilderness Act that stopped logging and defined the park boundaries. The remaining resorts were bought and razed under Federal eminent domain law. Motorboats and snowmobiles were eliminated in over eighty percent of the thousand lakes in the park. That pretty much left it to the canoes and hikers."

"I expect there were more than a few pissed off folks up here," Setty said.

Hansen nodded, "Still are. The skin is still pretty thin over the scars. Locals saw it as nothing less than a government seizure and occupation of private land. There are still plenty in the local populace suspicious of any government intervention into their daily lives. Ely's got it worse. They're probably one 'Ruby Ridge' away from establishing the Minnesota chapter of the Montana Freemen."

"What's Ely?" Setty asked.

"It's a little outfitting town smack dab in the middle of the BW."

Hansen pointed off in to the right, which helped Setty not at all. He looked in that direction and simply saw more of the trees, hills and lakes he saw when he looked to the left.

"Grand Marais is a little less reactionary, mainly due to a recent influx of liberal-minded artists and former city dwellers looking to live on the big lake. They fall for the romance of wilderness and big water—you know, endless vistas and waves crashing on jagged rocks, cute little animals in the yard. Of course, none of these people had to watch their hard-working family and friends lose their jobs and a way of life. As long as they've got electricity, plumbing and a latte, they couldn't care less about the people that came before and pioneer …whoa, what the hell…?"

Hansen clammed up and looked down onto the surface of a large lake. He banked the plane sharply to the left and lost altitude dramatically.

Setty hung onto his seat.

"What?" he managed. "Did we hit something?"

Hansen straightened the craft out and took another pass over the lake, lower this time.

"Look down there, out your side. Put those Polaroids on and look under the water."

Setty took the pair of sunglasses from their perch on the sun visor, put them on and looked down at the lake's surface. The polarizing glasses removed the sun's glare and revealed clearly rocks, logs, weed beds, reefs and sand bars…and a canoe. He could see a yellowish glow from under the water and as they passed over it looked like a canoe filled with gear, but it was hard to tell at one hundred and twenty miles per hour.

Setty glanced over and saw Hansen mark the spot with a handheld GPS. Hansen took the plane to the lake's westernmost end, banked it around and brought it down for a smooth landing on the water, the pontoons cutting white slices through the tranquil surface of the lake. Following the GPS, he taxied to the spot he had marked. The plane slowed to a stop in the water, bobbing slightly on its own wake.

Hansen stepped out of the plane onto the pontoon and told Setty, "There's a boat hook in the back, on the floor. Get it. Hurry up, we're drifting off it!"

Setty jumped up and found the telescoping aluminum pole with a rubber-tipped hook on one end. He handed it to Hansen, who immediately thrust it into the water and snagged something. With great effort he hauled a green backpack out of the water. Setty stepped gingerly onto the slippery float and helped him bring the pack aboard. They opened it up and found large rocks piled on top of clothing, a sleeping bag and a tent.

"It's Mark's," said Hansen.

The officer stared dejectedly into the backpack as it drained water through the seams. Shaking his head slowly, he seemed lost, baffled.

"This just doesn't make any damn sense. Who the hell would've done...?"

His words trailed off into silence as he stood there rocking slowly with the movement of the airplane on the water. As if finally putting several things together that were swirling around his head, Hansen looked sharply at Setty.

"What in the hell is going on? You know something, don't you?"

He motioned toward the sunken canoe. Nodding his head he said, "You know about this." It was not a question.

Before he could respond, Setty's satellite phone rang. Brian was genuinely pleased to hear Beth Adams' voice and not only because it provided a perfectly timed diversion. But by the time she was through talking, he would wish she hadn't called.

FORTY-FOUR

Agent Beth Adams sat in a HumVee on the Dulles tarmac waiting for the C-130 that would take her to Minneapolis and speaking to Brian Setty on the phone.

"I'm telling you, they're already in the woods!"

Beth tried to be emphatic without sounding shrill. She knew that could happen when she was excited about something. Her father used to say "Nobody hears Beth scream, but all the neighborhood dogs come running!" Absently she twirled the heart locket on its chain. She was excited to be in the middle of this, despite all its terrible implications. Things were happening as she had said they would and her research and reasoning might just help prevent a horrible tragedy. Her rise from the faceless denizens of the Pentagon's cube city had been meteoric. Though exhilarating, she was afraid to look down.

"How do you know they're still there…here?" Setty asked.

"They're either still in the Boundary Waters or just getting out. Hell, they could be at the mall by tomorrow!"

Beth could almost hear Setty's brain spinning over the phone.

He asked, "And they're sure about the cesium?"

"Brian, the guy they interrogated played a key role in the plot. He was the courier, exchanging information between the organization and the terrorists. He's credible."

She heard an odd warbling sound come over the phone.

"Uh…what was that? Where are you?"

She heard him repeat her question to someone away from the phone but could not hear the distant answer. "I'm told that was a loon," he told her. "I'm…well, I'm standing on the pontoon of a seaplane in the middle of a lake. It's a long story."

"A loon?" Beth paused a moment, wondering if she heard him right.

"Never mind, I'll fill you in later," he said.

"Listen, there's nobody in the Duluth field office right now. They're in Seattle for some conference. The Bureau is flying about fifty agents to Duluth, then they'll helicopter to the Grand Marais airport. They're not notifying local agencies of every detail yet, because of the nature of the threat, but it won't take long for word to get out. If the cell gets wind of anything, I'm worried they'll let it loose wherever they are."

"You're damn right they will, he said. "We can't afford some Barney Fife blasting a hole in the container or worse, hitting a suicide belt and doing their work for them. Same goes for our guys. Getting that many agents up here is a mistake. I'm surprised Williams let this happen. Doesn't sound like him."

"It wasn't him," Beth said. "The plan came from higher up."

"That's what I figured. For what it's worth, please pass along this prediction from the agent on the ground—it will be a cluster fuck! It'll make Waco look like a play date. I'm just hoping we can find them before they get out of the park."

"Do you have someone there to help you?" she asked.

"Uh, yeah, I've got plenty of help," said Setty, though his response lacked confidence. "Anyway, I think we may have just found their trail."

FORTY-FIVE

Boundary Waters Canoe Area Wilderness, Minnesota
May, 2002
Thursday, 2:00 PM

Setty was not happy to be in the air with Hansen. He could tell the man was noticeably shaken by the uncertain status of his friend and the information the FBI agent had just shared with him. The hardest thing was getting Hansen to agree that they couldn't get help in the search for Mark Toftey until the terrorist threat was resolved. More people in the woods was a bad idea right now. Setty glanced at the big man who was looking in the right direction, but could just as easily have been watching I Love Lucy as flying the plane. He was distraught, miles away.

"Hey," said Setty, "you ok? I know this is a lot to deal with all at once—would be for anybody."

"So, you're tellin' me these terrorists have probably killed him," Hansen said flatly.

"I don't think so," said Setty. "I think they sunk your friend's canoe because they didn't want him using it to get out and warn anybody. They could have more easily thrown it in the woods, off the trail, if he was already dead."

Hansen considered this possibility in silence for several minutes.

"Maybe you're right," he said finally.

Right or not, the possibility seemed to perk him up. He straightened in the seat and checked his instrumentation. That was good. Setty needed his head in the game. They agreed to finish what they started, following the route that Toftey would have taken in reverse. Finding the sunken canoe was a lucky stroke. Hansen guessed the bad guys just left once the canoe started to sink, not realizing they were on a large gravel bar that lay only eight feet under the surface of the lake. The canoe glowed in the sun like a neon banana and was easy to spot from above. Once they finished the flyover, they would head south and try to find the terrorists and report their location.

But they reached sprawling Saganaga Lake with no sign of the Forest Service ranger. Hansen's funk returned.

"I should have come out here sooner," he said, shaking his head. "Always a fucking day late and a dollar short!"

Setty took a breath to speak, but thought better of it. This guy had more than a few personal demons fluttering around upstairs and Setty had learned the hard way it was best to stay out of such conversations.

Next stop was for fuel at Gunflint Lake. From there they would head south to Alpine Lake where they had found Toftey's canoe and then, continue south until they reached a remote dirt road called the Grade.

"Back in the thirties," Hansen told Setty, "it was a railway for logging operations. Now it's a forestry road. You can get to several Boundary Waters entry points from the Grade."

"Much traffic on it?" asked Setty.

"Moose mainly. It's the perfect place for these guys to get out of the wilderness without being seen, if that's what you're getting at."

"I am," Setty said.

"We better get the Cook County Sheriff and State Patrol on the way to check licenses on every vehicle parked in those entry point parking lots along the Grade,"

Hansen said, switching radio frequencies to make the call. "They either have a getaway vehicle parked there or someone's going to pick them up."

To Setty, the latter seemed unlikely given the difficulty in coordinating schedules amid a plethora of variables conspiring against them—weather, physical obstacles, navigational miscues. No, there had to be a truck parked somewhere. Probably a panel van to allow them the privacy they would need to prepare for the attack.

"I'm going to circle down over Seagull," Hansen said as the plane banked right. "Just in case he had to get off the portage. If they got his gear, he probably had to run. The guy's a rabbit," Hansen laughed as though recalling an amusing story, but kept it to himself.

"If anybody had to escape through the woods, I'd put my money on Toftey every time."

Setty tentatively ventured a question. "So, you guys are pretty good friends?"

"Yeah," Hansen said, "you could say that. He's the closest thing I ever had to a brother. He helps me keep my head on straight. Keeps me grounded, you know? Ever have someone like that?" he asked, though it seemed like he was talking to himself now.

"You're out there bobbing around like a kite in a hurricane, dipping and diving, no way to get down other than crash. But there's someone at the other end to reel you in, help you get back on the ground. And now I can't even help when he needs me."

Hansen paused a moment and looked at Setty, as though suddenly noticing him, and laughed, "Christ. Sounds like I'm queer for him."

You probably are, Setty thought, but you're so fucked up by the testosterone overload of this wood-chopping, ice-fishing, log cabin-living, deer-hunting, truck-driving, beer-drinking, uber-lumberjack trip you're all on up here you'd go to your grave before you admit it.

Instead, he said, "You sound like you're beating yourself up for something that's out of your hands."

Hansen shrugged. "Well, I'm getting pretty damn sick of showing up after the parade, just in time to walk through the piles of shit."

FORTY-SIX

Setty stopped talking and Hansen let the drone of the plane fill the silence as his mind wandered back to a BW duck-hunting trip he took with Toftey one cold October on Big Sag. He remembered it with shame, even after several years. He remembered the cold seeping into his body and the precise moment he gave up. It had come so easily, like blinking or breathing, as if resignation were always waiting there, stalking, blending with the swaying grasses, whispering, "Give up, let go, it could all be over so easily."

Hansen blamed it on Toftey's dog, an excitable black lab with a skull of concrete. While Hansen leaned over to retrieve a duck he had just shot, Barney broke for it as well, ignoring the command to sit he'd just been given by his master. The one hundred-pound dog slipped on the gunwale and hung there for a precarious moment, then tipped into the water along with the canoe, two men, their shotguns and gear. Panicked, the dog paddled out into the steel-gray waters of Saganaga. Toftey and Hansen screamed at the struggling animal but he showed no sign of hearing. They watched his head bobbing north, toward the Canadian shore, almost two miles away. After roughly one hundred-yards of frantic paddling, Barney's big black head disappeared behind a wave and was gone.

They'd been dumped between American Point and Englishmen Island. Toftey retrieved one paddle, but they could not find the other. They righted the canoe and simultaneously pulled themselves into the boat from opposite sides to avoid swamping it again. Both men began to shiver as the biting wind hit their exposed faces and hands. Though the nearest shoreline was almost a quarter mile away, the crashing of waves on the rocks was the only sound to penetrate the steady howling of the wind. Hansen hugged himself tightly, rocking back and forth on the front seat, facing the stern, while Toftey drove the canoe inches at a time.

He was twelve again, in his father's boat on Superior. The little silver, open-stern dory pitched drunkenly over six-foot swells, making the job of pulling in herring nets a Herculean effort. But asking for help was not an option. His father was bringing in a net on the other side of the boat, dealing with the same biting, wind-driven spray and numb hands and fingers. There were gale warnings for the big lake that morning, but the catch had to come in. Garrett's muscles burned beneath his freezing skin as he pulled hand over hand, every pull of the rope turning a child's hands into the callused, leather mitts of his father. He was cold. He hurt. He would go to school later, after working harder than any other kid, working like a man, and he would be ridiculed for it, shamed. He could not complain, he could not cry. Not that he would be reprimanded. In fact, expressed emotions were met with bewilderment and suspicion in the Hansen house. Nobody knew what to do with them. So, he pulled and pulled and pulled.

The deck was slippery with spray and fish slime. His rubber boots normally provided sound purchase on the deck, but at the very moment he pulled mightily on the net, the boat dropped out from under him as it plunged unexpectedly off a huge swell. He pulled himself overboard into the frigid waters of Superior. The cold squeezed the breath from his body and his lungs responded by instinctively rushing to fill up again. But now he was below the waves and instead of air drew in great draughts of water. There was a moment of clarity as he looked up through the crystal waters, expecting to see his father reach in to grab and pull him back into the boat. Where are you, Dad, where are you? His question went unspoken and unanswered as his vision narrowed and closed around him.

And then he died.

At least that's what they told him. What little he remembered, after waking up in his bed, bore no resemblance to the stories he'd heard of floating above one's body, seeing dead relatives, bright lights, euphoria and peace—something after. Instead, he saw the emptiness of space, he saw blackness—not the color of ravens, but the darkness of desolation. He woke afraid, afraid of sleep, afraid of the boat, afraid of the lake, afraid of death, for now he knew the difference between life and nothingness could be as tenuous as a father's distraction. He would discover that he had lost the inherent human denial of his own mortality. From that day forward, happiness ran out of him like water through his fingers.

His father was the first to see him after twenty-four hours of coma-like sleep.

"You lost the net," he said.

Hansen had thought of this, huddled soaking wet and shivering, while Toftey paddled, the cold October waters washing over the gunwales and slapping their numb faces. The difference was he no longer expected anybody to save him. But when Hansen felt the canoe surge forward he opened his eyes to see the wilderness ranger paddling hard, fighting violent gusts that pushed them into open water to the north. Toftey was in charge, confident. It made Hansen feel safe, or at least comfortably resigned to his fate.

Darkness was upon them, the trees along the distant shore only slightly darker than the featureless charcoal sky above. Toftey held the salvaged paddle and stroked mightily to get the boat turned into the waves so he could ride over the crests and avoid taking one at the low point of the skinny craft. Slowly he made headway, as gently as possible quartering the waves, trying to gain a subtle change in direction. Hansen could not bring himself to speak. The power of the memory had paralyzed him. It was as though he had returned to the coma. His inability to act made him more miserable. And though he knew he should be better, as usual his expectations of himself were higher than he could reach. He only curled tighter, closed his eyes and let nothingness wash over him while Toftey eventually pulled them into the shelter of Long Island.

He remembered that feeling now, as the Cessna's engine droned and the plane bounced along in the volatile, low-altitude air. He longed to let someone else take charge of his life, if only for a little while, to flip on the autopilot and take his hands off the wheel. But he knew he couldn't. Toftey never mentioned that day and for that, more than for saving his life, Hansen felt a boundless debt of gratitude.

FORTY-SEVEN

Toftey heard the plane droning in the distance for what seemed like hours—faintly, then louder, then fading into the distance once again. He knew it was Hansen.

He figured he had traveled a couple miles along the western shore of Seagull, making his way northeast toward Trail's End, the settlement near the north end of the big lake. Now he fought through head-high brush and deadfalls to the shoreline, looking for a suitable bare rock outcrop upon which he could perch and make himself seen from the air.

He found a large boulder and leapt onto it. Quickly he gathered dead cedar and balsam boughs from the surrounding woods and made a sizable pile on the rock. Opening the match case he took from the dead man, he removed a single wooden match and struck its white phosphorous head against the rough gray granite boulder. The match flared brightly and he placed it under the tinder-dry, rust-colored needles in the pile. They began to sputter and crackle like bacon in a hot pan, sending smoke into the sky. He grabbed some larger branches and fed them into the growing flames, which roared and snapped loudly. He could no longer hear the sound of the plane, but he believed Hansen would see the smoke eventually. Toftey looked up and watched it rise high into the clear blue sky. The sight made him laugh. Part of his job was enforcing burning restrictions in the park. After winter's snow-pack melted, but before green-up, the woods were vulnerable to fires and no campfires were allowed unless it had been a particularly wet spring. The irony that an illegal campfire outside an approved U.S.F.S. fire grate would save his life made him smile. He felt giddy, euphoric. Standing on a rock alone in the middle of wilderness, Mark Toftey laughed out loud, waiting for rescue.

FORTY-EIGHT

Boundary Waters Canoe Area Wilderness, Minnesota
May, 2002
Thursday, 2:30

"There!" Setty followed Hansen's finger, pointing insistently at something outside the cockpit window.

"Over there. Smoke!"

"I see it, I see it!"

Setty saw the thin tendril rising from the shoreline of the large lake before them. It was Seagull Lake and somebody on shore had a fire going.

"It has to be him," Hansen said. "He must have run from the portage after they grabbed his gear. He was heading for Trail's End."

As the Cessna flew to the fire, Setty hoped it was not someone else. He didn't think either of them would survive the disappointment. After their earlier conversation he wondered just how co-dependent Officer Hansen was and what losing someone important would do to his grip on the world.

Hansen flew the plane low over the treetops, right through the smoke, and banked around sharply over the lake. As they turned they could see a man standing next to a roaring fire on a large rock outcrop. The man was frantically waving at the plane. As they passed over him once more they could see his wide smile from the air.

The Cessna passed once more over the lake as Hansen searched the surface for a stretch of water free from shallow rocks. The water was smooth and featureless, like a glass-top table.

"I hate glassy-water landings," Hansen said. "It's tough to judge your distance from the water. I always come down hard."

Setty wasn't sure what "come down hard" meant, but he nonchalantly tightened his grip on the seat, just in case it involved an experience similar to bouncing through the woods in a pickup truck.

Hansen brought the plane close to the shoreline, running parallel to the line of tall cedars growing just beyond the rocks.

Almost as if he were talking to himself, Hansen mumbled, "You have to keep the trees in sight. When you drop below the tops you keep your power and airspeed constant until you feel the floats hit the water."

Setty felt his stomach lurch slightly, like a brief elevator ride, as the plane dropped quickly then thumped onto the water's surface. The plane was quickly slowed down by the resistance of the water. After about five hundred feet the little blue and white Cessna smoothly settled down and floated to a stop just offshore from a slender, grinning, bearded man in a brown U.S.F.S. shirt and pants, badge glinting in the sun.

Hansen opened the cockpit window and yelled, "You sorry son of a bitch, you lost your canoe, didn't you?"

The plane taxied to a low ridge of rocks where Toftey quickly clambered onto the right pontoon and, with Setty's help, into the cockpit, collapsing in a heap onto the floor.

Hansen moved the plane away from the rocky shoreline and out toward the middle of the lake. Only then did he leave the pilot's seat to check on his exhausted friend.

"My god, you're a mess!" he said, placing a big hand on Toftey's shoulder.

"You ok?"

He drank lustily from a large bottle of spring water which Setty had given him after he flopped into the plane. Toftey's hands and face were covered with red welts and scratches. Dried blood and dirt mottled his Forest Service uniform.

"You got a candy bar?" he asked.

"Yeah, in my bag." Hansen looked at Setty and pointed to his camouflage backpack on the floor at the back of the plane.

"Hey, Setty, can you dig in there and find him a Snickers?"

Setty crawled back and found the bag. He noticed a perceptible change in Hansen's demeanor since finding Toftey alive. It was as though some missing self-confidence had suddenly been found there on this wilderness shoreline. The bag was heavy. He reached in and pulled out a Beretta .45 caliber semi-automatic pistol. The boy's ready for anything, he thought. Setty knew Border Patrol officers carried handguns. There was just something ominous about finding a gun where you didn't expect to find one. He returned the pistol, dug deeper, and pulled out two candy bars. The agent brought them back to Toftey, who wolfed them down in seconds.

"Thanks," he managed between gulps of water. Setting down the empty water bottle, he extended a hand to Setty.

"Mark Toftey, U.S. Forest Service."

Setty clasped his outstretched hand gingerly, aware of the angry-looking lacerations on the man's skin.

"Brian Setty," he said, "FBI. Pleased to finally meet you. I have to say, a bit relieved too!"

"Yeah," said Hansen who had returned to the cockpit to keep the plane from drifting into any obstacles. "You've missed some excitement around here."

At that, Toftey looked up at the FBI agent, then over his shoulder to his friend sitting in the pilot's chair.

"Begging your pardon, gentlemen," the ranger said, "but you don't know excitement from your ass!"

FORTY-NINE

The sun was low in the sky when they reached the canoe landing at Kawishiwi Lake. Asad was particularly relieved when he saw the clearing and road on shore. He had been fighting the canoe by himself for almost two days now, while Saad and Anwar in the other canoe seemed to glide ahead of him effortlessly, mocking, he believed, his own struggle. For that reason alone he regretted Kadir's death and hated these men more with every passing hour. Their deaths, he thought, could not come soon enough for him. His own martyrdom, however, had seemed to him less inevitable over the last few days. The solitude of wilderness was growing on him. If it was not for these sheep he now led, this place would be a blessing—a gift from Allah.

At the landing, Asad suppressed his growing ambivalence and went to look for the white van that was to be parked in the landing's gravel lot. Saad and Anwar remained behind and unloaded the canoes. The canoes would not go with them. They would be hidden in the woods, though permanent concealment was not the goal. In fact, it was something to be avoided. Their trail was an important part of their mission, as the Sheik's messenger had told them. Without advertising their presence immediately, they were to leave the impression with these infidels that their country is easily penetrated and attacked. Nobody is safe, ever.

Ahead of him, Asad saw an opening in the pine trees and several vehicles parked there. It struck Asad as odd how, other than the ranger and the old man, they had seen no one. There were apparently other campers in these woods, but the wilderness just swallowed them up. At the far corner of the lot sat a white panel van with a keypad on the driver's door. Asad entered the code they had all memorized before leaving Toronto. He opened the door and reached under the seat where the ignition key had been hidden. The van was empty except for four copies of the Qur'an on the floor between the front seats. Asad climbed in, sat behind the steering wheel and adjusted the seat for his large frame. He closed the door, inserted the key and the engine roared to life. The fuel gauge rose to "F."

He sat with the van's motor running, looking at the trees across the road. He could kill them both, he knew. It would be easy to kill these two peons and disappear. I am invisible, he thought. With his impeccable documents, his education, his indeterminate "American" features, his knowledge of the country. The United States, like the wilderness around him, would swallow him whole.

A sharp rapping on the window startled Asad from his daydream. The stern, weathered countenance of Saad stood outside the van. A cloud of tiny black flies circled his head and lit on his exposed skin, adding to the red welts that disfigured his forehead, neck and ears. Asad rolled down the window.

"There is an airplane approaching," he barked. "Hurry up and drive the van to the water so we can load it!" He turned abruptly and walked quickly back toward the canoes.

Asad, the pretend prince, seethed. For a moment, his smoldering brain could not form a coherent thought. The sight of Saad's back, after his flash of anger directed at the leader of the cell, the leader chosen by the Sheik. It was insubordination, mutiny, blasphemy! This ignorant peasant, with his ancient Bedouin sensibilities, still smelling of putrid sweat and camels, the lines in his brown, weather-checked skin filled with sand, this man who held only disdain and bile for Asad's authority and favor with the Sheik….

Asad jerked the shift lever to "D" and smashed the gas pedal to the floor. The truck lurched into gear, tires spinning, spraying gravel into the woods and with a clatter against nearby vehicles. He saw the man as through a red tunnel, or the scope of a rifle, gaining size as the van gained speed. Saad was expecting to hear the truck approaching and did not turn around until it was clear that it was moving faster than necessary. Saad turned to see the front of the van bearing down on him. He tried to jump out of the vehicle's path, but it was moving too fast for him to react appropriately. The edge of the bumper caught Saad at the right knee, shattering the kneecap and spinning him around. Asad hit the brakes and sent the truck skidding over the coarse gravel, shuddering to a stop just before the water's edge. He ignored Anwar, who was running toward him, waving his arms. Asad threw the van into reverse. Looking in the mirror he aimed the accelerating van at the disabled man struggling to stand. The tires spun and chattered over the rough gravel as the heavy vehicle gained momentum. Saad disappeared from Asad's view and for the briefest moment, he thought the old man had somehow escaped. But then he was relieved to hear a tremendous crunching thump against the back doors of the van. He did not release the accelerator until he felt the wheels bounce roughly over Saad's body. He brought the truck to a halt and got out.

A cloud of dust billowed around the white van then quickly settled, revealing Saad's crumpled form on the ground, bleeding from a host of lacerations including protruding bones and patches of skin removed by the undercarriage of the vehicle. Only his face seem unchanged, staring almost longingly at the sky, his scar a red line slashing diagonally across his face. Asad took it as a final insult, that the man's face remained defiantly unchanged. Asad, teeth clenched and grinding, raised his steel-toed hiking boot and brought it down on Saad's slack face, again and again, hearing the bones in the nose and jaw break with sickening liquid pops. He was lost in his rage when Anwar reached him. The smaller man threw his weight at Asad, who stumbled away from Saad then regained his balance. For a moment, he stared at Anwar, breathing heavily, as if unsure who the man was.

"What have you done?" Anwar screamed.

Asad seemed to regain his composure. He looked up to the sky from Saad's mutilated body, and then recited from the Qur'an.

"`Allah is He Who sends the winds so they raise a cloud, then we drive it on to a dead country, and therewith we give life to the earth after its death.' Anwar, or whatever your name may be," the big man made an all-encompassing motion with his outstretched hands, "here we are, alive in a dead country."

Asad moved back to the bloody corpse on the ground and looked at it admiringly.

"Well, some of us," he said, without irony. "We have come to this godless place to raise a cloud and free Islam.

We are the wind! Can your peasant's brain comprehend this?"

Anwar said, his anger rising "I am a soldier in a war. My faith is strong, my objective is clear."

Anwar looked questioningly at Asad, then shook his head slowly.

"Your double-talk does not confuse me," Anwar said. "We have been sent here to fight for our homes, our families and our religion. You did not send us here, Allah has sent us. We have been chosen for paradise, yet you sabotage us at every turn!"

Anwar pointed to the dead man on the ground.

"That was not Allah's will. That was your own."

A cloud passed over Asad's once animated face, turning it to stone.

"That was swift punishment for his incredible arrogance and disdain for authority."

He stared unblinking at Anwar as his hand slid toward the blade sheathed in his belt.

"It was his choice and he chose poorly. What is your choice, Anwar?"

The question went unanswered as the sound of a rapidly approaching airplane interrupted them. They ran to the canoes.

FIFTY

Save for the steady drone of the engine, there was silence in the cockpit of the little Cessna float plane. Toftey had just finished recounting his last forty-eight hours in the woods, chased by what were apparently suicidal terrorists heading for the Twin Cities. Each party had only pieces of the story, but together the picture was clear. Their next steps, however, were not.

"If they get into a vehicle," ventured Hansen, "we're screwed. We won't know what it looks like."

"Well," said Setty, "from what you told me, they have very few options. They're heading south and there's only so many places they can get out of the BWCAW. So, let's fly over them and see if we can find these guys."

"And if we find them?" asked Toftey.

Setty looked at the tired, bedraggled man still sitting on the floor of the plane.

"I don't know yet."

Toftey chuckled and took another big swig of water.

"You don't know yet? Well, I hate to be blunt, but you better get a fucking clue `cause these guys are not your ordinary fugitives. They're playing to win."

Hansen spoke up from the front of the plane.

"I don't think it's all that complicated. We blow their brains out."

Setty ignored the offhand comment and looked out the window, then said, "How many routes are there to an entry point from where we found your canoe?"

"Lots. I mean, out here you've got options. Many ways to get to the same place. If you're not looking to lollygag, I'd say you've got three primary choices—Kawishiwi, Sawbill or Baker."

"Which one is the least traveled?"

"Baker," said Toftey.

"Which is fastest?" asked Setty.

"Kawishiwi," Toftey said without hesitation.

Setty thought for a moment, looking out the window of the plane. You've got a rendezvous with destiny, he thought. You wouldn't want to be late.

He turned to Hansen and said, "Let's head to Kawishiwi."

Hansen turned the plane slightly, asking Toftey, "Mark, you thinking Gabi, Little Sag, Makwa, Malberg, down that way?"

"That would be my guess," said the wilderness ranger. "Little Sag is where they would decide on Baker or Kawishiwi. They were hauling ass. I expect they could be at Kawishiwi already."

"Let's go see, Mr. Hansen," said Setty. "Kick this little bird in the ass."

FIFTY-ONE

Boundary Waters Canoe Area Wilderness, Minnesota
May, 2002
Thursday, 4:20 PM

The two men worked quickly, carrying the heavy
packs to the van. While Anwar pulled the canoes into the
woods, Asad dragged Saad's body to the side of the road
and rolled it into the ditch. Asad spit on the man.

"Peasant," he said.

"Now!" Anwar was already in the van, its engine
running, sitting behind the wheel.

Asad didn't like it, but the sound of the airplane was
growing nearer and there was no time to argue. He
jumped into the passenger seat and slammed the door.
Anwar put the truck in gear and they sped down the
narrow road.

Neither man knew where they were. They had in
essence been taken from their homes, blindfolded, and
dropped into the middle of a place so foreign that it may
as well have been on another planet. The language, though
they could understand and speak it, was not their own.
The countryside, its vegetation and animals, insects, were
all exotic and unfamiliar. There were no lakes, no forests,
no waterfowl, no moose, no canoes in their homeland.
Now they had to drive to a city they had never seen.

Anwar had his GPS unit sitting on the dashboard,
where it was acquiring signals from up to twelve orbiting
satellites out of a constellation of twenty-four circling the
globe. The unit's software would triangulate their position
and orient them on visible maps according to the simple

data it received from the satellites, which consisted of strings of numbers representing degrees, minutes and seconds of longitude, latitude and time in a configuration the unit could understand. Preset waypoints, specific positions defined as longitude and latitude, had been preloaded before the mission and now led them out of the wilderness and ultimately onto a major interstate highway, then to their final destination. The unit showed them every turn and every significant landmark. The only thing that could defeat them now was their own carelessness.

"Can you see the plane?" Anwar asked, showing no hint of their recent enmity

Asad opened his window and stuck his head out, looking behind the van and into the sky. The lake would soon be out of sight. There was nothing in the darkening sky. Allah was still with them, it appeared.

"There is nothing there," Asad said, back inside the van. "Soon it will be dark and we will simply be another car on a U.S. freeway, driving to the city."

Anwar handed the GPS to Asad. "Please," he said, "tell me when to turn."

Asad took the device and watched the map change along with their position.

"Soon you will turn right onto Lake County Highway Seven. This will take us to state highway 61, the road that leads us to Duluth and the interstate highway."

Anwar fought the urge to drive as fast as he could. They had to avoid stupid mistakes. There had been enough of those already. He saw the sign for highway seven and turned right. He glanced over at his remaining teammate.

"Tell me something," he said.

Asad looked over at the man. "Of course."

"Why are you here, on this mission?"

Asad considered this question carefully. It was easy to forget that nothing he said now had any consequence, now that he was heading to his death. Only this man and Allah would know what he said. And if he was not prepared to die, then perhaps God had failed. There should be no question in his mind when the moment arrived.

"I was asked to lead this mission, by the Sheik," he said. "I have proven myself, I have done great things, and this was my idea. I was destined to lead it."

"And yet," Anwar said, "you sabotage it at every turn. The mission called for four men. We are now two. You are the reason for this discrepancy. You have taken it into your hands to keep two men from paradise. Only God can change men's destiny."

"Then there is nothing to worry about, is there?" Asad asked. "Your hypocrisy exhausts me. You accuse me of changing the course of a man's life then contend that only God may do so. I believe it was their stupidity that killed them, their incompetence. Better their weaknesses were discovered now, before they could jeopardize the mission."

"How close are you to killing me?" Anwar asked.

Asad looked out the windshield of the van and into the darkening woods. "I was a man of privilege, like the Sheik. I am not ashamed of that. Allah has put me here to do as he wishes. I am comfortable with what I've done and what lies before me."

"You avoid my question," said Anwar.

Asad looked at him, his green eyes intense, and flashed an engaging, effortless smile.

"Perhaps, my friend, you should not press me to answer it? You know as well as I do that our mission can be accomplished by one man. One explosion is as powerful as ten in this place. We are killing their strutting arrogance, their dreams of world domination, their crusade. You and I can do that."

Asad looked out the window at the passing trees. He could no longer distinguish individual tree trunks in the growing darkness.

"Or I can do it alone."

Suddenly, the van jerked several times and then the engine almost died. It would be disaster if they ended up stuck on the side of the road, asking the next passerby for a ride. Anwar pulled over to the side of the road.

"There is something wrong with the engine." He looked at the big man helplessly. "I don't know what to do. Do you know anything about engines?"

Asad opened the passenger side door and stepped out. "Open the hood," he ordered. Anwar did as he was told and then got out of the van. Asad noted that the engine now seemed to be running just fine. The ignorant ass probably did it himself. Asad paused. A disturbing thought was there, but it was amorphous. He struggled to grasp it. It was important. He reached underneath the hood to flip the safety catch. Then he felt something hit him in the back of the head and saw a splash of red streak across the front of the van. The realization that it was his brains coincided perfectly with his death.

FIFTY-TWO

Billy Cosgrove figured he'd poisoned himself with his own cooking. Sometime before dawn he'd awoken with incredible nausea, barely making it outside the tent before puking his guts out. To his great disappointment, the sickness continued along with the violent heaving. Libby's gonna love this, he thought as he pushed the loaded canoe off the rocks and away from his campsite. He had caught a few nice lake trout the night before and kept one for dinner. In his pack he'd brought his famous fish breading mixture—a combination of homemade cracker crumbs, flour, salt and pepper they used at the lodge, a large potato and a bottle of squeeze margarine. After filleting the fish, Billy dropped it into a plastic bag with the mixture. He would have dipped it in milk first had he been at the lodge, and shook it until the damp fillet was completely coated. Before cooking the fish, he cut the potato into small squares and fried them with a squirt of margarine and a little salt and pepper over his single-burner propane camp stove. About twenty minutes later he added the fish to the pan. He couldn't imagine what could have made him this ill. Unless maybe the damn margarine was bad.

He had a long trip ahead of him. He didn't relish the thought of portaging and paddling while sicker than a dog, but whatever it was, it seemed to be getting worse. If it was botulism, alone in the wilderness was not a good place to be. As he paddled he noticed a stinging pain in his hands, as if he were getting blisters. Billy Cosgrove's hands were like leather vise grips. After years of work in the boat livery and as a mechanic, plumber, electrician, logger, a blister was the last thing he expected on an overnight canoe trip. He looked at his hands and a red rash covered them. He put down the paddle and looked at his palms. They were an angry red, as though they had been burned.

"What the hell?" he said.

Grabbing the paddle, he continued stroking, picking up the pace, trying to ignore the pain. He concentrated as best he could on the far shoreline. There was a large white pine leaning over the portage. It was a great landmark for folks who didn't know the area. In his years as a guide and lodge owner in this country he had helped hundreds of people experience wilderness. In that time nobody had ever been seriously hurt on his watch, and most, by far, had left the woods knowing more about themselves and their connection to nature. He treated this place with the same common sense and respect you'd give any dangerous, indifferent thing you fall in love with. He felt it was his job to provide a dose of reality for those well-meaning folks who arrived for their BW trip all dressed up and accessorized like they were going out on a date, ready to share a bottle of fine wine and an evening of witty conversation. But when their date shows up, they find a four hundred pound gorilla at the door, all full of raging storms, torturous parasites and physical and mental trials. As he liked to say, "They want to understand and be held. All he wants to do is fuck em and forget em."

After several portages and a few miles of paddling, Billy was certainly feeling fucked. He sat and rested a moment at the portage into Little Rush Lake. His body was weak and the last few bouts of heaving left spots of blood in the water. His palms had blistered and were filling with fluid. They would tear soon, he could tell. And now, with about three miles of paddling and two portages ahead of him, one nearly a mile long, he had begun to cough. There was blood in that too. It was like he was falling apart by the minute. All he could do was keep moving. He knew Libby would be worried if he didn't get back when she expected him. The thought of her helped him to pick up the canoe once more, lift it gingerly onto his shoulders and keep walking.

FIFTY-THREE

Cook County Airport, Grand Marais, Minnesota
May, 2002
Thursday, Noon

Fritz Anderson sat in the small blue arrival/departures building at the Grand Marais airport, listening to the occasional broadcast from Dale Arndt, a local entrepreneur who gave plane rides in his 1963 bright yellow DeHavilland Beaver, and reading through the delinquent tax notices in the Cook County paper. Anderson always thought Arndt was uppity. He wasn't a local, not really. He showed up with money enough to retire 25 years ago. Apparently he had flown single-engine reconnaissance planes in the Navy and then crop dusters in southern Minnesota. "Farm country," Fritz would say, in a disparaging tone; disdainful of its checkerboard-flat patchwork of tilled 40-acre squares stretching for hundreds of monotonous miles. "Anything south of Duluth," he often said, "is Iowa." He didn't think much of the "little planes" in which Arndt had gained his proficiency. Anderson flew C130 Spectre gunships in Viet Nam – 9 months "in the shit," flying around 40 **close air support missions** before Nixon called it quits. At about 80 tons with four 5,000hp Allie turboprops it looked like a flying whale and handled like one, at least that was how he imagined a flying whale would handle. When he spoke of Arndt at the VFW, he would say, "While that pig farmer was killin' bugs, I was killin' gooks." There was no proof that Arndt had ever farmed, but that was not important to Fritz's story.

The little airport facility sat almost eighteen hundred feet above sea level, straight north of Grand Marais, near Devil's Track Lake. The airspace around Grand Marais was uncontrolled, so no tower oversaw the comings and goings of the mostly small planes crossing its skies. The mile and a quarter runway oriented east-west. Five buildings comprised the airport facility: two hangars, two for housing maintenance equipment and the glass-fronted terminal in which Fritz now sat. To the east lay a motley collection of hangers, maybe a dozen metal buildings of various design and level of investment. Many were in rusting disrepair, squatting like some forgotten Cannery Row along a narrow taxiway carved out of the forest

Fritz always recognized a few names in the paper. It was good fodder for gossip at the VFW. Tonight there was a pool tournament and he expected to be there until they closed the doors and kicked him out. He would then stagger to his truck, concentrate mightily on keeping it out of the ditches and on his half of the road, park in his driveway and sleep there until morning. He was not allowed inside drunk. It was either that, his wife had said, or never come inside again, ever. It seemed to him a fair compromise. Suddenly the radio crackled to life. Fully expecting to hear Arndt announcing "Beaver Whisky Tango Zebra 785 on approach," Fritz jumped when an unfamiliar voice came through the speaker.

"USAF Chinook seven-niner, Zulu, approaching from the southwest at 3,800 beginning descent for landing."

Fritz went out the door and looked to the southwest. He couldn't see anything in the bright sunlight, but he sure enough knew the growing deep death-rattle of a CH-47's dual rotors cutting the air. The sound never failed to send a shiver down his spine. He fully expected to hear a fusillade of .50 cal music grace his ears any second. Instead, the door was still closing behind him when he heard another broadcast.

"USAF Chinook thirteen-eight, Tango, approaching from the southwest at 4,000 feet, beginning descent for landing."

And another.

"USAF Chinook niner-four, Whiskey, approaching from the southwest at 3,200 beginning descent for landing."

What the hell? Then he heard Arndt and the panic in the voice made him smile.

"Uh, B…B…Beaver Whiskey T…Tango…uh…shit! Fritz? Fritz, there's choppers everywhere. EVERYWHERE! It looks like…like…an invasion!"

Anderson did not answer, but took note of the stuttering, which he had never heard before, with amusement. He would save that little gem for the VFW tonight. Back outside the building he heard what was now the thundering staccato chop of big helicopters. The large windows of the terminal were vibrating. They came out of the sun and all he could think of is Apocalypse Now and Robert Duval commanding his "air calv" into battle, blasting Wagner's "Ride of the Valkyries" from stadium speakers mounted on the struts of his choppers. Fritz could see three, big, double-prop Chinooks dropping out of the sky toward the runway. Prop wash from the big blades blew his hair back and swept away anything not nailed down. He felt sand stinging his face and hitting his glasses. They landed along the length of the runway. Spaced equally apart and parked diagonally, they took up almost the entire strip of concrete.

"Jesus!"

No sooner had the helicopters hit the ground than the side doors slid open and people began emerging from the aircraft. Dozens of mostly men hopped from each craft, all similarly dressed in dark suits, white shirts and sunglasses. Behind them the thick coniferous forest provided an incongruous backdrop. From a distance they looked like clones of the first man to disembark. Fritz was not prepared for what he was seeing. He had worked at the airport for the past 12 years and there had been very few things sufficiently out of the ordinary to garner more than ten minutes' discussion at the VFW. This would provide fodder for years.

As the well-dressed men walked briskly toward him, Fritz found himself backing up. The first one to reach him extended a hand. Fritz saw a tiny reflection of himself in the man's dark sunglasses. The man spoke.

"Good morning, Mr. Anderson."

FIFTY-FOUR

Anwar Masoud had nothing with which to wipe the blood, brain and skull fragments from the hood and windshield of the van. He removed the fleece jacket from Asad's lifeless body and used it to clean up the mess. Then he dragged the man off the road and into the woods. He laid him face up so the scavengers would have easy access to the arrogant, swaggering countenance Anwar had come to loathe these last few days. He returned to the van, which had no mechanical difficulties, and drove off toward highway 61.

I should have acted sooner, he thought. It had been clear, after Kadir's death, that the man was a hindrance. Now it was up to him alone to do this thing. It was a scenario they had each trained for, but it made the outcome less assured. With only one man detonating a device he wondered if enough material could be dispersed to ensure the contamination of the entire building. That was the key. He had to render the structure unusable. Stationing a man on each level had been the way to ensure that. Now it would be much more difficult. He would have to improvise.

As he drove, Anwar prayed. For the first time in this mission, he felt loneliness. He feared it was a harbinger of doubt and he needed Allah's strength and the Prophet's resolve to dispel it. He thought of his sons in Yemen. His wife was a strong woman and would take care of them.

Their future was assured. The Sheik had given his word. They would grow up holy and, with Allah's grace, would find a righteous path as he had. They would learn by his example. They would live to see a world after Jihad when Muslims had become one united people under God, living according to the teachings of the Prophet. Finally, the **dream** would be realized. Nothing would prevent him from making his contribution to that future. His reward for unwavering faith was an eternity of such indescribable beauty and pleasure that he was truly eager to effect his own demise. He pressed down on the accelerator and the van sped south, a cloud of reddish dust rising behind him. For a fleeting moment, the sight filling his mirrors reminded him of home and made him smile. Tomorrow would surely be a great day.

FIFTY-FIVE

Boundary Waters Canoe Area Wilderness, Minnesota
May, 2002
Thursday, 5:20

Hansen banked the Cessna over the Kawishiwi landing and saw nothing, at first. Setty had already relayed Toftey's fantastic story to Washington, which would coordinate with local authorities and FBI agents now on the ground in Grand Marais. Setty would have paid to see those field agents heading into the woods in canoes. Not even investigating federal agents could compromise the wilderness rules with motorboats. Local businesses would do well. They were about to have sixty or so tourists in their town who brought no food and no appropriate clothing. Terrorists: bust for the nation, boon for the local economy.

"There, what the hell is that?" Hansen was pointing at the ground.

"It's a body," said Setty. "Land."

———————————

"Was this one of the guys?" Setty asked Toftey, once they were on the ground. They were looking at what was left of a man's face. It had been stomped by a large boot. The print was clearly visible as an angry blue bruise on what was left of the left cheek.

"I'd say yes, judging by the clothing."

Toftey walked around the body to get a different perspective.

"Kind of hard to tell which one," he said.

"His face is hamburger. One of them was a bit older and had a pretty wicked scar on his face. I think this is him."

Brian got down next to the mangled body. He could see gravel and dirt driven into the skin, along with tire marks. He had been run over and beaten. Setty searched his pockets but found nothing.

"Over here," said Hansen.

He followed drag marks from the shore into the woods and found their canoes. They left nothing else.

"So," said Setty, "they're down to two, unless someone picked them up here."

Setty bent over and put his hand on the man's neck.

Hansen watched him and said, "You don't think he's still alive, do you? Look at him."

"No," Setty answered. "But he's still warm. This just happened twenty or thirty minutes ago." He looked at Hansen, then Toftey.

"Come on, we have to get back in that plane. They don't have much of a jump on us."

"Sorry, we can't," said Hansen. "I have just enough fuel to get back, maybe. You better call it in and let somebody else get a bird in the air. At least until I get some fuel. I'm not going to risk ditching this thing."

Setty dialed Washington once again.

FIFTY-SIX

After she picked up her rental car, Beth received vague directions to the Mall of America from an infuriatingly slow and distracted hotel desk clerk with a barbell piercing hanging from her nose, which swung back and forth slightly as she spoke. Beth found it difficult not to stare at the silver thing, which, she assumed, was the whole point. She didn't approve of exhibitionism, whether it was tattoos or piercings or outrageous clothing. It all seemed so pathetic, to feel that you have to define yourself by advertising or mutilating your body. It just perpetuated that destructive cultural fallacy that the outside was what really mattered—that what was inside was so weak and fragile, it could not stand on its own.

The Mall of America was a monument to exhibitionism and obviousness, a tribute to the strength and power of the American capitalist ideal. Its hulking mass squatted on **sixty** acres of Twin Cities suburbia, casting a six-story shadow over thirteen thousand parking spaces servicing a constant stream of automobiles and buses. Inside, throngs of shoppers and sightseers from every country in the world—though by far the bulk were from Canada, Japan and Europe—wandered four levels with **two and a half million** square feet of retail space and a **seven-acre** amusement park sitting in the center of it all, like some giant whirring, flashing, undulating mechanical heart spreading an aura of energy and vitality throughout the cavernous structure.

Beth found the place easily—it was virtually impossible to miss. She entered the rambling labyrinth of parking ramps and settled on the Alligator lot near the west entrance. She entered the building behind a family with a double stroller and a toddler in tow. She held the door for them as they struggled with the unwieldy contraption. There was architectural brilliance in the design of the place. As soon as she was inside the door she felt compelled to move forward by the promise of open space and movement ahead.

On the way in or out visitors passed eating establishments, positioned conveniently near the entrances to catch weary shoppers on their way out, or hungry ones looking to fuel up before wandering the marketing gauntlet that lay ahead. Walking further she passed a set of elevators and came to a crossroads with wide hallways, bustling with people, stretching left and right, circling the mall as the main pedestrian thoroughfares. Past long escalators carrying shoppers from one level to the next, Beth came to a landing that looked out over "Camp Snoopy," the amusement park named after Minnesota native Charles Schulz's famous cartoon dog. Before her, beneath a giant dome of metal and glass, two crowded roller coasters twisted and turned, while people-filled log cars emerged from a mountain and dropped with a waterfall into the river below. A giant axe with seats on top, at the handle, swung like a pendulum in greater and greater arcs to the screaming delight of its riders. Below that were dozens of other rides and carnival games. Adults and children swarmed the various attractions like ants at a picnic.

"Oh my God," Beth said quietly to herself as the enormity of the situation washed over her in cold waves.

Before she had left D.C., Chief Williams, after the briefing, asked her to meet him in his office. When his secretary led Beth into his office she was surprised to see him in conference with two other men. She recognized them as Colonel Kimball and General Westguard. All three men stood as she entered, shook her hand and sat down after her. Though they were welcoming, with no hint of patronizing or condescension, it was hard not to feel like a little girl at the adult's table, her feet swinging underneath. Though it was exciting, sitting with the big people usually meant a bowl of Brussels sprouts was on its way...and not a napkin or family dog in sight.

"Thanks for coming, Beth," said the chief. "We were just talking after the briefing and we agreed there were a few details you should know before you head up to Minnesota. As you walk into that mall, you need to be thinking like these guys. You have to keep their objectives in mind. Once you do that, you can get ahead of them. As it stands, we've got a lot of catching up to do." He looked over to the general to hand off the conversation.

Westguard fixed his deep blue eyes on hers. He smiled, but there was a sober determination in his face she hadn't noticed before, his game face, she supposed.

"The stuff they carry probably came from the Location C storage facility at al-Tawaitha," Westguard said. "I'm sure you know that was Saddam's largest nuclear research facility."

"Yes," she said. "It's near Bagdad."

"Correct," he said in his subtle Texas drawl. She thought he sounded a bit like the actor Sam Elliot.

"When we rolled into town, we didn't get over there to secure that place for...well, for a long time. Too damn long. We dropped the ball, big time. People were runnin' in and outta that place for weeks, takin' anything they thought they could use or sell. There was a lot of bad stuff in there. They dumped pounds of yellow cake on the ground just to use the barrels for drinking water. Ignorant bastards. That raw uranium isn't the most deadly stuff but it sure as hell ain't one of the four food groups. Regardless, we accounted for most all of that. Unfortunately, there were about four hundred radioactive sources that remain unaccounted for. We know there was a lot of cesium in there. And that's all gone."

"Didn't the Soviets have a lot of cesium as well?" Beth asked, trying not to let the previous disturbing revelation seize her up. She felt her mouth growing dry.

"Yes," said the general. "They used it for irradiating seeds, trying to improve yields I think. It certainly could have come from there. Hell, it could have come from here, for all I know. It just seems more likely this stuff came from Location C, given the proximity of our enemies in the Middle East to Iraq and the security problems inherent in war. It's a hell of a lot cheaper to steal it or buy it from some poor camel rancher than buy it from a black market enterprise in republics of the former Soviet Union. There's a lot more sympathy for OBL in Iraq these days than in the Commonwealth of Independent States." Apparently finished, Westguard turned to Kimball expectantly.

There was something very dark about Kimball, Beth observed. He emanated cold malice, but she couldn't find visible evidence supporting that conclusion. It was just a feeling. It made her think of cancer in remission. Loosed, she believed, the man could render black a countryside without the distraction of inner conflict.

"Mr. al-Takar shared with me, in great detail, nuances of the plot I left out of my briefing earlier," he said in his smooth, deep voice. "I did not believe them relevant for that audience. But nuance is exactly what you need, Agent Adams. It is important to realize that although the 9-11 attack was dramatic and successful beyond their wildest dreams, it is over. Though the ripples are still hitting the shore, we have moved on, to our credit, to our strength. The towers are gone and we will build over their corpses. This is an insult to Bin Laden. He realizes that he has simply raised the bar for shock value. He believes that now he must place in our midst a constant reminder of the pain we have inflicted on his part of the world, his religion. A permanent tribute to Jihad to eclipse all we hold dear, our freedom, our wealth, our religion, our way of life." Kimball paused a moment, as though giving his audience time to catch up.

"When Chernobyl melted down," he continued, "the Russians encased it in concrete. Hundreds of thousands of tons of concrete were poured over it from helicopters above. It's still sitting there, most likely the burning graphite core still smolders in its tomb. More concrete will need to be added, because concrete crumbles after years of exposure to weather and the core will be radioactive for hundreds of years."

Kimball looked at the faces across from him. There was no expression on his gaunt face as his brown eyes swept across theirs.

"Blocks of Goiaina, Brazil lie beneath their own concrete tomb because two hundred and fifty-five people walked those streets with cesium on their hands and feet."

"This will be a monolith rising hundreds of feet above the suburban Midwest—Middle America, casting a shadow across everything we do from that day forward, far darker than the missing towers. That is their goal, their mission. And they are well on their way to accomplishing it."

FBI agent Beth Adams did not want to be at the big person's table any longer. The Brussels sprouts were here and she wouldn't be leaving until she'd eaten every last one.

FIFTY-SEVEN

Silver Bay, Minnesota, May, 2002
Thursday, 6:00 PM

Anwar drove the white van into the little mining town of Silver Bay, on the north shore of Lake Superior. He drove into the village's neighborhoods, cruising for an opportunity. One presented itself almost immediately. It was almost dark when he parked on a quiet street and walked uphill to a house that was isolated by a thick stand of low cedars on either side. Across from the house was a large garage or storage building with a fenced-in yard. It was important he not be seen.

He chose this house for those reasons and because there was a garage where he would hide the van and inside the garage, which had been open, he had seen a single car. It was unlikely there were more than two people in the house. He was confident he could overcome two people without a weapon. He had trained for years in the camps of Afghanistan. Extensive teaching in advanced military tactics wrapped in fanatical Islamic doctrine had prepared him for virtually any eventuality. Al-Qaeda knew guns and God were the most lethal combination and they offered both in copious amounts.

Anwar stepped up to the door and knocked. Strangers use the doorbell, he knew, friends knock. He felt no hesitation, no fear, no doubt that what he was doing was right. Allah was strong within him and he had been praying aloud as he drove southwest on highway 61, "Those who reject Faith, Allah will not forgive them nor guide them to any path except the way to Hell, to dwell therein forever." He prayed as he passed the infidels' monuments to their false beliefs, their crosses and their flags. He would soon raise a new monument to the one true God, Allah be praised, and it would stand as a constant reminder of Allah's greatness and power.

The moment the handle turned, Anwar kicked the door open and sent an old woman flying backwards. She fell on the floor and lay there moaning. He walked in quickly, his gaze flying around the house, looking for resistance. A noise down a hall, to his left. He ran toward it and met an old man walking out of a room into the hallway. He kicked the fragile, white-haired man in the groin and watched him crumble to the carpet. Then he drove his foot into the man's side and heard ribs crack.

Anwar quickly searched the bedroom for a telephone. There was none. He left the man in the dark hallway gasping for breath and went to find the kitchen. Just outside the kitchen was a round dining table on which sat the woman's purse. He dumped the contents on the table and a set of keys tumbled out. He verified there was a car key attached, and then went into the kitchen where he opened drawers until he found a sharp knife. Returning to the elderly couple writhing in pain on the floor of their home, the holy warrior, in the name of Allah, slit their throats as easily as he would sacrifice a goat after the Hajj, the annual pilgrimage to Mecca. It seemed fitting, their blood flowing over his hands as he neared the end of his own final pilgrimage to join Allah. There would be many more sacrifices before his journey was over.

FIFTY-EIGHT

Cook County Hospital, Grand Marais, Minnesota
May, 2002
Friday, 2:40 PM

Libby Cosgrove was inconsolable. Hansen held her as she wept, anger and frustration sweeping through him in waves. They sat in the Cook County Hospital waiting room, decorated to feel like home with crafty nick-knacks, calico-covered pillows with lacy fringe that matched the fringe on the couch and lounge chair. Hansen hated it all. How could anybody think that a few decorations could ease the pain and suffering found in this place? He'd only ever lost people in hospitals. And now he was here once again, with the two most important people remaining in his life, watching them suffer, helpless as always.

A TV hung suspended in one corner, tuned to a twenty-four hour news show, flashing incessantly, muted but still demanding attention. Nothing there about what was going on here in the wilderness of northern Minnesota. Terrorism on U.S. soil had already claimed three in the last couple of days—two dead and one lying in a hospital bed, his body disintegrating before their eyes. He longed for an outlet for his anger—just one chance to take these guys down hard.

As they were flying back to Gunflint Lake to refuel and drop off Toftey, who needed a long hot shower and sleep, Hansen had been summoned over the radio.

"Garrett," Mary Silvan, another border patrol officer, sounded afraid, though it may have been the scratchy quality of the signal.

"Billy Cosgrove is in the hospital. He got hurt somehow…out in the woods. Might be food poisoning. He's really sick. Libby asked you to meet her at the hospital as soon as you get back. Garrett?" Mary's crackly voice added, "Libby said Billy was saying something about drug smugglers and blue cocaine. He wanted you to know."

It was then that Setty asked if he could drive Hansen into town. If this wasn't related, it was quite a coincidence. Hansen gladly agreed. He was too worried and distracted to make the trip safely. Now, Hansen looked out into the hall and saw Setty in conference with the doctor who had correctly diagnosed Billy's condition as radiation sickness, though he had a hard time believing his own diagnosis. He immediately contacted Miller Dwan Hospital and Burn Center in Duluth to confirm his diagnosis and get a helicopter for transport. There was nothing they could do for him in Grand Marais. Hansen saw the doctor walk away and Setty motioned for Hansen to join him.

"Libby, hon, I need to go out for a sec. Drink some of that coffee. I'll be back."

He looked into her teary red-rimmed eyes and bent down to kiss her forehead then walked out, barely holding back his own tears. "What's he say?" he asked Setty, leading him away from the waiting room and Libby's earshot.

"Well, of course they didn't know what kind of radiation they were dealing with until now, so it's a good thing we came in when we did. They have to administer Prussian Blue—Ferric ferrocyanide, an iron compound, as soon as possible. It binds with the cesium so the radioactivity can be excreted. The key is to get it out before moves from the blood into his tissues. He's already getting antibiotics to fight infection. They'll probably give him a transfusion when he gets to Duluth to help keep him from hemorrhaging."

"Why would he be hemorrhaging?" asked Hansen.

"The radiation is attacking his blood cells. They'll have trouble clotting unless he gets new platelets," Setty told him. Brian could see Hansen was struggling.

"Look, Garrett, why don't you stay here with her. Looks like she could use you. I have to get this info to Washington and then check in with the agents that came in today."

Hansen looked at him, trying to suppress his growing rage.

"I know we've had our differences and I haven't exactly added a lot of value to all this so far, but don't cut me out now. I can't sit around with my thumb up my ass while you're out there looking for these worthless bastards. I have to do something useful, Setty."

Brian Setty considered this, staring down at his shoes.

"After they transport your friend, come down to the Harbor Inn. That's where the Bureau's set up shop."

"I thought they were still closed for the season," said Hansen.

"Let's just say we convinced them to open early."

FIFTY-NINE

Grand Marais, Minnesota
May, 2002
Thursday, 6:40 PM

"Hey! Good to hear from you, Agent Adams."

Setty slumped in a recliner in his second-floor room at the Harbor Inn, overlooking the smooth Grand Marais harbor, with its picturesque break-walls and flashing lighthouse. Between the concrete barriers, Lake Superior's vast steely blue plain stretched unbroken to the horizon, uncharacteristically placid, but menacing, even in repose. It was a rare reprieve for the FBI agent, who had been trying to coordinate the activities of the throng of field agents milling around the Harbor Inn. In his lap lay a legal pad and a pen. There was an official reason for the call, but that didn't make it any less pleasant to hear Agent Adams' voice.

"Agent Setty, I think you called me?"

"Always the analyst! Anyway, I thought you might want an update. Actually, I want to give you an update because it helps me put it all together."

"I would love an update. Your boss told me I was to 'keep their objectives in mind' in order to get ahead of them. I still feel like I'm playing catch-up."

"Okay, here's what I've got so far, the Reader's Digest version. The principals thus far include three dead terrorists, one very lucky U.S. Wilderness ranger, one very radioactive local citizen. How's that for a hook?"

"I'm hooked," she said. "You're telling me you've killed three members of the cell?"

"Nope, they killed each other."

"Trouble in paradise?"

"Trouble getting there, certainly," he said. "Best I can tell, the first one was just unlucky. He was injured by a bear and they couldn't afford the delay."

"Sorry, did you say a bear?" Beth asked.

"Yeah," he said. "A big black bear."

"Okay, I won't ask all the obvious questions. Go on."

"The next two are tougher to figure. I think personalities within the cell contributed to some sort of implosion. The next guy was run over by their escape vehicle, then stomped on a few times for good measure. The third was found a ways down the road in the woods shot in the back of the head at close range. So unless he has local manpower, it's down to one guy heading for the target."

"Somebody left that vehicle sitting there," she said. "Isn't it possible somebody joined them? Maybe there was another team in the woods?"

"Until we hear something concrete to the contrary, I have to assume one team. If the OGA had a source who compromised the mission to this extent, they would have heard the whole story. Unless, of course, the source left the interview."

It took Beth a moment to interpret the field agent jargon. OGA, or "Other Government Agency" was a term she had heard field agents use when referring to the CIA.

"What makes you think a deep-cover CIA operative would tell us everything he knew?" she asked. "Especially if the guy died during questioning?" Colonel Kimball's foreboding visage stalked through her memory, leaving her chilled. Her certainly seemed capable of an overzealous interrogation.

"This seems more like a probe to me," said Setty. "I think they're sending a small team to see how easy it is to come in through an unprotected border. Besides, we don't have enough time to deal with another cell. We know this guy's real and where he's going. We have to concentrate on that right now."

"You're right," she said, temporarily dropping the notion of another cell. "You said there were other principals?"

"Yes," he said, moving the phone to his other ear. "A forest ranger came across them in the wilderness a couple days ago and he's been running through the woods ever since. We picked him up today. He said they tried to kill him. He was just lucky they didn't want the attention of a gunshot."

"How did someone get exposed?" Beth asked.

Setty answered, "That isn't completely clear either, and unfortunately the guy's too sick to communicate. He said something about drug smugglers on the trail and finding 'blue cocaine.' My guess is he came across one of their packs or they dropped one of the balloons and he picked it up. He must have got it on his hands because the skin of his palms is sloughing off. He's on a helicopter to a burn center as we speak."

"Great," said Beth. "This is going to be in the papers by tomorrow."

"We still control most of the details…"

"I beg to differ, Agent Setty," she said. "Since when does a little thing like a lack of facts stop a news story?"

"True," he agreed. "Bottom line, with all this stuff we know, we still don't know the most important thing."

"Let me guess," she said. "Where he is right now? Or, maybe, where they are?"

"Agent Adams...," he said in a warning tone.

"Okay," Beth said. "I'm backing off. Promise!"

"We've got birds in the air with infrared, but we don't exactly know what we're looking for. Forensic guys cast the tracks at the canoe landing and their best guess is a full-sized SUV of some kind, or a van. Since that's about all people drive up here, it doesn't help us much. We figure he has to be on state highway 61, but he'll be hitting Duluth soon and there he'll get on Interstate 35, heading south to the mall."

"Have you ever seen this place?" she asked. "The Mall of America, I mean?"

"No, I'm not much for shopping centers, especially gigantic ones."

"Well, it's a security nightmare. Constant activity, noise, movement, an international demographic. Identification of a subject is going to be incredibly difficult. It really is going to be a needle in a haystack."

Setty said, "Sorry, but I've gotta get back to the troops. If you want my advice, take the chief's advice. Finding this guy before he gets to the mall is going to be virtually impossible. The only advantage we have is that we know where he's heading. We'll have agents at every entrance. Anyone looking the slightest bit odd will be detained, with prejudice. We'll deal with the fallout."

"No pun intended," she said humorlessly.

"Yeah," Setty chuckled, equally mirthless. "You have to get to where he's going before he does. That's the only chance we've got. Get inside his head. He's one guy now. He has to make up for three missing soldiers. What can he do to quadruple his impact? Figure that out, agent Adams, and that's where we'll be."

"You coming down here?" she asked, immediately afraid the question sounded imploring.

"Yeah. I'm catching a chopper in about an hour. I'm bringing a friend. You'll like him—he's a neurotic with a gun. You're an analyst and he could certainly use some analysis."

"I think we're all going to need some analysis when this is all over."

SIXTY

The silver Buick Regal pulled into the Airport Marriott, stretching twenty two stories above Bloomington's suburban sprawl, just south of the Twin Cities, minutes from the Mall of America. In the van, Anwar Masoud had found forged Minnesota drivers' licenses and credit cards for each of the men on the mission. Those documents and the packs, he had transferred to the stolen car and left the van in the elderly couple's locked garage.

At the front desk he inquired about a room, an executive suite if possible. The young woman at the desk was rude and seemed suspicious of his request for a premium room, given his shabby appearance. She flaunted her body with mutilation and frivolous decoration. It was an effort to smile at her, with the silver ring in her nose and the flowers tattooed on her right hand. Her body and face should be covered not adorned to tempt and shock.

"You're in luck," she said. "There's an executive penthouse suite available."

"Allah be praised!" he thought to himself. He handed over his bogus identification and the credit card, which had been opened by a fictitious business based on a hefty checking account that of course no longer existed. The suite was $568 per night. He would carry his own bags, thank you.

Anwar wheeled the cart with the Duluth packs into the suite and closed and locked the heavy door. He removed his filthy boots and socks. He had several changes of clothing, but only one pair of footwear—waterproof leather hiking boots. He looked around the expansive room—such opulence, such waste, he observed. At the window he pulled aside the curtains and looked out over a large complex of parking ramps surrounding an enormous building. He suddenly realized he was looking at the mall. The sight of it – after all these miles, the trials he had endured, the sacrifice, the complete and willing loss of self – made his legs grow weak and quiver. It was enormous! The pictures and blueprints and diagrams he had studied for months before the mission did not prepare him for the scale of the structure laid out before him. He fought off a sudden, nauseating wave of doubt and turned from the window.

To his left, sunken into a platform at the corner of the room, beneath the large window, was a whirlpool bath. Anwar longed to be clean. He turned on the tap, adjusted the temperature so that steam rolled off the water, then plugged the drain, letting the tub fill while he undressed before the open window.

He saw his reflection in the glass. His body was lean and muscular. Training for this mission had been good for him. He had never felt better. He would be clean and fit for his journey tomorrow. Excitement and anticipation fluttered in his stomach. How long had he waited for this moment? It seemed like his entire life was an exercise, preparing him for this, his chance to share in Allah's glory. He had known the fleeting pleasures of his earthbound existence, but they were few and muted, tempered with the suffering and hopelessness he saw around him every day. He was now ready to live.

In the bathroom he found a clean robe hanging from the door along with a full complement of towels. He took the toiletries from the sink and brought them to the tub, now full of steaming water. The hot water was a shock to his body at first, but as he lowered himself into it, he felt the tension and exhaustion ebb from his body. He slid under the water and let the warmth envelop him, surfacing only when his lungs protested. He turned on the jets and closed his eyes, submitting entirely to the massage for several minutes, his mind empty of all thought and worry.

After bathing, thoroughly washing his body and hair, he rinsed in the shower, put on the white terry cloth robe and called for room service. He ordered a Caesar salad, a rare porterhouse with garlic mashed potatoes, asparagus and chocolate cheesecake. He also asked for two Diet Cokes, an extra-large glass of milk and a bunch of grapes. Green or red? It did not matter.

He hungrily devoured the salad, and then more slowly savored the steak and potatoes. The asparagus was cold and not sufficiently cooked. After finishing his meal, he took several sips of milk to lubricate his throat, then plucked five of the largest grapes and swallowed them whole, one at a time. They went down easily. He had mastered this skill only after extensive practice on larger and larger objects. The advantage of the powder-filled balloons was that they were malleable and conformed to the shape of the esophagus as they slid through to the stomach. Within hours his digestive juices and peristalsis would break open the balloons and kill him. Even if they did not open, sufficient radioactivity would eventually pass through the plastic barrier and enter his system quickly. But, Allah willing, he would be dead long before there was any danger of such a lingering death.

Anwar opened the Duluth packs and carefully removed all the items, spreading them out across the floor. The explosive vests were designed to spread more explosive thinly over the entire torso of the martyr, back and front, to be easily worn beneath a regular shirt. He laid these on top of one another. He would wear two of them, a detonator in each hand. That should substantially extend the range of the material. He was told to wear the vest inside-out, to direct the blast inward, opposite of the usual desired effect which was to blow external shrapnel outward, toward the intended victims. The intention here was to force the blast inward, like two opposing waves, forcing the contents of his body upward and out. The pattern of material dispersion would look somewhat like a mushroom, sending radioactive powder and organic material high into the air where it would fall to the ground in a wide circle, leaving an immediate perimeter of radioactivity perhaps one thousand feet across. Suspended particles of cesium powder would find their way through the ventilation system and would, within hours, have coated all air exchanges, rendering all breathable air in the structure deadly.

From another Duluth pack he removed the heavy lead-lined silver box that contained the silicone balloons filled with cesium-137. He did not open the box. He was told to limit contact with the balloons until immediately before implementing his mission. He set it on the floor, near the jackets. Next he removed three semiautomatic pistols and twelve boxes of ammunition. He also pulled out all four GPS units from the fanny packs and erased all the routes and waypoints from each. It was possible that someone might be able to reconstruct the data, but there was no sense making it easy.

Moving to the window, he stood and watched the GPS acquire a signal from one satellite, then another, and another until he had a reasonably accurate fix on his position. With that, he could now find the direction for prayer. Ironically, it lay in the direction of the giant temple to American pretension and extravagance which tomorrow he would destroy. On the carpet of the penthouse suite of the Airport Marriott hotel, Anwar Masoud, soldier for the Jihad, bent his head toward the Mall of America and prayed for courage, strength and a successful trip to paradise.

SIXTY-ONE

The Mall of America closed its doors at one o'clock in the morning, after the bars closed, but Beth Adams was given unlimited access all night. Security was ordered to let her into any room, maintenance tunnel, catwalk, amusement ride…she had total freedom to poke around.

It was 11:20 Friday night and she was looking out over the attractions of Camp Snoopy, now quiet and lifeless, its great mechanical heart resting before the Friday onslaught of shoppers. Tomorrow, through these doors would enter a cross-section of America: singles and families, young and old, lovers and the un-loved, rich and poor, winners and losers, the hopeful and the hateful, citizens and visitors, Republicans and Democrats, xenophobes and xenophiles. And, she thought, one man who sees the suffering of humanity as a tool to further his cause. How could a cause that punishes such a representative sample of the world's human beings, in all their various forms and beliefs, be anything other than a cause against mankind? Such a cause could not be less holy, less in league with the creator of man.

Diversity was at the very heart of our species. We have no control over it, she thought. We are all different and we struggle to belong. We struggle because we feel we can only belong to those like us. What if, she wondered, we strived to belong to groups of individuals different than ourselves? What if we were drawn to distinguishing characteristics and beliefs, embracing them instead of fearing them? Then we could stop fighting to make everyone like ourselves. Her father taught her to look for the similarities in things instead of concentrating on the differences. "People never hate each other because of the ways they are alike," she heard him say. She pulled the heart-shaped locket away from her breast and opened it to reveal the sunrise inside. "They learn to hate the differences," she finished quietly, quoting him in her own voice.

She snapped the locket closed and fingered its smooth gold exterior. The heart. The heart was the key. She had been looking at it all this time. It was there in front of her, larger than life.

"You have one shot in your gun. You want to kill the elephant. Where do you aim?"

She was on the phone with Setty once again. He was in the helicopter heading to the Twin Cities and could hardly hear her. Hansen was sitting next to him, asleep.

"The heart?"

"Exactly! You shoot it in the heart. That's Camp Snoopy—it's the heart of the mall. He has to get in there, up high, to make this work. If he can contaminate the amusement park, he destroys the whole building. He can either take a catwalk across the top of the dome, or he can use one of the rides. The catwalks are easy to secure. They can be locked. But the rides are open to anybody."

"Even terrorists," he said.

"It will be easier to watch the amusement park entrances," Beth said. "Then, if we have an agent assisting with each ride, we can be sure to find him."

"Then what do we do with him?"

"You kill him as quickly as possible," she said.

"But if he's got one hand on the button of the belt, we're still screwed."

"We have to somehow get both hands out in the open."

Beth pondered the issue for a moment, then said, "I have an idea that I think just might work. But we've got a lot of work to do before this place opens in the morning."

"Well, lay it on me and we'll get started."

SIXTY-TWO

Anwar woke feeling rested. He relieved himself, dressed, prayed. It was 6:05. He looked out at the mall. The weakness in his knees upon seeing it for the first time, was gone. Traffic already streamed along nearby highway 494. In the distance he could see planes taking off and landing at the Minneapolis-St. Paul International Airport. The sky looked threatening. Anwar saw that as a positive development—rain would mean more people inside the building. More contaminated people rushing out of the mall compounds the crisis for the Americans. In some ways, Anwar thought, it works almost like a biological agent. The cesium powder can be spread to other surfaces and substances, causing illness and panic far from the original site of the explosion. The world was about to change, once again. He would live on forever in the hearts and minds of Muslims everywhere. He could feel it, like the electricity in the approaching storm. Allah was with him today.

Over his skin, Anwar carefully donned the first explosive vest. He treated it gingerly, though the Composition 4, a mixture of a powerful explosive, malleable plastic compound, motor oil and a binder to stabilize the substance, would not detonate without sufficient percussive spark. The material had been molded into rectangular blocks and sewn into the fabric of the vest. The vest itself was actually a lifejacket with the foam flotation removed to make room for the C-4. Ignition would be provided by blasting caps inserted in each block and wired to a common detonator—a simple device fashioned from a butane fire lighter. Pushing the button sent a spark simultaneously to each blasting cap and ignited the C-4. Really, only one blasting cap had to work. A single explosion would instantaneously ignite all the nearby C-4 and the result would be the same.

He slipped the second vest over his head. A detonator hung on either side of him at his hips. Over the vests went a bulky, hooded Minnesota Golden Gopher Hockey sweatshirt. Below the logo were two large pockets. Inside each a hole had been cut to allow for the detonator to pass through. Hidden in the large pockets, they could be reached easily and quickly. With everything in place, he looked at himself one last time in the mirror. As he stood there, a cloud passed over his serene countenance. His brow knitted and he spoke quietly to the figure in the mirror. "Will I ever see you again, Anwar, my old friend?"

SIXTY-THREE

Brian Setty met Beth Adams at her hotel for breakfast. It was six o'clock, Friday morning. They had spent all night preparing for the next fourteen to sixteen hours, as had sixty other agents with the FBI, CIA, Minnesota BCA, Secret Service and one twitchy U.S. Border Patrol agent. There was nothing to do but wait. Setty wanted breakfast. Beth's stomach would not allow it, so she watched him eat eggs and drink coffee at a restaurant on the second floor.

"I don't know how you can do that," she said, shaking her head. "My gut's full of butterflies tied in knots."

"Ah, the lady likes her metaphors mixed." Brian signaled the waitress for a coffee refill. "Food settles my stomach—makes me happy. Those were my best memories of childhood, family meals. Me and my sisters would laugh so hard we could blow mashed potatoes out our noses."

"Your parents must have been proud," she said

"Yeah," he said, sounding far off. "I figure my folks had some kind of agreement about the dinner table. Like it was some sacred place the old man wasn't allowed to desecrate with booze. I never once saw a bottle on that table."

"Your father drank?" she asked.

Setty looked at her and smiled, his face an odd contortion of conflicting emotion. "No," he said, shaking his head slowly, "he worshipped."

Beth felt as if she were teetering at the edge of a precipice. She had kicked a pebble in and it echoed with a hollow sound far below. She backed away. He let her.

"I'm curious, why did you let this Hansen guy come, if you have doubts?" Beth asked.

"I couldn't say no," he told her, shrugging his shoulders and raising a fork full of ketchup-smothered scrambled eggs.

She shot him a puzzled look. "I find that really hard to believe."

"Look, in the past couple of days this guy almost lost his best friend and now a guy that might as well be his father may not live through the night, all because of this terrorist who's showing up today to bomb innocent civilians. Hansen's a veteran who's seen some tough duty...."

"Sorry, but all I hear are reasons he shouldn't be here."

"I know. I just feel like I owe him a chance. Plus, I feel guilty about hitting him."

"You hit him?" she asked, shocked. "Whatever for?"

"It's a long story," he said, "and we have very little time. Maybe we'll get a chance over dinner sometime."

"Perhaps," she said, "though I'm not sure I ever want to eat with you again."

She gestured toward his orange eggs. "That's about the grossest thing I've ever seen this early in the morning."

"What?" He looked down at his plate and used the egg on his fork to wipe up the last of the ketchup and popped it into his mouth.

"Bloody eggs. It's just wrong."

"You think this is bad," he said, "you should see me eat liver and peanut butter sandwiches."

She made a disgusted face, and then grew serious.

"There are so many ways this could go wrong, you know."

"I know," said Setty. "I stopped counting caveats somewhere around one hundred and forty."

"I don't mean this as an insult to anybody, but it's just hard to believe this is the best idea we can come up with."

"It is the best idea given the six or so hours we've had to develop it," he said, draining his orange juice glass.

"If you can tell me where he is right this moment, before he straps on the bomb and swallows some radioactive balloons, I'll go shoot the bastard right now. But since we're not going to find him until he's lethal, this is the only option."

Beth shook her head and said, "Can you imagine the panic in that place if the bomb does go off? People are going to die, crushed at the exits, trying to get out."

"By eight a.m. we'll have a Hazmat team and guards for every exit. They're waiting in trucks, out of sight until they're needed. If there is a release, we've got to get those people out of the building as quickly as possible, but we can't let any of them get away before they've been tested and decontaminated if necessary."

"Cross contamination?" Beth asked.

"Yep," Setty said. "If these people are contaminated, get home, make a few sandwiches for the kids, pet the dog, this problem gets a hell of a lot worse."

"Where can we take this many people?"

"The chief had the FAA order the local airport commission to clear out a maintenance hangar for us," said Setty. "Luckily we're close to the airport here, as well as the National Guard's 133rd Airlift Wing. They've got trucks on standby to haul people to the hangar."

Beth put her face in her hands and rubbed her eyes.

"I can't see the logic in any of this," she said. "They can't hope to change anything by coming over here, killing themselves, killing more of us. We're not going to leave Afghanistan or pull out of Kuwait or Qatar or Saudi Arabia or Morocco or Iraq or any other Islamic country. At least not until our interests change."

"I think they've already proven they can change things. Hell, in forty-five minutes they changed the world. They strengthened a right-wing movement in our country that led to an aggressive approach to defense, which in turn led to alienating our allies and the world. It led to a loss of personal freedoms while strengthening an evangelical Christian movement and building solidarity in the Muslim world. It led to idealistic polarization in our own country not seen since the Civil War." Setty paused, and then asked, "Do you go to church agent Adams?"

Odd question, she thought. "No, she said, "Not since my father died. He liked us to go as a family."

"You still went after you came out here?" he asked.

"I did find an old Lutheran church, out of habit I guess—respect for the family tradition. I went once after he died, you know, to see if the years I invested would pay out in a little comfort or at least piece of mind."

"Let me guess. You were disappointed."

"I sat there praying, really praying for God to show himself."

"Makes sense," he said. "A woman of science. Always looking for that empirical data."

"I wasn't looking to solve some faceless mystery. I wanted God to give me a reason for taking my dad."

"I'm sorry," he said, lowering his eyes. "I didn't mean to minimize it." She nodded and he continued.

"I was raised Catholic. Got a heavy dose of Sunday school, altar boy too. There's a lot to do as a Catholic: catechism, confirmations, a lot of weddings, lots of singing, get up, sit down, get up again, take communion, go to confession. You're too damn busy to ask why about anything. It's exhausting."

"But you still believe in God?" she asked.

"Of course I do. I'm not a regular churchgoer but I average at least once a month. Helps clear my mind."

"Confession, huh?"

"Not just confession," he said. "It's the sense of community. I think spirituality is a communal thing, meant to be shared. People are meant to worship together. It's the closest thing we have to a collective consciousness."

"Collective if you're a Catholic. Exclusionary if you're not."

"Kind of hard on us spiritual types, aren't you, Agent Adams?"

"Well look how these Muslim fanatics are celebrating their collective consciousness. Communing over a suicide bomb or a vial of anthrax. You could say they are the most committed people on the planet. I mean people who willingly end their lives to get into Heaven—kind of hard to argue the veracity of their belief."

"That's not a love of God. That's using God as a convenient excuse to further political ends. It's not religion they're practicing, it's an ideology."

"Maybe that's just the natural evolution of religion. Religion's legacy will be our destruction; it won't rest until all of us are in the other world."

"Oh come on now, that's pretty extreme," he said shaking his head.

"Think about it," she continued. "If you have a community of like-minded people who believe that not only is Heaven a better place, but that your destruction of this world and its people is a legitimate way to get you there then this world is doomed. This place is just becoming a battle ground for two sides trying to get out of the hell they've made here to their own version of paradise. Both sides believe you can kill in the name of God and still get there. Neither believes the other will be there when you show up. Which side is right?"

"So," he said, a note of irritation in his voice, "you think right or wrong is just a matter of perspective? It must be damn hard for you to go to work every day, with all that confusion in your head."

"I hear the "love it or leave it" in your voice."

"No. I just don't share your ambiguity. There is a God and he doesn't want his people killed in skyscrapers or trains or shopping malls by people claiming to be on his side."

"I don't have any hesitation about stopping these guys, agent Setty. I just think it's a good idea to remember that they think they're right just as much as you think you are."

They looked at each other for a moment in silence. Setty spoke first.

"Look, we've got a lot to do and not a hell of a lot of time to do it in. Let's agree to disagree and move on."

"Agreed," she said. "Let's catch this guy. We can always argue later."

———————————

After breakfast, Agents Adams and Setty walked into the west mall entrance, passing the small Bloomington cop shop on their right. The three-room facility contained several computer workstations, a radio base station for communicating with private mall security and the Bloomington Police Department's headquarters, a small secure holding facility and a break room/conference room. Now it served as the tactical operations center where frantic preparations were underway to secure the enormous building, without making it look suspicious. Blinds would be pulled before the doors opened to the public at eight o'clock, hiding the scrambling agents in the little room.

But even if they hadn't seen the busy cop shop, Adams and Setty would have felt the tension permeating the building's interior. FBI agents, state police and National Guard soldiers walked briskly throughout the complex, moving displays, statues, boxes, stuffed and inflated animals—anything to create a natural funnel at four locations, guiding visitors to the secure checkpoints. The workers had free reign to move anything that wasn't nailed down, and even a few things that were. "Legoland," a building-blocks store and display near the west end, was hit hard, with huge Lego statues of dinosaurs, buildings and animals moved into new positions blocking access to the park.

"Look out!"

The two agents looked up in time to see an eight-foot, multicolored Empire State Building complete with a Lego King Kong standing on top, tip over and shatter on the floor, scattering thousands of little plastic blocks with a sound like hail across a tin roof. An young National Guard soldier looked sheepishly over at the FBI agents, his face the color of Setty's rented truck.

He shrugged his shoulders and said, "Guess I better go find a broom."

"This is really amazing," said Beth, kicking aside a few stray blocks.

Setty nodded.

"I agree. It's impressive how much people can accomplish with a common goal and no time to worry about turf issues."

She turned to look at him.

"I'm sorry if I got a little heavy-handed at breakfast. I was out of line. I guess I'm nervous. What if I'm wrong?"

"You've got nothing to apologize for," he said. "I was being a hard ass. Anyway, what have you been wrong about so far?"

She thought for a moment, then answered, "You."

"What do you mean?" he asked as they continued walking around the perimeter of the park, last minute preparations winding down around them.

"I had a preconceived notion about male agents, that they were pretty much just good cops with slightly bigger egos..."

"Like I said," he interrupted, "what have you been wrong about so far?"

She smiled. "I'm just saying you've been open to my ideas from the first time you heard them. You listened, and I appreciate it."

"You're welcome, but in case you didn't notice, I'm not the only one listening. You've got a huge ally in Williams, no pun intended. And he's not easy to win over. I've seen analysts with twice your experience reduced to a quivering blob by the chief. But he respects your creativity. That's something you just can't train for. A lot of folks in the I.C. look at a tree and see nothing but leaves, bark and branches. You've got the gift of seeing the roots, the wood, the bugs, the lumber, the birds, the shade, the tire swing and the tree fort. Where they see a photograph, you see a picture. That's what makes you exceptional at this, Beth."

Beth looked down to hide the red rising in her face. It was the first time he had used her first name.

"Ok, head getting big now."

"Well," he said, pointing to the huge inflated Snoopy figure just inside the park, near the flume, "You're in the right place to grow a big round Charlie Brown head."

She laughed, "Thanks a lot!'

"Now, enough site-seeing. We've got work to do."

"What can I do?" Beth asked, feeling somewhat helpless without a lab to work in or at least a table and a computer.

"You like clothes?" he asked.

"Sure," she said. "They just don't like me."

"Well, I'm not asking you to do any modeling. I just want you to hand out T-shirts to the ground team. I had them printed and they should be arriving any minute."

She frowned and cocked her head at him. "You had shirts made?"

"Yeah. That's what I do with my free time while I'm driving cross country. They say 'I helped save the free world and all I got was this lousy t-shirt!'"

"Funny, but I don't believe you," she said, looking at him doubtfully

"Cynic. I'll let you know when they arrive. Have the boxes brought over there by the big Snoopy so people can find you easily. There will be three sizes—just hand 'em out as appropriate."

"What are you going to do?" she asked.

"I'll be the mother hen, coordinating the ground teams."

"You like this kind of thing, don't you?"

Setty thought for a moment before he answered.

"Yeah," he said, "I was born for it. I used to play detective when I was a kid, sneaking up on people, doing surveillance on my older sisters. We were Catholic, so I had three sexually repressed and guilty sisters. The intelligence gathered, not observed mind you, was pretty compelling for a ten-year-old boy. I guess I just always wanted to be a cop with an extra-large ego."

"You're going to make me sorry for that one, aren't you?"

"For a while longer, yes I am."

SIXTY-FOUR

Anwar was at peace as he knelt before the silver box on the carpeted hotel room floor, between the king-sized bed and the huge windows that looked out over the Mall of America and the airport. Farther away were the skylines of Minneapolis and St. Paul, difficult to discern on this gloomy gray day. Beside him sat a cold glass of milk which he had been keeping in the refrigerator since last night. He opened the lid for the first time and looked inside. It was almost completely full of oblong balloons roughly two inches long and one inch thick. He took several swallows of milk, took a deep breath and picked up one balloon. It may have been his imagination, or the cold of the milk glass, but the capsule felt warm to the touch. He looked at it, the luminescent powder shifting within its thick, clear membrane. It was a lovely, rich blue, glittering even in the dull light from an overcast morning sky.

This will be the end for my body, he thought, but the beginning for my soul.

He put it in his mouth and felt it slip down his tongue and into his throat, and then it was gone. He did this thirty-nine more times before driving to the mall.

SIXTY-FIVE

When Camp Snoopy opened there would be forty new employees, all wearing yellow T-shirts with the word "STAFF" printed on the back and a picture of Snoopy with his little yellow companion, Woodstock, on the front. At each entrance to the amusement park, tables had been set up with two attendants on one side and a single chair where another staff person sat on the other side. People entering the park would have to stop at the table where the backs of both hands would be stamped, one with Snoopy and one with Woodstock, to show they had paid. As they faced the table to get their hands stamped, they would have their backs to the man in the chair. Hopefully no one would walk around evaluating the situation first or they might notice that all the men sitting in the chairs were physically imposing specimens.

All agents had received an artist's rendition of Toftey's description. He was the only person to have seen the man, though his perception may have been colored by the frightening situation in which he had found himself. Of course, he remembered the big man most clearly, but he was dead. He had gone through a process of elimination in his head, removing the faces of the men who were dead, leaving one. That was the picture all the agents held and studied, though they were instructed to put it safely away before the mall opened. Seeing his picture would certainly compromise their only advantage—his belief that his mission was, as yet, unknown.

Undercover agents at each entrance to the mall would be looking for the man as well, hoping to give the Camp Snoopy teams a little warning before he got there. The more time they had to prepare for their delicately choreographed dance the better. Each agent was armed with a .45 caliber pistol in a holster secured beneath each table, or in a holster in the small of the back for agents in the chairs. A standing order had been given to shoot first, without hesitation. The large caliber weapon eliminated any possibility that a final moment of consciousness would allow the completion of the terrorist's deadly mission.

At eight a.m. the rides were started and the glittering cacophony began.

SIXTY-SIX

Garrett Hansen sat in a plastic chair wearing a yellow Camp Snoopy shirt with the word "STAFF" stretched across his broad back. It had taken a great deal of convincing to get Setty to let him in on their little FBI party, but he was more than qualified to subdue a difficult subject. And this was a subject he badly wanted a chance to subdue. Across from him was a table where a male and female agent sat with hand stamps. Both played their parts wonderfully, all smiles, putting pictures of Snoopy on one hand and Woodstock on the other, handing out free pens (another ploy to keep the terrorist's hands busy). They were quick and the line moved efficiently. Some parents grumbled about the "new procedure" but there was very little dissent and most people didn't think twice about getting both hands stamped. The few that asked were told, "Our security personnel have a hard time seeing a stamp when it's only on one hand. It makes it easier for them to ensure only authorized people are in the park. It's for your and your children's safety, ma'am or sir." Nobody argued with that one.

Every table had a coed team—the woman to stamp and the man to grab wrists if they identified the subject. The agent seated across the entry from the table, seeing the wrist grab, would jump up to lock the man's arms in a full nelson, a wrestling hold designed to disable the opponent's arms. That would make it impossible for him to return his hand to his pocket and detonate the suicide belt. He would then be handcuffed, hands and feet, with a long metal bar between and, hanging thus, hustled out of the mall like a missionary heading for the cannibals' soup pot. He would then be tossed into a bomb squad van, which would be sealed until…well, that part had not been discussed. Hansen suspected there was no discussion because there was no plan. Once you threw him in there, he thought, who would be dumb enough to open the door again and check on him? What if Houdini Muhammad had removed his bonds and was sitting in there lovingly fondling that little button, waiting for a visitor? Nobody spoke of all the ways this could go wrong. Everybody was told to think happy thoughts.

Hansen's nerves were stretched like guitar strings, vibrating with tension. He was expecting any moment to hear a bomb blast or gunfire—all hell breaking loose in some fashion. This Arab piece of shit, he thought, would not make it out of the mall alive, not if he had anything to say about it. He had been thinking about nothing else for the past couple of days, unable to sleep. The anger helped him avoid other more painful thoughts whirling around in his brain. It was a strategy he had learned growing up at odds with his father's narrow expectations, disappointing him at every turn. His "pissed-off" demeanor kept everyone at arm's length and questions to a bare minimum. His mother had been afraid of him, he was certain, though now it was too late to ask her. Some perspective on his father and their relationship would have been nice. What had she seen? Had she worried about it or was she just disappointed by her son's selfish behavior and disdain for what her husband, his father, had built with his own sweat and blood? Had his parents talked about the day their son would take over the business? How deeply had it touched them, his escape? Had it touched them at all?

A steady stream of people made their way through the gauntlet to join the crowd already in the park. As more and more people showed up, Hansen grew more worried. Where the hell do they all come from? He wondered. Finding one face in this mass of humanity seemed, well, impossible.

And then, just like that, there he was.

At least, it could be him, Hansen thought. The man was small. He wore a bulky sweatshirt with some sports team logo on the front. His pants were baggy and worn low, gang-banger style. The hood was over his head and Hansen couldn't get a look at the face to compare it to the sketch. His complexion was dark, or at least it seemed dark, but was that the shadow of the hood or the color of his skin? He seemed to be alone. Why go into the park by yourself? What made Hansen most nervous, however, were the man's hands. Or, more specifically, the fact that he didn't see them. They were buried in his pockets.

He watched the man look the place over, the rides, the tables, the people being stamped, and then he turned around and walked away.

Hansen didn't know what to do. He couldn't leave his spot in case that wasn't the guy and the real one came through. He turned away from the people milling at the door and spoke quietly into his radio.

"Camp West, Camp West. I think I just saw him. Subject about five six or seven, dark complexion wearing a bulky white sweatshirt, baggy jeans and hiking boots. Looks like a gang-banger but kept his hands hidden in his sweatshirt pockets. He looked over the scene then headed north from my location."

SIXTY-SEVEN

CIA agent Beth Adams wandered the ground level of the mall, circling like a bird of prey, searching for a man based on a vague artist's rendition of a brief eyewitness encounter. Brian Setty was doing the same, while monitoring identification efforts at both external and Camp Snoopy entrances. Beth was not especially confident of their chances at spotting this guy. There were so many people in the mall, their faces became a blur. She didn't want to be in this place if the guy got his way. Of course, she was in this place to help prevent that. So, she thought, I guess I'm stuck.

She passed Setty for the second time, walking the opposite direction. He winked, she smiled. He was another reason she didn't want anything to happen. My god, how can you be so selfish, she admonished herself. What about the other thousand or so people in here, the children? What about the country's future if he pulls it off? Our security, our freedoms, our economy?

But it really was quite something, she thought, her mind stubbornly wandering back to Setty once again. She wanted them to both be around when it was all over. Was that so wrong? It's not like she was hoping everybody else got hurt. She just wanted a little extra consideration for her and Brian. Praying for it seemed a bit of overkill, but hoping seemed appropriate. But she could pray for this to end without anybody getting hurt and that would cover her and Brian Setty, without being selfish. Praying was the way to go. She prayed for a positive outcome as she wandered around and around some of the over 4 miles of storefront, seeing new things at every turn, like a goldfish in a very big bowl.

Then she heard the radio: "…bulky white sweatshirt, baggy jeans and hiking boots." As she did, the man walked past her, head bent down, shuffling along beneath the hood, hands buried deep in pockets. She keyed her mike, but nothing seemed to happen. She announced her position anyway, and turned carefully to follow. What the hell do you do now, Agent Adams, she wondered. She had a weapon, but now even the thought that she could have to use it sent chills down her body. She watched him walk and noticed he primarily looked straight down, making no eye contact with anyone, not even looking at storefronts or food vendors. He never removed his hands from his pockets. She looked but saw nobody she recognized as law enforcement. She followed him and saw he was heading to some public restrooms. As soon as he was out of sight, she ran to catch up with Setty.

SIXTY-EIGHT

Chief Williams was summoned to the Vice President's office with no explanation. In his experience, that could mean only one thing: trouble.

When he entered the room he found the attorney general and colonel Gillis along with the vice president of the United States, John Quincy "JQ" Lester, or "Johnny Clueless" as they used to call him behind his back during a short and undistinguished career in the CIA.

Williams and the VP went way back. Williams was an Annapolis man who ascended quickly to the top of his class, demonstrating inspiring leadership and uncanny analytic skills in tactics and strategy. JQ went to West Point on family money and privilege and succeeded only in ascending the institution's bell tower after a night of drinking, falling fifty feet to a construction scaffold, breaking his clavicle and shattering his left ankle. Though he hid it well, the limp was still there. He and Williams ended up at the CIA together, where, within six months, JQ found himself reporting to the young agent Williams who had become an OTL, or operations team leader. After a year of failed assignments and embarrassing debacles it was suggested that if JQ insisted on serving his country, he try a less intellectually taxing method of doing so. Though his success in politics had been impressive, he still blamed Williams for getting him drummed out of the CIA, taking the chief's every promotion and commendation as a personal affront and reminder of his own failures.

"Ah, thank you for joining us, Chief, on such short notice!" said the VP in an insincere, sing-song voice that made Williams' skin crawl. "Colonel Gillis was filling us in on some disturbing details of the operation you have currently underway in Wisconsin, at that big mall?"

"Minnesota, sir," Gillis gently corrected.

"Yes, that's right, Minnesota. Tell me, Chief, is it true you're using several thousand people as human bait to foil an al-Qaeda plot? And not just any plot," he looked at Gillis and the AG with raised eyebrows, nodding stupidly, "this is a plot to explode a nuke-u-ler bomb in the Mall of America. I am surprised, Chief Williams. Surprised and disappointed by your questionable leadership on this issue."

Williams tried hard to respond without sounding defensive or condescending.

"Mr. Vice President, I think the term 'human bait' is sensational and frankly, irresponsible…"

Lester chuckled. "Irresponsible, exactly! It *is* irresponsible to put American civilians in harm's way to obfuscate your failures in planning and execution."

Williams had had enough. He raised his formidable voice a few decibels and dropped it an octave. His audience felt it vibrate their teeth.

"Sir, if I may finish? I cannot speak to the reasons our intelligence assets failed to discover this plot earlier. Perhaps it has something to do with the allocation of funds by your committee. Obviously that is not in my purview. However, I commend them for correlating some rather obscure and seemingly unrelated evidence. Their efforts have given us a chance, however slim, to stop another devastating terrorist attack in the United States. Given the timeline, we have few alternatives, Mr. Vice President.

Closing or evacuating the Mall of America will create widespread panic, both emotional and economic. And, if we do so, we send this man to Site B...."

"What? Where's Site B?" interrupted the VP.

"That's my point, sir. The only chance we have of capturing him is letting him come to us. Otherwise he will move to a predetermined contingency plan, a Site B, or pick a target of opportunity. Either way, he once again holds all the cards and we fold."

Williams leaned his eclipsing bulk in toward the VP and said, more quietly, "Sir, it would be far more irresponsible to create panic than to allow our people to continue living their lives normally, trusting us to protect them, according to our duty."

"Well, Ed, I must be blunt," said the VP, shaking his head. "This thing has gone too far for us to turn back now anyway. But don't think for a moment that even if this fiasco of yours bears fruit and all ends well, that I won't ask for your resignation. You know how the media is with this kind of thing. They'll be asking why we put thousands of Americans in harm's way with previous knowledge of imminent threat. Sound familiar?"

"You're painting some pretty broad stokes, John."

"The American people have a big brush," countered the VP.

"I am confident in our approach," said the chief. "It isn't ideal, but it's all we have. We have discussed this at great length, Mr. Vice President. We weighed all the scenarios carefully. This plan is the safest for the people in that mall and the nation as a whole."

"Well, confident or not, when this is all over I expect a letter of resignation on my desk the next morning. Thank you, Chief Williams, that will be all."

Williams stood and acknowledged the seated men with a curt nod. Then he turned an icy stare to Lester and said, "I serve at the pleasure of the President of the United States as directed by our Constitution. I will resign when he asks me to. Not before."

Williams saluted smartly and headed for the door, where he paused. Without looking back, he said over his shoulder, "Oh, and by the way, Sir…it's nu-CLEAR."

SIXTY-NINE

Agent Greg Tanaki was stationed to watch the west entrance. A young Asian man wearing shorts, a polo shirt, Nikes and glasses, he carried a camera and fit the stereotype of a Japanese tourist perfectly. He sat on a bench near the busy glass doors, fiddling with his camera and watching every person walking into the Mall of America. Some visitors he excluded without really even focusing on them—too young, too old, female, handicapped. Those who were closer to the description from the forest service guy – right height, weight, sex – he spent a split second more time on to bring their faces into focus. Then he noticed complexion, hair length and color, facial hair, and most importantly, general demeanor. That was a skill that, although there were strategies taught at Quantico and Langley, a person was born with. And Tanaki had it in spades. His classmates at the academy labeled him the "Surveillance Mutant" or just the Mutant for short. Some claimed he could read minds.

He knew they were looking for a terrorist—a suicide bomber—and that it was imperative he not suspect anything upon entering the building or all may be lost. The Mutant had filled similar roles in other public facilities, primarily airports, and he was currently on an eighteen-month streak of positive IDs without a single false read. He had brought down an amazing twenty-seven drug smugglers and other undesirables, many of those with balloons and nothing external on their person. Two months ago at LAX he'd marked two Arab men for airport security. Upon exiting the plane their eyes wandered too much, not with wonder, but with purpose. He'd seen thousands of foreign travelers, probably a couple hundred from Middle Eastern countries, disembark. Regardless of their feelings toward the West, they always expressed some awe at being in the United States. These men were arrested entering a van left for them in long-term parking. Along with a change of clothes, fake drivers licenses and $2,000 in cash, four automatic weapons and several boxes of ammunition awaited them inside the vehicle.

Today, as usual, Tanaki watched without watching. He sat with the camera sitting beside him, toward the glass so he could sit and work on its imaginary malfunction while facing the doors. He did not have to move his head at all. Only his eyes rising briefly above the rims of his glasses hinted at his true purpose.

Tanaki heard a commotion at the door and looked up from the camera. One had to take full advantage of natural attention-grabbing occurrences when they presented themselves. He watched as a group of kids bustled through both doors, talking loudly and laughing, excited. There were over a dozen pre-teen girls and boys, with two adults as chaperones. It was human nature to be distracted by such a sight—the noise and movement and energy. But the Mutant did not miss it. Behind the children he saw a man who didn't fit. The man seemed oblivious to the cacophony before him. He was looking past the motion and the screaming as though he was deaf and blind. His face was stone. It had not been more than five seconds when Tanaki returned his gaze to his camera. But he had seen enough: white Minnesota Golden Gopher hockey sweatshirt with hood, about five foot, nine inches tall, slender build but with an unusually large upper body out of proportion to the thickness of his limbs. His gait was somewhat lurching, as though he was fighting for balance. His complexion was olive and his skin was moist. He was sweating. Tanaki chanced another glance to confirm. Yes, his face was wincing slightly with each step. His hands were buried deep in the sweatshirt pockets and his shoulders were hunched as though against the cold.

Alarms sounded in Tanaki's head. Without question, this was the guy. The Mutant watched what he was certain would be his twenty-eighth positive ID lurch through his peripheral vision and activated his microphone.

SEVENTY

Anwar had seen hundreds of pictures of the place, including videos taken by their operatives as well as those from press kits freely available to any member of the public. But nothing he had seen prepared him for the scale and wonder of the place. Despite himself, he gazed in awe at the sound, colors and movement around him. Images of beautiful human beings or items of function and frivolity beckoned him at every turn, whispering to the impetuous child he once was, the lonely adolescent, the angry alienated young man—solutions offered in tempting packages. Hunger, desire and greed blossoming in overpowering covetous profusion, filling his head with echoes, exposing with ever more clarity the depth and darkness of his need. It was all here for him—happiness, beauty, fulfillment, offered in singsong, flashing promises.

Anwar looked at the people around him. They were mostly women with children. There were few adult men in the crowd. Odd, he thought, but acceptable. He saw it as yet another sign that his mission was just, inspired by the Prophet, in service to his God. Anwar recalled Muhammad's words, "I have not left after me turmoil for the people but the harm done to men by women." The Prophet would certainly be pleased, he thought, to see these houris, strutting around in their revealing clothing, their various mutilations and gaudy adornments, suddenly panicked as their selfish superficial world came crashing down around them. "I was shown the Hell Fire," the Prophet had said, "and the majority of its dwellers were women who are disbelievers or ungrateful."

His wife was ungrateful and selfish, just as Muhammad had described. The children, however, their sacrifice was a true test of his faith. He had struggled with the pain that accompanied the vision of his own children's faces, maddeningly superimposed upon those of his young bloodied and disfigured victims. He loved his own children—his young son most of all. Hassan was a quiet and tall stick of a boy who loved playing football in the streets around their modest Riyadh home. And his sweet daughter, with the dark bottomless wells of her eyes so intent and watchful of the world and people around her. When he gave himself to Jihad he had prayed for forgiveness and guidance and for Allah to relieve the pain he felt in his heart. His prayers were answered when he heard the Sheik speak once at the madrasah. On the subject of Jihad and the killing of children, he said, "One does not kill the fly but spare the maggot. To claim the right future you must destroy the wrong one." Anwar realized then that it was to *save* his children that he killed the infidel, in all its various forms. Burying his fatherly instincts was proof of his commitment to Allah. It did not come to him easily, but he learned to take pride in his ability to think and act decisively even amid the protests of his squirming conscience.

He grew dizzy and sat down on a nearby bench. It is Allah, he told himself, breaking me free of the spell of this place. He looked down at the floor, afraid to engage the evil around him once more. It was strong and he felt weak. God knew of his weakness, obviously, and had come to help him. Resting for a moment on the bench, Anwar attributed the warm fluttering in his stomach to nerves and anticipation of the glory he would soon realize. It followed that as Anwar drew closer to Allah, his physical being would tremble at the prospect of its own demise. Standing up, he turned back toward the amusement park, his resolve strengthened, his goal reaffirmed.

However, he had not counted on the line.

He walked to the Camp Snoopy amusement park entrance closest to the external door where he came in, expecting to simply walk into the park, purchase a ticket, and ascend to the highest point possible and fulfill his mission. Instead, he found a queue of people, most with children, standing and waiting to pass through some sort of checkpoint. Could they know about me, he wondered? He could not imagine how. Anwar stalked the perimeter of Camp Snoopy, looking for an alternative entry, but there was none free of a milling crowd. He returned to the first entrance and evaluated the line—the speed with which people were moving, what was expected of them when they reached the entry. People were leaning over a table, apparently purchasing tickets, and then were free to continue. He looked at his watch. Each transaction took about fifteen seconds, though getting children through seemed to double that. He quickly counted the people in line and calculated it would take him roughly twelve minutes to pass through.

There were other options, of course. He had considered going up to the top floor and jumping off, detonating his payload as he plummeted to the floor of the park. But he was uncertain of his ability to think rationally and detonate the device while the ground rose to meet him. Of course, Allah would be with him, but he had also learned to recognize and appreciate his own limitations as God's way of protecting him from foolhardiness. Even if he could have jumped with complete confidence, he might not have attained his goal as effectively as he would from the very center of the mall. To stab at the very heart of this monument to his enemy and transform it, in its death throes, into a monument to Allah and Jihad was his mission, his promise, his destiny.

As the line shuffled forward at its agonizing pace, he felt his stomach burning and bile rising in his throat. He was beginning to realize this sensation had less to do with Allah and more to do with the deadly substance he carried in his stomach. It was not supposed to affect him this quickly. He knew, however, that the chance a balloon could rupture, though remote, did exist. He tried to put that thought out of his mind, but the burning pain was growing in his gut along with the nausea. He saw the table now. He would be through soon and it would be glorious. But he felt the sickness would overwhelm him at any moment. He looked around and saw a restroom. Perhaps a moment to collect myself, he thought, some water on my face.

SEVENTY-ONE

"Wait, wait. Slow down a bit. Where did you see him?" Setty followed Beth as she spoke.

"He just walked into the restrooms. Over there."

She pointed to the restroom sign that directed people down a long narrow hallway with doors on either side.

"Stay here," he told her.

"Let me call for backup."

"No," he said. "If this isn't him and the cavalry comes galloping in, then we're screwed, we blow the whole thing."

Setty left Beth Adams standing at the railing and headed into the hallway. He passed a man and a small boy leaving the men's restroom. The door closed with a soft thud behind them. Setty felt for his gun in the small of his back and took comfort in its shape. He carefully opened the door and slipped inside. No one stood at the urinals, nobody washed their hands at the long row of sinks. Water was running from one of the faucets. He inhaled the oppressive smell of a strong air freshener attempting in vain to overpower more animal odors lurking beneath. The toilet stalls were all opened, save one in the middle. Setty quietly squatted down and saw hiking boots. He stood and briefly weighed his options. Either this is the guy and I take him out in here, hopefully containing the blast and dispersal if he goes off, or it's not the guy and we get sued. Of course, the first scenario ends very badly for everybody, himself included. He could live with the second option. Funny.

Setty stood in front of the toilet stall door and kicked it as hard as he could. A sharp yelp came from the other side as the door hit something, presumably the guy's knees. Setty drew his gun and rushed into the stall simultaneously, slipping the .45 into the man's mouth before he noticed anything else. He looked down first at the man's hands, which hung limp at his sides.

"Move your hands and your brains will be on the wall behind you. Do you understand English?"

He felt the man nod slightly and whimper. Setty left the gun's barrel in the man's mouth and for the first time looked down at his face. He pulled the sweatshirt hood back.

It was a kid of about fourteen. He was crying. And he was Asian.

SEVENTY-TWO

A few moments earlier the "all clear" was given and Hansen now felt like an ass.

"The redneck hick from up north got it wrong. Send him back to the woods."

He could make excuses all night. He was tired, he was worried about Billy and Libby, the past kept whispering in his ears, taunting him….

But this time, he was certain. This guy in the Minnesota Gophers sweatshirt wasn't right. He walked stiffly, gingerly, as though he were hurting, or carrying a crate of eggs on his head. He looked down, avoiding eye contact. His hands were in his pockets, even though it was uncomfortably warm in this part of the mall. His frame was thin, but his upper body was strangely out of proportion, thin neck, thin legs. Then, he tried to squeeze past the couple getting stamped at the table, sidestepping between them and Hansen. Hansen saw the hands disappearing into the pockets and he dared not take him down.

"Excuse me, sir. Sir?" Hansen smiled warmly, trying to be convincing, "Sorry. You need to get your hands stamped before you go in."

He pointed over to the table where the couple was just moving away. The man looked up at Hansen, who immediately saw that the guy was ill. He was sweating and very pale—his eyes glassy and wandering. In those dark eyes Hansen saw hesitation, confusion, anxiety and suffering, perhaps? He knew this guy was close to his goal, close enough to smell it. He wouldn't let a little thing like getting his hands stamped keep him from reaching it. Or would he?

"Sir, it'll only take a sec," Hansen cajoled, "then you can go in and have...." He almost said, "a blast," but instead said, "...a good time."

He blocked the man's forward progress with an outstretched hand, guiding him to the table.

"There you go, Missy and Jeff will get you stamped and on your way. Thank you, sir."

Hansen didn't know the agents' names—he just said the first thing that popped into his head. They were sharp, thank God. They caught his act and Hansen was able to give them a quick earnest nod. Here we go.

SEVENTY-THREE

Setty walked the kid to the operations center himself, trying to assuage his Catholic guilt and feeling genuinely bad about scaring the living shit out of him. He would see that he was given a very generous gift certificate to use in the mall for him and his family. But Setty knew there would be a subpoena coming soon. The way he saw it, it was the cost of protecting the public at large, that the public at small sometimes got stepped on.

"West two to Setty."

"This is Setty, go ahead West two."

He was walking back to his beat on the third floor when he got the call from Tanaki.

"SOI," said the agent over the radio. Tanaki pronounced it "soy," like the sauce.

"Confirm?" asked Setty, his heart racing.

He knew the Mutant—the world hung on this number. An eternity passed between transmissions.

"Ninety-nine point nine," Tanaki said. "Five foot eight or nine, short dark hair, slim build, over-large white Gopher Hockey sweatshirt, jeans. Looks like he's cold and he shouldn't be."

Setty began walking quickly toward the west Camp Snoopy entrance, speaking quietly but clearly into his wrist mike.

"Ok. Everybody, our guy just went past west two. I want the west side teams to look for a male, average height, slender build, big white Minnesota Gopher Hockey sweat…" Setty's description was interrupted by screaming somewhere ahead of him.

He ran toward the chaos, yelling into his radio as he ran, "I think we found him!"

SEVENTY-FOUR

Hansen watched the man's every movement. Nothing else entered his mind. The man seemed reluctant to remove his hands from the sweatshirt pockets. He was weighing his options, contemplating, Hansen assumed, whether his goal could be realized or if this was as far as he would get. But was this good enough? Hansen hoped the guy was a perfectionist. Behind him was a growing line of people waiting to get into the amusement park. They craned their necks, trying to see over each other and identify the source of the delay. Toward the back of the line, impatience was getting the better of some who freely expressed their frustration.

"Come on, what's the holdup?" "Let's go!"

Clearly the man heard the restless crowd. Hansen didn't know which way their behavior would push him. In your place, buddy, Hansen thought, I'd be tempted to blow up these rude sons-a-bitches right now. He kept his eyes fixed on the man's hands, or rather, where they would emerge if he decided to remove them from the pockets. The man was frozen. Hansen didn't want some dumb ass to push him the wrong way.

"Sir," Hansen said pleasantly, straining to hold back and not break the guy in half, bomb or not, "if you'd rather not enter the park at this time, would you please let these folks through. Only because they've got young kids who are waiting."

The man glanced from the table in front of him, over to the spinning, flashing rides, then up to the ceiling. Apparently, he made up his mind. Hansen saw the man's arms begin to move and prepared to grab him. He didn't need to think about what would happen if this didn't work. After seeing Billy dying in the hospital, blowing up, he figured, would be the easy way out.

SEVENTY-FIVE

Anwar did not know what to do. The pain was nearly unbearable and he tasted the sick in his mouth. He thought he might ignite from the inside, though self-immolation was not a method of martyrdom he was prepared for. He begged Allah to help him. He needed to climb high somewhere in the center of the park for maximum exposure, to ensure the total destruction of the building. Here, the overhang would contain the blast. He had to get out into the open. He clung tightly to each controller. He had promised himself he would not release them until his body did it of its own accord, after the explosion.

But now they would not let him enter the camp until he removed his fingers from the pockets, which meant releasing the detonators. He saw no sign of ulterior motives in these smiling fools, and yet…. He had come all this way, struggled through painful trials, toiled day and night, taken life. Now, he assumed, he was dying where he stood. Clearly it would take only a couple of seconds, and then he would be on his way with nobody left to stop him. His inaction was drawing unwanted attention and he was not sure how much longer he would be able to suppress the urge to vomit. He would have to remove his hands from his pockets, careful not to drag the detonators out with them. If they fall out onto the table, he thought, I will be forced to do it here. What will be my fate should I fail?

Anwar was a devout Muslim, a man of unwavering faith. He believed to the depth of his being that his God would lead him when he needed him most. Anwar prayed for direction, he prayed for a sign. And in his time of greatest need, like Moses and Abraham and Muhammad before him, Allah, be praised, spoke to him.

Slowly, he released the two detonators and removed his hands from the sweatshirt pockets.

SEVENTY-SIX

Over the usual white-noise din of the mall, Beth heard a scream, then yelling. She ran toward the commotion, past shops and through crowds of people who seemed like paper cutouts, or extras in a movie. They didn't have a clue. And part of her job to was to help keep them in ignorant bliss.

Her father had told her that she had to find satisfaction in her accomplishments within herself.

"Nobody believes in community service anymore," he told her once, after an especially difficult day on the job. "Folks just can't fathom that you might actually do something for a stranger and expect nothing in return. You can't understand a selfless act until you know what it's like to truly love someone," he said. "I have you to thank for that."

She remembered those words so clearly, because the next day he was dead.

A gunshot snapped her back to the present. Now people were paying attention—many had stopped in their tracks and from the milling throng questioning murmurs began to build. She ran faster.

SEVENTY-SEVEN

Minneapolis, MN
Friday, 10:00 AM

He had been staring so intently at the man's pockets that he almost didn't react when his hands appeared. But as he bent down to get marked with Snoopy and Woodstock tattoos, the FBI agent Hansen had named Jeff, lunged for his wrists. Too soon. The terrorist stepped back and Jeff fell across the table, grasping empty air.

Hansen's heart leapt into his throat as the man attempted to thrust his hands back into the sweatshirt pockets, but the bulky material had folded over and blocked access. He looked down and began to fumble with the shirt. Hansen jumped forward and thrust his fists under the man's arms lifting them up with his own, then interlacing his fingers behind the smaller man's head. He forced the terrorist's head forward using his neck for leverage as he pulled back against the man's shoulders. With his arms flailing helplessly at his sides, the bomber was unable to reach Hansen, or more importantly, the detonators in his pockets. He had him!

"Handcuffs!"

Hansen yelled, but the female agent he knew as Missy was already around the table, pulling out her cuffs. Jeff was struggling to get his handcuffs off his belt while calling in to the other agents on his radio. They needed both sets of cuffs to shackle this guy to the bar. But just as Missy reached the struggling men, the terrorist, whose legs were still free, kicked her savagely between her legs, dropping her to the floor where she balled up, writhing in pain. A woman waiting in line screamed. Then Hansen felt his captive stop struggling. Suddenly the man's body went limp and Hansen lost all leverage. The man slipped out of the sweatshirt like a molting snake leaving behind its empty shed skin. He ran haltingly into the park with Hansen seized by disbelief, clutching the empty shirt where once was a struggling terrorist.

"No!" Hansen roared.

He dropped the sweatshirt and ran after the man, who was lumbering forward as if he was drunk and losing control of his muscles. He wore only the explosive vests, two of them, over his torso, the dark skin of his arms and neck exposed and glistening, sweat staining the beige material below. The vests looked to Hansen like life jackets, the bulky strips which once held foam for floatation now bulged with explosives. The detonators swung wildly around suicide bomber's knees, eluding his reach. His movements were shaky and frantic, uncoordinated. His body was failing him.

Hansen reached around for the .44 snub-nose revolver in its holster tucked against the small of his back. With a deft flick of his finger, he unsnapped the flap and pulled the gun out. Hansen took a knee, leveled the pistol at the man's bobbing head and fired.

SEVENTY-EIGHT

Minneapolis, MN
Friday, 10:00 AM

Setty heard it on the radio and felt immediate, overwhelming relief.

"Camp West, we've got him! We've got him!"

Camp West? That's where he left Hansen. Way to go—home town boy makes good! Now, comes the dangerous part—securing this evil bastard and his gear. Setty ran to the location, gun drawn. The mall was full of shoppers already and he had trouble getting through without knocking people down. A few saw his gun and stepped aside. Some dropped to the ground. But most ignored him, like they were in a daze, like sheep watching a wolf running through the flock, all of them bleating "As long as he's not after me..." It was infuriating! He was about thirty yards from the West Camp Snoopy entrance when a large glob of people closed in front of him. He wanted to open fire.

There was a scream and then shouting toward the west entrance. A gunshot.

Setty stuck his left thumb and forefinger in his mouth, against his tongue and blew. A piercing shriek split the air and the all heads swiveled toward him in unison like some hydra-like beast.

"All you motherfuckers, get the fuck down!"

He raised his pistol over his head and brandished it sideways, "gangsta style," like people saw every night on TV, black kids in braids and dew rags, their guns held high and sideways like they were trying to shoot over a wall. A few of the hydra's heads screamed. All of them dissolved into a featureless lump on the ground. Setty ran around the huddled mass and on to the west park entrance.

For some reason he didn't understand, Beth Adams entered his mind. Had that been her scream? She didn't have any field experience. He shouldn't have let her come here. His heart sank. Apparently they were not out of the woods quite yet. He sprinted for the checkpoint.

SEVENTY-NINE

Beth reached the west checkpoint just as Setty did. She saw his gun was drawn and there was a grim look on his face.

He ran up to her and whispered in her ear, "Get outside, now."

His tone was tense and urgent, but not panicked. She looked into his eyes. Clearly it was an order he fully expected her to obey. Because it made her feel helpless and inadequate, her first instinct was to say "No." Setty saw the hesitation on her face.

"You got us here, Beth. When this is over, there's going to be a lot more to learn, to do. We need you for that. I need you," he added, sincerely. "Please go."

Then he turned and ran into the park. Watching him run past the giant Snoopy statue with his gun raised above his head was an image she stored in her brain, hoping they could laugh about it together sometime.

EIGHTY

Hansen's first bullet removed the man's right ear. He howled. The pain made him stumble and clutch at the right side of his head, the detonators hanging at his sides temporarily forgotten. Blood quickly seeped through his fingers but he stayed on his feet and disappeared on the other side of a steel support for the coaster. Hansen got off another round but it hit the column with a spark and echoing ricochet. He got up and ran after the man. It seemed the mall was full of screaming and crying children, but he heard little above his own wildly pumping heart and the ringing of the gunshots in his head. Above them the roller coaster still ran, its violent, rattling roar adding to the din. He closed the gap with the steel beam, expecting an explosion at any moment.

EIGHTY-ONE

Setty fought his way through the panicked crowd streaming from the park entrance. As he broke into the open where the carnival rides still spun, clattered and roared, he saw the big man, Hansen, running toward the steel columns supporting the roller coaster. They converged quickly on the same place. Setty sprinted. He was afraid Hansen would blow it, literally. He suddenly realized what a horrible lapse in judgment it had been to allow this emotionally charged guy into a situation like this. What the hell was he thinking? He was scared now, running as fast as he could, adrenaline driving him forward. It was an odd feeling, running *toward* a bomb. He didn't think he could live with parts of him missing, or worse yet, not even knowing they were gone. And then, only to die ten or twenty years later from cancer. If he had to, he'd jump on this fucker and smother him, ride him all the way to hell if he had to. His vision was crystalline. He saw everything around him in such exquisite detail—the flashing lights playing upon the floor, the confusion of shadows spinning and folding in upon themselves then fading into light, only to take form in darkness once again. Beth's face flashed through his mind. He needed more time. Stop it! Was this his life flashing before his eyes already? Maybe that whole near-death myth was crap, a self-fulfilling prophecy—you keep thinking about all the things you should've done before you kick it.

He arrived at the column across from Hansen. He caught his eye and was relieved to see the big man was focused and clearly in the game, poised beside the steel column in a two-handed shooter's stance. Setty took a few deep breaths to steady his hands and slow his pulse. It didn't work. Fuck it. Let's get this over with!

To Hansen he mouthed, "On three, one…two…"

EIGHTY-TWO

Anwar Masoud was dying. Or was he ascending?

"Blow the thing, you fool!"

It was Asad, hovering over him, a gaping hole in his head. He saw the big man smile, the white glistening teeth filed into points, his head undulating and turning inside out, then back again, like a jellyfish.

"You peasant," Asad said, then his jellyfish head exploded and Anwar could feel it hit the side of his own head, running down his neck. He raised his hand and felt the slipperiness there, where his ear should have been. He could not find it and his hand came away bloody.

Then, like the two tines of a vibrating tuning fork, fighting to bring themselves to stasis, tremulous reality stilled and his vision steadied. He fought to hold them still, clutching at the picture he saw now. His family stood before him, his children were crying and he could see his wife's tortured eyes, her disappointment in him, his failure. Did his son and daughter cry because he was dead or because he had failed? Suddenly the vision, like a distant mirage in the desert, wavered and then disappeared in a shimmering conflagration of pain and nausea which swept through his body. He saw eagles high over the clear water, locking talons and spinning, plummeting to the ground, like pieces of the sky falling. The bluest sky fell with them, pieces clutched in their savage hooked beaks and dropped upon his chest, which grew heavy under a lava-like flow of translucent blue. It was the sky above him and his friends, chasing gulls along a white Moroccan beach. His breathing grew more labored as he sank below the sparkling azure waves.

"Blow the bomb!" Asad screamed at him, his jellyfish head having reconstituted itself.

He hovered above once again, a demonic angel, herald of the apocalypse.

Anwar grabbed the detonators. The tuning fork was quivering once again. He stared straight ahead, trying to concentrate on the mission and the distant feeling of his hands on the detonators. He found the buttons. The tines of the fork vibrated wildly, making it hard for him to grasp the handles. The undulating sine waves left him numb and he could no longer feel his fingertips. The tuning fork rumbled overhead. The end was here. His martyrdom was assured. He pressed the buttons. Allah must have prepared him well. He felt nothing and smiled as peace consumed him.

EIGHTY-THREE

Out of the corner of his eye, Hansen saw movement. Glancing to his left, he saw Setty run to a neighboring steel support and stand, just out of sight of the bomber. They looked at each other and Hansen read the FBI agent's lips, "On three, one…two…"

They rounded the steel beam simultaneously, guns extended, fingers on triggers. But what they found made them both take a step backwards. The man was slumped on the floor, his suicide vests covered with the contents of his stomach—blue from a ruptured balloon of cesium and red from the disintegrating lining of his stomach and intestines. Bright crimson painted the side of his head where his right ear used to be and it ran in rivulets down his neck and over the shoulder of his shirt. He stared blankly straight ahead, his back against the rollercoaster support, legs stretched out stiff in front of him, hands at his sides. Most disturbing was the beatific smile on his face. Hansen's heart jumped into his throat when he noticed the man was rhythmically clicking some sort of button in his right hand. Over and over, his thumb flexed "click-click, click-click." Hansen took aim and his finger tightened on the trigger, but then he saw the man held a Snoopy ballpoint pen he'd taken from the check-in table. The detonator buttons lay on the floor beside him within reach. Instead, he unconsciously worked the pen, "click-click, click-click." Hansen reached into his pocket to grab a pair of handcuffs and moved toward the man.

Setty yelled at him. "Don't! Unless you want to end up like him. Move back as far as you can," Setty ordered. "Just make sure you can take his head off if he moves towards those detonators." Without lowering his gun, Setty said something into his wrist mike.

"Hazmat guys are coming," he told Hansen. "They'll secure and bag him and clean this up. They'll probably want to decontaminate us too."

It was growing very warm and stale in the mall. All ventilation systems had been turned off as soon as the doors opened that morning to help contain airborne contamination. The rides within the park began shutting down one by one and riders were led off as quickly as possible. As the mechanical sounds faded, the human ones overwhelmed the space. They could hear shouted orders, cries and the occasional scream as hundreds of people were evacuated from the building. Hansen figured most of the screams were from people reacting to the dozen or so guys in bulky white space suits trotting into the building.

Setty and Hansen watched the man clicking the ballpoint in his right hand. His left hand convulsed in time with his right, though the button beneath that thumb was imaginary. Then a retching sound began and the man brought up more blue balloons that rolled down his lap. The smell was overpowering, Hansen's repulsion magnified by the thought that radioactivity was spewing from this guy's body. He didn't know how long it took to contaminate an area with radioactive puke, but this guy was doing his best.

"Wouldn't it be better to keep that stuff inside him?" asked Hansen.

Setty looked intently at Hansen.

"Let's hang on, man. The cavalry's on its way. Besides, I'm not an executioner."

"How noble of you."

Hansen snorted and waved his gun at the man on the ground.

"This piece of shit walked right past hundreds of women and children, people he was ready to kill for no reason."

Hansen shook his head.

"I've got no problem putting a bullet in his brain. Self-defense, I say."

He leveled the gun once more, seemingly prepared to shoot.

"Hansen, wait. We've got the situation under control," said Setty, calmly. "Look, I understand. You almost lost one good friend and you've got another in the hospital because of this guy. But our duty is to protect the public—everybody. Taking revenge for your friends won't help them."

Hansen could feel the FBI agent studying him, seeing if these words had any effect.

"You don't need to tell me what my duty is," he snarled, his gun still trained on the terrorist's lolling head. "The only thing these fanatics understand is revenge. It's their creed. Religion's just an excuse for their hatred and jealousy. You know as well as I do the best thing I could do to protect the public is let a little light into this fucker's skull."

Setty was afraid of losing control of the situation. This Muslim, if he survived, could do more to protect the country than a hundred U.S. agents and a year of field work. Setty realized this murderous terrorist was worth more right now than the American standing next to him.

Following his train of thought to its ultimate end, Setty prayed, God, don't let it come to that. Thinking back to a conversation he had with Beth — was it days, weeks, hours ago? — he decided to try a different tactic. If that didn't work, he was out of ideas.

"Did you ever stop to think these guys may not be the only ones?" he asked. "If we can't interrogate him, then we'll never know."

The thought made Hansen's stomach lurch. He looked over at Setty, horrified.

"You think there's more?"

"There were four cells active on September 11, maybe more." Setty looked down at the sickening sight before them and continued.

"Do you really think this sorry-ass bunch was their A-team?"

Hansen had not considered that. The thought did nothing to slow his pounding heart. He still wanted to kill this piece of shit, but he could see the man was already a goner. All he would be doing is hastening the inevitable and ending his suffering. Rational thought was slowly returning to Hansen's adrenaline-soaked brain and he realized that euthanasia was the last thing he wanted for the man who may have killed one of his few friends in the world. He lowered his gun slightly.

"Maybe we can get something out of him," he said, "before he bites the dust."

EIGHTY-FOUR

Minneapolis, MN
Friday, 10:20 AM

Beth tried to get out of the nearest mall exit, but chaos reigned at each. She looked for a yellow shirt in the teeming mass and found an FBI agent to help her. From a distance, the female agent looked to be about Beth's age, but shorter. She looked up at just about everybody.

"Hey," Beth said, but the young woman did not hear her above the din. She was watching the crowd attentively, though Beth was not sure what the purpose was. "Excuse me," she tried again.

Finally the woman turned. She looked to be about twelve-years old.

"Sorry, ma'am, you'll need to get in line with everyone else and wait your turn...."

Please don't call me ma'am,' she thought.

"No," Beth said curtly, displaying her credentials.

The young agent looked at them carefully. "Okay, ma'am. Let's get you through then," she said.

The ma'am stung her again. I really don't like you, she thought, glaring at the back of the girl's head. Beth looked to the tightly-packed, writhing crowd of people jostling at the door then back to her diminutive guide.

"Yea, right," she chuckled.

"Follow me," the woman said. "Stay close."

With surprising grace that belied the substantial weight of the weapon, she pulled out her shining black sidearm and raised it in the air with one hand, her badge and picture with the other. Then she produced, from somewhere near her feet, Beth speculated, a voice that cut through the noise like a tornado siren—an unholy harmony, part Beverly Sills, part marine drill sergeant. "Make a hole, people!" she yelled. "Police! Make a hole!"

With her eyes downcast, suffering in painful embarrassment, Beth followed dutifully behind her tiny, gun-toting banshee, the clot of people, men, women and wide-eyed children, parting before them. At the door she was checked with the Geiger wand and passed on through, into the dreary gray light of late morning, Minnesota spring. She took a deep breath of fresh air and savored it. With her lungs full she realized she'd been taking sparse shallow breaths ever since the shooting began, subconsciously trying to avoid inhaling contaminated air. She could control her conscious fear, but fear of the atom, she believed, lay at the core of our collective being. There was no denial vast enough to soothe the horror inherent in dismantling the basic building blocks of existence.

People were quickly heading to their cars, unnecessarily urged on by mall security personnel. In hope of relieving the gnawing pang of worry in the pit of her stomach, Beth immediately began looking around for Brian Setty.

EIGHTY-FIVE

Five men in large hazmat suits entered and ran past Hansen, four carried a stretcher, while one man, the name "CURTIS" printed in black letters on his right breast, carried a bucket and a large waterproof "dry bag" over his shoulder. The men with the stretcher quickly unrolled and unzipped a very large white bag.

Hansen called out to the technician, "Hey, before you do anything, put these on him."

Hansen tossed the handcuffs to Curtis. The man swiped at them clumsily with one of his bulky white gloves, like a polar bear swatting at a high inside fastball. The cuffs dropped to the floor. The Hazmat guy looked helplessly at his gloves, then at the cuffs on the ground, then back at Hansen.

From behind the clear plastic mask came a muffled, but clearly irritated voice, "What do you want me to do? I got throw pillows for gloves over here!"

"Well your stuffing's gonna get blown all over the mall if he gets to those detonators next to him," Hansen told him.

The man thought about it a moment, then bent down and made a concerted and successful effort to shackle the man's listless hands. Setty pulled out his cuffs and threw them at the dying man's feet. Curtis heard them land. Setty said, "Put those on his ankles." The man glowered at him, but obeyed.

From behind his mask he shouted, "You guys better get the hell out of here. They're testing folks as they leave the mall. Make sure you get tested."

Setty and Hansen backed away slowly from the frantic scene before them, lingering to watch the proceedings with morbid fascination. The four men with the stretcher spread the opening of the plastic bag on the floor, then picked up the terrorist, blue puke and all, and lowered him gingerly into the center of the huge bag. After zipping it up, they opened another similar bag and slid the bagged man into that one, which was zipped up as well. Hansen noticed a small tube penetrating both bags. This was attached to a small tank, oxygen he assumed, and strapped to the external bag. They carried the double-bagged terrorist to the stretcher and laid him on top, covering the whole thing with yet another bag and zipped that as well. They walked it out quickly, past Setty and Hansen and through a crowd of panicked shoppers, held back by yellow T-shirt clad FBI agents until each person could be evaluated and released or treated if necessary. Seeing a stretcher carrying what all assumed to be a dead body did not serve to calm the crowd.

The remaining HAZMAT worker, Curtis, began the unenviable task of cleaning up the vomit and blood and expelled balloons that littered the area immediately surrounding the place where the would-be bomber finally collapsed. From his "spill kit" in the dry bag, he pulled out several items, including an assortment of absorbent pads and towels, a large white bottle of something called Radiac-Wash, a pair of blue, heavy-duty latex gloves, a couple of large red plastic bags, a disposable mop, a small disposable broom and dustpan and a large roll of yellow caution tape that read "Caution: Contaminated Area."

Curtis was thorough. After surrounding the area with yellow tape, he began by sweeping the man's stomach contents into the plastic dustpan, then dumping that into one of the large red bags. Then, using a generous amount of the Radiac-Wash solution, he scrubbed it carefully over a perimeter twenty-feet across. He used a large sponge to clean the floor and another sponge to rinse. He did this three times, and then mopped it all once more. When he was finished, he dropped all the cleaning supplies into the red bags, sealed the white bucket and dropped that in as well. Then Curtis lumbered out, bags over his shoulder like Santa Claus from outer space. As he left, yet another HAZMAT worker entered the park. This one carried a Geiger counter. As they neared the door, Setty and Hansen watched him begin sweeping the area with methodical, precision. It would take him several hours to test every nearby crack and crease in every surface surrounding the radioactive terrorist. But the Mall of America would open for business as usual at ten o'clock, Sunday morning.

EIGHTY-SIX

Hansen was not especially confident in the field decontamination procedures he underwent in the specially equipped Nuclear Regulatory Commission van.

"Tide?"

"Yeah," said the space-suit-clad NRC technician who was carefully applying a thick white paste of water and powdered laundry detergent to Hansen's arms, hands and fingers.

It smelled of lilacs. As if reading his mind, the tech looked up at Hansen and said, "April-fresh fragrance."

As people left the mall, they were tested by NRC teams with Geiger wands. The only people who tested positive were Setty, Hansen and the two FBI agents at the table who had tried to restrain Anwar. After testing their bodies for radiation, technicians found that Hansen carried significant contamination on his hands and arms, presumably from his wrestling hold on the terrorist. They were sent to a lead-lined recreational vehicle from the Nuclear Regulatory Commission, which contained a large shower and holding tanks for any contaminated water. While Setty got by with a soapy shower, Hansen was treated to the laundry detergent poultice. The detergent contained titanium dioxide, an effective oxidizer. Mixing the powder into a thick consistency and leaving it on the skin until it began to dry and cake oxidized the outermost layer of skin. Nuclear facilities found that the laundry detergent not only was an effective cleansing agent for the skin, but the familiar sight of the brand and packaging was comforting to employees, whose psychosomatic reactions often eclipsed any residual physical effects of exposure to radiation. Using something that people used every day to wash their clothes implied a level of normalcy to the whole process and reduced their anxiety.

When the NRC was finished with them, Hansen left Setty and walked to a nearby pay phone and called the hospital in Duluth to check on Billy. He got a hold of Libby, who sounded as though she had pulled herself together since their last conversation.

"Now they're transferring him to the Cities, to the University of Minnesota hospital," she said. "They said something about it getting into his tissues and his blood cells. The doctor said the transfusion bought him some time, but his bone marrow is affected."

This is a damn nightmare, Hansen thought. Every time he talked to Libby he found himself transported back in time several years when it seemed he spent every waking moment on the phone with his mother, listening to the latest nail being plunged into the old man's coffin. Collapsed lung, pneumonia, transfusions, dialysis. And from the base in Germany, he could do nothing. Finally, he requested a hardship leave, but he arrived too late to do much more than watch his father take his last breath. It would have been easier to lie to his mother and tell her they wouldn't let him come home due to terrorist threats recently made against the base. He wished he had not hesitated. Now that the man was gone not a day went by that Hansen did not confront the guilt and regret of waiting until the man was at death's door to see him. He felt doomed to relive the lie and the missed opportunity, over and over and over.

"So," he asked Libby, "what can they do for him at the U?"

Libby's brave façade began to crack.

"I don't know…there's some procedure they use for AIDS victims. It helps fix the bone marrow somehow. Something with a bunch of letters…GMS or CFS…something."

Hansen couldn't help but smile.

"Just wait till he hears they're treating him with an AIDS drug."

Libby giggled. It was good to hear her laugh.

"He'll be out of his gourd!"

"Are they flying him in?" Hansen asked.

"Yeah," she said. "They're taking him by helicopter right to the U of M hospital. We leave in about an hour."

"Ok hon, I'll meet you there. Don't worry, Libby," he added, "He's a tough man—a rock."

"It's not his head I'm worried about," she said.

Her humor in the face of this hit him right in the gut. He didn't feel that brave.

"I've gotta run. Talk to you soon," he said, and then abruptly hung up the phone before he lost it completely.

He stood in the booth for a moment, trying to collect himself. Tears burned in his eyes. He hated that feeling—it made him sick that he couldn't stop it.

"Fuck me!"

He opened the phone booth door and violently slammed it shut behind him. He did it again and again, until the threat of tears was gone.

EIGHTY-SEVEN

Silver Bay, MN
Friday, 11:20 AM

Lake County deputy sheriff Phil Pulaski parked his cruiser in front of Esther and Harold Olsen's small, nicely kept brown rambler. Harold was active in the Lions Club and had served on the county board once or twice in years past. Phil liked him—bit of a blowhard, but that was no sin up here. Most locals had a bit of a swagger that came from living in a place harder than most places in the country. If surviving the winters, the bugs, the storms, while somehow managing to scratch a living out of ancient stone, frigid waters and a million acres of road less forest didn't earn you some bragging rights, what the hell did?

"Lake County three-twelve, I'm 10-8 at location."

Pulaski's radio crackled in acknowledgement and he got out of the car. He'd received the "check the welfare" call about twenty minutes before, but he was having coffee and a Krispy Kreme at the Beaver Bay Holiday station. It had taken him that long to take the call, finish telling Sarah Rausch a joke, glance once more at her excessive breasts resting on the counter and jump in the cruiser to head the twenty-miles south, lights flashing, doing eighty miles per hour on every straightaway, fast enough to liquefy any animal that might stray from the woods. He loved driving fast.

A neighbor had called after Esther and Harold missed church that morning. The Olsens never missed church, ever. Pulaski crossed the manicured lawn. It had rained the day before, but this morning the sun was out and the grass was a surreal shade of green. Not a dandelion to be found. Harold doted on his lawn. The officer looked behind him and saw his footprints in the lush green carpet. He felt guilty and hastened over to the sidewalk. He could see the side door to the garage was open a crack, so he decided to look in there first. It was odd they didn't go to church. He didn't know them that well, but old folks around these parts didn't just suddenly change well-worn habits. He felt a growing sense of foreboding, but he would be a laughingstock if he called for backup and found that they both had the flu or had gone to see their grandkids in Duluth.

He pushed the garage door open and was surprised to find a large white van inside. His heart began to race as he realized that this must be it. He checked the plate number—he'd memorized it. Sure as shit, he thought. This was the van those terrorists used. And he, Lake County sheriff's deputy Phillip Pulaski, found it! He knew he should immediately call it in. There were Feds, state troopers, BCA guys from the Cities all looking for this damn thing. They're gonna crap when they get this call! And he would be in the papers, and not just the Duluth News Tribune. There would be interviews, maybe national. He walked into the garage, thinking of Katie Couric leaning over him, attaching his lapel microphone.

Absentmindedly he laid his hand on the door handle, and then jerked it away.

"Shit," he said out loud.

Now his fingerprints were there, damn it! Well, he was looking for the Olsens. Oh shit—the Olsens! Most likely dead in the house. He'd call in for that one. That's the last thing he wanted to see—a couple of old people dead in their own house. Who knows what these sadistic fucks did to them—probably gang-raped that poor old lady. Damn heathens. He stretched and pushed his nose against the passenger side window. There was something on the front seat—a couple of jackets piled there. Maybe there was a little something he could pick up—a souvenir. Shit, one of their Allah bibles could fetch a ton of cash on eBay! He had a cousin that served in the Gulf War—just a grease monkey, but he made a shit-load selling souvenirs on the internet. Pulaski pressed his nose harder against the glass trying to see further into the van. He couldn't see a damn thing. Well, he rationalized, my prints are on there already. What could it hurt? He placed his fingers under the chrome door handle, pulled up and opened the door.

The trip wire attached to the armrest detonated the two lifejackets filled with C-4 explosive, just as Anwar had planned. The explosion blew Deputy Pulaski into tiny unrecognizable fragments. Same with the garage and house, along with the Olsens, already lying dead inside. The house next door was also destroyed, as was the large storage building across the street. Nothing burned. The force of the blast blew out the flames and consumed the surrounding oxygen before fire could take hold. There had been enough C-4 in the booby-trapped vests laying on the van's passenger seat to propel two martyrs all the way to paradise. How far it had launched the Olsens and Deputy Pulaski was not immediately apparent.

EIGHTY-EIGHT

Setty stepped out of the NRC truck, hair still damp from his impromptu shower. With their subject secured and shipped off to the U of M, Setty's lead role was transferred to local agents. Now the investigation would be approached from two fronts—the first, urgent and tactical, would ensure that this was not a multi-cell, coordinated attack. The second would be a methodical, analytical and exhaustive deconstruction of the plot—backtracking the cell's journey and following the money trail. Setty expected to lead the former and he had someone in mind for the latter. He pulled out his cell phone and dialed.

"Where are you?"

Beth seemed caught off-guard.

"Uh...I was looking for you. Calling you hadn't occurred to me." She reached back and flipped her ponytail. "The blonde's natural."

"Dumb blonde? I'm not buyin' it. I'd say you give off more of a 'absent-minded professor' vibe," he said. "So, you didn't answer my question. I'm over here at the west entrance. I thought you'd come out here. Where'd you end up?"

"I kind of got herded toward the south. I'll head over that way. Are you ok? It looked a little hairy in there."

People were still milling about, waiting to be released in small groups to walk to their vehicles. The Mall of America was now fully evacuated and all shoppers were tested. Setty walked to an unoccupied spot on the sidewalk next to the building to speak more candidly.

"Hairy is one word for it," he said. "I obviously stopped thinking for a few minutes because if I had my wits about me, I'd have run the opposite direction. This had FUBAR written all over it."

"Your hometown boy came through, though."

Setty was silent for a moment, mulling that over.

"You know, he really did. I was a little concerned. He was wound pretty tight. I know at one point he wanted to save some taxpayer dollars out there, but he held it together."

Then Setty saw her walking toward the west entrance, looking toward the doors, away from him. The relief he felt at seeing her surprised him. He walked toward her.

"Where did they take the subject?"

"How about I tell you in person?" he said and then tapped her on the shoulder. She turned around, still holding the phone to her ear.

"Hi," he said. Setty was pleased that she seemed equally relieved to see him alive and well.

She smiled. "Hi there." They both holstered their phones.

"You know," he said, "this is far from over. We've got a lot of work to do."

"We?"

"Well, I can't think of anybody better suited to run the post-mortem investigation."

She looked at him in wide-eyed shock. "Run it?"

"It's primarily research, data analysis, hypothesis. You probably won't be running into shopping malls, shooting at radioactive suicide bombers, but it can't all be fun and games."

"I don't know what to say. Do you have that kind of power—to just assign me?"

"You doubt my omnipotence?"

"Of course not, your highness," she said, "but your boss might."

Setty's phone suddenly beeped and he answered it.

"This is Setty," he said into the phone. "Yeah? White Econoline? Oh, I see. Well usually the VIN tag survives, but it sounds like it could be anywhere within a one thousand foot perimeter. Well, seal it—if it needs to be a thousand, tape off a thousand. Anybody killed besides the deputy? Jesus. Let me know what you find." Setty looked at his watch. "I'll be there tonight." He ended the call then looked at Beth.

"They think they found the van," he said, replacing the phone on his belt. "Well, more accurately, a sheriff's deputy found it, then it disappeared, along with the deputy and a couple of nearby houses. Agents on the ground are suggesting several pounds of C-4 booby-trapped to the door handle."

"The other suicide vests?"

"I suspect you're right, Agent Adams. So, how about dinner tonight in beautiful Silver Bay, Minnesota, on the North Shore of Lake Superior? You packed?"

Beth looked at Setty, incredulous.

"You're serious? You want me to come with you?"

"Hey, didn't I just promote you? The least you could do is start acting like you earned it!"

His playful tone put her at ease. "Sounds like harassment," she said, "making me go up north with you under some official pretense."

"You think I arranged the explosion of an acre of small-town real estate just to get you to go out with me?"

Beth shrugged. "You are, after all, impotent."

"I believe the word your fumbling for is 'omnipotent'. Funny, but you're not impressing your new boss. Come on, Agent Adams. Let's blow this one-horse town."

"I hope that wasn't a pun, Agent Setty. And I didn't realize you had promoted yourself as well. Maybe I'll run it by Chief Williams, see what he thinks of it?"

"Uh…no, that won't be necessary," he said, shaking his head. "I'm fine with a partnership."

They walked to the gaggle of FBI agents near the mall's west entrance to bum rides to their respective hotels. To the west, the sun cleared the edge of the low gray clouds as it set, turning the sky to red and promising a better day tomorrow. Setty opened the door of a big Crown Vic and sunk into the brown leather seat. It felt so good to just sit. He hadn't done so in hours.

He sat and watched the slowly shifting colors in the sky as his brain purged the day's events in a free-form flood of images and perceptions. From the amorphous jumble of impressions, a single coherent thought took form, like a ghost resolving itself from an evening mist. There would be a lot of celebration over today's outcome. Hands would be shaken, medals pinned and pictures taken. But the fact remained that the terrorists had succeeded. No, they hadn't blown themselves up, but that was academic. This was really about psychology. And in that department, he thought, they got an "A." They made it to middle America and it was only luck that stopped them. Next time, luck might be on their side. Nothing was safe anymore.

EIGHTY-NINE

The hospital was quiet and dark when Hansen, slumped in a stiff chair in the corner unable to sleep, heard footsteps. Various monitors flashed and occasionally beeped over Billy's bed and a pie slice of weak yellow light from the hall illuminated the floor of the room. The timer on the IV had expired and a steady tone was sounding. After several seconds the light was briefly eclipsed and a nurse entered, as others had done regularly throughout the afternoon and night. And, as he had been doing all night, he watched intently as she pressed buttons on the devices, the IV monitor, the heart monitor, the respirator, temperature and humidity controls for the plastic tent that enclosed the top half of Billy's body. He memorized her movements—which device she addressed first, which buttons got pushed, how many times. He closed his eyes when she finished, feigning sleep. He looked at his watch. It was 3:10 a.m. He had taken Libby to a nearby hotel about four hours ago. She had been too exhausted to argue. She had looked so tiny and frail as he left her in that strange room, alone and so out of place, like a butterfly in a jar. The very essence of the woman, the things that made her Libby Cosgrove, the strength and independence, were stripped away and she sat on the edge of the mattress, on the quilt's bright floral print, defeated and helpless.

The doctors injected Billy's vena cava with granulocyte-macrophage colony-stimulating factor or GM-CSF, a substance present naturally in women during early pregnancy. Dr. Gharwala, a dark Indian man with a gentle manner and kind but sad brown eyes, explained to Hansen and Libby that it had been used successfully to treat many disorders.

"Physicians internationally have been applying this protocol to many issues over the last several years," Dr. Gharwala told them. "Infertility to encourage cell division after in-vitro fertilization, for arthritis to reduce inflammation and cartilage destruction and to slow its spread to other joints, to reduce sepsis in newborns and, most importantly to us at this moment, to stimulate the growth of white blood cells in the bone marrow for certain cancers and immunodeficiency diseases like AIDS."

"And this can cure Billy?" Libby had asked.

The hopeful desperation in her voice caused Hansen to put his arm over her shoulders protectively.

"Ms. Cosgrove…" the doctor began, quietly.

"Mrs., please," Libby interrupted. "It's *Mrs.* Cosgrove."

Dr. Gharwala smiled. "I am sorry. Habit. Mrs. Cosgrove, we hope this will help your husband's body fight off infection while it grows strong enough to do that on its own. But, as painful as it must be, you must accept that there are many other factors against your husband. He is a fighter, Mrs. Cosgrove. We have seen that already. But he needs more than I can give him to survive. He needs you and his friends," he said, looking at Hansen, "and God."

"So," Hansen nodded toward the room two doors down the hallway where a Minnesota state trooper sat outside the door, "is this the same treatment he's getting?"

The doctor looked down the hall, past Hansen.

"I am sorry, but I cannot discuss another patient's treatment, Mr. Hansen. I am sure you understand."

"Sure," said Hansen, disgusted.

He knew the answer anyway. Regardless of the information he might hold, caring for that murderer was an abomination. And there he lay, thirty feet away, receiving the best that American medicine had to offer. And then, if he survived, he would be fed and housed and coddled and filmed and reported on like some celebrity. They'd write books and make movies, lawyers would defend him and get rich. And terrorists all over the world would laugh as the years rolled by and no sign of justice, no vengeance was ever delivered. In their savage world view, Hansen knew, we will have yet again met moral strength with the weakness of empty gestures—bombs lobbed over their heads as we hide in our mansions, shivering under our canopy beds, while they, secure in their faith, know that, live or die, it will be God who has saved them or called them to paradise. You can't beat these people and you can't change their minds. So where the hell does that leave you?

In Billy's hospital room, Hansen rose from his chair and stretched his weary muscles. He was stiff and sore and hadn't slept in almost two days. He'd survived worse in the Marines, but he'd been younger then, screaming filthy marching cadences. They passed the time and helped occupy his brain, humping it over those damn courses, dripping sweat and hating your existence, cursing everything that led you to that place. Sometimes he recited a litany as he ran. He thought about being big and fat in a small-town school, he thought about being the son of a fisherman, hating the life and the smells, helping his father in the mornings pull nets and fillet herring, walking to school in the same shoes, teachers ordering him to leave them outside the schoolroom door. He sat at his desk in stocking feet while kids around him giggled and passed notes. The work made him strong and lean but his anger took root in the acidic soil of classroom taunts and ridicule. There were fights and suspensions. So he quit. And then he quit his father and the life of a fisherman and ran away. Anger was his salve for pain and guilt, so he found a profession where his anger was shaped, honed and rewarded. The Marines took an angry man, stripped him of his guilt, and conquered his conscience.

Now, in the University of Minnesota Hospital Center for Radiation Therapy, Hansen's guilt was back, mixing with anger and frustration. Billy was dying here in this room. And just down the hall was the man who killed him. Hansen looked at each of the monitors in the half light. They all had a touch-screen interface with some variation of "Menu, Options, Settings, Calibration and Alarm." He experimented with Hansen's saline IV. He pressed the button marked "alarm." A little picture of a bell appeared on the upper right corner of the screen. It had a red slash running through it diagonally. He watched the timer expire. Silence. He pressed the alarm button once more. The tone sounded and soon after, the nurse returned.

"You got some sleep?" she asked Hansen pleasantly as she reset the IV.

"Yeah," he said stretching. "A bit. Where can a guy get some coffee this time of night?"

"The cafeteria is downstairs on the first floor. Follow the signs. There's coffee, juice and rolls available all night and some vending machines."

"Thanks," he said, and then left the room.

He walked down the hall and stopped at the state trooper, who was slumped in his chair, asleep. Hansen had been visiting with the guy off and on throughout the day, gaining his confidence and trust.

"Hey, Todd."

The agent started, then looked up.

"Shit! Something wrong?"

"No, no, relax. I was just stretching my legs. Thought I'd get some coffee and a doughnut or something. Wanna join me?"

Todd rubbed his face with his hands.

"Sounds good, but I can't leave until I'm relieved." He checked his watch. "About forty-five minutes from now."

"Looks like you need it more than I do. Go ahead. I'll take your seat for a couple of minutes. Grab yourself some coffee and a roll."

"I'd like to, but, you know, this is a Federal thing...."

Hansen interrupted him.

"I'm a Fed, remember? Take a break. I'll be fine. Go on."

Todd looked up at the big Finn, and then he stood up.

"You're right. Hey, thanks a lot. My ass was getting numb in that thing. Want me to pick you up something?"

"Naw," said Hansen. "I'll want to walk down there myself when you get back."

Hansen sat down and watched Todd disappear through the ward's double doors. Looking down towards Billy's room he saw the nurse walk out into the hall and disappear around the corner, returning to the nurses' station. The time had come.

Hansen stuck his head into the room and saw a tent similar to Billy's hanging over the upper portion of a bedridden patient. He immediately noticed that there was less equipment. There was no respirator, only oxygen for the tent, a heart monitor and an IV. A light was on in the room. After one last look down the deserted hallway, he slipped in.

He walked immediately to the monitors and pressed the alarm button on each, disabling it. There was silence in the room save for the slight hiss of oxygen flowing into the clear plastic tent. He stepped to the bedside and looked down into the open, conscious eyes of Anwar Masoud.

This was not something he expected. In his head, all he had seen was a faceless man, eyes closed, as fragile and close to death as Billy Cosgrove. He had not prepared to kill a conscious human being. He looked down at the man through the distorting haze of the plastic sheet. The man looked up at him, his eyes wide in recognition and fear. Hansen took pleasure in that look and his apprehension faded. The side of the man's head was bandaged, covering the missing ear. Hansen unzipped the tent and said, pointing to the bandage.

"I did that. Remember me?"

The man in the bed nodded.

"Good, you speak English," Hansen said. "I don't have a lot of time, so I just want you to know that I've come here to kill you. I want to tell you first that you failed. I want to tell you that the only people dead because of your mission are your own. I'm pretty sure that me coming in here and strangling you while you lie here, under the care of American doctors and American medicines, won't get you into paradise. I'm pretty sure your deeds won't be forgiven by Allah—murdering your Jihad brothers and all."

Hansen placed his hands around the man's neck, hands large and strong like those of men that came before him, generations spent hauling nets bejeweled with the glittering silver bodies of herring caught in the mesh.

"And last of all," he said as his thumbs tightened over the stiff ridges of the windpipe which he would soon collapse, "I'll never be afraid of you."

He squeezed and the man in his grasp convulsed and scratched feebly at Hansen's hands, knuckles white and veins bulging. Hansen thought of nothing. His rage had overwhelmed all but the most primitive thoughts. No sound escaped the man's throat as the cartilage began to tear and sink under Hansen's thumbs. There was silence except for the rustling of the bedclothes and from somewhere a soft rhythmic clicking, click, click, click. The familiarity of it broke through Hansen's vicious trance. He looked down to see in the man's hand the nurse call button, thumb pressing spastically. There were footsteps in the hallway, running. His grip failed and Hansen's hands pulled away as though from something hot or forbidden. And like a child immersed in a game of wild destruction, suddenly facing certain discovery, eyes casting about for escape or a plausible explanation he backed away from the bed and watched a shadow grow larger as the nurse neared the door. He could only think of one thing to do. He called for help.

"What happened?" said the nurse, flicking on the light over the man's bed.

"It…it sounded like he was struggling, so I ran in. I thought he was suffocating," Hansen said, "so I opened the tent."

Hansen watched her check the monitors.

"Did you touch these?"

"I just tapped them to see if they were working," he told her. "Sorry, I was just trying to help."

He watched her warily as she examined the man on the bed who had since passed out, most likely from the exertion of the struggle his weakened body had just survived. She ran her fingertips over his neck, inspecting the red marks encircling the Arab's throat. She looked up at Hansen and he saw that she knew.

"You'd better stay outside now," she told him quietly. "You've done all you can do."

Hansen silently slipped out of the open door and into the hallway. Defeated, his legs felt like lead as he shuffled slowly over the shining white tiles, retreating to Billy's room, back to what he was best at—waiting for something to happen.

NINETY

It could have gone either way. Bureau Chief Edwin Williams knew that better than most, having been on both ends of the media's big stick—the shit end, and…well, anything at the other end was an improvement. The mood in the country was decidedly conservative and like any entity with something to sell, the media gave the people what they wanted. Protecting the country through legislation, diplomacy and covert ops was complex and most Americans couldn't grasp all the nuances in a sixty-second snippet during that half hour between Law and Order and Letterman. No, the public wanted a hero— someone who stuck his or her neck out, accomplished something daring and lived to tell about it. For the Mall of America attack, the media flipped the stick around and handed Williams the shitless end. And he grabbed on with both hands.

Now he would receive his due. He looked in the mirror and straightened an elegant tie in teal and navy horizontal stripes. It looked good with his charcoal suit, he observed. In print and electronic media, Williams' quotes were the hottest thing going. He got so tired of hearing himself he even stopped listening to NPR, his favorite source for news. He had to admit, the way they described it, they had done something quite remarkable. In the span of twelve hours mobilizing three hundred agents, state and local law enforcement, coordinating their efforts and creating a successful ruse within a 4.2 million square foot mouse trap. Of course, there was some controversy over the bait used, but since none of the thirty-two hundred civilians in the mall that day was injured seriously—a few minor bruises and scrapes during the initial stampede to the exits—that fact received very little press. Besides, that detracted from the real story.

The real story, so the press proclaimed, was the FBI regaining past glory, establishing itself once again as the pre-eminent domestic police agency, clearly capable of protecting the citizens of the United States from the worst of the worst. The Bureau had taken some hard knocks from the popular media since the glory days of Hoover, when prime- time TV showed virile Efrem Zimbalist Jr. as the FBI's Inspector Lewis Erskine always getting his man. But even then, the role of the agency was blurred by Hoover-led lapses into McCarthyism, left-wing witch-hunts, even overseas operations in Puerto Rico and El Salvador. After the death of Hoover, news of his eccentricities and notable lapses in judgment and tactics—Ruby Ridge, Pine Ridge—created within the agency a general confusion as to their mission. Morale took a nosedive. As if to illustrate its descent into the bizarre, the next popular FBI show on TV would be The X Files, where FBI agents Mulder and Scully routinely investigated alien abductions, circus geeks and a variety of nightmarish creatures, all steeped in a rich broth of government conspiracy and cover-up.

But those days were gone. Now everyone could feel safe again—the old FBI, well-dressed and straight-shooting, was back! Though he didn't like the hype, he had to admit it was nice to feel good about what he did and have others appreciate it as well.

From his house in Annandale, Williams took the Little River Turnpike into D.C. proper and parked in one of the many secured government ramps his credentials allowed him to use. The ceremony would be on the steps of the Lincoln Memorial, looking out upon the Mall, toward the Washington Monument and its mirror image in the reflecting pool. It was a beautiful spring day in the capital, Williams noted, though the cherry trees had long since dropped their blossoms. He loved the smell of those blooms. He would forever associate it with the feeling of patriotic euphoria that never failed to overcome him in this place. He walked around with chills, through the monuments, past the Wall, the White House, the museums, Arlington. From this place he loved his country without question and his faith in it was supreme.

The press was out in force, he noticed as he walked along the reflecting pool. Lots of cameras. The president himself had called him yesterday at home, apologizing for his absence. The director would be there, of course, senators and congressmen, the head of the Department of Homeland Security, the attorney general. And then, of course, a dignitary of the president's choosing to bestow the honor. He climbed the wide marble steps and commenced the requisite schmoozing. He enjoyed it, now that his stock was high. Then it was time and he took his place next to the podium.

"Bravery," said the vice president of the United States to the sizable crowd gathered at the base of the steps. As always, his singsong voice grated mightily on Williams' nerves. "It is a word too often saved for those who have already given their lives on the field of battle, too late to hear the appreciation of a grateful nation," said the VP. "That is not the case today. I have with me a man I have known for many years. Since our early days in the CIA, we fought for the safety of our nation together."

Williams lowered his face to his hand for a moment and rubbed his brow, afraid his eyes might roll of their own volition or, worse yet, that he would laugh.

"And we continue that fight today. Sometimes we fight in quiet ways such as passing the Homeland Security Act and removing obstacles that hamper the efforts of our country's intelligence community. And then, sometimes, we get to do something spectacular."

The Vice President turned to Williams with a wide grin and an outstretched hand. Williams, the good soldier, shook it firmly, though he wanted to crush it, to hear bones snap and watch this fawning hypocrite crumple in pain and humiliation before the American people and Abe. Instead, he stood while the Medal of Honor was pinned to his chest. It was enough to know JQ would never get one of these himself. And, looking into the Vice President's eyes, he knew that JQ knew it too. That made him even happier.

NINETY-ONE

CIA field Agent Beth Adams stood in her underwear, staring at a large black suitcase that sat on the hotel's double bed, overflowing with clothes. On the floor lay all her shoes. She hadn't even tried to fit any in yet. Unsure of what to take, she tried to take everything, substituting the immediate vacillation over what she should take, with the impending vacillation over what she should wear when she arrived at her destination. What does a female agent wear in the field? She was an analyst, used to hiding beneath a formless white robe.

"What the hell do you think you're doing?" she asked herself, staring at the suitcase. Only yesterday she had been running through a crowded shopping mall trying to stop terrorists from killing people. Now she was heading up to the woods to retrace their steps. Thinking back to the last few days, it was hard enough to retrace her own steps, from the Pentagon to the capitol to Minnesota to the Canadian border.

She knew her father would be pleased. "Adams Apple of Father's Eye." Minnesota was a lot like Wisconsin and it made her think of home. She'd forgotten how comfortable the Midwest made her feel, or maybe it was simply how uncomfortable she felt out east. It took a long time for Midwest folks to accept you completely, but once they did, they'd be with you forever. Out east things happened a lot faster, but as usually is the case with speed, a certain recklessness always accompanies it. Nothing seemed as permanent or as sincere since moving out there.

She remembered there was a zipper pouch on the outside of the suitcase. She began stuffing shoes into it. She would have to make with four pair. According to Setty, she would probably have to get a pair of hiking boots and maybe some rain gear as well.

Today she felt an excitement and optimism she hadn't felt in a long time. She didn't know how much of her anticipation was a result of the rapport she'd developed with Brian Setty, but she knew that was part of it. More compelling than that, however, was the taste of doing something important for others, for her country. Of course, she'd been doing that all along. But this was different, more immediate and tangible. Then there was the thrill of the chase mixed up in there as well. It was a motivating, addictive cocktail she'd been drinking lately. She was looking forward to her next sip.

Beth closed the suitcase as best she could, holding the items inside as she flipped it over. Pushing down on the case was not sufficient to get the zipper to circumnavigate the bulging material. She had feared it would come to this. She climbed onto the bed and sat on the case, reaching around to pull the zipper closed. Finally successful, she got off the bed and looked back to admire her work. Satisfied by the sight of the corpulent bag, now sealed but straining at its seams, she turned to get dressed and catch the flight to Duluth. She looked around. She looked back to the suitcase.

"Yes, Beth," she said, "they're in there."

NINETY-TWO

Gunflint Trail, Cook County, MN
June, 2002

Garrett Hansen watched the sparks fly into the chill evening air, mingling as they rose with the stars that sparkled brilliantly overhead. He wore a dark blue flannel shirt and jeans and a fleece vest against the cold. The campfire's crackling warmth was welcoming and he added another large spruce log to make it more so. He sat in a folding chair with armrests and a cup holder, beer in his hand. A similar, but empty chair sat opposite him, on the other side of the fire. His friend Mark Toftey would be stopping by at some point to share a beer and some conversation. It was the first time they'd been together since their adventure two weeks ago. It was Hansen who'd been avoiding it, not knowing how he would react on certain subjects, especially after a six-pack.

He'd done well. Everybody said so. He received a commendation from the Department of Homeland Security. The secretary himself came out to Grand Portage to present him with the medal. He wouldn't admit that it meant anything to him and he stowed it in his underwear drawer. Nor would he admit that he looked at it every time he went to grab a clean pair of undies. His border patrol colleagues threw him a big drunken bash at the Gunflint Tavern in Grand Marais. Malorie even showed up to hang on his arm until he was drunk enough to forget how much she pissed him off. They ended up at her house where he spent the night, though they were both too drunk to have sex and passed out simultaneously upon hitting the mattress. In the morning their animosity returned and he left to the familiar tune of her screaming.

He thought it odd how quickly his world returned to normal after coming so close to disaster. Maybe that was because his world was so small to start with. Of course, normal, he observed, was sort of a slippery thing. Sure, sitting in front of a campfire holding a beer outside his log cabin in the woods was normal. Getting up at six every morning, putting on his uniform and going to work was normal. Taking the canoe over to the Brule River for a long paddle on a Saturday or Sunday still felt normal. But waking up in a sweat trying to blink away the image of Billy in a hospital bed, his hands bandaged and hanging like white clubs at the ends of his wrists, face red and swollen, disfigured—that was pretty damn far from normal. Then there was the feeling that he'd missed an opportunity to put it right. Missed opportunity—put another check mark in the normal column.

Hansen looked up into the treetops and saw them illuminated eerily by approaching headlights, alternately glowing then disappearing again into shadow. Then he heard Toftey's jeep making its way down the driveway. He went to the cooler and got him a beer.

"So, what's the word?" Hansen said in greeting.

"Thirsty," answered Toftey.

They took their positions on either side of the fire and diddled it with sticks, sending more sparks into the sky.

"Heard from Libby?" Toftey asked.

"I talked to her today. Anybody else would've been dead ten times over. She said he was in the canoe this morning. Caught two twenty-seven-inch walleyes before breakfast."

"What is he—about sixty?" asked Toftey. "Hell, even if the radiation was gonna cause him cancer, he'll be too old to care by the time it shows up. Do they know anything else about the terrorists?"

Hansen shrugged. "I don't know. It's not like they're calling me with updates. I'm just supposed to keep my mouth shut about what I know while they investigate. Matter of national security, don't ya know?"

"You saved a lot of people, you know," said Toftey.

Hansen laughed. "Whoever tied his little balloons shut is the hero. Luckily they don't have Boy Scouts in Saudi Arabia or the knots might not have failed. You saw the pictures of Silver Bay. Just imagine if that had happened in that mall, tossing radioactive innards into the air and onto everything for hundreds of feet in all directions."

"Yeah, I saw it," Toftey said. "But that was two explosive vests, right?"

"That's how many this guy was wearing. He wanted the fast train to paradise, so he borrowed one of his buddies' and wore it over his own."

Hansen poked at the fire and sent an eruption of sparks into the air. "I still wake up with that fucker every night. That is," he said and held up his beer, "if I haven't had enough medication."

"So, no career in the FBI, Garrett?"

"You know, that did run through my mind a couple of times. But that mall was an ice-cold shower, I'll tell ya. I'm looking around at the mass of humanity, a cross-section of America, thinking, 'Am I going to throw my life away for these fat, selfish, arrogant, greedy people?' I've been thinking a lot about that. What am I protecting?"

Toftey took a long pull on his beer and looked up at the stars.

"The question you need to ask yourself," he said, "is do you believe that America is a sum of its parts, or an idea that transcends them? Right now, I'm not very hopeful about what the folks in charge are doing to this place and worse yet, like you said, look who they're leading. Folks who consider it a hard day of work when they have to get off their ass and actually talk to somebody instead of just send them an email. They're exhausted by business lunches and negotiating the cost of staplers and tracking toilet paper use by the sheet. But this place can get better—it's that good of an idea, that it can survive a few years of dumbasses and bounce right back."

"I wish I had your glasses, man," Hansen said.

"Say your terrorist had blown up instead of blown chow," Toftey speculated, rising to get his second beer. "A few people die, big headlines, outcry cause we're afraid to go get a loofah at Bath and Body Works. We throw a few more bombs at somebody, we post dogs and machine guns at mall entrances. We all feel better, we forget. Life goes on. How about another beer?"

Hansen nodded and tossed another spruce log on the fire, losing a fountain of sparks.

"That's kind of cynical coming from you, Toftey."

"Not at all," he said, returning with the beers.

"It's optimistic. I'm just sayin' that for all the greed and assholishness in this country, we're really great about moving on and not feeling sorry for ourselves. I see that as a strength. Hell, if we spent our days thinking about how bad yesterday was, we'd all be passing around the spicy Kool-Aid."

Hansen couldn't think of anything to say in response. Toftey didn't push it. They spent the next several minutes in silence, their eyes following the intermittent stream of orange and yellow cinders rising on the updraft, past the dark jagged silhouettes of scrub pine until they flickered out, swallowed by the black cold of space.

NINETY-THREE

White Mountains, Afghanistan
June, 2002

About seven thousand miles away, an open fire burned in the depths of an Afghanistan cave, high in the rugged White Mountains. They burned narrow dense logs cut from scrubby, windblown juniper. Its high resin content made it easy to light, but created an unruly crackling flame. The two men sat back from the flames lest their robes catch a flying spark. But the penetrating chill in the cave drove them closer, chancing the errant exploding coal.

They sat cross-legged on folded blankets. A plastic tray sat between them, holding a pot of steaming brewed and bitter tea. They followed the sparks and smoke up toward the hole in the cave's high, dark ceiling.

"Have we failed Allah?" asked one man, bringing a teacup to his mouth and sipping it quietly.

"Of course not," said the other man, the shadows playing across a long determined face and full black beard.

"We have served Allah, praise be to him. We have learned much, we have accomplished much. They cower in fear. They have begun to understand that our commitment to Jihad is as deep as our faith, and our faith knows no earthly bounds, Allah be praised."

"They treat it as a victory for their diligence, their intelligence. It seems to only have inflated their haughtiness and arrogance. They prance about bestowing great honor on those who stood in our way."

"Ah, but you see, my brother, they stand in the way of nothing. But believing they do is their weakness. With each operation we lay the stepping stones in a long and glorious journey. There are no failures in serving Allah if you are pure and unwavering in your faith. All of us who wage this holy war will be rewarded with an eternity of unimaginable beauty and pleasure under God's loving gaze."

"I admire the strength of your faith, brother. I aspire to share them with equal conviction. You are truly an inspiration."

"Allah must be your inspiration. Human beings are flawed and will fail you, even under God's guiding hand. But Allah himself will not fail you. Aspire to his ideal," the man said, smiling and placing his hand gently on his companion's arm in a gesture of fatherly intimacy, "and you will achieve greatness despite the obstacles in your path. Allah will remove them all in due time."

The men returned to their tea in silence. They smiled as they brought the cups to their lips, enjoying the bitter strength of the drink while watching the fire crackle before them, feeling renewed warmth in their camaraderie and the certainty of the path that lay before them. Victory was assured and every death, no matter who's, was a battle won.

THE END

Kevin Woodward lives in Saint Paul and
Grand Marais, Minnesota with his wife and two children.